PRAISE FOR *GLASS A*

"This anthology is a welcome relief from dystopias and postapocalyptic wastelands, and a reassurance that the future need not be relentlessly bleak."

—Publishers Weekly

"Each of these stories is a window into a world where issues like climate change and food shortages are approached with a joyful creativity."

—Booklist

"Humans have spent generations destroying the planet. These seventeen stories explore the various ways to work with the world to improve it. From technological solutions to simple planning, the characters in these stories find a way to work with the world."

—SFRevu

"This anthology gives you just enough story, science, and hope…I've been needing a book like this in my life."

—Utopia State of Mind

"[T]he seventeen stories in this anthology are speculative in the very best sense of the word: They speculate on how our future could be, rather than how it must be, and provide an optimistic view which somehow manages to escape being escapism."

—SFF Reviews

"If you like your science fiction and fantasy with a hopeful outlook and a diverse cast of characters, you're likely to find many of the stories in *Glass and Gardens* to your liking!"

—Mad Scientist Journal

Glass and Gardens: Solarpunk Summers

an anthology

Edited by Sarena Ulibarri

World Weaver Press

GLASS AND GARDENS: SOLARPUNK SUMMERS

Published by World Weaver Press, LLC
Albuquerque, NM
www.WorldWeaverPress.com

Cover layout and design by Sarena Ulibarri.
Cover images used under license from Shutterstock.com.

*

First edition: June 2018
ISBN-13: 978-0998702278

Also available as an ebook

GLASS AND GARDENS: SOLARPUNK SUMMERS

CONTENTS

INTRODUCTION

In his well-circulated Ozy article about solarpunk, Tom Cassauwers writes, "Imagine a scene, set in the future, where a child in Burning Man-style punk clothing is standing in front of a yurt powered by solar panels." To be honest, there isn't a single story in *Glass and Gardens: Solarpunk Summers* that contains that scene, though I am quite curious about this child and would love to read their adventure. Nor do any of these stories look quite like the towering tree-covered skyscrapers so prominent in solarpunk artwork. Still, those evocative images have spurred interest in this developing subgenre of optimistic, environmentally-conscious science fiction, and maybe the stories in those settings just haven't been written yet.

A lot of the tropes and requirements of solarpunk are still being negotiated, among both the writers and artists producing solarpunk works and the bloggers and critics discussing it. Does it have to explicitly deal with energy technology? Does it have to be anti- or post-capitalist? Does it have to be utopian? Does it even have to be science fiction? When I was reading through submissions, I settled on a couple of requirements: stories had to touch on environmental issues and/or climate change, and they had to have an overall optimistic tone. But beyond that, these worlds each look quite different. The stories in this anthology present a number of different possibilities for what the label "solarpunk" could mean.

Science fiction has a bad habit toward homogeneity, whether it's the depiction of a single-ecosystem planet, ubiquitous and monotone cultures, three-course-meal food pills, or futuristic silver jumpsuits for all. It would be an insult to the decentralized, localized nature of solarpunk to pin it down as only one thing. Single visions of the future ignore the cultural and ideological variations that make us human. They also ignore the interconnectivity of eco-systems, and the variations of landscape and climate that make up a world.

I think M. Lopes da Silva's vision of a desert city reconstructed from collapsed skyscrapers is just as much solarpunk as the domed garden oasis envisioned by D.K. Mok. The rural aesthetic of Sam S. Kepfield's underground farmhouse has just as much to add to this genre as Jerri Jerreat's rooftop gardens and SkyCities. It wasn't actually the mention of solar collectors in Blake Jessop's "New Siberia" that gave me the solarpunk vibe, but rather the way his space explorers face the consequences of their past mistakes and choose *not* to take the same colonial, exploitative path again. There's hardly even a mention of renewable energy in the panoramic narrative of "Midsummer Night's Heist," a contemporary story of non-violent protest through art that exemplifies the "punk" part of solarpunk. Helen Kenwright's quiet tale of clairvoyance and family secrets might be better classified as lunarpunk, and no one would bat an eye to simply call Edward Edmonds' weather manipulator murder mystery "cli-fi," but these terms all have nebulous overlap. They circle around the same ideas.

A couple of quasi-dystopias and environmental apocalypses did sneak in here, and while none of the utopias are quite *Omelas*, some of them do have a darker underbelly. But I tried to choose stories that depict adaptation and compromise rather than destruction and conquest, stories that value empathy and cooperation over greed and competition. Once you've read them, I'd love to hear how you think these stories stand up to those expectations. Honest reviews are one of the best tools to help readers find the kinds of stories they're craving.

If you'd like to read more solarpunk, check out *EcoPunk!: Speculative Tales of Radical Futures*, *Wings of Renewal*, and *Sunvault: Stories of Solarpunk and Eco-Speculation*, as well as novels such as *New York 2140* by Kim Stanley Robinson, *Walkaway* by Cory Doctorow, and *The Fifth Sacred Thing* by Starhawk. Or, try writing your own. There's plenty of space for varied visions of brighter futures.

Sarena Ulibarri, June 2018

CAUGHT ROOT

Julia K. Patt

I.

I arrive at the gates of the New-Ur settlement just after dawn.

It is so different from my home in Hillside, some three hundred miles away. Where Hillside's shining towers reach for the blue sky, New-Ur seems born from the very rock, all adobe and stucco and low-sitting buildings. Here and there, I can see where green relieves the brown, and this is the only similarity between the two.

The wide-eyed guard, only a teenager, scuttles away when I try to speak to him. Will they let me in at all? I told Arthur this was a fool's errand, that New-Ur and Hillside would never trust one another. But you don't say no to Arthur, especially when an idea's taken hold.

Finally, a woman appears; she introduces herself as Safiya. Am I lost? Injured?

"No, ma'am," I explain. "I represent the Hillside Project. We wrote two months ago, asking to meet Dr. Khadir for an exchange of ideas."

Safiya studies me, considering. Eventually, she nods and enters the code that opens the gate. Not *all* low-tech, I see.

II.

"You can go in," Safiya says. Her dark eyes crinkle in secret amusement.

This room, like the rest of the complex, smells like water and fresh-turned earth. It's designed to cool passively, and entering it is like walking into a cave: the air chill, damp. Shade plants—ferns, hostas, bleeding hearts—line the walls. Skylights drop sunbeams throughout.

Khadir stands at his desk, reading a report on paper, of all things, and frowning. He's a tall man, olive-skinned, with a scattering of ivy, twigs, and flowers in his curly hair.

He brushes them off self-consciously when he sees me looking. "The children…sometimes," he offers by way of explanation. "You must be Dr. Orkney."

"Ewan is fine," I say. I stoop to examine the discarded blossoms, most of them dark purple. "These are lovely."

"A newer varietal. We need more dry season plants, especially edibles." He covers them with the papers so I can't study them further.

Such distrust. I should be pleased they allowed me in at all. Somehow, I'm meant to change this, much as I insisted—at length—that I am a scientist, not a diplomat. I clear my throat. "To that end," I say. Awkward. "These are for you." I drop a packet of seeds into his palm.

He plucks one out to study, his movements delicate. This is a man accustomed to handling the smallest tendrils of life without bruising them. "Are these…?"

"Pears. They'll bear fruit in the second year. We've crossed them with an Asian near-arid to boost their water efficiency," I say. And can't help adding: "They're my own work."

Khadir regards me, amused. "And we can keep working with these seeds? They won't require a second visit or your permission for replanting?"

"We're giving them freely," I say. Trying not to let my offense show. "We're not some hard-hearted corporation, Dr. Khadir, just because we're well-funded. We have the same goal as New-Ur: to re-imagine civilization. Surely we can help one another? Exchange ideas freely?"

"Call me Bari, especially when you appeal to my humanist sensibilities." He smiles. "Come, let me show you around."

III.

The more I see of New-Ur, the more I understand it is both like and completely unlike Hillside. They use the same conical structures for multi-layered planting that we do, but their base materials are reclaimed and reused metals, whereas ours are recycled, unblemished, new-looking. They live in the same circular configuration we do: concentric rings interspersed with lush gardens and communal spaces, each section self-sustaining and yet part of the greater whole. Nothing goes to waste at either settlement, but here they use less to begin with—no need for extra tech.

Khadir doesn't object when he sees me taking notes, even sketching portions of their water purification system, made from porous clay. He flinches, however, whenever I pause to examine a leaf or bud, or gently turn a still-green tomato on its stem.

"You'll have to forgive him," Safiya—his sister, I learn—tells me at the communal dinner. The whole settlement gathers at the center of the complex, passing dishes around several tables and talking, laughing, sharing the end of the day, and enjoying the cooling air of the desert. "He's protective of this place."

I think of Arthur and Hillside, his passion for the community and the technology, his determination, his willingness to hear any idea from anyone. "I understand. We're not so different, you know. Aesthetically, we might appear to be opposites, but we share the same goals."

"Not entirely," Khadir corrects me from across the table. "Hillside doesn't care about searching our past for solutions. It's all new, new, new. The shinier the better." His smile eases the criticism, but I can see in his eyes that he means what he says.

"Bari," Safiya chastises him. "Don't be rude."

I wave her off. "It's fine. It's true that Hillsiders aren't overly burdened by sentimentality, but we do incorporate lessons and methods from every culture. Tiered planting, like you do, for example."

"But you still rely heavily on automation, even if it is solar-powered," Khadir counters. He gesticulates with his fork, a piece of sweet potato speared on the end. "There's no connection between the work and the workers. You'll take us right back to a divided labor force, alienated from the meaning of the task."

I gesture back with a hunk of naan. "Automation means our workers can choose their tasks more freely, can devote more time to study, creativity. They're invested in bettering their society through innovation."

"But what is this measure of *better*—" Khadir starts to reply.

"*Gentlemen*," Safiya interrupts. "While we certainly don't object to intellectual discussion at the dinner table, perhaps you should save your debating prowess for another venue. We'll sell tickets."

Everyone around us laughs; Khadir subsides, offering me a sheepish smile, which I return. This, too, is like Hillside, where conversation stretches long into the night, only to be resumed, unabated, the next morning.

"A proposition, then," I say. "I will stay and work with you all for the next three weeks, and if I survive—" More laughter here. "—you will send an emissary to Hillside to live among us, too."

It's quiet for a moment, thoughtfully so, and I begin to fear I've overstepped. Safiya's eyes twinkle, catching the illumination from the solar lamps that light the complex; their once-faint blue glows more powerfully as the night settles around us.

Khadir extends his hand across the table to me. "It's a deal."

IV.

The first week, I work on the maintenance crew. We replace the terracotta tile roofing on the exterior ring of the complex. A recent storm has damaged the tiles. It's sweaty work in the sun, even in the morning. Khadir surely thought this would deter me, but it doesn't. Where Hillside is climate-controlled, New-Ur adapts to the seasons, shifting work schedules with the demands of summer and winter. We spend the hot afternoons resting in the shade and in quiet contemplation. The children bring us water and flowers, the purple blooms from the day before. "Where do these grow?" I ask, on the third day.

They lead me to a garden tower ringed with the same plants. The others don't have them yet, so they're clearly experimental. Maybe a deterrent for pests? Khadir said they were edible, but I'm not sure which part. The petals are bitter when I taste them; the children laugh. "We eat the leaves," one girl tells me. "And the shoots."

It's tempting to take samples, even a complete specimen, but instead I rejoin the crew. At dinner every night, Khadir and I resume our debates, much to the amusement of the others. I sleep well that week, deep and dreamless.

V.

The second week, they place me with the school. This is happier work than replacing tiles, although no less exhausting. The children's lessons roll continuous from one subject to another, uninhibited by rigid structures. If a question demands one explain Algebra or Chemistry or Chaucer, we discuss Algebra or Chemistry or Chaucer. Nothing in the settlement is off limits, either, and the children visit the water purifiers and the gardens and the chicken coops at will. It is apparently tradition for the teachers to end up with flowers and leaves in their hair; I am no exception. Khadir teases me at dinner one night. Despite my spaceman clothes, as he calls them—the standard-issue jumpsuits we wear at Hillside—I am starting to look like I belong at New-Ur.

At the end of the week, I find the trestle with the purple flowers ringing it again. Although I feel a pang of shame, I uproot one plant and carry it away with me. Only for examination, I tell myself, but really, I feel the need to bring something of this place back to Arthur and the others.

VI.

The third week, I find myself on kitchen duty. More surprising, however, is the sight of Khadir waiting for me on Monday morning, his apron already dusty with flour. "Everyone takes part in everything," he explains. "No one is too important for any work."

I think of Arthur mending water silos or giving immunizations to toddlers. "I think you would get along better at Hillside than you imagine."

"Perhaps I will see it one day." Khadir smiles and returns to kneading dough, slapping it against the countertop.

We spend the week in lively conversation, debating the merits of hydro-electrics in this climate, the natural airflow of the buildings in Hillside vs. New-Ur, the cultivation of interbred varietals as opposed to the preservation of heirlooms. Several times, I see the other cooks rolling their eyes and sighing. "We're boring them," I tell Khadir.

"They hear it all too often, I'm afraid," he confesses. "It's nice to have someone here who is still passionate about such things."

He looks away; something tightens in my chest. I almost blurt out the truth about the plant I took, but our conversation turns to other topics.

VII.

After dinner on my last Friday in New-Ur, we walk under the stars. Khadir shows me the night-blooming lilies; their color reminds me of the bioluminescent lanterns at Hillside, which I try to describe to him and fail. Midway through, he leans down and kisses me, once and then twice more.

We stumble back to my quarters, entirely too impatient, fumbling under each other's clothes. I push him onto my bed and he tumbles, boneless and smiling, looking up at me.

Come to Hillside with me, I want to say.

We wake up curled together. The dawn fills the corners of my room, the skylight above my desk illuminating everything, including that small cluster of leaves and buds.

How could he miss the purple flowers he knows so well, tucked among my books?

He doesn't even look angry, just blank. "Ah," he says. "I see."

VIII.

Safiya sees me off.

She has been appointed emissary to Hillside, she tells me. She will depart at the end of the summer.

"We'll look forward to your arrival," I say, sincere. "I hope you'll find it as pleasant as I have your home."

She kisses my cheeks in farewell. Hesitates. "My brother…"

I haven't seen Khadir since that morning. I shake my head. "It was my fault."

It's a two-mile walk to the hovercraft station and my trip back to Hillside. The day is still cool; the hills are pink and green with vegetation.

I spare a look back at New-Ur, the plants blooming among the stucco and terracotta. Arthur will understand my regret despite our success.

At first, I think the figure approaching me is an illusion, summoned by my heartache and the strengthening sun.

But it's him, Khadir, carrying the plant in a small translucent capsule. "You left this behind," he pants when he reaches me. "Why?"

I shake my head. "Bari—I'm sorry. Truly. It was wrong of me."

He presses the pod into my palm, covering both with his hands. "The greens aren't quite right. Too bitter. And they don't keep long. There's still work to do. The truth is," he continues. "We need another talented botanist. Someone willing to experiment, debate merits. That kind of thing. Know anyone?"

His eyes are earnest, searching mine. *Stay with me*, he doesn't say.

There are, I see, flowers and leaves and twigs in his hair again. I reach to pluck one out with my free hand. Caress his cheek. "Yes, I believe I do."

THE SPIDER AND THE STARS

D.K. Mok

Del's childhood, like many others, was woven from enchanted tales. Every night, as the warmth of the day radiated back through the glass water-wall of her bedroom, Del curled up with her plush quokka and listened, enthralled, as her mother spun wondrous stories.

These were never stories of dragons and fairies, mermaids and centaurs. No, these were stories of fierce young women with flocks of tree-planting drones, firing seeds into the barren sands and rolling back the desert. Or tales of ravenous locusts sweeping across the land in suffocating plagues, and the farmers who responded by cultivating carnivorous wheat.

But tonight, there had been no story. Del waited in bed until even Quokka's genial features seemed to furrow with impatience.

"Wait here," whispered Del. She was almost five, and therefore officially allowed to negotiate the terms of Bedtime. Stories were a requirement under Article Three, since she had fulfilled the conditions of Article Two: specifically, the Brushing of Teeth.

She trod softly towards the sound of voices in the kitchen. Her mother sounded uncharacteristically frustrated; her father, uncharacteristically chipper.

"It's their loss," he was saying. "There'll be other competitions—"

"Not like the Solaria Grande Exhibition." Her mother's voice was thick with disappointment. "It'll be twenty years before it comes this way again—"

"So we'll travel to the next one—"

"With all this gear? What if the truck overturns? The last thing we need is a hysterical headline like *Mutant Bugs on Rampage!* It's hard enough getting people not to gag at the word 'entomophagy'—"

"Maybe we shouldn't use that word next time. How about 'alternative protein'?"

There was a soul-crushing sigh. "People won't eat spiders because they have too many legs, but they'll happily eat crabs. They won't eat shea caterpillars because they're too gooey, but they'll slurp down oysters. Gram for gram, insect protein is cheaper, healthier and more sustainable than red meat. To make a single beef patty, it takes two thousand litres of water. To make the same amount of cricket flour, you need a moist towelette and a tolerance for swarms—"

"I know. And *that's* why you'll make this work. You don't need some fancy prize. You have your passion, and your entomology degree. And you have me and my winning way with a hot wok and spices—"

"And me," Del blurted from the doorway. "I'll help you look after the bugs."

"Oh, Del, daughter of mine…" Her mother scooped her up like a rugby ball, the comforting scent of ripe apricots and jasmine lingering in her mother's thick brown hair. "Am I late for story time?"

As the cicadas bleated their one-note love songs from the eucalypts outside, Del settled onto her sleeping mat, the straw cool against her skin. She slid her night terrarium a little closer, the bioluminescent mushrooms and glow-worms suffusing the room with a gentle blue-green radiance.

"Can I have a story about ogres?" Del's playmates at preschool had terrified each other with stories of child-guzzling ogres, and Del wondered if the ogre had considered eating cricket damper and jam instead.

"Hmm… I don't know many stories about ogres. Oh, wait, there is one very special ogre—the ogre-faced spider, *Deinopis ravida*. A huntress of the night who stalks her prey with a silken net, with eyes so keen and clever she can see the galaxy Andromeda."

And it was in this moment—her mind filled beyond capacity with this wordless, moonlit image of a stargazing spider—that Del chose her destiny.

***

Ten Years Later

It had rained all summer, and the water tanks were overflowing, but the local frogs kept the mosquitos at bay. Even so, citronella candles lined the backyard deck, adding their fragrant glow to the festive solar fairy lights. Del wove through the convivial crowd, carrying one last platter of crispy garlic tortilla chips, setting it down between the creamy mango curry and the crunchy lime and chilli beer snacks.

Del glimpsed her mother in lively conversation with the mayor, while her father manned the barbecue, an aroma like char-grilled prawns and capsicum infusing the balmy air. On the bandstand, a woman on an electric oud was trying to drown out an enthusiastic accordionist, and Del's temples twinged.

Her work done, she slipped quietly into an adjoining paddock and down a wide stone stairwell that descended into the earth. The wall console blinked as it recognised her wrist-chip, and she passed through the airlock, entering a sprawling underground chamber. The humid air smelled of fresh oats and loam, and the room was almost entirely dark. Dim red guide-strips marked the floor, and overhead, the ceiling was studded with thousands of pinprick lights.

Countless rows of two-metre tall racks stretched into the distance, each filled with shallow drawers constructed from corn-starch plastic. A ventilation gap separated each drawer from its neighbour, so that the room resembled a cross between a bakery and library. Large signs were affixed to the end of each row, along with smaller labels on each drawer:

CRICKETS (ACHETA DOMESTICUS)
MEALWORMS (TENEBRIO MOLITOR)
SILKWORMS (BOMBYX MORI)

Del's father had been right. They hadn't needed some fancy prize to realise her mother's vision; just a few years, a new marketing angle, an environmental emergency, and a gutful of hard work. A faint flush of pride warmed Del as she surveyed the tidy insect farm, her mother's colourful logo printed on every crate and carton.

KOUMI'S ORGANIC FOODS:
DELICIOUS SUSTAINABLE PROTEIN

Overcoming people's aversion to creepy crawlies had been their greatest challenge, until they realised that cultural attitudes weren't an obstacle, but an asset. If most people hadn't cared when their corn chips were made from palm oil and the tears of orangutans, why would they care now that their cheese-powder fix was made from sustainably farmed, gluten-free crickets? As long as it looked and tasted like a corn chip, most people didn't care where it came from.

Lilana Koumi's banquet parties had become a thing of local legend. They'd started as sales and networking events for potential clients, but as the business prospered, they'd become an annual victory celebration for the family. And it was true, no one really cared that the tortilla chips were made from cricket flour, or that the mango curry included pepper-roasted termite puree, or that the beer snacks consisted of deep-fried, salt-and-pepper grasshoppers. Everything was delicious, and almost nothing looked like bugs.

Del walked down the softly lit aisle, the chorus of *chirrups* washing over her. While most of the crickets' songs were probably entomological booty-calls, she couldn't help imagining that some were wistful odes to waving grass and summer rain. She lifted the mesh of a passing drawer and tossed in a few pieces of carrot. The facility had automated feeding systems, but Del still liked to drop them extra snacks.

The underground chamber was naturally climate-controlled, and the lights were powered by biogas from the nearby cheese factory. And while Del knew it was only her imagination, she sometimes thought the light smelled faintly of cheddar.

At the far end of the subterranean shed, through a small, plain door, lay Del's realm. It had been intended as a supply closet, but Del had begged her mother for the cosy space.

You have a big lab in the warehouse upstairs, Del had said. *Let this be mine.*

And so it was.

Tanks and terrariums and trays and aquariums crammed the small space, brimming with grasses and ferns and multi-legged residents. Giant water bugs paddled lazily, while peacock spiders danced their nervous rhumbas. Charts covered the walls, and boxes of slides were neatly arranged around a scuffed microscope. Stern signs were prominently attached to every insect residence: NOT FOR EATING!

Del reached into a leafy terrarium and gently lifted out a delicate, caramel-coloured spider about the size of a dime. The ogre-faced spider scurried up Del's arm and perched on her shoulder, staring at her with limpid black eyes.

"Hello, Artemis," Del smiled. "Ready to go stargazing again?"

Artemis continued to stare, and, not for the first time, Del wondered if deciphering the expression on a tiny arachnid face was like trying to read a poem inked onto a grain of rice.

While Del's mother spent much of her time researching the nutritional value of insects, Del had become fascinated by the engineering marvel of termite mounds and the dazzling aerodynamics of dragonflies' wings. Her mind sprouted with possibilities, imagining how this knowledge might transform her own world. She envisioned gigantic skyscrapers with convection ventilation systems, requiring no artificial heating or cooling, and agile drones flying through dense jungles in urgent search-and-rescue missions.

Often, as Del peered down her microscope, Artemis would keep her company, ambling thoughtfully across Del's pages of notes, or hanging upside-down from a potted fern, occasionally waving a leg as though in encouragement. Or perhaps telling her to hurry up so they could go outside.

Del conducted a routine check of the room's filters and meshes, double-checking the seals on a tall cylindrical terrarium. Inside, the fire ants were forming another tower, climbing determinedly on top of one another to create a sturdy latticework that resembled an Eiffel Tower of ants. They seemed to do this every time they outgrew their existing home, but Del wondered how high they might go if left unchecked, and if, perhaps, somewhere in that seething lattice, there was a fire ant who longed to reach the clouds.

She would have to get them a larger tank.

Back outside, Del found a quiet spot by the jacarandas, the fallen purple blooms already wilting into potpourri. From her perch, Artemis turned her gaze towards the sky.

Someone coughed from the shadows.

"Hey, am I interrupting?"

A teenage boy with light brown skin and an easy smile stood holding a rustic wooden plate. Del returned the smile.

"Hey, Ziad. Thanks for coming."

Ziad's family ran a busy bakery in town. They were vegetarians, but they came to every banquet, bearing pastries and warm wishes.

"Well, Dad loves a good party. I saw you were frantically busy, as usual. I thought you might be hungry."

He offered the unfamiliar plate, which seemed to bear a delicate sculptural work of contemporary art.

"Wow," said Del. "That looks like it belongs in a gallery."

Ziad beamed. "It's a kangaroo grass sable with lemon myrtle ice cream, quandong tart and a sweet potato twill."

Just as meat had become a luxury in an increasingly arid world, so too, thirsty crops like rice and wheat were beginning to attract concern. Those with foresight were turning to plants like kangaroo grass and saltbush, which required no irrigation, no synthetic fertilisers and no pesticides. Unfortunately, the palate of the masses was yet to be convinced.

Del took a bite of the warm, buttery pastry and tried not to salivate as the tangy quandong jam hit her tastebuds.

"It tastes like a perfect day. I'm sure you'll have your own patisserie in no time."

"Not just a patisserie. It'll have its own garden, its own farm, with heirloom vegetables and heritage fruits and exciting new varieties of grains and berries and honeys." He sighed. "Or, at least, that's the dream."

"Maybe this'll help." Del bumped her wrist-chip gently against his, and a holographic screen blinked into life between them. An ornate certificate shimmered briefly before being replaced by a page of dense disclaimers. Finally, a large title *swooshed* into view:

WELCOME TO CRISPR FOR BEGINNERS.

PLEASE EDIT GENES RESPONSIBLY.

Ziad's wide-eyed expression made him look almost like a human version of Artemis. "You got a CRISPR kit?"

"*We* got a CRISPR kit. Don't get too excited; it's just the student version with a vial of *Drosophila*, but we can share the equipment. Now you can make your pest-resistant chives—"

"And you can make your flame-resistant moths!"

They grinned at each other as bogong moths fluttered through the sultry air, and Artemis gazed at the stars.

***

Another Ten Years Later

In the canopy of the scrubland, perched on ten-metre stilts, there nestled a sleek cabin of photovoltaic glass and reclaimed timber. In the eaves, elderly spiders knitted cobwebs, while on the roof, corellas rode the spinning ventilators, cackling uproariously.

Within the airy sunlit rooms, Del rushed from bench to shelf, flicking items off a holographic list that hovered to her right. She slotted one last carefully sealed terrarium into her trolley case before plucking a pristine flyer from her corkboard.

THE SOLARIA GRANDE EXHIBITION AND PRIZE

INNOVATORS, VISIONARIES, INVENTORS,

ENTREPRENEURS, ACTIVISTS
COMING TO TERRARIUM CITY

Del pressed the flyer to her chest. Terrarium City was only twelve hours away by levitation train. Her mother's experience at the exhibition had been less than heartening, but her descriptions of the magnificent halls and cosmopolitan crowd had ignited Del's imagination. And while Del loved her cabin in the canopy, and her job at the local Community Knowledge Centre, she longed to venture beyond the red dust and scribbly gum trees of her home town. Far beyond.

A quiet *pitter-patter* announced the arrival of her housemate. A tawny spider the size of a Labrador skittered into the room, clutching a ruffled net of cobweb silk between her forelegs. At the sight of the trolley case, her huge black eyes shone with worried disapproval.

Del clipped the case shut. "Sorry, Devana. I wish I could bring you with me, but I just know someone's going to panic and try to squish you."

Devana was a distant daughter of Artemis, and the benefactor of Del's years of tinkering with CRISPR. However, the more Del probed the cryptic genome of insects and arachnids, and the more she studied their complex behaviours, the less inclined she felt to modify them, and the more she longed to understand their strange and alluring worlds.

Del withdrew a translucent golden pod from a warming cabinet and tossed it to Devana, who snatched it from the air and sank her fangs through the soft gel skin, greedily drinking up the bottlebrush nectar. It had taken Del almost a year to devise this latest formulation, but Devana seemed to find it palatable, and it gave her carapace a healthy sheen.

"Be good," said Del. "Make sure the cockatoos don't chew my house to sawdust while I'm away."

"Everything will be here when you get back," said a voice from the foyer. Del's mother leaned against the gently curving doorframe, an insulated lunchbox in one hand. "Your father sends his love, and dumplings. Vegetarian."

It had been a wrenching decision for Del, many years ago, when she'd excised meat from her diet, including insect protein. But having spent so much time with her tiny companions, having seen their rich, complex lives filled with as much hope, tragedy and delight as her own, in the end, it had hardly been a decision at all. The choice had wounded her parents, but they understood. Or, at least, they said they did.

"All the filters have been changed," said Del. "The cabinet is full of nectar pods. You don't have to do anything with the incubators, but if the fire-ants start building again—"

"It'll be fine. Just enjoy yourself, and remember, the prize doesn't matter."

"I know." Del tucked the flyer into her jacket, her stomach suddenly fluttering. "It's just…what if they laugh at me?"

"Then it'll be a family tradition. My dearest Del, daughter of mine, they can laugh at us, but they can't stop us."

Del's mother drew her into a hug, and for a brief moment, it was twenty summers ago, when the days smelled of ripe apricots and jasmine.

As Del walked down the leafy track away from her cabin, she turned to see Devana standing on the roof, waving her forelegs. Whether in farewell or in the hopes of netting an unwary cockatoo, Del couldn't be sure, but she waved back.

***

Ziad was already waiting for her at the levitation station, his two storage drones following him obediently. Their sleek cylindrical forms made them look like a pair of patisserie refrigerators moonlighting as henchmen. As Del jogged over with her luggage, Ziad gave her an excited grin.

"Ready to transform the world with your entomology research?"

"We'll see. Ready to make incremental but meaningful change

with your climate-resilient crops and nutritionally responsible, mind-blowing desserts?"

"I have two tower-cases of pastries, puddings and cakes, so whatever happens, I'll be having a good time."

The station was a curving sandstone platform, partially enclosed by lofty timber beams and tinted skylights. Even in the baking summer heat, the angular design of the roof drew cool air in from the surrounding native gardens and exhaled warm air through the ceiling vents. A bell-like tone signalled the arrival of the train, and Del watched with anxious delight as it snaked across the sand.

Affectionately known as the Wyrm, the silver, serpentine locomotive glided a metre above the trackless ground. It was guided by GPS and location beacons stationed every kilometre along its path, and powered by a crucible of geomagnetism, photovoltaics, and lightning in a bottle.

The interior was part Orient Express, part Star Trek, with panoramic windows on every side. Del and Ziad settled into an economy booth, sipping ginger tea and practising their presentations. But the changing landscape outside kept tugging at Del's attention: there were towns, just like hers, speckled with solar arrays and water tanks. But there were also villages floating on inland seas, their bustling markets a crowd of floating tea houses and creaking junks with patchwork sails. There were forests of typhoon turbines ready to capture the rage of mighty storms, and enormous greenhouses in the desert, flanked by desalination plants powered by the sun.

As the terrain outside grew more arid—the parched earth puckering into shingles—an oasis slowly rose on the horizon. A gigantic dome of glass—a garden city in a bell jar, infused with greenery and flecked with iridescent butterflies and scarlet macaws.

Terrarium City.

***

Terrarium City Exhibition Centre was an enormous labyrinth of adjoining halls, and the registration foyer resembled a fusion of intergalactic spaceport and overgrown conservatory. Climbing roses spiralled up the stone columns, reaching towards a ceiling that was little more than a glassy frame for the sky. Full-grown fig trees towered around them, their roots sinking deep into the floor, and it was hard to tell where the carpet stopped and the moss began.

At a registration booth wreathed in delicate pink mandevillas, Del and Ziad finally received their convention passes.

Ziad quietly pumped a fist. "Yes! I'm in Meadow Hall. That's supposed to be one of the fun ones. How about you?"

Del looked at her pass. "I'm in Tundra Hall."

"Uh, I'm sure that's fun too. I'll come visit your booth."

Del glanced at the sprawling map overhead. "No, that's all right. It makes sense that they'd situate the live exhibits far away from the food exhibits."

As it turned out, Del's neighbouring booth was technically a food exhibit.

"Hi, I'm Xiaren Appelhof," said an angular woman with rosy cheeks and a smile like a flash of steel. "Distributed biogas generation. You?"

"Del Koumi. Entomological research." She tried not to stare at the tall, complicated tanks lining Xiaren's booth. They resembled a more militant version of Ziad's storage drones.

Xiaren followed her gaze. "Ah, I see you've noticed my portable domestic biogas system. Normally, biogas harvesting systems require thousands of tonnes of cheese to create a commercially viable amount of whey for anaerobic digestion. My system utilises less than twenty kilos of cheese, and generates enough gas for heating and cooking in a typical home. I call it the *Fromagerie 5000*!"

Xiaren swung open a panel in the tank to reveal five shelves of ripening cheeses surrounded by gurgling pipes and humming canisters. Del rocked back on her heels, the intense smell of gorgonzola hitting her with almost physical force.

"That's...powerful."

"I've specially cultivated the microorganisms to generate vastly more biogas than normal. And the cheese tastes amazing."

Xiaren cut a gooey wedge from a creamy blue and offered it to Del, who, after a moment's hesitation, took a bite. Notes of chilli and lychee simmered beneath the pungent flavour, and her eyes watered.

"This would make an insanely good pasta sauce." She gave herself a moment for the sparkles to disappear from her vision. "So, why did you go into cheese?"

Xiaren shrugged. "My hometown isn't overly fond of dairy, but we needed clean energy. And in my mind, gas is gas, whether it's happening inside a cow or a star. Or a round of cheese."

Del looked at the racks of peaceful cheeses, and wondered if they knew they had the heart of stars.

Over the next four days, she and Xiaren bonded over rice-paper rolls and grilled cheese sandwiches, listening to each other delivering their spiels to the curious visitors who streamed endlessly through the halls. Some people seemed interested in Del's collection of giant phasmids and burrowing cockroaches. Less so in her infographics, research papers and posters of 'fun facts.'

"Koumi?" said one middle-aged man, studying her information screen as it hovered over his wrist-chip. "Any relation to Lilana?"

"That's my mother."

The man's smile broadened. "I saw her presentation nearly twenty years ago. She knew her stuff. Generous, too. My pitch for a café run by homeless ex-cons sank at the panel, but your mum gave me a cricket flour starter kit and a recipe for butterscotch pancakes. It's still a bestseller at the café now. I was so tickled when I saw her Caramelised Onion Protein Bars in my local supermarket a few years back. Tell your mother, 'Irvine says hi'."

However, not every visitor was as supportive as Irvine. Del's stand elicited as many 'ew's as Xiaren's elicited 'phew's. Many potential investors scurried past, eyes averted, handkerchiefs over their noses. By the time Del's convention pass flashed with her presentation alert, she was feeling less than buoyed by the public's reaction.

"Hey," said Xiaren. "It doesn't matter what people say. What matters is what you do about it. I'm sure your bugs think you're awesome."

Del made her way through the seething crowd, clutching a single terrarium. Every exhibitor was granted one ninety-second pitch slot with minimal props. If the panel wanted more information, they'd investigate your online portfolio, and, if you were lucky, they'd visit your booth.

She took a slight detour through Meadow Hall, marvelling at the glittering lights, colourful holograms and delicious aromas. One stand billowed gently with cumulous clouds, while another promised neural-implant learning modules.

She finally spotted Ziad's booth. His glistening displays of pastries had tempted a large crowd, and he was enthusiastically describing the carbon footprint of a regular egg tart, compared to the carbon footprint of his regeneratively farmed eggs and macadamia butter pastry egg tarts. Del noted, with considerable satisfaction, that Ziad's onlookers included a significant number of snappily dressed proxy droids, favoured by professional investors who wanted to inspect potential ventures without leaving the house. Del glimpsed one or two faceports that seemed to show the bleary expression of someone who was probably still in their pyjamas.

Del's pass flashed more urgently, and she hurried the rest of the way to Galaxy Hall. The cavernous theatre was almost pitch-black, lit only by twinkling beads of lights on the ceiling and softly coruscating guide-strips on the floor. The hall was largely empty—most people preferred to watch the presentations on their displays, but Del's heart still stuck in her throat as she walked down the aisle and onto the stage.

Her courage almost failed her as she saw the panel of five judges seated near the front. Metres away from her sat Solaria Grande, her brown skin dusted with holographic flecks, her frohawk teased with grey and threaded with light-emitting filaments. Cybernetic contacts made her irises a sigil of golden circuitry, and she looked every inch the ecological goddess who'd forced the desert into retreat. Her seed-planting drones had strafed the land with precisely mapped grasslands, scrub and forests. Her educational programs and support networks had empowered communities to manage the natural regeneration of dormant vegetation systems.

Del felt her voice evaporating as those golden eyes fixed onto her.

"Adelie Koumi," said Solaria Grande. "What do you have for us?"

With shaking hands, Del set the covered terrarium onto the presentation table. "Dung..." Her voice cracked, and the silence seemed to swallow her. She took a slow, deep breath, and imagined she could see Andromeda. "Dung beetles navigate by the stars. Bogong moths migrate thousands of kilometres by starlight. We still know so little about insects and their relationship with the constellations, yet they could hold the key to our off-world aspirations.

"Our ability to colonise other planets hinges upon how well we can recreate functioning ecosystems. How can we do that without the pollinators and the decomposers? Without the complex web of organisms that sustains life on Earth? If we intend to make our home on other worlds, that home will need insects.

"Furthermore, space radiation remains one of our biggest obstacles to interstellar travel. However, tardigrade cells contain a protein that protects DNA from radiation damage, and not only could this protein allow humans to travel beyond the safety of our planet, it could also have implications for protecting us against cancers, radiation therapy, and cellular degeneration.

"Another challenge is developing resilient materials that can withstand physical and radioactive assault, but remain sufficiently lightweight and versatile for launch and operational needs. However, I've experimented with the proteins in spider silk, and I believe there are potential applications in the development of self-healing spaceships, habitats and safety lines.

"Finally, orbital junk poses a threat not only to space travel, but to the safety of our satellites and space stations. I've been studying the movement of spiders in zero-gravity, and I believe that automated arachnoid robots and mesh snares could play a key role in the retrieval of dangerous orbital refuse.

"Now, I don't have a product to sell or a business to implement. What I'm hoping to do is spark interest, encourage collaborations, spur research. What I'm proposing is a space station dedicated to the study of invertebrate organisms in non-terrestrial environments. Because when we eventually journey to the stars, I believe our tiny colleagues not only deserve to, but essentially must, come with us."

Del pulled the cloth from the terrarium to reveal a zero-gravity chamber containing a model spaceship surrounded by tiny floating balls of aluminium foil. She flashed a laser pointer across the porthole of the ship, and an ogre-faced spider excitedly scurried out. It launched into a gently swimming motion through the weightless space and proceeded to collect the nectar-daubed foil with a silken snare.

It wasn't a product, or a service, or a design. It was probably rather silly.

But it was memorable.

She finally dared to look at the panel, whose expressions ranged from bemused to stony.

"Thank you," said Grande. "Please enjoy the rest of the exhibition."

With a mixture of embarrassment and elation, Del left the stage. As she walked past the panel, she thought she caught a flicker of a smile on Grande's lips, but it might have been a trick of the starlight.

***

On the final day of the exhibition, hardly anyone came through Tundra Hall. It would seem that word had spread, and a consensus had been reached that there was little to see here.

"I'm sure it has nothing to do with your presentation," said Xiaren. "It was cute. I mean interesting. Hardly anyone said it was weird."

"Uh, thanks…"

A familiar figure trotted over. "Actually, it was slightly weird. But also very cool." Ziad graciously set down a tray laden with eclairs, baklava, mochi, and raspberry strudels.

Del struggled, and failed, to keep her mood in a trench. "They're about to announce the winner. Shouldn't you be networking in the Investor's Lounge?"

"My details are online," he replied. "And I saw this irresistible presentation about these incredible exploding cheeses."

Xiaren sighed. "No one was hurt. And I've figured out the problem."

As Ziad sampled Xiaren's tasting plate, Del started on an eclair, interrupted only by an impatient '*ahem*'.

A heavy-set woman with brown skin and scarlet-lacquered nails stood before Del's booth, arms crossed, wearing an expression like someone who spends her day maintaining a polite tone of voice while suppressing a category-five rage-hurricane.

"Are you the one who wants to build rocketships for spiders?"

"Well…" Del wondered if she were about to be subjected to another rant about scientists and taxpayer money. She reached for her 'Fun Facts About Science' leaflet, complete with a helpful infographic about the 90% return on investment. "Well, yes, but I have this leaflet—"

"My Jada has something to say to you." The woman clearly had no time for infographics. She nudged her charge.

Del peered over the counter, and a small girl with a vigorous puff of brown hair thrust a large piece of paper towards her. The crayon drawing depicted a shuttle sloshing with spiders, and a puff-haired girl sitting at the controls, smiling like the sun.

"Jada wants to pilot one of your ships when she grows up," said the woman. "Shuttling spiders into space to keep the planet safe."

The girl nodded vigorously, thrusting the picture towards Del again as though presenting her CV. Del tenderly accepted it, not mentioning that free-range probably wasn't the best way to transport a colony of spiders.

"Thank you. I'll keep you in mind."

The girl saluted ferociously before marching away with her mother.

"That was also weird," said Ziad. "But adorable."

A chord of music rippled from the front of the hall, accompanied by a mesmerising aurora. The stage suffused with light, coalescing into a holographic broadcast of the closing ceremony concurrently taking place in Celebration Hall. The convener thanked all the attendees, and a series of guests gave stirring speeches about innovation and persistence. But everyone was waiting for the final speaker, and the final announcement.

Solaria Grande was resplendent in an emerald suit that appeared to generate its own micro-ecosystem, seeming to ripple with grass one moment and shimmer with moss the next.

"The prize is not about the prestige," she declared, "although it has launched careers and established reputations. The prize is not about the money, although it has seeded ambitious projects and turned dreams into flourishing businesses. The prize is what you brought here with you. The prize is what you take away. The prize is what you've shared with all the people who passed through those doors. But that's not what most of you came here for, is it? So, without further ado—"

In the breathless silence of the hall, Del, Ziad and Xiaren linked hands, grinning with the inexpressible joy of being *here* and *now*, on the cusp of something extraordinary, no matter what came next.

"—the winner of the Solaria Grande Exhibition Prize is—"

***

Another Thirty Years Later

The shuttle docked with barely a bump, and Del released the armrests of her business-class seat. She'd made this trip countless times now, but that final *click* of the docking clamps always sent electric shivers to the very tips of her fingers. She brought her face close to the passenger-side window, her nose almost touching the cold, transparent matrix.

In the dizzying expanse of space, the station hung in the star-dusted void. It resembled a complicated molecule, with large glassy nodes interconnected via semi-rigid passageways. Its surface rippled with tiny photovoltaic scales, all turning to lap up the passing sun. In the half-light of space, it looked almost like a slumbering snake, curling itself into Celtic knots.

A coppery octobot jetted gracefully past, trailing a net of captured space debris. Del watched with a faint ache of pride as it climbed in through a station hatch and disappeared with its haul.

Del passed through decontamination and stepped into the arrival hall. She'd imagined, once, that space would be all chrome and glass and pulsing lights. Clinical, synthetic, easy to clean. But, back on Earth, past efforts to eliminate germs and bugs from human habitations had led to an explosion in allergies, inflammatory diseases and decimated microbiomes. Successful, long-term space exploration would not—could not—be a sterile venture, and what humanity needed now was a sandpit to experiment in.

Throughout the hall, aluminium trusses were laced with lilac wisteria, and mesh walls brimmed with ferns and bromeliads, forming an avenue of vertical gardens. Despite the softly humming filtration systems, the scent of orange blossom and pear tarts wafted from the nearby cafés. Del's mouth twitched into a smile—as it always did—at the sleek sign emblazoned over the entrance arch.

TERRARIUM SPACE STATION

Del had few rituals, but this one she had maintained for twelve years, since the day of her first visit. She made her way to the Summer Arboretum, past aromatic lemon trees and velvety bushes of French lavender. In a small grove, curtained off by bottlebrush, there stood a little bronze statue of an ogre-faced spider holding a small moon aloft in her forelegs.

DEDICATED TO ARTEMIS,
WHOSE CHILDREN REACHED THE STARS

Del gazed up at the large circular skylight, the cloud-dappled Earth a delicate sphere hanging in the darkness, and wondered what Artemis would have made of this.

"Del! I only just saw your name on the arrival logs." A lean young woman with a short mane of curly brown hair walked across the flowering grasses, her navy flight suit marked with the epaulettes of a captain. "Why didn't you tell us you were coming?"

"Jada! I thought you weren't due back for another week."

"We had a biomechanics team from Astroviva scheduled to arrive yesterday, so I thought I'd come back early. They're trying to design an asteroid rover with variable terrain mobility, emergency aerial capabilities, flexible anchoring technology, and a compact folding solar array."

"Peacock spiders," said Del automatically, and Jada grinned.

"They're with the arachnology team as we speak."

"You've been busy. I saw the new Phasmid and Mantis Habitat Pods on the inflight preview."

"Yes, those opened last month. I don't think the stick insects have realised it's zero-g yet, and I don't think the mantids care. Oh, and in other exciting news—it's still under wraps, but we're planning to build a Cephalo Pod. Because who doesn't want to see octopuses in space?"

Del's heart somersaulted in anticipation as she imagined the mischief an octopus might get up to in space. "Save me a ticket to the opening."

"Will do. So, are you here for work or pleasure this time?"

"It's always a bit of both. But I'm meeting an old friend here later."

"Let me know if you need anything. And say 'hi' to your folks for me."

"I will."

Del visited the various research pods, listening as each scientist enthused about their latest project. It was hard to imagine that, thirty years ago, all she had was a room full of bugs and a dream. As it turned out, others had shared that dream.

In the end, the Solaria Grande Prize had gone to a non-profit organisation that coordinated teams of teachers, librarians, and androids, sending them out in nimble airships to help communities build, equip, and staff schools for girls in remote regions.

But Del's wobbly video of a weightless spider gripping a wad of aluminium had captured the imagination of a few people out there, some of whom had looked into Del's projects and reached out to her, and to each other. And, like a colony of spiders, the web of connections had grown until it was strong enough to catch an elephant. Or launch a space station.

Later that night, Del enjoyed dinner at one of the station's restaurants—spicy eggplant stew and mango pancakes—before she made her way back to the Summer Arboretum. The dome had drifted into its nocturnal cycle, the lights dimmed so that only moonlight shone through the skylights. Del strolled the gentle slopes, and from a distant pod, disoriented crickets sang odes to memories of 'up' and 'down.'

"Hi, Del. I brought you something."

Del turned to see Ziad standing beside a sandstone water feature, holding a plate of something that resembled a swirl of light.

Del laughed, wrapping her friend in a warm embrace. "How was your flight?"

"Terrifying. I refer to the ticket price, not the journey."

Del winced. "Space tourism is still in its infancy—"

"You mean poorly regulated monopolies are still gouging consumers."

"Speaking of monopolies, how's Xiaren?"

"She's well. Still irritated every time the press calls her a 'biofuels magnate'."

"Ah, she'll always be a fromager at heart."

Ziad smiled, his gaze coming to rest on the tiny statue of a spider and her moon. "Well, we all managed to follow our hearts, didn't we?"

Del considered this. "I think, perhaps, we followed the science and the necessity. And our hearts just didn't allow us to give up."

A breeze stirred in the microclimate of the arboretum, and Del could almost taste the smoky summers of long ago. She and Ziad stood side by side, watching the Earth swirl gently with the seasons.

From up here, all of humanity was little more than a microcosm, every living speck indistinguishable from any other. And yet, if you looked closer, you'd see the breathtaking complexity of every single soul; you'd see new stories constantly unfolding, new journeys constantly beginning.

Somewhere, down there, a pair of ambitious teenagers shared their hopes beneath a gibbous moon.

Somewhere, down there, a campfire burned beneath a sky streaked with galaxies, and a moth fluttered, unscathed, through the flames.

And somewhere, down there, an ogre-faced spider watched a strange star moving across the midnight sky, and dreamed.

RIOT OF THE WIND AND SUN

Jennifer Lee Rossman

"'Riot of the Wind and Sun. Coming soon to a city near you'," Zeph read aloud from her tablet while the nail polish dried.

The girls laughed, the sound echoing off the carved cave walls along with the energetic song blaring from their music player. It was Kirra's favorite, a protest song called "Always, Always."

"Not likely," Kirra said, reaching into the nearest glass bowl. She scattered a handful of red beads in her lap, her dress forming a nice little hammock for them in the valley between her outstretched legs. "Even if we had better roads into town, they wouldn't come." She speared a tiny seed bead on her needle. "No one knows we exist."

"Will you stop moving!" Zeph chided, grabbing Kirra's foot. She painted the final coat on her big toe with a steady hand. The bright yellow polish complemented Kirra's dark skin, like the rising sun over the Outback.

The lights flickered and dimmed. Not a total blackout this time, but the girls' nails still glowed, along with their clothes and the beads. It would be brighter in the front of the shop, where Kirra's aunt had installed phosphorescent backup lighting, but no one could criticize the volume of their music if they stayed in the storeroom.

"Aw, potch," Zeph swore. "You wanted your whole foot yellow, yeah?"

Kirra looked at the glowing streak across her foot. "No!"

Zeph tried to wipe it off, but succeeded only in smearing it. "Eh. Tell people you're starting a trend." She went back to reading from her tablet. "They're doing pop-up concerts. Just showing up in random towns and asking to play."

"Entire town living in old opal mines? We're nothing if not

random." Kirra squinted at the design she was beading. Just random patches of color right now, but they'd soon morph into the dingos and lizards she saw in her mind.

"Just have to get us on the map," Zeph announced, tossing her tablet aside. The last page of the weekly news blast glowed eerily in the semidarkness: a poster for Riot of the Wind and Sun's summer concert tour, featuring a stylized wind turbine slashing the coat of arms of Adelaide.

Known for being edgy and rebellious, the band was made up of people who had fought in the war for the rights of little outpost towns like Coober Pedy. They were the people who had made it possible for them to use some of the energy they generated on their massive wind and solar farms, instead of having all of it diverted to Adelaide and the other big cities.

Kirra stared at the poster as the lights dimmed further around them, the screen illuminating her face and glinting on all the beads in her hair.

Coober Pedy was exactly the kind of place Riot of the Wind and Sun would love to play an impromptu concert.

If only they knew it existed.

***

Kirra sat on the stone floor of her aunt's shop, sewing beads onto dresses made of smart fabric that felt like cool water in her hands. A luxury in the underground city, but an absolute necessity for those that braved the outside, like the turbine mechanics and the people who swept the red Outback dust from the acres of solar panels.

In addition to adding a little flair to otherwise plain tans and whites, the beads absorbed light, like her nail polish and the backup lighting that ran along the ceilings of most of the caves and tunnels, and emitted a bright glow in case of a power outage. Some people had their entire homes and furniture painted with glow, so they'd never be inconvenienced on days when the capital took all the power.

Some of the dresses were just beaded on the edge. Simple

geometric patterns. But the really fancy gowns, the ones they made special for weddings and birthdays, they were elaborate as the night sky, each design passed down from the first people of Australia who had lived there even before the Europeans came. Those dresses were her favorite, like family scrapbooks you could wear.

Her aunt worked from a pattern, but Kirra could see it in her mind, work out what bead had to go where to create the Rainbow Serpent motif.

While she worked, she hummed Riot songs and imagined the thrill of seeing them play live. It'd have to be a night concert—the old opal mines the town was built in were expansive, but not even the chapel could hold the audience of a rock concert, and the heat of the day was too oppressive.

They could set up the stage on that little hill overlooking town, with the turbines in the background, and everyone would be there in their best beaded clothes. The night would glow with music.

A plain gown draped across the counter caught Kirra's eye, and she started absent-mindedly imagining the design she'd bead onto it to wear for the concert that would never happen.

Soft greens like the first shoots of spring, beiges and rusts like the Outback, all swirled together in a spiraling pattern that would glow like the great river of stars in the night sky.

Curious, she had just stood up to see what shades of green they had in storage when Zeph came running into the shop, waving her tablet.

"They're coming!"

Kirra's heart stopped, and forgot to start again for a few seconds.

"No, no," Zeph said quickly, "not *them*." She thrust the tablet in her friend's face.

This week's news blast featured an announcement that a census survey would take place in five days.

Kirra looked up at the most recent census map from a decade before, displayed on the shop's smooth rock wall. Australia was a dark patch in the ocean, the lights of big cities a bright fringe on either coast. A black swath in the middle was the Outback, its expanse dotted with the occasional tiny point of light at the location of a bigger solar or wind farm, the kind that could afford cooling biodomes over their aboveground settlements.

Coober Pedy had exactly one light on the surface, a little red one that blinked a warning so hovercraft wouldn't get too close to the open mine shafts, and no one but turbine inspectors and the odd parcel delivery ever came to town.

On the map, Kirra's aunt had circled a dark patch at the southern end of the old Stuart Highway and scrawled "Coober Pedy" in bright letters.

"They'd see something that big," Zeph said with a laugh. "'Coober Pedy' written across the desert? But anyway, I thought we could go up topways that night, see if we can spot the plane?"

Kirra didn't answer, her attention fixated on the map.

Five days.

Yeah, they could do it in five days.

She nodded to herself. "Let's put Coober Pedy on the map."

***

Long shadows swept across the desert as the turbine giants swung their arms in the last orange rays of sunlight. The ground radiated heat, but the air was starting to cool enough that it no longer felt like inhaling an oven.

Kirra sat on the hill where she hoped the band would play, idly pushing beads around in the soil.

"What are we waiting for?" Zeph asked again.

"You'll see."

Or so Kirra hoped.

She pushed the beads into the shape of letters, variations on the pattern springing into her mind fully formed. In the simplest font, each letter was three beads by five. That meant thirty-eight across, with spaces, fewer if she put the words on top of each other. She imagined a swooping arrow curving off the end of the Y, pointing directly at the city.

She stared down at the beads and chewed her lip in thought. How did tiny beads translate to meters and acres? Would they have enough glow to embellish the desert?

Kirra's nails began to emit a faint yellow light as the sun finally dipped below the horizon.

Zeph stood, craning her neck. "What's that?"

Grinning, Kirra scrambled to her feet. Way out beyond the first row of solar panels, a multicolored glow pierced the endless black of night.

"That," she said, grabbing Zeph's arm in excitement, "is a big pile of every luminescent thing I own."

Zeph tilted her head to the side. "What did you go and do that for?"

In response, Kirra gestured grandly to the beads.

"'Coober Pedy'," Zeph read.

"Now pretend each letter's an acre tall. The plane can't miss us if they try."

***

The sun gave life to the Earth. Nurtured her with light and warmth and made her vibrant and beautiful. When it struck the blue-black photovoltaic cells that carpeted the Outback, its light was transformed into energy that brought warmth and life to the most inhospitable caverns.

It also turned the air to liquid fire, or so it felt as Kirra and Zeph sped along the solar fields with Zeph's father. Their scarves fluttered over their faces in the wind, the built-in filters keeping the blowing sand from entering their mouths, but Kirra felt her lungs burning with every breath.

When they stopped to sweep the dust from the shimmering panels, which required getting out of the shaded hovercraft, she thought her skin would burst into flames, even though not a centimeter of it was exposed to the harsh rays.

Zeph's father welcomed the help. Zeph, having been volunteered without her knowledge, glared from beneath her floppy hat, but dutifully took measurements on her tablet and scattered the glowing beads like breadcrumbs.

"It's too big," she reported. "Everything you own made a spot the size of the space inside one of the Os." She showed Kirra the diagram, all math and squiggles that didn't mean anything.

In her mind, Kirra saw the fields from above, saw the path of their hover as it scrawled the words across the Outback. Big, yes. Massive. But *too* big? No, she thought. Just big enough to put them on the map.

***

For the next two nights, they worked. Every kid in Coober Pedy, and a good number of the adults, trudging back and forth from town to the fields with backup lights and spare clothes and household items.

The beads Kirra and Zeph had left in the desert shone with the absorbed light of day, a million points of light in the black sand. Like a reflection of the sky and all its stars.

Kirra flitted from letter to letter, helping her townspeople fill in the outlines that would label them, would bring their little town back to the world for the first time in a hundred years.

It used to be no one came to the outposts. Left them to fend for themselves and live only to supply the capital with power. Then the outposts rebelled, cut off the power entirely. Then people came, people with guns and explosives. They came every time the towns dared to fight back.

The war fixed that. People from all across Australia, risking their lives to travel thousands of kilometers to round up the other towns and fight. People as young as Kirra had led armies into the capital itself.

Now that they had power, they got news from outside and seasonal visits from the mail truck. But no one else came. No one cared.

They would come once Coober Pedy was on the map. Tourists to buy some beaded dresses and the opals the town had been built upon, geologists to study the old mines.

Bands like Riot of the Wind and Sun.

Kirra's heart sang out in joy as the letters came into being, each a shining beacon shouting news of their existence into the void.

A breeze picked up, billowing her skirt and throwing sharp projectiles of sand at her face. It showed no signs of stopping and by the end of the night, a sloped pile had accumulated at the base of each turbine.

***

The winds continued all through the day. The sweepers had to fight to keep the sand from accumulating on the panels, leaving no time to uncover the now-buried letters.

Kirra stood in the shade of what had once been the entrance to one of the larger mines, watching the sun in its freefall. Soon it would hit the ground, splash stars up into the sky. All over Australia, lights would come on and the planes would fly over to map them all.

And Coober Pedy would be forgotten once again.

It took every bit of strength for Kirra not to crumble to the floor and cry. Her beautiful words would never be seen now, and Riot of the Wind and Sun would never come. The summer would end without a concert, their town little more than a blank spot on the map.

Echoing footsteps preceded Zeph's arrival at her side. She took her friend's hand wordlessly, their nails glowing yellow and pink in the twilight.

"There's no time to dig them out," Kirra whispered. "Not before the plane comes by. All I've done is get sand on all our spare clothes."

"Just the spares," Zeph pointed out.

Kirra looked at her curiously, the seed of an idea taking root. Zeph had donated most of her luminescent wardrobe to the cause, but like the rest of the three thousand citizens, she'd kept a few items for safety's sake. Wasn't good to be caught in the dark when the lights went out.

Zeph's loose blouse glowed a soft blue, her pants a rainbow of beaded trim. Kirra wore something similar, her shirt accented with cutouts around the shoulder, and lighted threads wound through her braids completed her pink aura.

Most everyone in town would glow, if the lights went out. Or if they went out in the night.

"Go get everyone," Kirra said suddenly.

"Everyone?" Zeph asked. "Everyone who?"

"*Everyone.* The whole town. Get them and meet me in the fields."

Kirra took off at a run, her feet striking the sunbaked earth, and didn't stop until she reached the mounds of sand where her letters should have been. She couldn't make out the shapes, but she saw the image in her mind, and that was all that mattered.

The townsfolk appeared on the horizon, their brightest clothes turning the procession into a winding ribbon of light. Kirra wasted no time in directing them as the low hum of a distant plane cut through the night.

When everyone else was in position, Kirra laid herself on the warm ground, her body making the very point of the arrow.

One of the stars blinked overhead, slowly tracking across the sky. Kirra waved at the pilots. They couldn't see her; she was far too small. But maybe they could see the town.

She imagined their surprise as they passed over an empty stretch of Outback, only to see a great swath of color. A neon sign shouting "Coober Pedy" with the voice of every one of its citizens.

***

The new map came out. Adelaide had gotten a little brighter, Sydney had dimmed as people fled the rising sea levels, and a few new outposts had cropped up out west.

But no one talked about that.

All the news articles wanted to know: what was that little patch of light along Stuart Highway? It was faint, so tiny as to be barely visible, but didn't it look like words? And an arrow?

Kirra had printed her copy quickly, before they lost the connection, and now sat with it on the hill overlooking the town she had put on the map, beading her dress in the last sunrise of summer.

"Truck," Zeph reported, shielding her eyes from the sun.

Kirra heard it too, that bumbling rumble of tires on the old road, and stood to greet their guests. As the masterminds of the plan, the girls had taken it upon themselves to welcome news crews who came to document Coober Pedy, the so-called "hidden gem of New South Wales."

But this wasn't a news crew. The truck—no, *trucks*, plural—were too big and fancy.

Kirra's heart caught in her throat as the lead truck turned and its side became visible. There, painted in big letters…

"Can't be," Zeph said, but her voice shook with excitement.

"It is." Kirra hugged her before they ran down to meet the band. "Coober Pedy is a city near you!"

The whole town came out that night to dance, their light rivaling the stars above as Riot of the Wind and Sun played on the hill. Kirra twirled in her beaded gown, her braids cutting the air like the blades of a turbine.

FYREWALL

Stefani Cox

It only took an hour on the trail for Daesha to lose Talia. Or rather, that's all it took for Talia to give her the slip. They'd headed out of the city and into the dusty, dry hills together, feet crunching in three separate pairs though the sticklike yellow grass. But eventually, Daesha realized one set of footsteps was missing. *I am never having kids,* thought Daesha. *I'm supposed to be doing a job, not running an internship program.* Saddling her with two teenagers fulfilling their community justice agreements was yet one more sign that The Council didn't take her position seriously. *And why should they?* she mused. *It's not like they really need me anyway.*

Daesha felt the sweat run down the base of her neck and underneath her shirt. Her scalp felt scratchy and hot, even though she had tied her locs up into a topknot earlier. The sun made her tired and grouchy every time.

"Hey, Ms. Daesha," said Carlos next to where she stopped. "Where did Talia get to? How come she gets to do whatever she wants?"

Her remaining charge looked irritated. He slapped at his neck to kill a gnat and then wiped his hand on his khaki pants. The mop of his black hair, shiny and freshly washed when Daesha picked him up at five this morning, was already silty with airborne dirt and debris from the bushes and trees lining the trail. She noticed that Carlos was twirling a thin metal object that looked just like her—"How did you get my particlemeter?" asked Daesha, swiping it back. She was sure she had stuffed it into the bottom of her bag. Carlos gave her a cheeky half-smile through his translucent facemask.

"I wanted to see what it does."

Never kids. Daesha took a slow breath through her own filter. No matter. She needed to check on the air quality levels at this spot anyway. She pushed a button on the side of the particlemeter and waited for the reading to sync and flash across her Ocu-contacts. Normal ranges. Or rather, abnormal ranges for human health, but nothing higher than expected.

"Go make yourself useful and see if you can find Talia," Daesha said to Carlos.

"What if I don't feel like it?"

"Well, then I guess I can put that in my progress report for The Council. I'm sure they'll be happy to hear an update on how you've been feeling."

He glowered and then slowly sauntered off toward the next hill, looking back at her once to see if she was still watching him.

Daesha patted her pockets. "You better not have taken anything else," she muttered. She fanned her face with a hand, and hoped that Talia wasn't off playing with fire as she was known to do. The destructive habit had been the reason The Council placed her with Daesha in the first place. *Let her see why fire is so dangerous. Help her contribute to the resistance of fire,* they'd intoned. For Carlos, they'd told her simply, *There's not much he can steal out there. Expose him to other ways of occupying his mind.*

It was hot. At least one hundred and thirty degrees hot. But the thermo-screen that they all used whenever leaving the cooled sphere of the city did its job, and Daesha was glad to know that at least her skin wouldn't burn and peel off in flaky scales later. She'd heard stories from Grandma Jean about how that used to happen before drugstores started selling thermo-screen over the counter. First, only the light-skinned kids had to get the ointments and deep burn treatments for sun exposure. Then, as California continued to warm, even her own family members started to experience the negative effects.

Daesha turned back the way they had come and scanned the

horizon for Talia. From her vantage point among the hills she could see all of Los Angeles spread out before her. The city seemed to sparkle through the gentle translucence of the Fyrewall.

The view of the city was a stark contrast from these dead, lonely hills she trekked among on a regular basis. Daesha remembered what Grandma Jean had said about LA being a bare desert more than a thousand years ago, which then grew to a sprawling, congested city where everyone coughed and hacked amidst brown air. She'd seen pictures in classroom holographics, but it still seemed hard to believe.

As long as Daesha had known her hometown, it had been dense and tall, with skyscrapers filling most of the land inside the wall, and trains snaking between the buildings at all times of day and night. Walking back and forth from school, she remembered coming across lush green pocket parks full of drought-resistant plants and little shaded nooks for studying or talking. Sometimes she would bike through her neighborhood's greenways to the edge of downtown, where she leaned against the guardrails and watched the expansive river flow past.

Surrounding everything was the wall itself, a blue, shimmering sheet of compressed oceanwater that Grandma Jean's team had engineered into a dome shape. It enveloped the city and protected it from the flames that used to ravage LA during summers just like this. Squinting now, Daesha could see the yellow-marked, guarded portal where she and the teens had come through the Fyrewall.

Daesha shook her head to clear it and put her back to the city again to continue up the trail. She was always floating away in a daydream; there was not much else to do out here. With the Fyrewall pretty much maintaining itself, she felt largely irrelevant. Daesha tried not to think about what industrious, brilliant Grandma Jean would think of her only living descendent aimlessly meandering the hills. But she wasn't alone today—she was in charge of the teens—and now she had to find both of them.

Her instruments began to beep. A table of columns, numbers, and percentages flashed across her vision. It was a compilation that her computer had just synthesized of all the local environmental readings—air quality, temperature, moisture levels, barometric pressure, and a million other measurements she didn't fully understand. Some of the numbers were pulsing in red. The beeping continued.

Daesha flicked the fingers of her right hand to trigger the bar chart mode, so that she could better understand what she was seeing. In the moment that it took her to absorb the red and blue rectangles, her heart jumped. She flicked her fingers again to put the data on a timeline and saw the dip clear as anything.

For some reason, the energy output readings from the past month were low. Abnormally low. The Fyrewall was losing power.

Daesha continued scanning the charts with a lump in her throat, but there was no denying it. The wall was built to be self-sustaining. In fact, it did more than sustain itself; it provided power for the whole city. But she could see that the output was going to lower soon, if the information was correct.

Daesha swallowed. She would have to tell The Council about this, and then they would want her to tell them what to do.

Something else was also bothering Daesha, but she couldn't put her finger on it. It was something outside of the sensors and readings themselves, something that her body was taking in about the physical environment, tingling at the edge of her awareness.

Whatever it was triggered a memory of Grandma Jean and the times she would read to Daesha at night when her parents worked late. The two of them would cuddle in Daesha's small bed, and she would breath in the lilac soap-scented heaven of her grandma, who was really her great-grandmother, as she listened to today's tale. Something about the past. Something about history.

...tore through the city...

"Yo, Ms. Daesha," shouted a familiar voice. "I found Talia. She's got something you should look at." Carlos appeared at the edge of her vison with a silent Talia in tow. The black girl was covered from head-to-toe, despite the heat. She wore a gray hoodie, dark skater shoes, and a sullen frown to complete the picture. She stared off into space next to Daesha's head.

"Talia!" Daesha scolded. "Where have you been? You can't just wander off like that!" Talia's expression didn't change.

"She's not going to talk to you," said Carlos. "She won't say anything. But she found something."

"What do you mean?"

Talia blinked and pointed over the east ridge. Daesha paused. It was the direction of the Fyrewall, though a different section than the one they had come through. She was still mad at Talia, but she did need to find out what was happening to the technology. She tapped her foot against the ground impatiently, then readjusted her shoulder bag.

"Fine," said Daesha. "Let's go."

She followed as Talia led the three of them down through the low brush and scraggly trees. They walked in silence for five minutes, drawing closer and closer to the blue shimmer. Something was still bothering Daesha, but she was distracted again as they neared the wall and her sensors started beeping faster.

The three of them kept going until they were just a few yards from the wall, where Talia stopped and pointed again. Daesha's instruments reached a crescendo. She was having a hard time seeing through all the data popping up in her Ocu-contacts. With an annoyed wave of her hand she turned them all off—the contacts, the sensors, everything. Her vision returned to normal, and the blue shimmer became more immediate.

That was when she saw the tear in the Fyrewall, a gap that was hard to notice if you weren't looking straight at it. It was a zigzag of blank air, surrounded by the water in the rest of the wall. The teenagers looked at her, but they didn't need Daesha to tell them this was a very bad sign.

It was also then that Daesha finally noticed the smell of smoke, faraway in the breeze.

***

People referred to The Council as though it were a small circle of government officials, when in reality it was a chaotic mixture of, well, *everyone.* That was how The Council worked. You could elect someone to represent your group based almost any factor—geographic area, race, age, gender identity…the list went on. You could elect multiple representatives, and there was no limit, as long as representatives were active in participating with The Council and in fulfilling their assigned roles and duties.

So when Daesha and the teenagers stood before The Council via the holoconference she set up next to the wall tear, there were actually thousands of representatives uplinking to listen in on the conversation. And since the meetings were open to the entire city, any resident could theoretically tune in. Imagining the size of the audience that might be opening the feed from numerous points throughout the city made Daesha nervous. She swallowed to wet her throat in hopes that her voice wouldn't wobble anymore the way it had when she'd informed The Council of the problem.

"The active fire is the biggest concern," said one Councilmember, an older Latina woman with white-gray hair framing her face in crisp waves. "If it travels just a few miles, it could arrive at the wall and rip right through the tear. Our buildings would be immediately at risk."

"My community is concerned with the evacuation plan," said a mid-thirties man in a wheelchair with caramel-toned skin. He rolled closer to the device he was using to project into the meeting. "The maps are outdated, and we haven't been keeping up with accessibility plans the way we should have been. That's why I kept bringing it up in—"

"The Fyrewall is our only source of power," said a member who represented the nonbinary South Asian community. They raised a leather-cuffed arm to trigger the holoconference technology to amplify their screen. "We have backup power stored up to last us for a year or two, but we'll have to figure out how to keep the air purifiers running past that point if we want the city to stay livable."

"Forget the air purifiers. What about the other cities who come barging down to our door whenever they sense a weakness?" asked a precocious youth member. "Selling them the Fyrewall tech and keeping the barrier flowing has been the only way to keep them away long-term, right?"

Daesha crossed her arms over her chest and closed her eyes for a moment. She hated Council meetings for this very reason. Too many voices, and not enough leadership. Sure, it was more fair, but it amazed Daesha that anything got done at all within this system. She suspected it was due to the multitude of citizens who ran the sub-committees for budgeting, resource management, and security. They kept the city running, while those who wanted air time made a ruckus in holoconference convenings.

Another part of her dreaded the moment when they would stop talking and turn to her for a solution. She was the one who inherited the responsibility of maintaining Grandma Jean's wall when everyone else in her family had passed on or moved away.

Daesha had never been as brilliant as Grandma Jean. Yes, she'd followed along as her great-grandmother did her rounds, and learned about the various instruments for keeping an eye on the wall. Daesha mastered the data science to inform The Council of the expected energy output each week, and she'd quickly learned what ranges were normal. But she'd never *understood* the Fyrewall in the same way. She'd never been taught what to do in the face of an emergency, because there had never been an emergency. For Grandma Jean, it had been as though the wall were an extension of her own body, not simply an engineered structure to maintain. In comparison, Daesha felt like a fraud.

At her sides, she could sense Carlos and Talia watching her, waiting to see if she would intervene in the conversation, if she would speak up. Daesha looked over and noticed that Carlos had gotten his hands on the special thermo-screened water bottle she kept clipped to her shoulder bag. She'd purchased it last week, since it kept water ice cold, even outside of the city, but she didn't have the energy or attention to try and get it back right now. The Council representatives kept talking, until one voice quieter than all the rest somehow cut through the noise.

"The Fyrewall can be fixed," it said. The projection in front of Daesha switched to an ancient woman. The lines in her face were not wrinkles so much as deep grooves carved throughout the passage of time. She had to be one hundred and twenty or thirty at least. The wrinkles furrowed her expression into incomprehensible twists and turns, but her deep brown eyes were alive and gentle.

It was clear that, even in the non-hierarchical structure of The Council, this woman commanded a certain weight. No one talked as she gathered herself to speak again.

"I remember a time when wildfires conquered this city," she said.

...tore through...

"We were scared every summer that all the progress we made in making Los Angeles bigger, more inclusive, and self-sustaining, would get wiped away by the next burn. And it wasn't just us. So many cities fought the heat and failed in those early years."

The Council remained rapt. Even Carlos and Talia seemed to be paying more attention now. Their eyes were dreamy, as though the bedtime stories that Grandma Jean used to tell were being passed on to them now.

"Then your great-grandmother, my friend, came up with the Fyrewall," said the old woman, looking right at Daesha. "We all knew immediately that she had just saved us—our sovereignty and our progress." The woman took a long, slow breath that heaved her full body up and down. "But the wall is not a miracle," she said. "It's made up of earth, and minerals, and water, just like the rest of us. The wall can be fixed, and Jean believed you could do it, Daesha. She taught you, and she chose you."

The Council remained silent after that, since no one knew what else to say.

"Well, that sounds like an order," said Talia, speaking up for the first time since they'd left the city. "Guess you have to figure out how to fix this thing."

***

Once the three of them disconnected from the holoconference, Daesha noticed the smoky smell had grown stronger. A light breeze blew the scent of ashes and embers from what couldn't be more than a couple of hills away. Even though she knew they were in no immediate danger—the next portal was close and the thermo-screen protected against fire burns—the smell still triggered a fear in her, and made her hesitate.

"So what are you going to do about this hole?" asked Carlos, handing Daesha back her water bottle.

"Klepto," said Talia.

Carlos shrugged, but he did look a little apologetic. "Sorry, I can't help it. It's just too easy. But I always give stuff back."

Talia was looking at Daesha intently. "You're scared, aren't you?" she asked. "My sister always gets tense like you when she's worried about her kids."

Daesha felt a quick surge of warmth for Talia, which caught her by surprise. Didn't teenagers always think about themselves? When had Talia been paying enough attention to others to notice something like that?

She let the moment pass. "I'm going to try some reprogramming functions, just give me a few moments of quiet. Maybe I can figure this out."

The teens promptly wandered closer to the wall and started to throw pebbles at it. The stones pinged off the Fyrewall with enough force to make the activity a game. Talia and Carlos ended up dodging the little bullets as they shot back at them like squash balls. A couple of stones went through the gap in the wall instead of ricocheting off of it.

Daesha did her best to ignore their game and turned all her equipment back on. The first thing the sensors picked up was the approaching fire. Ten miles away and moving slowly. Good. No need to head back to the city yet. The next thing she figured out was how to pick up the size and location of the hole through a 3D rendering of the Fyrewall that she projected in front of her. It looked as though…no, that couldn't be right…

"Hey Ms. Daesha, did you know there are other cracks in the wall too?" It was Talia. She'd noticed the same thing that Daesha was picking up on her computers. The giant hole that Talia found earlier was actually flanked by tiny streaks of nothingness where the blue of the wall should be. *Why do I even bother with these gadgets at all?* Daesha wondered, toggling another control.

"Okay," Daesha snapped at Talia. "I'm working on it." She flipped through stats using the Ocu-contact set. Gravity hold, normal. Flow speed, normal. Wall width three to five feet, normal. She triggered the size controls anyway and heard the entire dome groan as it contracted by an inch. The adjustment didn't seem to do anything to close the gaps, even the small ones.

"Cool!" said Carlos. At least she had an appreciative audience.

Daesha didn't know what else to do. She'd never encountered a situation like this before, where the Fyrewall wasn't capable of fixing itself. Daesha sighed, and buried her eyes in her hands, near tears. She tried to channel the supportive gaze she remembered from Grandma Jean's Council friend, but she felt so alone out here above the city. What would The Council say when they realized that she wasn't who they thought she was? That the city was going to fall prey to the same problems it used to have long ago?

Daesha heard a metallic zip. Once. Twice. Again. She pulled her hands away from her face to see Talia flicking an e-lighter on and off. The stone game exhausted, Talia and Carlos were both sitting immediately next to the gap in the wall, watching the flame.

"Talia, you know you aren't supposed to have that," said Daesha. She readied herself to go into authoritative mode, which she had read somewhere was the best way to get defiant kids to listen.

Then something extraordinary happened. The Fyrewall reached out.

Talia screamed and nearly dropped the lighter she was holding. Carlos shimmied away from it faster than Daesha would have thought him capable. The bulge in the Fyrewall remained, a mass of it that had shifted to be closer to Talia.

"Do it one more time," said Daesha, a spark of inspiration hitting her.

Talia flicked the lighter, and the wall streamed out to touch it, absorbing only the flame. The color in the piece of wall that reached out brightened from aqua to a rich green. As the wall pulled itself back into place, it looked different somehow, newer.

Healed.

The section of the wall that had reached out was now completely smooth, with no cracks marring its surface. Talia looked up at Daesha, realizing what this could mean. She stood, walked to a new section of wall and flicked the lighter again.

The same process happened. The wall healed in the place where Talia fed it fire. Talia moved to try a third time.

As Talia flowed along the wall, the proof flitted across Daesha's contacts. The sensors were detecting bigger energy waves from the wall again—a spike each time Talia fed it fire. Based on what she was seeing, the new sections would have enough strength to both power the city and withstand external fire threats.

Carlos recovered from his startled state and went over to Talia.

"It's like it needs the fire to get better," he said, examining the latest healed spot. Daesha realized he was exactly right.

"It's gone symbiotic," she exclaimed. "The wall was created as standalone technology, but it's been absorbing the power of the fire that hits it! The wildfires don't damage the wall, they make it stronger. The wall needs the flames." She realized what she was saying. "This isn't the same wall that Grandma Jean built. It's…it's evolved."

The next idea seemed to come to her at the same time as the teenagers, who were already poised to move. "Gather branches," Daesha told them.

Carlos and Talia nodded and ran off to find some. When they came back, Daesha wrapped the bottom of three of the branches in strips from the heat-dispelling fabric she kept in her kit for emergencies. She handed each of the kids a piece of wood and kept one for herself. Then, she nodded at Talia to do the honors.

Talia flicked the lighter and touched it to the unwrapped portion of Daesha's branch, which caught immediately, dry as it was. Daesha held her flame out to Carlos' stick, and Carlos held his to Talia's. Together the three of them approached the original gaping hole they had found, and thrust the branches toward it.

For a moment, nothing happened. The break in the wall held its shape. And then, slowly, the edges of the Fyrewall seemed to sigh outward and pick up the energy of nearby light and heat. The structure reached and drank from the flames for several long minutes. Daesha and the teenagers held their arms steady, feeding the wall patiently.

Finally, the undulating matter relaxed back into place, freshly-knitted together and whole. The green of the new portion spread into the surface and healed several nearby cracks as well. *It's beautiful,* thought Daesha. *I never needed to fix the wall, just nourish it.*

Daesha turned to her charges with a grin. "Looks like there might be some more work out here for you two. Want to stay and help me repair the rest?"

"Really?" asked Carlos. "I thought you hated us." Talia looked confused too.

Daesha smiled, and thrust the final, smoldering embers of her stick into the emerald expanse. She watched the kaleidoscope effect unfold and laughed a little.

"I'm realizing I could use a couple of assistants who know what they're doing," she answered.

Talia studied Daesha carefully, then nodded and fed the remains of her charred branch to the Fyrewall too. "I guess I might have some time," she said. "As long as I get to keep my lighter."

"Too late," replied Carlos, as he flipped the metal device into the air and caught it in the palm of his hand.

WATCH OUT, RED CRUSHER!

Shel Graves

The mind-matriarch glowed faint luminescent pink—the most beautiful shade Andee had ever seen. Andee sat in the circle of students under the great willow tree while Madame Morell chanted words of solace, eyes closed. Although Andee knew it was just a side effect of the solar nanites that Aberdonia injected into the cells of all of its citizens, the pink glow still made Madame Morell look magical. Andee wished Madame Morell was, as she looked, a wish-granting fairy godmother. Instead, she was chanting, "Practice. Focus. Patience," as usual and reminding her students that, "A shade can't be forced, it must be found."

But I'm not patient. I don't have time to be patient, Andee thought. *I have to get my shade under control.*

For this First Summer celebration the community would still consider Andee a child and excuse her shifting shades. Soon though, as an adult, she'd be expected to settle in. It wasn't enough that the nanites glowing beneath her skin helped power the community, providing electricity, running water, and warming the algae production ponds. In addition, every resident of Aberdonia had to pick an occupation and be formally welcomed into the community at the autumn Sun Ceremony or face exile to the uncivilized Freeway—home to murderers and thieves. Everyone told Andee she was wrong to fear exile. Her parents were farmers and she would be, too.

"Oh, Andee, of course you'll be welcome," her mother said.

But Andee wasn't sure. She saw the way the elders looked at her blue shine with distaste. And she didn't want to be a farmer.

The elders thought Madame Morell was a charlatan, but the shade-changing classes were Andee's last hope. Unfortunately, the more she listened to Morell's soothing words, the more hopeless she felt. The nanites within her betrayed her feeling, making her glow a despondent blue. Everyone could see her insecurity and that made Andee feel even worse no matter how she tried to hide it. She glanced to the side through her blue glow at Irwin Hunter, who glowed red on the edge of the class. He'd come into class brick red and his shade hadn't dimmed despite Morell's guidance, deep slow breathing, and chanting, "Love. Peace. Love."

Irwin was also trying to gain acceptance by moderating his shade display, but his predicament was even worse than Andee's. His red betrayed an aggressive anger and most Aberdonians, including his own parents, feared him.

At least people don't think I'm *a monster*, Andee thought.

"Go in peace," Madame Morell said when the class ended, but Andee stayed, hoping to ask a question. As usual, Madame Morell was spending extra time with Irwin. Andee hovered nearby, overhearing their conversation.

"I went to Council Leader Gordon like you suggested," Irwin said. "He was welcoming. It was daytime so he couldn't see my shade and judge me by it, but I think I was keeping calm. I was excited, but not angry. You know, orange, at least. I let him know I was interested in apprenticing like you said."

"Good, good," Madame Morell said.

"Yeah, but then he asked me about my politics, my passion, and I…"

"Oh, Irwin."

"I got worked up. I can't lie! I told him I disagreed with the Solar Pact. I said I had some other ideas. I—I just talked too much."

"People do when they are passionate," Morell said.

"Sure, well, that's fine if you have ideas other people agree with…if not… Anyway, he got kind of mad. I got madder and then, well, he had this little Solar Pact monument on his desk, and I picked it up, threw it. Stupid thing."

"Oh, Irwin."

"It gets worse."

"Oh, Irwin."

"I threw it *at* him."

"You threw The Spiked Sun at the Council Leader?"

"It hit him in the face. There was blood."

Madame Morell's glow flickered, but then she stepped forward and hugged Irwin. He relaxed into the hug and shimmered soothing orange, but then seeing Andee watching he broke away. "I don't deserve it! Any of this! I didn't ask for this!" He stormed away, glowing bright red as a warning.

Andee turned, embarrassed. Throughout it all, Madame Morell hadn't lost her calm powder pink.

"Andee, is there something you wanted?"

"Yes, Madame, I've just been wondering about your glow, so light. Why did you choose such a low dose?"

"It's true," she said. "I got the smallest injection of nanites the Council would allow, so I glow very faintly. I was unsure about this whole idea and I was right to be wary. While the solar cells in our bodies have solved many problems, this side effect has created new ones."

Andee was afraid to ask her next question. "Did you consider going Unseen?"

"I did," Madame Morell said. "I could have refused the Solar Pact, refused the injection of nanites altogether. But then I wouldn't have been a part of the community. I would have been cast out. Maybe they wouldn't have done it right away, but eventually…I saw where things were headed. I can do more good here than out on the Freeway."

"Our generation wasn't given a choice," Andee said.

"I know. I'm sorry. You were injected at birth and you have to deal with these unintended consequences. Just know you're not alone. Others struggle, too. A shade can't be forced, it must be found." Andee knew Madame Morell was encouraging her to reach out to Irwin. "You have things in common," she said.

But Andee didn't like to think of herself as like him. Her struggles were different. She was depressed, not dangerous. She wouldn't risk her place in Aberdonia for him. The last time she'd tried to befriend Irwin, it hadn't gone well.

***

There was an incident in school when they were all quite young. Andee's mother had brought in a red velvet cake covered in raspberries, Andee's favorite. No one knew exactly what had happened, but Irwin had ended up stomping and smashing the red treat into a mush and none of them had gotten to eat any of it. After that, the kids had teased Irwin mercilessly, bringing in red foods and toys and asking Irwin to crush them in a myriad of violent outbursts, gleefully squealing when he had gone along with it. Irwin had earned the nickname Red Crusher. It got so no one called him by his real name.

Finally, the teacher had put a stop to it.

"No more Red Crusher," she'd said. "I'm introducing a new student, Irwin Hunter. Let's give him a fresh start."

The children had complied, pretending to forget the incident and playing nice, but behind his back, and the teacher's, Irwin had remained Red Crusher.

Nowadays, Red Crusher was synonymous with any uncontrolled red glow—a potentially violent person. Even the adults had picked up the term.

***

First Summer night celebrated the passage of Aberdonia's youth into adulthood. Everyone would be there. Andee knew she couldn't miss the social event of the year, but she was stuck in her indie sun dome glowing a wrong shade—a deep, sad blue—and she couldn't shake it. Dusk was turning the inside of her dome pale blue, reflected off of Andee's own solar skin shade. All she wanted was to stay inside, look at the nature scenes reflected on the walls of her sun dome, drink lavender tea, and go to sleep, but soon the community would be gathering for the evening festival. Andee closed her eyes and attempted Madame Morell's shade-shifting techniques. When she opened her eyes, she imagined she could see pleasing winks of green from the corner of her eyes.

"Please, please be green," she thought, as she turned toward her reflection in the concave mirrored wall behind her.

She heard Madame Morell's words, *A shade can't be forced, it must be found.*

That might be true, but if she couldn't shake her sad shade quickly, no one would hire her and she could be cast out of Aberdonia's utopia onto the Freeway. Andee didn't have time before the festival to wait for an acceptable hue to emerge. So, she begged. Her desperation worked, kind of. Squinting, *maybe*, maybe there was a sea green glint to her skin, but definitely the glow around her head and torso remained a depressed periwinkle blue.

Andee knew if she really wanted to change her mood, as Madame Morell often said, she needed to get out and be around her friends. Even if that didn't feel like what she wanted to do right now, it would help.

But she couldn't show up to the party blue. She needed pale green at least.

Fretting in the mirror, her shade lost all green and dropped to worried blue again.

Ugh, she thought, disgusted. *Why can't I just be right?*

Just then, a colored light—aquamarine—flashed over the dome, indicating the arrival of a guest.

"Oh no, Marina," Andee said, irritated by the interruption even though Marina was one of her favorite classmates.

She went to the side of the dome and an arc of light opened for her friend. Marina stepped in, glowing a radiant green, a nourishing sea shade around her hemp halter-top and wrap skirt.

"So beautiful," Andee said, saying the first thing that came to mind.

Marina smiled and her lush aquamarine brightened. She embraced Andee. Marina was going to be an ocean protector. Her parents were forest protectors, but they encouraged Marina's love of the sea. Comparing herself to confident Marina made Andee's own color dip and fade to sickly gray.

"Hey, happy First Summer," Marina said. She gazed pointedly into Andee's eyes, clearly trying not to look too closely at her friend's off color. "Do you want to walk with me?"

"I'm not quite ready yet," Andee said, ashamed. She needed more time to present a better shade. Sometimes she envied her mother for the old days when they had to "get ready" for parties. Nowadays, makeup was a thing of the past and everyone wore similar clothes. No one cared about external trappings. Your internal glow, your solar skin shade, was what mattered.

"You're going though, right?" Marina asked. "We haven't seen you in awhile. I'm worried."

"I've been spending a lot of time in classes," Andee said. "With Morell."

If it were anyone else, Andee wouldn't have wanted to admit that she was studying shade shifting; most people thought it was weird and "inauthentic." Your natural color was supposed to shine through. You weren't supposed to have to try. But Marina knew that Andee struggled.

"Oh, okay," Marina said, her eyes betraying concern. "Well, be careful if you walk alone. There's a Red Crusher out tonight. I heard stomping and swearing and saw some red flashes."

At this, Andee lost all traces of her green equanimity. She hated it when people talked about Red Crushers. Marina was kinder about it than some of her friends, but Andee couldn't help but imagine if it were her. She had wrong shades, too. What would they say about her?

"Hey," Marina said, noticing Andee's color shift. "It's okay. Come on, walk with me, we'll be safe together."

Marina had mistaken Andee's color for fear. At least there was that. People could see your emotion, but they couldn't always tell why.

"No, I'll be down in a bit," she said. "Marina, the Red Crusher could be Irwin."

"Oh, not again." Even Marina's color waned at that. He'd been one of their classmates and now rumor had it he was in danger of exile. "Still, be careful, okay? He's red like that for a reason. It's not safe. I'm glad you're coming out. I'll be by the beach, if you want to go down."

***

After Marina left, Andee felt more guilt and shame. Why couldn't she have gone with her friend? She liked Marina, but all Andee could think about was herself, her own dark mood, and her ill shade.

Her failure made her want to give up, but she sat down, turned away from the mirror, and closed her eyes. She recited Morell's "Green Poem" in her head.

Peace and calm they keep me free,
Like the sea of deepest green.
Act from love and not from fear,
Come color, color, color clear.

Andee let the calm settle into her. When she turned around again, she was a light shade of green. It wasn't perfect and it wasn't attractive, but it would pass. She wouldn't be embarrassed by this mood anyway.

She put on a hemp halter-top and wrap skirt identical to Marina's. Her green skin glowed lightly through her clothes. The sun had lowered, but there were still hours of light. She had plenty of time to walk to Abersea Park.

The crushed rock lining the ped path glowed a solar-powered blue as it wound its way to the sea. Andee looked up into the overhanging willow trees that lined the path. As she walked, she noted how her shade settled into a steadier green glow. Getting out of her dome was good for her. Walking made her feel better, but it was easy to forget when she was inside and her entire dome was glowing gray. Slowly, she relaxed and her forced green shade settled into her skin along with her uplifted mood.

As she rounded the ped path's last bend, she dipped under dark trees and then stepped into the park, alit with people shining like lanterns. She saw her friends, beacons of pink, orange, and yellow by the cliff overlooking the sea. The Spiked Sun statue towered over them and caught the last rays of sunlight in its tips. Her friends bounced and shone in a cascade of laughter and waves. Unsure whether she could match their enthusiasm just yet, she turned away from her friends' bright lights toward the parents' softer glows. Banquet tables were arranged under the park dome in the arboretum.

Andee had lived under her parents' sun dome longer than most and she missed them. She found her indie sun dome lonely, and her shade struggles had begun after she had left her parents' bigger communal dome. She had lost the verdant color her parents expected of "their darling farm girl," settling for a peaceful green when she could manage it.

Outside, colorful children darted around the circle of the elders' dome, flashing like fireworks. They turned the merry-go-round into an arc of striped multicolored light. With a couple of exceptions, most of the community elders had softer glows. Like Madame Morell, they had opted for lower doses of the bioluminescent solar-collecting nanites that made their skin cells glow at night. Everything in Aberdonia, from ped paths to domes to the Spiked Sun Solar Pact statue itself, did its best to capture the waning sun and power the community—and that included its people.

"The glow keeps me up at night," Andee's mother had complained once, but later said, "Nowadays, I find it soothing. To see your father beside me glowing like a peach at night makes me happy."

It was a completely unintended side effect, but being able to see each other's mood clearly, at night anyway, was now something the community counted on. Andee wasn't sure how she'd relate to someone if she didn't know they were baseline green, blue, orange, yellow, or pink. A violet glow was common among creatives and everyone knew to avoid Red Crushers—people in the throes of unacceptable anger or violence.

Andee quickly found her mom's comforting green glow among the crowd.

"Oh, you made it," her mother said. "Did you have any trouble on the path? People are saying there's a Red Crusher out tonight."

"I know. Marina warned me. I'll be careful," Andee said. Before the Solar Pact and Aberdonia's creation, her mother had been a Victim of Violence in the old regime. Andee didn't like to worry her.

"Honey, you look lovely," her mother said, and Andee's skin flashed a bright green response. "I'm so jealous. In my day, we had so much struggle over what to wear."

"You look nice too, Mom."

Her mother was wearing loose hemp slacks and a billowing blouse. Andee had thought it weird how much time her mother used to spend selecting clothes. Teens in Aberdonia wore uncolored hemp basics. Andee was glad to see her mother finally embracing the modern style. The old fashion industry had been such a waste. Though sometimes she wished she could worry about clothes and makeup instead of her solar skin glow.

Andee found her father next to a buffet table snacking off a platter of colorful vegetables and talking with his friend, Council Leader Gordon.

"Hey, Andee." He hugged her. "I was worried about you walking alone, because of the Red Crusher."

"That Hunter boy, I suppose," Gordon said. "The Council is talking of banishing him."

"Andee, good to see you." Gordon winced as he smiled. Three red punctures puckered below his eye.

Where The Spiked Sun hit him, Andee thought.

Out of the corner of her eye, she saw her shade gray with horror. So it was true; Irwin could be exiled.

***

When they were younger, the kids had teased Irwin Hunter mercilessly about his temper. His red glow didn't show during the day, but his acting out did and everyone knew he was quick to anger. Finally, their parents had intervened. Andee remembered the night her own parents had sat her down to talk about Irwin.

"We don't shun people for being different, Andee," her father had said. "That's not who Aberdonians are. You have to make an effort."

Unfortunately, Andee had already watched a number of her more sociable, attractive, and outgoing classmates try to befriend the ill-tempered boy. Sorcha, Xollo, and even Marina had all failed. Irwin grew red and turned them away.

So Andee was surprised when Irwin talked to her and she started to get to know him. He would sometimes turn a soft yellow, a sunny color she enjoyed. In school and around the other children, he never showed that calm.

The other children began to make fun of her for her closeness to him.

"Watch out, you'll get red, too," they teased.

In fact, she could feel it flaring up in her.

"You were all told to make friends with him, too," she said one day, red with anger.

Soon, she stopped making an effort to be nice to Irwin and they had grown apart. For a while, they were classmates, nothing more.

***

"Father," Andee said, throwing his own words back at him now on First Summer night. "We don't shun people for being different."

"We tried," Council Leader Gordon said. "It's not something we take lightly, but now..." He touched his bruised cheek. "People are afraid."

"It's a matter of safety, Andee," her father said. "You know we can't allow violent behavior."

"Andee, what are you doing once work starts?" Gordon asked, changing the topic.

It was an honest question, but Andee bristled. If she didn't say, "farmer," if she flashed red anger, would the Council Leader consider exiling her, too? Red prickled across her green glow. Andee shrugged, trying to calm herself.

"You'll decide soon," the Council Leader said.

"I'd better get to my classmates," she said, and turned toward the cliff overlooking the ocean. They were easy to spot: bright yellow Sorcha, orange sherbet Blair, and hot pink Chris.

"Andee!" Sorcha cried as soon as she spotted her. She picked her up and swung her around. Blair and Chris had to step back so as not to be hit by Andee's swinging feet. As soon as Andee was on solid ground again, they had to warn her about the Red Crusher.

"Did you see that Red Crusher? So brick. Out of control. I saw the flash earlier up the ped path," Blair said.

"Yeah, I heard," Andee said. "It might be Irwin. Did you know the Council is talking banishment?"

"That's terrible," Sorcha said.

"Probably for the best though, don't you think?" said Chris. "I mean, if he's really dangerous."

***

When Andee had gotten older, she'd connected with Irwin again and for a while they'd been more than classmates. They'd started to take evening walks together. He'd told her what had happened that day in school when he'd been dubbed Red Crusher.

"Somehow I was carrying your stupid cake and I tripped and I dropped it. And I was so ashamed and embarrassed, that I decided to make it like I'd done it on purpose. I stomped. I screamed. I totally destroyed that cake. I don't know why I did that. Now I wish I hadn't, of course, but it's not like anyone was going to eat it once I'd dropped it anyway. I had no idea it was going to stick with me so long."

Irwin was still angry, but he talked about why he didn't like Aberdonia. Andee didn't agree with a lot of what he said, the source of his deep-seated anger, but she started to understand his reasons.

"The adults at least had a choice about whether to be injected with these solar cells. They never gave us any choice. And now we're judged by this side effect. A freakin' side effect." He would start to flash red as he talked. "You know, Aberdonia, it isn't perfect for everyone."

She had listened to his angry ideas and some of what he'd said made sense. He was frustrated with the Solar Pact and its unfair provisions.

They'd sat together through the night under the dome at Abersea Park. They'd talked about what it would be like to not glow at night, to be Unseen. They'd talked about the sun, its waning power, and its color.

"I don't know about the night glow, but I'm glad to have some of that beauty and power inside of me," Andee said.

One summer night as they sat on the merry-go-round, Irwin turned a serene shade of yellow like the summer sun. She'd liked him that way.

"What are you feeling?" she'd asked shyly.

"It's none of your business," he'd said, but his shade had stayed strong. It hadn't shifted.

So she knew it was okay that she had asked and that he hadn't answered.

They'd walked to the cliff and sat on the edge overlooking the sea, listening to it crash beneath them. They'd stayed together just holding hands and mostly silent until the real sun came up, and the Solar Pact monument began to pull in its rays.

He could kiss me, she'd thought. It had seemed like a dangerous, rebellious idea at the time. What would her classmates think? *I would let him*, she'd thought.

But he hadn't.

So for a while, Andee had become fascinated with Xollo, a talented storyteller. She'd gathered with her classmates around his violet glow. He told Red Crusher stories featuring wild characters with violent outbursts made ridiculous. Andee could see herself in his stories, see the absurdity, and she had laughed loudly along with the others.

Irwin never saw the humor. He grew distant again.

Still, Andee remembered when he had confided in her. He'd told her what he really wanted, what he was dreaming about for his life in Aberdonia. It had surprised her.

***

"Irwin wanted to be on the Aberdonian Council someday," Andee told her friends. "He wanted to have a say, to help change things, to update the Solar Pact, and make it fair."

"Well, anger won't help," Blair said.

"Come on, it's First Summer," Chris said, picking up some solar balls and beginning to juggle them. "Let's enjoy it. We can worry tomorrow."

Andee spent the rest of First Summer night in the company of her bright classmates. They ran around posing like light statuettes, making art out of their shining bodies, and playing Solar Ball. When Andee tired of their neon antics, she took the walkway cliffside to the beach to look for Xollo and Marina.

Marina was swimming, a blue flash in the dark sea. Xollo was in the corner of a stone cave by the beach, glowing violet. His shade was not as bright, but it was alluring. People were gathered around listening to his stories, his work. She wandered over to listen, too. He was telling a beautiful story about selkies and water nymphs that betrayed his love for Marina.

Xollo stopped telling stories after Marina came out of the water.

His audience wandered off in pairs or trios down the beach. Marina gave Andee and Xollo wet, salty hugs. Xollo lingered by Marina's side and Andee decided to let the couple be alone together.

"Be careful walking back by yourself," Marina said.

"Yeah, watch out for the Red Crusher," Xollo said.

"Thanks." Andee turned away. "I've been warned."

Again, she thought and rolled her eyes.

She began walking back to her indie sun dome alone, away from the scent of lavender and sea salt, along the ped path with its solar-blue light.

As she walked she caught a glimpse of red and fear flared up in her. She thought about what could happen to her out here. A Red Crusher could take their anger out upon her body, and she was small, weak against their wrath. Everyone who warned her would have been right, and she would be proved wrong and stupid. What had she been thinking walking alone when she knew there was a dangerous person on the rampage?

As she grew closer to the red, she saw she had mistaken the color. The red shade was pinker, more passionate. She heard a giggle, a rustle, and glimpsed a couple glowing amorous, pink-red through the trees.

Andee sighed. Her shoulders relaxed. She took a deep breath and walked on. Maybe she should be scared, but she was happy to be alone. It had been exhausting worrying about her mood and how it might affect others. She was glad to relax with herself and glow blue if she must.

What if she wasn't meant to be a farmer as expected? Maybe she didn't want to feel the peacefulness of green.

What if she became a counselor, a listener, someone like Madame Morell? Even if others scorned them, she liked Madame Morell's classes. She thought about Irwin sitting near her in the outdoor classes at dusk. She'd seen the classes work for him sometimes. He'd come in red, but then that true-sun color would rise in him and burst through his thin hemp wrap as the night bloomed.

She started to think she understood that color, knew what it meant: acceptance.

Maybe she could be blue and that would be okay and let other people know they weren't alone. She could listen, maybe tease out of people a lighter, warmer color, and see them shine that yellow glow. Yes, she'd like that. It would be satisfying to help others.

But would it be allowed?

It's easier to exile people, she thought, growing angry.

On the path, she saw the red light ahead of her. This time the red anger was unmistakable. She heard shouting. Andee knew she should veer down another path and avoid confrontation.

Act from love and not from fear, she remembered the words of Morell's poem.

But acting out of fear had served her well. Sometimes, she was sure it kept her safe. Certainly, it paid to trust her instincts. Her mother had told her about violence in the time before solar cells, when it wasn't easy to spot and avoid dangerous people...*he held me against the tree, I tried to fight*...bits of her story, just enough to make Andee listen. It was terrifying how, back then, you couldn't know someone's mind in the dark until it was too late.

"Now we can see them coming," her mother said. "There's no reason not to use that knowledge, avoid danger."

Thinking about this and looking at that Red Crusher, Andee felt her heart beat faster.

It wasn't fear, though. How did that person know she was a target? How could they assume she was powerless?

Maybe she was the angry one. Maybe she was the danger. No one knew what she might do. She was tired of people assuming they knew her. Maybe this time, *they* should hide.

Out of the corner of her eye, Andee could see her own solar cells reddening as she headed toward the brick glow on the path.

Then she saw it, the lit pearl of luminescent pink in the wall of red.

Madame Morell. And someone else. A spark of peace and love surrounded by hate.

Andee charged forward.

She wanted to find a stranger there, some exile, some outsider. She didn't want the danger to be someone she knew, but when she got close enough to see limbs and faces among the light, Irwin looked up at her. In his eyes she saw someone she had agreed with and someone—she saw it now—she had loved.

She screamed, no words, a bright animal call of alarm.

Irwin froze. Madame Morell shrugged him off, scrambled to her feet and to Andee's side.

Irwin crouched and rose.

"We were just talking. It got out of control," he said. "I didn't mean to."

"Go." Andee said, trembling with rage.

He stepped toward her. "You think I'm a monster."

"No. I never did. It's what you're doing. Go now. Don't wait for the Council to tell you. I'm telling you. You can't be here. That's not who we are."

Irwin looked at her. His shade wavered, rippling lines of red.

I'll never move. Hurt him if I have to, Andee thought.

Finally, he turned and walked away.

The red glow remained, a sumac flare around Andee as her body relaxed and her breathing slowed. She smoothed Madame Morell's mangled hemp wrap and covered the welts rising on her shoulder and collarbone. Andee hugged her teacher.

"I'm fine," Madame Morell said. "I'm okay. Really. Thank you." She reached for Andee's hand and held it. "I see. You have found your shade."

"It's unacceptable," Andee said, her voice shaking. "It's wrong."

"Maybe. But beautiful. I needed a fiery sun, and you shone."

THE CALL OF THE WOLD

Holly Schofield

Pedalling out of the shade of the Douglas firs, I heard the farming collective before I saw it. Squawking, bleating, angry barking—and that was just the people. I ground to a stop in front of the gate, careful to avoid the wild sorrel poking through the damp, crumbling pavement. "Olly Olly Umphrey!" I called over in my cracked old woman voice. The nearest person, a lanky man with a brown pony tail pulled exceptionally tight, frowned at my shout. His foot rested on a rusted cage with something brown and feathery in it.

He glanced at me, my bicycle, and the small bike trailer that held my possessions, then back at the other two. The woman was waving a large and shiny cleaver in the face of a stocky, acne-scarred man. I wasn't one to judge—well, I *was*—but my calves ached and my stomach was tired of deer jerky. I raised my voice a notch or four. "I don't want to join your discussion, I was just hoping I could do a few chores—"

"We don't need any trade goods," yelled the cleaver-wielder. "Go away, old woman!"

"Ageist, much?" I yelled back. The driest summer in Vancouver Island's recorded history meant my scalp itched continually, and a guest bunk sure beat out a dusty tent, but I didn't let such comments slip past me. Not since I turned seventy last year.

"Let her in," the lanky man said.

I pushed my bike along the high chain-link fence—the height of it intended to keep out the overly-numerous deer rather than human intruders—until I reached the gate.

Neither of the other two had moved.

The lanky guy sighed long and low. "By the power vested in me by Henkel's Wold, let her in." At his feet, the caged guinea fowl backed him up with an ear-piercing shriek.

The short guy moved first, walking up to the lock and looking into the biometric screen. It gave a loud click. My heart did the hokey pokey as the smartcam swivelled toward me and facial recognition software did its thing.

"Keeps out the riffraff, eh," I remarked to the guy as the gate clicked again and swung open.

"So what? We breed our own criminals," he said, glaring back at the woman.

She waggled the cleaver at him. "Sez you, Riley."

"Gah!" Riley turned to the skinny guy. "Did you see that? Whatcha gonna do about it, Aaron, waffle as usual?"

With a sigh, I scanned the dark clouds overhead. Was a bit of comfort really worth enduring such an unhappy crowd? But I knew my solitary life wasn't mentally healthy, any more than my cheese addiction. Surely I could hang my frayed Tilley here for one night.

Besides, maybe I could help settle the dispute. I hadn't been much use to anyone lately, maybe I could use my rusty people skills to at least calm 'em down. I sucked in a breath. "I think you people are the flea's pajamas, doing what you do, way out here in the bush," I said and smiled blankly like the kindly old woman I hoped I looked like. "A bunch of nice people like you, nothing more to talk about than some chicken." My tactic worked—they all looked as sheepish as ewes at a shearing competition. I stuck my hand out toward the one named Riley. "Julie Leung, traveller extraordinaire."

"Pleased, and all that," said Riley as he gripped my fingers with a callused palm. "Come on in. We got some lentil stew with your name on it. Always glad to have a few helping hands around the farm."

"Yeah," said Laura. "We'll settle this later. I've got to get back to chopping carrots for dinner." She ran a finger along the cleaver and flicked a fleck of orange off it, grinning at me. "Betcha thought I had other plans with this beauty, huh?"

I grinned back.

Riley gestured me to follow him. "How are you at tapping maple trees?"

I regaled him with my expertise in syrup extraction skills as I followed him across the communal yard. Up on the roof of the sculpted concrete main building, a bearded guy waved, solar paint dripping from his brush. We proceeded down a ferny green trail to some tiny guest cabins. The wooden walls were streaked with the ironically pleasant blue of mountain pine beetle damage. I parked my bike in a rack made from repurposed car parts and grabbed my backpack. Dinner and bed would certainly warm the cockroaches in my heart. But, with the smartcam's capabilities in figuring out my real identity, I could only stay a couple of days.

***

My aging Ikea chair and borrowed quilt had just grown comfy when the argument started up again.

About ten of us had lingered after dinner in the common room by the months-cold methane gas stove. Next to me, on an old Forest Service park bench, a woman opened her shirt and began to feed her baby, while an older guy stroked his long beard in mindful contemplation of something, and a teenager tapped away on a tablet designing a cranberry harvester. Riley sprawled in a handmade chair across the fire from me, and Aaron, the collective's leader, slouched beside him in an ancient armchair.

My twelve years bicycling throughout western Canada meant I'd seen a few hundred of these "intentional communities." By now, I could spot the reasons why they worked—or didn't—as quickly as I could gather Canada goose eggs for lunch. The way this bunch had all made a conscious effort to back down from their verbal scuffle at the gate told me Henkel's was a community of the sort I would have leaped to have joined in my thirties, or even my forties. That and the swoon-worthy food. Riley's lentil soup had been fragrant with fresh spinach, flavorful carrots, and a couple of spices I couldn't immediately recall: coriander maybe, and cardamom. It had been accompanied by a salad of miner's lettuce, sorrel, clover, and various greens such as I might collect for myself but with a much better dressing of raspberry vinaigrette. And that had been followed by a piece of excellent goat cheese made by the angry-woman-who-was-no-longer-angry and went by the name of Laura. The woman, that is, not the cheese.

But, despite the appeal, would I want to join *any* collective nowadays? I'd always been an introvert and, now, after over a decade of unpeopled solitude, a little peopling was all I could stand. A murmur from the baby, another beard stroke, and a tappy-tap-tap, and I edged my chair away a little bit.

Laura backed in through the kitchen swing door and began handing out cups of rosehip tea to a chorus of appreciative murmurs. She ended with Riley, thrusting the tray at him, mouth tight.

"It's just a guinea hen," Riley said, taking the last cup with both hands.

"Yeah, sure, and its eggs are just scrambled genes," she said, slapping the tray against her thigh.

"We need a decision," Riley said, gripping his mug like death heated up.

Laura nodded. "It's impairing our happiness levels."

They both turned to glare at Aaron, whose face was in shadow under the hood of a faded gray UBC hoodie. "I—I—I think that Laura had better start—"

"At least you agree on something," I interrupted brightly. Whatever he'd been about to say, telling just one of 'em what to do wouldn't resolve anything. I hadn't worked for a wildlife foundation for twenty-five years without learning something about negotiation.

"Phone home, gramma," said Laura, then looked abashed as the nursing mother raised her head and the teenager tsked. Each collective tended to develop its own slang so I wasn't sure what that meant—although I could grok the essence.

I said lightly, "Haven't owned one in years." Taking her literally might de-escalate the situation, and, besides, I hadn't. In the solar-powered communities of the New West Coast, where every kilowatt counted, one of the few advanced technologies everyone made sure to prioritize was cell coverage—generally, people agreed that a transparent society with almost all information freely available mostly worked to everyone's advantage. But no way was I going to carry a phone, even though the maps and other data would be damned handy.

When you—meaning me—are an environmental activist working for your older brother's charitable foundation and you—meaning me—become the director when he takes two years off to be a new dad, it's a big deal. And when you—yup, me again—finally have enough of whining, bickering humanity and walk out on one of the endless meetings about a federal wildlife law that affects a provincial law that affects a local bylaw that would affect the water rights of a multinational company that may or may not be leaning toward a tax-favored donation to the foundation, it's…liable to leave the foundation in the lurch. Especially after you walk out of the office building, across Bayview Avenue, and down to the Don River, and your black pleather oxfords fill up with warm algae-tinted water and you stand there and stand there until a passing mourning dove shits on you.

Meaning me. Shit on *me*.

I'd left the shoes in the mucky silt, along with my blue wool blazer, and walked unshod and unblazered for miles. And I'd never gone back despite Willi's endless phone calls and messages. I'd ditched my phone, my Toronto condo, and gone off-grid, driving north. Eventually, reading historical biographies in a rented Muskoka cottage had palled and I'd bought the bike and cart and never looked back. (Unless the cart got a flat tire. Which it occasionally did.)

I'd had a close call last month. I'd paused by a roadside hawker in Coquitlam under several streetcams. My hand had hovered indecisively over several solar-powered miniature water filters. The hawker's cell phone, close by my hand, rang and we both jumped.

"Who? Who's Julie Leung? Is this a prank?" she'd yelled into it before I'd bustled my hump along Highway 7, pumping my pedals like a well handle in a six-month Saskatchewan drought. Twelve years later, and Willi was still needing me back. I just *knew* he was. I'd been the best damn activist my brother had ever hired. One look into his pleading black eyes and I'd return to that soul-sucking city life in a hurtbeat.

So, no phone.

Problem solved.

Maybe I could solve this problem as well. Aaron gulped down his tea, hand shaking. Laura and Riley both crossed their arms.

"Tell me, what do this collective's rules say about ownership of the bird?" I squinted, trying to see Aaron through the growing dimness.

"Ownership isn't the issue. I actually own it all," Aaron said.

"Wowsy," I said.

He leaned forward into the light. "My mom, Helen Henkel—"

Everyone made a slow fist of respect.

"—most decent person I ever knew."

"—peace be upon her."

"—she never phoned it in."

Ah, that explained Aaron's clumsy handling of the incident at the gate. The mantle of leadership was XXL and he was an extra-small. He muttered, "Mom set this place up as a formal trust—everyone signed over their assets to her in return for lifetime rights to live here."

"And that *worked*? A dictator telling you folks what to do?" My voice squawked like the poor guinea fowl. I'd see that style of intentional community before—usually the people had a fundamentalist religious doctrine or another form of abhorrent behavior. Or a commercial agenda, like when marijuana went legal. Some of those communities made a small fortune—by starting out with a large fortune.

They were all smiling at my naïveté, or maybe I had spinach in my teeth.

Aaron spoke from the depths of his hoodie. "A benevolent dictator is actually the best form of government. *If* you can find the right person." He scrubbed his face with a hand. "Trouble is, I'm not the person Mom was."

The protesting murmurs from the other people weren't even loud enough to drown out the baby's slurps. Poor guy.

"Okay. Here's my decision." He spoke firmly, for once. Maybe I'd underestimated him. "I'm going to ask Julie to decide. It'll be impartial and it'll count as her chores, a win-win."

Yup, underestimated. He'd neatly passed the bucking bronco to me. After I hit the road tomorrow, they could collectively hate me instead of him.

I twisted in my chair. My past career meant I was pretty good at that kind of stuff, despite it not coming naturally. Plus, lack of internet meant I'd read my way through all the classics in the past decade, from *Art of War* to *Callahan's Crosstime Saloon*. Further, my arthritic wrists hated the idea of three hours of drilling holes in big leaf maples and running sap lines tomorrow. My nimbility wasn't what it once was. I squirmed again and my hip twanged like a cheap guitar. That decided me. "Okay, deal. What's the scoop?"

They all looked blank for a minute, even the guy with the beard. Hooboy, you know you're getting old when what you consider normal slang has become unintelligible. "Just tell me the problem."

"Laura says she bred the hen from two she'd paid particular attention to. Tracking software shows it eats more ticks than most and she wants to keep it for breeding. It lost its leg band and Riley says she's mistaken about which hen it is—" Riley snorted. "—and it's one of several he's bred to taste better and it's now at its peak age for meat production. That about cover it?" Aaron turned to both of 'em and they nodded.

I thought it over. Whether they had a fancy genetics lab set up in one of the outbuildings or whether they were cross-breeding the old-fashioned way didn't matter. Nobody relied on fancy tech solely any more. We all wanted backups to the backups and there was no backup like a live hen strutting her stuff in the farmyard. Plus black-legged ticks had benefited like few other critters from the long hot climate-changed summers and the dumb-ass ban on deer culling. All ticks needed were deer and humidity to spread Lyme disease, a deadly risk to us all. Out here in the wilds, they were all over humans like, well, ticks on a hound. I was picking a few of the evil beasties off myself every night. Most British Columbia collectives donated extra profits to the Lyme Research Collective in Vancouver, hoping for a cheap, reliable vaccine.

I tilted my head left and right a few times, considering both sides. Maybe a classic solution was in order. "Have the hen lay a clutch and then kill it. The eggs go to Laura and the meat goes to Riley." Solomon has nothin' on me, hooboy.

All ten of 'em erupted into arguments as to why that wouldn't work. I let 'em go on for a bit, hoping they'd settle. Sure enough they began to batten down the hatchets and discuss it more rationally. Laura spoke above the rest: "I suppose if I had a dozen eggs, I could work with those. We do need the meat for the smokehouse or we'll be hungry come January."

"But if the hen is killed, you'd be betting on the eggs," Riley said. "And I do hate ticks with the passion of a—"

"— lipstick-covered pig," I cut in.

"Yeah, sure," he said and laughed. Laura giggled and, just like that, the tension was broken.

Laura and Riley agreed to leave the hen alive for now and work together tomorrow to construct yet another floating platform of mussel ropes. It'd have to be situated in a less convenient location than most of the existing ones, but it would help replace the protein lost by keeping the hen.

Aaron was looking at me steadily, open-mouthed. I smiled, shrugged, and sipped my cold tea.

Later, as I walked toward the cabin and its very appealing cot, Aaron took me aside. "Teach me how to do that?"

I opened my mouth, about to explain the complexities of the interpersonal techniques I'd used and the micro-expressions I'd interpreted. I opened the cabin's door. My hip twanged, this time like a whole banjo orchestra. "It's, um, complicated," I said. "G'night."

He trudged away, head down.

Hours later, I'd tossed and turned so much that the bedsheets were trussed and torn. I felt like the world's biggest meanie. The selfish kind, the kind Willi thought I was. But there was no easy way to tell Aaron how draining it was to be around people, face-to-face, aura-to-aura.

Willi had never understood that either.

***

By the second day at Henkel's, I'd been given a potted tomato plant and a woven hemp hat and been asked to settle four disputes. This morning's involved two new mothers and the last remaining frozen bagel. I could forgive 'em their anger—teething babies without teething rings could set anyone's teeth on edge. At least, one of the mothers had brought me a duck egg omelet, full of mushrooms and chives, still steaming from the kitchens. The mother, *and* the omelet.

I was forking in the yellow fluff of heaven when Aaron stopped by. His faded corduroy shirt hanging on his thin frame made him look a scarecrow, or maybe a scarevulture.

"Help me figure out this puzzle?" His tablet held some accounts and preliminary number-crushing. It resembled the decision-making matrices that I used to discuss with Willi.

I swallowed the last bite, washing it down with some chicory coffee. "Does the super-fiddly hand-threshing of lentils balance their higher production volume per hectare versus the ease of chick peas?

Damnifino. Use some cost-benefit software, like HappyEconomics freeware."

"But it's not that simple." He sighed. "How do you know if—"

"Aaron, there's *never* enough information. You could collect it until the crows come home and still there'd be something you missed."

"I don't think I'll ever grow into this job." He blew out a long breath. I felt sorry for him—adapting to something you aren't suited for is an uphill climb, made especially tougher by putting on the wrong suit. Or an itchy blue blazer. All I could do was give him permission to make a decision. "Sometimes you just have to fish or cut loose."

He ran a hand through his hair. "I suppose. I'll figure it out, later. Come help me in the truffle orchard?"

"So they grow on trees now?" I said, determined to lighten his mood.

He only grunted and shoved the tablet in his pocket.

We stopped by the tool shed and he handed me a narrow tree planting shovel, taking an odd-looking rake for himself. I had no idea what the black plastic box affixed to the handle near the tines could be for.

The truffle orchard was down by the shore, staggered rows of hazelnuts and Garry oaks marching toward the high tide mark.

"My nose may be big but it's not all that sensitive," I said, accustomed to other collectives' use of trained dogs to sniff out the tasty underground fungi.

"We spent most of last year's discretionary funds on this baby." He patted the rake's black box proudly, then flicked a switch. The box emitted a cheery *pew pew pew* sound.

"Raygun?" I asked. I approved of the new trend of replacing the annoying *dings* and *beeps* of most electronics with music but this concert was disconcerting.

"Texan elf owl," he answered.

After a while, we got it down to a routine. He used the fancy sniffing device like it was a metal detector wand to locate the truffles under the trees. It would go *pew pew pew* when it sensed truffle spores and he'd rake away leaves and twigs and other detritus, exposing the good dark soil. I'd dig up a handful or two of thumb-sized deliciousness, and then he'd carefully rake the duff back over.

"I'll be leaving tomorrow," I said, when I felt the moment was ripe. "Don't get to relying on me." My brother would trace me through the publicly available images the gate's smartcam had taken of my face, probably in a day or two. I could be far up island by then. I bit down on the usual wave of failure, humiliation, and regret. I'd cracked under the strain of leading his foundation and I was continually paying the price. Or pricing the pain. Or something.

"Julie." Aaron swung the rake under the next tree. "I'm...thinking of quitting, too. Collapse the community trust and give their money back. Let them run it like a democracy, with voting and everything."

"And run off?"

"Travel. Like you are."

Pew pew pew.

His raking this time was vicious, sending crisp, dry oak leaves flying in all directions.

"I've got my reasons," I said. I didn't need a home, not me, I was as self-sufficient as a...well, as a...come to think of it, *nothing* was truly self-sufficient. But this conversation wasn't about me. "Without you, Aaron, that bunch would fall apart in a week. You just need to work on a few arbitration skills," I said.

"I need *you*," he countered with a firmness that belied his shaking hands. "If you stay, I'll stay. You could give me advice behind the scenes. Just feed me what to say and I'll spout it out to them."

I dug a few cautious shovelfuls. "Like Cyrano de Bergerac? Or like Edgar Bergen?"

He frowned. "Who—"

"Never mind." I carefully eased several black lumps from the near-dry soil. "You'd really want to run things that way?" The musky funky truffles wafted their funky musk over us and we both breathed deeply.

"I'll just tell them that you've bought your way in but I won't actually charge you a single loonie."

"And one farmhand washes the other? Doesn't sound very benevolent to me."

"No one will know. Look, the night you came, I was about to kick Laura out for non-compliance to the rules."

"So you're giving yourself a choice between being Charlie McCarthy or Joe McCarthy?"

"Who are—"

"Never mind. You haven't studied history. You just know how to grow cabbage and broccoli. You're doomed to repeat."

He looked at me suspiciously. "I don't know if that was a fart joke or what, but I'm serious. I'm offering you a permanent place here."

"You don't need me, damn it." I laid the truffles in the wicker basket. "The only thing you have to fear is...spiders. How about I give you some books to read—"

"Books! That won't help, not right away. But *you* can! Please." He grabbed my cuff and I jerked away instinctively. "At least say you'll think about it."

He kept on badgering me as we filled the basket.

"Enough!" I finally said and handed him the shovel.

My pulse was racing like a racecar and I couldn't think straight. I had to get away from him. I tore off across the orchard like a deer in flight, if deer could fly.

A few gallops and gulps later I was out of the bright sun and in my tiny cabin. The blankets were itchy-scratchy and the air was hot and close. Just outside the window, the rest of Henkel's was busy with the bustle of people. Finally, I strode out to the back pasture and commenced pretending to ignore the one resident—a goat on a staked rope. Its face was as surly as mine must be.

As the goat tore at the grass within reach, my mind raced a mile an hour...which actually seems a pretty fast speed if it's circling the same tiny topic.

What *was* I doing here?

Before my travels had started, I'd been a bit of a homebuddy and getting used to the road had been hard. My fancy would be tickled pink to settle down somewhere and not have to pitch a tent every night. I'd parked my big city pay cheques in a credit union and left it alone ever since I'd fled the city lights—maybe signing it over to Henkel's Trust would be enough to get me in legitimately? After all, good things come to those with a bird in the hand.

I licked my lips, still tasting the omelet's wild chanterelles—it really *had* been a breakfast of champignons.

Yesterday, I'd borrowed Aaron's tablet and looked up some stats. According to the Simon Fraser University Collective, more than half of the people in BC's Lower Mainland, both urban and rural, had changed to collectives. More than a third in the interior and a quarter of Alberta, too. The cognitive limit that a person could maintain interpersonal relationships, known as Dunbar's number, was about one hundred and fifty, and such small communities had proved both viable and robust—to expropriate some of my former corporate vocabulary. At that size, you always knew what your neighbor was doing so crime wasn't a problem. Basically, with Dunbar's number, the criminal element's number was up.

And, Henkel's Wold ranked near the top of all the collectives I'd stopped at. With good reasons (as well as good raisins). Over the last few days, I'd spent time with Laura and learned she'd been evicted from her Winnipeg apartment when her alcoholic ex-husband had destroyed her front door. Riley had been raised in Kelowna by parents who were strong on a self-sustaining lifestyle but supplemented their indifferent crops with a break-and-enter during his final year of high school. Of course, they'd been caught right away. Riley had worked at various high tech jobs around the country for years before ending up at Henkel's. Aaron's mother's up-close-and-personal government was a combination that worked for him.

The others I'd talked to here had similar stories—they'd joined due to personal beliefs, total commitment, and a work ethic that would leave a colony of ants speechless.

In the distance, Laura carried a pail of goat's milk to the cheese shed. My mouth watered while my thoughts tumbled like mismatched socks in a dryer. Opportunities like this didn't come along like streetcars.

But, maybe I couldn't see the forest for the cheese.

I'd always known that, as an introvert in a world of extroverts, I'd needed to adapt more than most folks to meet social expectations. Why would I think that Henkel's would be any different? After my soothing life in the woods, the daily interactions would rub me raw. It wouldn't smooth off my rough edges but it would rough up my soothed edges. I should retreat back to the forest where the only aggression came from the hummingbirds when their nests got disturbed. Let someone else step up to the plane.

But, then, I'd be letting down Aaron, and Riley, and Laura, and all the rest, just like I'd let down Willi and all the wildlife his foundation helped protect.

Maybe I *should* stay.

For once, I'd found a place I might fit in.

It wasn't just wistful thinking this time.

It was possible. And, in the back of my heart, I'd always known that Willi would find me eventually.

"Hey!" While I'd been cogitating, the goat had eaten through its rope, some bamboo fencing, and most of the raspberry bushes beyond. I grabbed its collar and yanked it back into the pasture. "Well, *you* sure learned to adapt to your environment," I told it. Then I stood humming and hawing until the dinner gong rang clear as a bell.

***

Pedaling hard, I got a ways past Nanaimo by nightfall. At first, Aaron's refurbished cellphone in my pack had weighed me down much more than its hundred grams should have but, after it didn't ring and didn't ring, I began to whistle while I pumped along past brown grasses and dull-leaved trees. Aaron wouldn't phone unless he needed to, and perhaps just being able to would mean he didn't need to. Meanwhile, I could nestle in the solitude of giant fir trees and huge ferns like the tough old woodlands creature I was.

As the sun dipped below a ridge, I pulled in by a narrow creek that chortled at my whirlpool of thoughts. I began to set up camp, a twinkle in my step. My travels were confirming that humanity, once on the path to doom, was instead becoming what both Willi and I had envisioned it could be. The new-style collectives were a success, phasering out some old-school beliefs, yet retaining the good stuff along with new tech. And—I glanced at the cell phone perched on a log—I was energized again. If I felt like chatting to Laura about cheese flavorings or Riley about enviro-politics, they were only a phone call away. And, after a bit of back-and-force, Aaron had agreed that my future advice would be presented openly to the collective, without hiding or pretense. I sat on the log and popped the last bite of Laura's truffle-smothered cheese in my mouth.

At some point, the phone would ring with an unknown call display. And Willi's soft, persuasive voice would ask me to come back. I knew what I'd tell him. My sanity needed both peopling and solituding, and, like a clown on a beach ball, I'd finally managed to find my balance point.

CAMPING WITH CITY BOY

Jerri Jerreat

This was my first time taking Rich out, *bare-arm*, to show him my world. I'd grown up with summer camping trips with family, loved it. He was from Toronto, that monster city with people living in the air, connected by pedestrian walkways. Some people rarely touched down. Oh, sure, his Skycities had gorgeous parklands on their rooftops, a paradise of small woods, pruned topiary gardens, even Japanese gardens with brooks. There were fiscus game fields and massive play structures designed like undersea worlds. It was amazing, but still…

I grew up in Bancroft, only 300,000 people strong. We had a small Skycity downtown of twenty-two buildings, but none higher than ten stories. My family lived in one, a nice three-bedroom with a river view. Their greenways were connected, and although ours weren't fancy-pants Toronto, they were something. We grew most of our food up there. My grandparents were on the team of caretakers, so I'd grown up fixing greywater systems (every drop to the food gardens), or repairing southern walls where the solar paint wasn't creating enough energy. I understood the giant rain catchment system off the roofs, and the water cyclator. I'd gone to schools and shopped in the stores on the ground floor.

Still, compared to Rich, I was a hick. Secretly, I nurtured that image. My favourite part of the year had always been the time I was heading into the woods and lakes. So, bringing newbies on a canoe trip was fine. I was finally introducing Kojo, one of *my* friends to Rich, but this was a tricky time—Rich had been hinting he wanted to make the Exclusive patch permanent. I just wasn't sure I was ready. It's a big step.

It's not an e-boat, I wanted to shout at Kojo's new boyfriend, Luiz. *You have to actually paddle.*

I forced myself to stop looking. Watching that canoe zigzag was painful. I'd offered a few tips but Luiz had shrugged them off.

"I've got it," he'd said, and used a delicate curved paddle tip to shove off the rocks.

I cringed. At least he wasn't *my* boyfriend. *My* boyfriend had been *irrepressibly* cheerful despite having to refill at water stations twice on the way. (Something wrong with the fuel cell engine.) Rich was handsome, fit, and confident. He was the fastest thrower on his fiscus team, and one sexy jolsta dancer. I'd practically drooled the first time I'd watched him. So had everyone else. He was the centre of fun, always making people feel a little bit better. I don't know how he did it, touching a shoulder here, dropping a question there, but it was a gift. *I* was quiet, had met him while taking a pre-astro course to see if I'd like it. He knew someone who knew my sister. I'm just ordinary, no fashion sense. (Loved his striped silver and gold hair and the wavy tattoo across his teeth.) I was smart, perhaps, but not like him.

Rich was in LifeFinance and could do weather stats in his head while I was still pulling on socks. And romantic? Yes. He'd brought me a real basil plant in a genuine clay pot after our first date six months ago. Classy, right?

We'd gone dancing a few times (me, content to watch his solos), and to 5-sense films but there were a lot of nostalgic ones that year about the failed Mao25 settlement. Tragic, right? Who can watch those without tearing up? We'd also taken many hikes through that incredible Skycity. He'd shown me hidden statues, little known trails through desert gardens where you'd *swear* you were in the plains of New Jersey, complete with cacti. We Ziptrained with his friends to Collingwood and Quebec City for his fiscus tourneys and explored the cities. Beautiful. The GreenStrips beside us looked rich with life. Repairing the planet. Just imagine—they used to be paved highways, jammed with Solo cars. Maybe our best date was the concert in

Montreal, just two of us, for the month anniversary of our Exclusive patch. (You can barely feel it on your inner thigh, and it ensures that *his* sperm, coded to his DNA, weren't dancing with *my* eggs.)

There weren't any Ziptrains north of Bancroft yet, so I'd booked a Solo and let it take us on the back roads past Algonquin Park to the larger Peace and Reconciliation Park (from North Bay to New Liskeard). Despite the water stops, we were in good spirits. Luiz seemed friendly, reticent compared to Rich, who could charm vivarium off a shiptrader. We had to stop at the Temagami checkpoint to get directions and serious reminders about no garbage/no zaps etc.

Finally we unloaded two canoes into Long Lake, one a plasbred lighter than a baby, and the other painted red with fake wood gunwales to look antique. My grandfather's, and it weighed a few grams more, mostly duct tape. I'd learned to J-stroke in that canoe, watched fireflies ("magic lights"), and fallen asleep, snuggled up to my sister. Mom would paddle us around, looking up. She loved the stars, an astropilot. An early pregnancy had grounded her temporarily. I used to tease Lorid that it was her fault we weren't born on Proxima B. (Frankly, I prefer Earth. When mom's on a mission we don't see her for two years. Seriously. Plus, they don't have trees or lakes like ours). Nana Mpenzi and Gramps were Park Volunteers, and took us on many overnights from toddler age. Great people, despite their music.

Kojo's boyfriend went right for the stern. *System error*.

Rich helped me get everything to the shore, then asked which end to get into. I tossed him a chuksnack for not tipping us (close call) when he clambered in. I snapped our gear in, gave us a push and slipped aboard. It took a moment to get my knees comfortable, then straighten the canoe. *There*.

It felt fantastic, like I'd been holding my breath for a *year* and could finally exhale. I gave some tips to Rich, then felt myself move into the rhythm of the 2-blade paddle. Loved that spin of water off each stroke. Art.

I'd seen water as art in that Skycity Japanese garden—a hundred fountains blowing water into shapes. Stunning. But give me this feeling of pulling the water myself, pushing it behind me, setting it free. Breathing in the river smell, seaweed, fish, these scents like a silk scarf run across your face.

Rich's knuckles were white, so I suggested he widen his grip and trace the horizon line.

"Stay in the centre," I called to Kojo as their canoe zigzagged drunkenly. "There's branches to snag you on the sides." I gave a few hard pulls to move away. "You okay, Rich?" I asked. "Shoulders comfortable?"

"Sure. Thanks."

***

We rafted up under a maple tree. "It's going well, eh?" I asked Rich, passing him the food.

He nodded. "Easy. Making camp soon?"

I almost snorted water, laughing. "We're about halfway."

"We'll get there before bugfall, though, right?" asked Luiz, bumping their canoe into ours.

"I hope to. But we all had vaccines, and I have pills and net hats."

"I'm not depending on nets," scoffed Luiz. "I packed Z420."

"That's illegal!"

"Tough. Skeeters ought to be eliminated. The feds are considering mass sprays. I'm just helping them along."

I blinked, wondering whether to smack him with my paddle or try logic. I tried logic. "Look, Luiz. People come out here to appreciate the wild in all its—diversity. We can protect ourselves. If we use Z420, it'll wipe out skeeters and the dragonflies and bats who feed on them, then the next level of predators. Sicken the whole water ecosystem. The point is—"

"So I won't offer it to you, but don't push your religion on me." He pushed off from our canoe. "C'mon Kojo. Let's make some time."

I hissed at Rich. "Can you believe that asshole?"

"Well, he's not spraying the entire woods. Just himself."

"Did you hear a word I said?"

Rich lifted his hands. "I didn't pack a secret can of Nature Killer. I'm just saying it's a small thing."

I tidied up, then paddled in silence, thinking it over. The women in my family were often Rangers. I'd always been shown the big environmental picture.

I smacked my blade onto the water surface and startled a long-legged walker who flipped in the air and skated away. I laughed and murmured an apology to the little guy.

I decided to nickname Luiz, "Laxy." For "laxative." It made me feel better. "Well, Rich. There's a small rapids ahead. Should be fun. Shall we beat them to it?"

I began to enjoy it again. The sun bounced off every water ripple. The rocky shore rose high and glinted rusty reds and pinks. Feisty green cedars curved up out of impossible crevices. No museum could rival it.

An hour later there was a darker blue line ahead in the water, and a sign on the right shore.

"It's the portage," I explained. "Around a rapids. Let's have a look!" I showed him how to exit carefully, then I pulled the canoe up on sand between rocks, and led the way uphill. The rapids was full of deadly rocks with a gradual drop of nearly my height. Water gushed forward, was split by a jammed log and boulders and sprayed up. It hit more rocks, arcing up at each, and joyfully raced downstream. A mist caught the sun and created a kaleidoscope effect of light and refracted colours. Arcobaleno. Qaansoroobaad.

When Rich joined me I reached for his hand. How incredible it must be to see for the first time.

"Nice spot," he commented. "Are we *carrying* the canoe around this?"

The magic cracked. "It's not as bad as it looks. There's a path off to the left."

He let go of my hand. "Why didn't we bring a jet pack? Or hire a guide?"

Surely he was kidding. "We went *bare-arm*," I reminded him, "And if *I* can do it, *you* can. C'mon."

He muttered as he followed me back but I didn't ask him to clarify. It was his first time. He'd learn it wasn't a big deal.

I hoisted the packs to the side, out of the way of Kojo and Laxy, approaching. Beginners usually carried a canoe tandem just to get the balance and way of it, so…

"If you'll stand on this side with me," I directed Rich, pointing, "and reach over like this…" I waited for him to follow suit.

Grunting with disapproval, he did. I rolled my eyes. We lifted the canoe up easily, then proceeded to walk up the bank. "Watch your footing," I called. "Slow down please," I had to add a moment later. At a sharp turn in the path, "Whoa! Watch out or you'll knock me over the edge!"

Rich complained about the heat, the sand in his shoes, flies, and that he couldn't see anything. It was a relief to reach the end, 300 metres. I splashed water over my face and neck, took a deep breath, then turned. "Coming?" I asked mildly.

We pulled on packs then scooped up paddles and small things. I smiled at Kojo, pulling their gear out. Laxy was washing mud off his shoes.

"Is it long?" she asked.

I shook my head. "Easy."

Rich made pleasant small talk this time, which, I understood, was his way of apologizing for whining. I debated aloud the merit of a quick swim. Tempting, for the current would be fun, pushing you downriver a little.

"That's safety allowed?" he asked, then blushed. His skin was so pale, emotions were written clearly on his cheeks.

"It's a good question," I said. "You wear the safevest to play in rapids, and you keep your shoes up on the surface, pointing downriver. It's fun. Especially if you're hot." We set our gear in the canoe and Rich started to laugh. I looked up.

Laxy was standing at the crest of the rapids, pants open, urinating. "Streams away!" he shouted.

You idiot, I thought. I turned on Rich, who was chuckling. "That's *not* funny. That's disgusting."

"What? Are you uncomfortable with healthy body functions?"

"No. I'm delighted his urinary system works and his sense of humour is an eight-year-old's. Perhaps next, he can defecate in your Japanese garden."

Rich frowned. "It was just a moment of—play."

He's an asshole, I thought. "Well, if you'd like to swim in his urine, now's your chance."

"That volume would be dissolved in seconds."

I handed him his safevest. "Fine. Just swim over, then float on your back. It's fun."

Rich took the safevest and put it on. "Well, I'm not that hot. By the way, where's the sunmist?

I flipped open a pocket on the pack and handed it to him. "Good idea, whitey," I teased. I didn't mind his colouring. Inconvenient for him, but it made me look gorgeous beside him, I'd said once to be funny. (It was true.) He made the most of his genetics, though. His light hair looked stunning in those metallic stripes and he'd had his eyes dyed aquamarine.

I pulled out the skeeterpills. "Despite vaccines, I usually take one before twilight." We each popped one and sucked on it. Raspberry cinnamon flavour.

"Thanks." He had misted himself. "Anything to munch on?"

I gave him a bar. "You are more tolerant of that guy—" I gestured backward. "—than me. This is a special place to me."

"Your Sacred Church of the Woods?"

"Ha ha." I arranged the canoe to point downstream and motioned him in. "No. But there is a lot of beauty here. His attitude bothers me. I'd appreciate it if you talked to him when necessary and let me—avoid him."

"I can do that." He was seated now, bony white knees poking up above the gunwale. "Spare you."

"Thanks." I was about to push off when I heard footsteps. "Hey Koji! Everything all right?"

"Good, thanks." She was carrying their canoe solo. I'd follow her lead from now on.

"We'll head down. Next stop will be our campsite," I said pleasantly, then pushed off and hopped in.

***

We'd already yanked our tent in the air to fill the tubes, pegged it down, and set up the cooking area when the others arrived.

"A loon popped up just in front of us," enthused Koji. "It fluttered its wings then dove under."

I nodded. "They're rare now. They're shy and they've moved north."

"Like everyone," said Koji.

Laxy strutted up like a peacock. "Good day! So, who wants a beer?"

"You're kidding, right?" I blurted.

Laxy arched one eyebrow at me then dug into their gear and pulled out two cans. He held one out to Rich… who took it.

I counted to five. "So guys, you all signed the forms in Temagami. No alcohol. No cans. No drugs. No garbage. So…" I looked at them as mild-mannered as was humanly possible, given that I was pissed. "What gives?"

Rich gave his sexy bad boy smile. The spiral on his right eye tooth glittered. "It's just a beer, Makemba. It's not a forest fire."

"I promise to pee it out," said Laxy. "A firefighter technique."

Both men laughed, raised cans, then drank.

I tried to channel my meditation teacher's advice but it was no use. Like most things in life, it was excellent in a classroom. Useless with annoying real people.

"Well. You two are on dinner. I'll go find the privy area. No peeing around the campsite," I said, mock sternly, though I meant it.

"Women," muttered Laxy. "Just because they can't."

I stopped. "Do you think, because you have a penis, only men can pee anywhere?" I held my hands out. "Women can pee wherever they like. With no hands." I took a couple of steps forward then paused. "We just choose not to soil our nests."

"Nor attract wildlife," added Kojo mildly. "Luiz, do you care where we put the tent?"

I turned down a narrow path toward the "latrine." The plasbox was pristine with no odour—a testament to science, a full powder dispenser, and good campers before us. I followed the trail farther, winding up a narrow ridge, then found a glacial erratic with a 180 degree view.

Spread out below me were mixed woods, coniferous and deciduous, a swampy inlet (mental note re: skeeters), and the river curving away. Directly below was our camp on the point, but dense woods concealed it. I let my legs dangle, spread out my hands on the warm rock and took long, slow breaths, concentrating on making the exhalation longer.

Even the clouds seemed more alive out here. There was a small one with rabbit ears chasing a large one with a grey bottom. *Chase it away from here,* I thought. I'd prefer no rain if possible.

Pine, earth, and river smells floated past. My Nana could sometimes identify the vegetation in front of her if you blindfolded her. We used to do that, as kids. I drummed my heels against the rock. I wished Lorid had been free for this trip. Her partner, Mara, was a music-scientist who loved camping too. They'd been accepted for a sperm donor and I think I was more excited about it than Lorid, who thought it was simply the next step.

How was it Lorid had come out of the womb knowing what she wanted to do with her life? She'd been working with Mexican and American refugees, counselling, filling out paperwork, accompanying them to courts. I'd seen her shouting in protest marches, even running a bubble booth at a New Canadians Festival.

I wrapped my arms around myself and shook my head. I had no idea what to be. I was a whiz at Astro-Mathematics, but also liked solving where the leak was coming from, or why a generator had stopped. It was like putting a puzzle together. Mom was nudging me toward the Canadian Space Agency but...maybe I should be a Ranger. A badge would help with jerks like Laxy.

The clouds had changed completely, which meant I had been too long.

The pasta was fine if a little soggy. What isn't good in pawmu? I could taste mangoes and pineapples in this one. The conversation was sports, Toronto politics, and the weather, predictable and polite. I made sure everyone had a pill before bed and the skeeter nets were snug. Malaria was not something to flirt with.

***

I slept like a log but poor Rich found the loon's calls creepy. He snapped his bracelet on, tapped in sleep EEGs, and thus, was groggy in the morning.

"What happened to *bare-arm*?" was my only comment. It's bad enough that slim band stored your health, academic, and personal stats, but if he started taking work emails...

I whipped up curried pea omelettes and toasted plantains, hoping dense protein and carbs would see them through. Lunch would be late today. Laxy thanked me and I complimented his hair, jokingly. It was all on one side of his face. He laughed and I hoped we were good.

This was the challenging day, I warned them, but the prize was the cave at the end. Amazing. Four portages—a chance to use your legs—and an untouched waterfall.

"Prettier than yesterday's rapids?" asked Kojo, flipping her long black hair into a ponytail.

"I think so. See what you think. But the portage can be tricky. Watch your footing."

"I'll warn Mr. Tough," she said, and we shared a grin.

It was a fine day to paddle surrounded by walls of green in every shade possible. I hummed and thought about Rich. In Toronto, he was funny, dramatic, always even-tempered. He made people laugh. Out with his friends, he was the one everyone turned to, the corners of their mouths already turning up.

At the first portage I told him I wanted to solo the boat today.

"What, I wasn't good enough?"

"No. It's just awkward with two people. It's easier to maneuver solo."

"Then *I* should take it." He mock-flexed his bicep. "I'm stronger. Fact."

"Right." I dumped the food pack at his feet. "So this is heavier. All yours."

I flipped the canoe up on my shoulder pads and began to walk. Once we were on a path of pine needles, I started whistling.

"What's that you're doing?" he shouted.

"Whistling?" I waited for him to catch up.

"Is that a real thing?"

I laughed. "It's music." I whistled a quick tune.

"You're like a twisted bird."

"Try it. Purse your lips and blow out."

He looked hilarious, like a toddler with his first straw. I nearly dropped the canoe.

"Hey. I'm trying. Explain it better."

"I will. Let's finish this trip first." My grandfather, a greybeard with kind brown eyes, was a champion whistler. He whistled at work, and sometimes a dance tune, whirling Nana Mpenzi around, her cheeks flushed. I smiled, remembering.

Kojo was sterning so they were on our tail all day. I was pleased she kept enough distance for private conversations. And silence. How I loved the sounds of the birds and our paddles. In Bancroft there was steady air traffic and hydro cars. Toronto was far worse, even up in their Skycity. Every air molecule vibrated with electricity, machines, people talking, beeping. People wore earpads to sleep or to stroll outside. Here, you didn't want to miss a single sound.

By the third portage, Rich's mood was sinking. I walked behind him, asking him to tell me about some of the exotic travels he'd taken, urging him toward pleasant memories. It backfired.

"Even hiking in the Falklands, guides brought our luggage by hydroplane to each campsite. This is primitive!"

I agreed. "That's why we do it, Rich. To remember that we can. To get away from machines."

"We're an advanced species. We created machines for a reason."

I was silent, groping for a topic. After a minute, I tried whistling one of his favourite songs.

Rich stopped abruptly, causing me to stumble and veer the boat to the right to avoid him.

"Must you? Are you trying to ruin a good song?"

Shocked, I said nothing. I wanted to stride past him but the path was too narrow. I had to wait until he'd glared at me, then turned. We continued on in silence.

***

We paddled for over an hour under the cloud of his sulk. I felt it would be rude to whistle, and my attempts at pointing out things—the Caspian tern diving for a fish—were rebuffed. I tried to look at it from his angle. He was new to this, accustomed to success in physical endeavours such as jolsta dancing and playing fiscus in an adult league. He was, in fact, a bit of a star. This trip was...humbling. It was a "growth experience", Nana Mpenzi would say. I gave up, and let him grow.

The river had widened into West Lake but now it narrowed and turned east. A great blue heron was standing, poised over a fish, exactly like the giant statue in one of his parks. "Look," I breathed, pointing with my paddle.

The heron did his sorcery. He crouched, bent his long neck into an "S" and turned into a pterodactyl. His wings swept down, then up so hard that you could hear the wind from them. He stayed low over the water. In a few flaps he swept up and disappeared over the trees.

"We're going into shore!"

"What?" To my surprise, Rich had continued to paddle, so we'd turned around. I straightened us with wide sweeps, asking, "Wasn't that incredible? Have you ever seen one, alive?"

"Of course I have. In zoos. Plenty of times. What machine is that?"

"Machine?" I listened, and heard the rumbling ahead. "That's the waterfall," I answered. "Keep an eye out for the portage. I don't fancy going over."

The falls were the main reason I'd chosen this route, for there was another way to reach the cave. Rich was tired and cranky, so I fed him a chuksnack bar and started taking our gear halfway up the trail. After my second trip he'd recovered. "I'll take the boat," he said, trying to make amends.

I helped him get it up, adjusted the shoulder pads, then donned the food pack and led him forward. He couldn't take the few flies who circled us, and kept dodging and cursing.

"You're immune," I soothed. "They won't bite you. Try to relax."

"What do you know? You love this stuff." He flung the canoe off and let it bounce on the dirt and rock trail. "How did you fake it in Toronto?"

I quickly knelt at the canoe, feeling the keel for a split. "Are you crazy? We need this to get home!"

"I'm sure you can whip us up a new one from a moose or something."

I looked up directly into his lagoon blue eyes. His face was red from heat and emotion, sweat plastering his striped hair over his forehead and neck quite…unattractively. His nose was still straight and long, but his nostrils were flared like a horse. I wondered idly how much money it had cost to tattoo his teeth. It suddenly seemed tawdry.

"What? Why are you looking at me like that?" he demanded.

I pulled my gaze away. "Well, Rich," I said calmly, studying the eggshell-thin surface of our canoe, "I was looking for signs of growth."

"Growth?"

I flipped open my waist pack, pulled out duct tape and cut off a piece with the flipknife. "Maturing. Improving." It only took two patches to repair, but I felt emotions heating up inside. Lorid had likened me to a volcano: slow to heat up, then—boom. "I'm sorry you're not enjoying our trip, Rich." I kept my voice flat. "Maybe it's not your thing. That's okay. But you need to treat me and our equipment with respect. We're *supposed* to be bare-arm out here. We have to work together."

"You *said* it was a holiday!"

"To me, it is."

"I thought you were going into the Canadian Space Agency, not—the Primitive Aboriginal Society."

I blinked. "What are you talking about?"

"You've been playing a role."

"As what?"

"Sweet and friendly."

Boom. I was standing up before I realized it, pointing at him. "And you? Mr. Popular? Mr. *Look-At-Me* on the dance floor or the fiscus team? Would you behave any better if I gave you a gold star for pulling your weight? For not complaining?"

Eruption. I'd never spoken in anger once in the eight months I'd known him. Though I'd been irritated a number of times. I turned, and shut my mouth firmly.

He seemed to be having some thoughts. I didn't want to hear

them. I dropped the food pack, flipped the canoe up and stormed the rest of the trail. At the shore, it was very tempting to keep going. Alone. *Jerk.* Instead, I swam hard to the falls, tried to get behind the curtain of water, then let the current spin me away.

When I reached the canoe again, everyone was there.

"Gorgeous falls!" said Kojo brightly, her eyes darting from me to Rich, standing stiffly to the side. "Can we have a snack here?"

I nodded. "Have you brought the food yet, Rich?" I gave him a fake smile. "I left it halfway up the trail for you." As he turned to go, I couldn't resist adding, "Careful. It's heavy."

I took another long swim. *You know, Makemba,* I told myself, *you just have to get through this trip civilly. Then the two of you could see a counsellor.* I'd kicked him right in his pride, and that wasn't nice. *He started it,* another voice said. Well, true, but what are we learning here? I am a volcano (news to him), not always so quiet, and he is not the minor god he'd seemed to be in the city.

I took another swim.

***

I studied the plasmap. Perhaps I'd booked too grueling a trip. I'd been so keen to show them the "Crystal Cave" (as Nana had named it) but, on second thought, did I want to have him even crankier? He'd been patient and kind in Toronto, showing me around, escorting me back to my aunt's when I grew weary of his busy social life. He once left a dance bar before his time because I was falling asleep at his table of friends. I could show the same generosity here.

That night I confided to Kojo that I was shortening the days and route. She agreed.

I asked Rich to help set up the tent when we arrived but he seemed not to hear me. I waffled, then did it myself. He was busy schmoozing with Laxy, recalling past glories in fiscus games. Laxy was rapt, slapping his knee at all the right places. Rich drew the guy out too, getting Laxy to tell some of his own stories, high school days, for gods' sake! I rolled my eyes at Kojo, but she didn't catch it. Just as well.

Watching the men out of the corner of my eye, I recalled that Rich had worked on the Greyson Chai political campaign. When I'd asked him about it, he'd flapped a hand and said simply that it was fun, but his eyes had lit up. (I, personally, shuddered at the thought of large crowds, non-stop enthusiasm and a smile painted on.) I looked over at his smile. There it was.

I went to bed and slept.

The next day we had a truce, unspoken. I was polite and friendly as to a paid client, and stopped offering him any guidance. He lily dipped. I cooked for everyone, assisted by Kojo. I took down the tent, our gear, the stove, etc. and packed it all efficiently. I only allowed myself pretty sunflower thoughts.

On the following day, it poured. We made it a layover. The sky was charcoal, the wind gusting full showers over us in waves. It was as though the river and sky had reversed themselves.

I read in the tent for two hours, then, in rain gear, walked the shore and drew possible greywater systems in the sand. I'd been thinking that the flattened copper wrapped around our building's hot water pipes wasn't absorbing enough heat for stored water. What about different metal? Wrapping the exit pipes too? I wished I'd taken more practical Earth courses rather than astro physics and astro geometry. Was it too late?

The next day it rained again.

That day I began to mess around with ideas Gramps and I'd talked about for capturing the field energy surrounding all the electrical wires through the building. I know other systems have been tried, but none have been truly successful. Perhaps a more sensitive receptor?

Laxy threw up in the party tent that night. Kojo was livid but I, removed from them more each passing hour, administered the remedy from the kit, gave cleaning supplies to Rich and dragged Kojo outside for a refreshing walk. I wanted to fly my ideas to someone and Kojo was a ChemEng with a sharp mind. Outside of her boyfriend choices.

"What does La—Luiz do for a living?" I asked mildly as our discussion wound down.

She grinned with only one side of her face. "Paramedic. In the HamBurlOakton tricity. Met him online."

I shrugged. "Gramps and Nana met that way." I bit my tongue from asking if she thought he was a potential mate for life. I couldn't see it, personally, but people are different.

"He's great with my Hiro," she said, wiping out our drawings with her foot. "Not everyone is good with a four year-old girl."

I laughed. "A four-year-old *genius*! Hiro practically beat me in double-level chess last time." I paused and squeezed her shoulder. "She's a gem. Extremely lovable, like you. Anyone would be lucky to pair with you."

Rich kindly threw up *outside* of our tent before he stumbled in and fell onto his windbed. He was snoring loudly so I pressed a snore patch to his sinus, shoved him over, then slept myself.

***

We turned back the next day despite the off and on drizzle through a hypocritical sky—first cheery and blue, then, in a minute, puffy grey clouds soaking us for half an hour. Unpredictable.

Rich and Laxy had been no help taking down the soaking camp, griping loudly about the weather and famous storms they'd seen on screen. I kept pace with Kojo to let the men schmooze. I was beginning to worry more about Kojo and Hiro's future than my own. It turned out that taking a partner camping was a swift personality test. It ought to be in Astro 101. You were away from your work, family, friends, your screens, and spending hour after hour together. As well, you faced mosquitoes, deer flies, ticks, rain, storms, cold nights or sweltering days. It gave you both a chance to see how you dealt with adversity.

Inside my head, a door closed gently.

We had to portage around the waterfalls again and both men spent so much time shouting insults at it that I wanted to toss Kojo in my canoe and let them find their own way back.

"I'll take the canoe, but can you take the gear pack this time, Rich?" I asked politely.

"I'm the food pack guy."

I hesitated. "We've nearly emptied the food pack, so I was going to wear it with the canoe. But you could take both if you like."

He paused, his eyes snaking from pack to pack, clearly aware of listeners. "Sure. No problem. This place is shit. Let's get out of here!"

Laxy grunted approval. I loaded up and left, waiting for no one.

After two more portages, and one good soaking, we rafted up and I handed out food. "So what do you all want to do? Our campsite is around the corner, but if you want to get home a day early, we could go another hour. There's a site further on."

"What happened to those big caves of yours, eh?" demanded Laxy.

I felt my nostrils flare and tried to school my face into zen. "Well, the weather turned pretty challenging, wouldn't you say? So, we decided to turn back."

"I don't remember anyone asking *me*," he demanded, suddenly aggressive. "Anyone ask you, Rich?"

"Makemba thinks she's the Prime Minister," snarled Rich.

Kojo jumped in. "We discussed it the evening you both threw up. We voted. You two were pretty sick of the rain, I remember."

Laxy backed down.

"Let's get the hell out of here," announced Rich. "I need civilization. Soon."

Everyone agreed, for different reasons.

***

We all paddled hard for another two hours and made significant progress. It was sunset before we pulled over to a free site. It meant we could be back in a city tomorrow.

When have I *ever* thought that?

I took a deep breath and wondered how and when was the appropriate time and way to break up with Rich. Would he be upset? He'd pushed for the Exclusive patch and hinted lately at more. And his friends seemed to really like me. But there were many attractive men and women who'd cast admiring glances at him, even with me there, and some obvious flirting. It had, I admitted, made me feel a secret thrill that he'd chosen *me*. It had made me feel special.

I wanted to gag. How pathetic was that?

Back to the problem at hand. I handed out skeeter pills before we landed, then asked everyone to set up camp quickly, before bugfall. That scared the men enough to make them actually help. I unfolded the stove and got working. Might as well eat heartily, I thought, since it was our last. Thus, I had both stoves and three meals going for a smorgasbord. At least they couldn't accuse me later of starving them.

I met an unexpected roadblock when I called them out to eat. Rich ordered me to bring the meal into the party tent.

First of all, I was cooking out of the kindness of my heart. For the last time. But no one barks orders at me.

"We don't eat inside a tent." My voice was brisk and no-nonsense.

"Get over it. We're not eating out there with the skeeters!"

I set the small picnic table, laid out all the dishes and helped myself. "We can't eat in the tent unless you want predators larger than you in there. Food's out! Dig in!"

There was a muttered argument in the tent, Kojo's voice soothing, then more grumbling. It helped me, I think, mentally. I had time to picture a balloon full of pretty images of Rich and me with kids in those Skycity parks. Beautiful, floating nearby, such a pretty future. Then I raised my fork and popped it.

I turned a broad smile to Rich, who emerged first, and waved my fork at the spread. "Hope you're hungry!"

He looked at me strangely.

Over dinner, which was pretty darn tasty, I felt myself growing unnaturally ebullient. I told a funny story about leading a camping trip with adolescent social climbers, each trying to outdo the others. Laxy laughed. When Rich waxed nostalgic about the technolight shows back home, I compared him to a buffoon robot in a recent 5-sense film who misses everything because he's busy complaining. Both Laxy and Koji exploded in laughter, then quickly muffled it. I winked at them. What did I care? I no longer had to struggle to fit in with his sycophantic crowd, nor to unruffle him when he was bad-tempered.

"Well," I concluded. "I know it didn't turn out to be your kind of vacation, you two." I nodded at each man, "But you weathered it pretty well. It'll be a good tale back in the city, right? Feel free to embellish it."

Kojo giggled. "Perhaps we met a rogue bear? Came between her and her cub?"

I shuddered. "A polar bear!" I stood to clear dishes and stretched out both arms and growled.

Laxy added, "A grizzly bear!"

This made both Kojo and I laugh and his face reddened. He demanded to know what was funny.

I stacked a few plates. "Grizzlies are out west, in the Rockies. But throw in a grizzly if you want. Why not? It's your story."

Humming, I brought the dishes to a flat rock and went to get water to heat for washing up.

Rich appeared by my side while I was adding soap. "What the hell are you playing at?" he hissed.

I blinked and took two cups from him. "Huh?"

"Since when does a backwoods hick make fun of me? In the city you'd be *nothing*. Less than a skeeter."

I frowned at my hands, working. "A skeeter? Do you have them in the city?"

"Don't deliberately misunderstand me. You—you," he stuttered, "You've *changed*."

I thought about it, then nodded. "Maybe so. Or, I've changed back." I turned to look at his artificially coloured irises. "I've come back to who I am. This," I pointed a soapy finger at my chest, "is me."

"Well, you might have let me know a little while ago. Before I got the damn patch. Do you know how many offers I've turned down because of you?"

I was overwhelmed with questions. Why me? Why did you do this? Why are you such a spoiled jerk? Since when do you treat your partner as a slave? All that emerged was a strangled, "Why?"

He misunderstood me. Ooh—I had an epiphany—that was the core of our relationship! He. Misunderstood. Me!

Meanwhile, Rich was lecturing me sotto voce on the New Sun party and the usefulness of a wife who would be a public darling, like a minor astronaut, someone of average attractiveness, shy, or…

"A virgin blueblood for the prince?" I blurted.

"What?"

"Never mind." Clearly I'd read too many fairy tales. I paused. "What made you think I was going to be an astronaut?"

"Your mother is one. High ranking, though you don't even realize it. Well respected. Conservative. And your sister told—"

"—so you sussed me out for my suitability for your career?" I started to giggle. Breaking up had been something I'd been dreading! I'd worried about how upset he might be. How I'd disappoint my mother, who'd approved of him, and his friends, who seemed fond of me. I laughed harder then and had to wipe my eyes on my sleeve.

As if my mother would have approved if she'd known of this. Hah! He didn't know my mother at all. She was a General, 2 star, and did have connections, it was true. (I wondered if this was going to backfire for him.) My mother loved the skies, loved adventures, diplomatic challenges, but had hated leaving her daughters behind. She'd wept the first two weeks of each mission, called us several times a day for a month until she'd adjusted. Lorid and I had always adjusted a lot faster. After all, we had Nana Mpenzi and Gramps, school, friends, camping trips, and our own adventures. Mom was always coming back to us. We knew it, deep down. And she had, every time.

I set the last plate aside and walked down to the river edge to wash my face with clean water. My thoughts had raced along so fast, I'd simply forgotten Rich was still there.

He followed me, livid, and pushed me in.

I floundered, swallowed a bit of water and stood up, dripping and seriously pissed. "These are my Warm Clothes," I said, in an excellent imitation of a 3 star General sounding off at troops. "My boots, warm socks, leggings, my only long sleeved top and jacket." I deepened my voice. "You. Have. Crossed. The. Line."

The other two appeared on the small ledge behind Rich, both nervous.

I shoved Rich back roughly and strode up to the others. "I've had it with prissy boy. It turns out he only dates people who might further his *career*. He thought I was going to follow my mother." I peeled off my boots, socks, and leggings right there. You're supposed to have the patch softened with a special cream then gently removed by a medico. Screw that. I ripped it off and tossed it at Rich, now a shadow on the beach.

Drunk with righteousness and giddy relief, I dug in the bag for his Moscovian knit leggings and his New Zealand wool slant-top (with the finicky opening under the left ear). I pulled them on. I liked anything from New Zealand and these were extremely expensive. I packed all my gear, set his outside in a small bundle, then stuffed the tent back into its tiny sack. I'd have to airwash it later.

Laxy was talking with Rich in a low voice inside his tent. Kojo was at the shoreline, setting the stove and food bag neatly inside my canoe, which was already back in the water. I looked around, discombobulated. Everything had been cleared up. All that was left was their tent and their canoe, which could hold three.

Kojo was looking at me from the shore, her head tilted patiently.

Right, I thought. I gave her a warm hug and kissed her cheek. "I owe you a week of babysitting."

"And don't think I won't take it. Because I need to get out there more."

I grinned. "Me too." I handed her Rich's safevest and paddle.

"Dating," she said, giving my stern a nice shove homeward, "can be difficult."

I laughed.

The stars were beautiful tonight. I thought I'd give my folks a 4-star hug when I reached home.

A FIELD OF SAPPHIRES AND SUNSHINE

Jaymee Goh

When Nurul Alina binti Safia Shamsia boarded the Trans-Pacific Sunship of Borneo Airways, she was still thinking of her boyfriend. Ex-boyfriend. She dragged her trunk behind her, its wheels making a soft clunking sound, marking overuse and replacement time. Though she wouldn't have minded economy seats, so long as she had somewhere to prop her feet up, all Trans-Pacific ships were kitted out with small cabins for long-haul flights. She set her trunk in the corner, pushed it onto its end, opened it, and locked it into place.

The frosted acrylic glass trunk had followed her for six years, seven moves, two continents, and many more long-haul airship flights. Her mother had joked that it would last longer than marriage. It had definitely been there before and after Jason, Alina thought wryly. When standing, Alina could unlatch it and spread it open, displaying the drawers of clothing and other essentials one needed: for Alina, that would be stationery, toiletries, travel records, and electronics. Built for the single, or single again, traveler who didn't need much, didn't accumulate a lot, and was constantly on the go, the trunk was perfectly suited for airship travel. Once standing, Alina could pull out corner braces to keep it steady even on the most turbulent of flights—not that air travel was that turbulent anymore.

The trans-Pacific flight would take a week, so Alina decided to wander the airship and get to know her neighbors. Most of them would be retirees, using the airship as a second retirement home. Some would be fellow international students, done with their cheap American degrees and going home, like her, maybe even leaving American sweethearts behind, too. And a few would be jetsetters, businesspeople with skills and projects that could not be done electronically.

She adjusted her tudung before she went out, humming as she re-pinned it into place. This was a new class of Sunship, rolled out with a special surau for its Muslim passengers. The surau was a half-spherical room with glass walls. On its ceiling floated two arrows, one pointing towards Mecca, and other towards the north. The airship also had its own food farm on the topmost floor, under the solar panels that fed energy to the ship.

Perpetual flight had long been a dream for engineers. Nurul Alina didn't pretend to understand it, but it did strike her as quite nifty, a ship that never had to touch the ground. She was more interested in the agricultural techniques they were using. Did they automate the farms? She had spoken to Jason about digitally-driven agriculture once, back when they could talk to each other about such things.

She was trying not to dwell on the slow death of her relationship; her mother had told her not to, but it was harder than it looked. It began a little before graduation, on a beautiful spring post-lunch walk in a park, and Jason had been blithely talking about moving to the Midwest. There was a little Muslim community there, and he would be close enough to work in case of an in-person emergency.

"First of all," she had said, "your work you can do anywhere in the world. Why does it have to be in America?"

He'd blinked at her owlishly—she'd decided that's how owls looked, anyway—and replied in his most reasonable tone, "Because this is where the most jobs are," and it took her a long time before she realized he'd heard only the second sentence.

"Okay, but what makes you think there won't be jobs in Asia? Remote jobs, even? You're a programmer; everywhere also can find this work," she'd continued.

"Don't tell me you want to go back all the way to Malaysia," he'd replied. "This is where the best jobs are."

"That's not true..."

He'd smiled at her. "And what do you know about my field and

America?"

What did she know, indeed? Only that after years of economic recession, America was finally on the upswing, catching up with the rest of the world. She'd come here because it was cheaper to study here than in her home country, where she hadn't been chosen for a scholarship and schools were so competitive; it was more expensive to qualify to study there than it was to simply shell out money for a desperate American university.

And she'd liked America. She'd liked most of Turtle Island, generally. She liked its old cities, and the suburban towns quite reminded her of home. The country was so big its airship industry was thriving, lumbering across the skies like scintillating pregnant whales. That didn't mean she wanted to stay forever, though. "He's not going to get it," her best friend had warned her, months earlier.

But she was loath to leave Jason: calm-tempered, cheerful, always willing to pull his weight around the house. He wasn't particularly funny or outstanding in any way, and sometimes he was a little passive-aggressive, not really much of a person to just outright state what he wanted. Since she was the same way, she had never minded, because they often anticipated each other's needs.

But it had been this need they had not anticipated: the need to go home. Of course they had thought about going home, and had talked about being home together, making a home together. The problem was that their ideas of *where* home would be, physically, had been very, very different, which they had not discussed, having taken for granted that of course the other would follow.

The walls of the surau were illuminated with a hologram of the Kaaba, as if trying to take people in prayer as close to Mecca as possible. Alina thought the Arabization was a little ostentatious. It was enough to know the direction to Mecca; not everyone had to pretend they were on hajj every time they prayed.

As she murmured her prayers, she forced thoughts of Jason out of her mind: she refused those blue eyes and gold hair, refused the pale cheekbones and easy smile. She focused instead on her family's paddy fields and towering angsana trees, vines of bright blue morning glories and ruby red jasmines. And the crocodiles, too. Jason had never been able to get over the fact that her family owned a crocodile farm.

The cafeteria was full by the time she was hungry enough to go. She got a small rice bowl with curry fish to go, picked up a newspaper, and went to the top floor.

As she expected, there was an aquaponics setup. Fish swam cheerfully past her, chasing each other between the hairy roots of the plants they fertilized. There was a person in the corner who seemed to draw their especial attention, possibly because of the bag on the utility belt. Alina watched, as did the other visitors, as the fish trailed after this magic food-giving gardener who pottered about, pruning. The sun streamed down through the solar-glass roof, its energy-collecting veins scattering rainbow prisms across the leaves and floor.

She sat down on a bench and got comfortable with the newspaper. NEW TOMB FOUND, its front-page headline announced.

Slow news day, she chuckled to herself. If the recovery of some Old Rich was the biggest news of the day, it was a sign that the science labs were taking their time releasing their findings to the public. She read the article anyway, to see where it had been found.

The "apocalypse" that the 21st century had predicted, with nuclear wars or zombie invasions or food scarcity or outright violence, had not happened. That didn't stop paranoid people from building bunkers and food stores in preparation for the end of the world. As the American and European economies had seesawed, sending out their armies to stabilize their hold on the world and reap other nations' natural resources, the refugee crisis had come to a head with outright racist violence all over the world. This prompted the doomsday preppers to duck into their bunkers. By the 22nd century there had been an entire network of wealthy elites living underground in their specially-made homes.

Rumor had it that insurrectionists took the opportunity to

sabotage these bunkers and bury their inhabitants alive. Some others suggested that unfortunate bunker placement led to them never coming out; after all, these were oil barons who knew that consistent pumping led to geological instability but didn't care, and this short-sightedness had led them to choose unsafe sites for their bunkers. Because history was filled with much more interesting events of social and engineering accomplishments, the Old Rich became nothing more than a footnote of morality.

This site was in Old Megajaya. Nurul Alina sighed. That meant work waiting for her when she got home.

She perused the rest of the newspaper, mostly the science and sports sections. She glanced through the racing pages, and barely paid attention to the socio-philosophical pages. Those she saved for bedtime, when she could properly mull over them in comfort and process their implications in her dreams.

She called several friends over the afternoon, sometimes to cry about her breakup, and sometimes to pretend she was okay, depending on the friend.

"I told you so," sighed a cousin. "Omputeh do not understand these things. A lot of them still can't really imagine a world outside America."

Alina dabbed at her cheeks. "But Azwa, he did four study abroads! He has a passport and everything!"

"A'lahai, just because he got passport doesn't mean he wants to live elsewhere. That's like saying you want to live in America just because you study there."

"True…"

"And anyway it's not like you can't find a boyfriend at home. I'm sure there must be someone who—"

"There isn't," Alina bit in, her voice flat. "What makes you think I haven't tried? Ibu tried three different matchmakers."

"Four." She could hear Azwa pressing her lips together, nonplussed. "Difficult to find someone who wants to be in your family's business."

"Like I don't know," Alina groused.

"So... how is the new Sunship?"

Alina was glad for the change in topic. She stretched her feet under the blanket and wiggled her toes, trying to imagine being in a cramped seat, as she described the innovations in the new 389 Airship Class. They were really grander than she had expected.

After the fossil fuel crisis, and the so-called apocalypse, profiting off energy became unacceptable, morally. It was slow-going, lobbying the government to increase solar power sources, because governments all over the world had militarized. Airplanes, with their awful "economy class" seating, had fallen out of favor when airships made a comeback, this time with solar power. The memory of the Hindenburg no longer haunted the 22nd century. A new generation of entrepreneurs poured into the airship industry, competing with each other with improvements to mechanical efficiency, meteorological instruments, and internal architecture.

When she finally called her family's home, saving the best for last, she frowned at how long it took for her mother to pick up.

"Aina!" her mother finally replied, sounding breathless.

"Ibu!" Alina's mind jumped to the worst conclusion. "Is everything okay? Or did the deal with Megajaya not happen?"

"What? Oh, no, that's not a problem at all. We'll be taking that contract, of course. But Aina, best news, we may have found you a partner after all!"

"A part—"

"Business only lah, of course, but who knows! Quite good looking."

"Ibu!" Alina rolled her eyes to the ceiling in exasperation. "You know I just broke up with my boyfriend."

"Yah, best timing my girl. Now you can focus on this one."

She hadn't missed the fact that her mother was speaking in Malay, and most pronouns were gender-neutral. Her mother knew she was bisexual, of course, which should have made matchmaking easier, but apparently not. "So, uh, laki ke perempuan?" she inquired.

Safia Shamsia paused for a moment, then laughed. "I'll let you wait and see!"

"Ibu! You can't do this to me!"

"Yes, I can. So, tell me your itinerary. I know you send me but I accidentally delete the e-mail."

"It's okay, Ibu, I also sent it to Bala, so he should be able to come get me."

"Cannot lah, Aina, Bala's wife is pregnant and due any moment now. If I come get you then we can also plan a dinner so you can meet the new partner."

Alina took a deep breath. She half-wished her mother was less of a tropical storm, but that would make Safia Shamsia binti Khairunissa Jamaluddin less than her best. Her mother wasn't the best at gauging men, judging by the divorces she'd been through, but she was also just not very well suited to marriage in general. At some point in Alina's teens, her mother had given up on marriage completely and taken on a string of lovers, becoming the family scandal.

But where her mother lacked in romantic commitment, she more than compensated with business sense. None of her business partnerships ever failed, so much so Alina remained friendly with three of her former stepfathers, who had all chipped in to help send Alina to school overseas.

"All right. I'll trust in you."

"Good! Now, tell me what you think—" and her mother launched into a comparison between two big-box book vendors.

Looking back, she had known that her relationship to Jason was doomed, and not from any fault of her mother's. Not when Safia Shamsia had stepped off the airship platform to greet Jason effusively and then insist on treating them to dinner. Not when Alina watched Jason speak to Safia Shamsia about his career plans, to be a software engineer. Her mother had queried him his thoughts on the new models of calculating machines that would help replace several computer functions, moving away from the use of rare minerals into more sustainable hardware. Not even when he had floundered a little, nervously joking that such a development would render his job obsolete. Safia had laughed, pointed out to him, rather gently, that his field was dependent on planned obsolescence. Then he had asked about the family business, more from courtesy than actual curiosity, and it was all over.

How had Alina found his basic decency charming, when he was so, so conservative otherwise? How had she let him get away with speaking about a future together as if he were indulging her, rather than collaborating with her on something they both wanted?

It would not do to dwell. Only thing to do was move forward. And Nurul Alina did look forward, to returning home and taking on the paddy fields. It was time to rejuvenate the hills bordering the land again. The village nearby would welcome the revitalization of terraced rice-farming, even if they'd lost whole generations to urban vertical farms.

Still, it took only two days before she called her cousin again. "Azwa, what do you know about my mother's new business partnerships?"

***

She had missed the air. Despite her mother's wealth, it had not been enough to finance much beyond schooling, so Alina had not seen her home since leaving for university. What little money she had earned on her own, her mother had encouraged her to use for traveling elsewhere. When would she return to Turtle Island next?

Her childhood home had undergone many renovations over the decades. When it had first been built, a few generations ago, it had been a colonial mansion, with high ceilings and stately pillars. There were remnants of that old house still, its courtyards with still ponds, and walls with paint that reached only as high as soldiers could reach. But otherwise the floors were now high off the ground, on stilts, adapted from older traditional styles. Gently-sloping walkways joined the various wings and rooms of the house, protected from the elements with elegant sunroofs upon which vines crept. Here and there, colorful painted solarglass windows depicted various folktales.

Touches of the contemporary were clear: a hint of chrome marking a concession elderly inhabitants made, to allow for easy wheelchair transport when they became too infirm to walk. While most of Alina's elderly relatives were hale and hearty, growing old gracefully also meant accepting when assistive devices were convenient. The front door was new, too—a double-door with the latest in glass technology, double-reinforced, frosted, and brightly-colored. Geroda on one side, Jentayu on the other, and Cenderawasih on the large fanlight above, wings spread as if to hug the other two legendary birds across the doorframe. It took a moment for Alina to see that lights were actually installed within the thick glass itself, making the mythical creatures light up with an unearthly glow, even in broad daylight.

Her mother was definitely living it up. Alina wondered what she would have to do to match that level of classy eccentricity. Solar panels made to resemble old nipah roofs, maybe.

There were already people in the reception wakaf beyond the front door. Alina sighed inwardly—she had hoped for some quiet time to get used to being home. She recognized several of the guests: some relatives, two stepfathers and their families, a few of her mother's business partners. They greeted her enthusiastically, congratulating her on her graduation from university. Her stepfathers had already done so, taking the opportunity to tour Turtle Island when they had visited for her ceremony, but they repeated their felicitations.

Finally she was introduced to the strangers, especially to one Fairuz Mohamed Jafri, and it was clear this was the new *proposed partner*.

Over the course of lunch, it was also clear that Fairuz—Alina wasn't sure how Fairuz identified, and she couldn't tell—was very new acquaintances with Alina's family. An entrepreneur in mineral engineering, with connections to the Old Rich without being an Old Rich. Also recently finished a course of study, but in Ireland. Spoke Gaelic haltingly, Semai flawlessly.

Alina found herself quickly feeling out-classed, and balked at the idea of being set up with this perfect stranger who was, well, perfect.

After lunch, most of the visitors went home, although a few stayed to nap in guestrooms. Alina and her mother took the new partners on a tour of the estate.

Most of the fields were bordered by walkways, with pondok at particular junctions for the workers to rest in. Alina caught up with many of her mother's staff that way. As they approached the side of the land that wasn't farmland, the side that was swamp instead, she found herself nervous.

This was the family business that led so many people to be leery of associating with her family. The crocodile farm had been some great-grandfather's idea, after a plague had infected local cattle. It was in the lowest part of the land that was difficult to drain and, even before the crocodile farm had been established, had been fetid marshland. Safia cheerily handed out masks to the guests before they arrived at the edge of the place where it would begin to stink.

It was a local joke that this part of the estate was called "Lembah Maut," Death Valley. Tomorrow, Alina would be in the processing plant at the mouth of the valley, cutting up carcasses. They would throw it into the marsh for the crocodiles to devour. Some of the crocodiles would be ready for harvesting as a delicacy overseas.

They took carcasses from everywhere. Veterinarians did their best to mitigate sickness in animals, but they would never be able to stop nature from taking its toll. And there was also always the odd human body to be disposed of. Lembah Maut served as regional body disposal whenever tombs like Megajaya were discovered. They took contracts from across the Nusantara region, sometimes as far north as Viet Nam. People across all the local faiths couldn't condone it, but looked the other way, in embarrassment that the morality of their religion couldn't have stopped the greed of the Old Rich. Sometimes, Alina's family was even paid for their silence by governments wanting to wipe their Old Rich from historical record.

What would Fairuz, with Old Rich connections, think of it?

Jason had balked. He had had no Old Rich connections, but he still thought what Alina's family did was heinous.

"Have you no respect for the dead?" he had demanded, when Alina finally told him.

Alina had thought about this question before, and was ready with an answer. "No. They didn't have respect for us when they were alive, so why should we respect them now that they're dead? And anyway, they're usually long dead by the time they get to us."

He had gagged. They hadn't spoken for weeks.

The Megajaya corpses had already been brought in, lying in glass coolers. Some of them had been mummified to some degree. Others just looked disgusting, covered in slime, failing to decompose because they hadn't been exposed to the proper elements.

It was one thing to feed cattle carcasses to crocodiles, quite another to use human ones. Sometimes, however, one just took one's food wherever possible. Who would mourn the Old Rich? What had they done to deserve lament?

As these justifications ran through Alina's mind, she went through the rote introduction of the process, the figures of crocodile populations and species, and the various clients that bought crocodile meat from them, as well as the rigorous testing the meat went through to ensure no pathogens remained that would infect humans. She had rehearsed it for several years.

"This makes selling the meat trickier, of course," she found herself babbling to Fairuz afterwards, who only nodded gravely.

"Of course, what with the awareness of pathogen theory these days," Fairuz replied. "But then, crocodiles have always eaten rotten meat, and we have eaten them in turn with no ill effects, for hundreds of years. I have some contacts in the medical fields who might be interested, actually, in procuring some of this meat. I mean, who knows what the Old Rich might have ingested?"

"Yes." Alina practically sighed in relief.

They walked up a set of stairs to a balcony overlooking the marsh. Her mother and the other guests were taking their time. From this standpoint, the sordid business was made clear. The bluebottle flies buzzed around the marsh flowers that stank like the meats they grew in between. Alina had always found it a brilliant sight. She was also delighted to see new flowers—she had sent home yellow lotus seeds in her second year. Many of the flowers in the marsh were yellow, a quirk some relative had started which she and her mother gladly continued.

"This is usually where people start screaming and losing their minds," she joked, gesturing to the limbs and organs strewn across the shallows or floating next to crocodile heads.

"Is this where you've done that?"

"No… I grew up here, so, I guess I can see its beauty." She flushed a little, and was sure it was visible around her face mask.

Fairuz's eyes crinkled a little—a smile. "The flies really add something to the landscape. It looks like a field of sapphires and sunshine. If you'll pardon my overly-romantic streak."

She returned the smile. "I'm jealous of the swamp now, for getting such a nice compliment."

And for a brief, blossoming moment, they stared at each other, both aware that they were on the cusp of something a bit more than a business partnership.

MIDSUMMER NIGHT'S HEIST

Commando Jugendstil
and
Tales from the EV Studio

Imagine a summer night in Milano…

The day had been torrid, 35 degrees with 80% humidity, and every activity felt like wading through lukewarm soup, but it rained in the evening, a heavy downpour with all the trimmings of thunder, lightning, and hailstones the size of grapes. The air is fresh now, the city looks clean, freshly washed, and the mosquitos have wisely decided to take cover for the night, just in case, so on the Navigli every bar has thrown windows and doors wide open to let the night in.

In one such bar, at a corner table, sits a gang of dreamers. At first glance they don't look like much, just ordinary young people, of the kind that opinion-peddlers love to hate: close to thirty, too many piercings and tattoos, fixed-term contracts, not a single mortgage between the five of them, and no money or credit to get one even if they wanted to. Just garden variety millennials having a night out with friends.

It takes a deeper look to notice the look in their eyes—a glint of defiance and determination—a keener ear to discern cryptic hints in their conversation—to perceive the barely repressed euphoria—a bit of attention to notice that they are drinking only gazzosa and fruit juice.

It would take an extremely keen and knowledgeable observer to spot the discreet enamel pins on their clothing: ivy leaves, because like ivy they will hang on and persist, slowly spreading until they have cleaned up all hydrocarbons and other filth from the city.

These folks are famous, notorious even, their name is on everybody's mouth, either acclaimed as the best new thing in art, some sort of local, hippie version of Banksy, or decried as a bunch of subversives and potential threats to the public order, depending on who you ask.

They are Commando Jugendstil.

Well, *part* of Commando Jugendstil, the core of the group. Since their first action about a year prior, they have managed to pick up quite a few extra hands who occasionally collaborate with them on some heists. They're spreading, teaching trustworthy affiliates and empowering more young folks like them, and mobilising local communities for ever larger and more impactful actions.

Loopy is the heart of the outfit. He had the original idea of conjugating art, green technology, and bioremediation to produce energy and create communities across the city during his master thesis at the Politecnico and has been trying to make it real ever since. His dreams are what have kept the group alive through years of short-term jobs and dissatisfaction, and his are the amazing Art Nouveau-inspired artworks for which the group is famous. He is doodling on a piece of napkin now, nervous, deep lines that furrow the paper like a ploughed field.

Sparky is an engineer from the same university. She makes lasers, coolers, and bits of spacecraft as a day job, and knows how to build almost anything from scratch and scraps, like a five-foot-tall, cherub-faced MacGyver. Most of the tech used in the heists comes from her lab via a detour through the shed of her mum and granny's house in the outskirts of the city. They are very supportive and discreet, and are now feeding a family of refugees with the hydroponics/aquaculture integrated system their daughter has built. The keys to her van jingle between her fingers, her foot taps impatiently on the floor.

Dotty is a chemist with a major photonics bent. Quantum dots are her speciality, hence her codename, and she knows everything about them, or at least enough to brew up enough raw materials for the Commando to work on. Her group never notices when the leftovers from an experiment disappear, only to reappear across the city as art. She's a brilliant scientist, and confident enough to waltz into Renzo Piano's or Norman Foster's office with a presentation on why they should change all the windows in their next skyscraper to solar concentrators, but at the moment she's munching nervously on a bruschetta and toying with her rainbow-hued dreadlocks, her ebony skin overlaid by a veil of pallor.

Sprouty is a botanist who studies bioremediation and sustainable urban farming. His thumb is greener than grass and he propagates ivy and other beneficial plants with an almost religious zeal. He also had the idea of recreating the Etruscan tradition of nomadic, riverine apiculture; the first harvests of water-lily honey are something to die for. He grows the best weed in Milan, and smokes a lot, but now his dark eyes sparkle alert and sharp and his strong, loam-stained fingers drum impatiently on the table-top. He never smokes before driving or before a heist.

Last but not least, Stabby, Loopy's partner, is the most unlikely member of the team, a structural biologist with a couple of papers in *Nature* and yet another piddling two-year contract. Zie is the nerdiest of their group of nerds, with a slightly unhealthy passion for D&D, extreme sports, and martial arts, and is the unofficial strategist of the gang, scouting locations, arranging getaways and pulling off diversionary actions to allow zir friends to do their jobs. At the moment zie is treating the group to yet another hyper-caffeinated rant about politics in *Star Wars*, to which the rest of the group nods distractedly.

No one is really paying attention, but not out of malice. They actually like to hear zir theories, but they are an hour away, tops, from their most risky heist yet, and nerves are strung high like violin strings.

"Hey, Stabby, what about a round of table football?" Sprouty stands up suddenly, jerking his head towards the now-unoccupied playing table.

Stabby closes zir mouth midway through an argument about the economic imperialism of the Galactic Republic and nods, standing and cracking zir knuckles.

"Ready to get trashed?" zie challenges.

"Keep dreaming." Sprouty laughs, propelling his lanky, stringy body towards the table with his customary lack of grace.

Sparky shakes her head, her Shirley Temple-style golden curls bouncing around her shoulders, and stands to join their game.

Dotty picks up her phone and starts texting her girlfriend Webby over the Commando's encrypted chat channel.

Loopy puts his mechanical pencil back in his bag and stands, stretching fully and yawning. He looks tired, his black curls are tousled, and his eyes are circled by deep, dark shadows.

It's Friday evening after a crunch week. The planning and preparation for the new heist has absorbed whatever little spare time they had, and they won't be going home to sleep for a while longer. Even longer if the police catch them in the act.

This time it's not just a little bit of guerrilla gardening or some night-time redecorating in a peripheral housing estate or private property.

This time it's big and loud and, even though their support network is as solid as ever, things could go south pretty easily.

Loopy tries not to think about it. They all have jobs; Sprouty even has a little kid. They have a whole lot left to lose, and yet they are there, planning to fool the entire law enforcement of Milan to make art and take a stand for the city they love and against those who, though talking of supposed past greatness, would turn it into something sclerotised, close-minded, and pitiful.

"From great insanity comes great power..." he thinks, casting a glance at his life-partner, who is still valiantly trying to hold zir own in table football against Sparky and Sprouty all on zir lonesome.

He yawns again and strolls to the table, taking his customary place at Stabby's side, manning the attack.

"Now we're talking!" Stabby exclaims, grinning and stabbing the handle forward to make the ball ricochet against the side wall.

***

When the bar closes at half past one in the morning, the gang slips out among the crowd of late-night revellers, splitting up as agreed and eventually converging to collect their gear.

Sparky opens the passenger door of her nondescript but spacious white van and pulls out a huge, battered duffel bag with the name of a local football team printed on the side in large, faded white letters. Stuffed in it to maximum capacity are a bunch of green overalls and some dark green t-shirts.

"Wow, Sparky! Your mum and gran really went above and beyond…" Dotty comments with a low whistle, pulling out one of the overalls from the bag. They're printed all over with stylised, deep green ivy leaves in a sort of elegant camo.

Loopy picks up another one, a hint of tears in his eyes.

"We're going to look like Ghostbusters…" he whispers, the nerd, then lets his bag fall to the floor and kicks away his shoes, shimmying into the suit as quickly as he can.

"What are the t-shirts for?" Sprouty asks, pulling one up with the tips of his fingers, as if he fears it will bite him.

"Ninja masks!" Stabby exclaims.

Zie picks up another shirt and quickly demonstrates, reversing, tying and tucking the garment until the only things that show from underneath it are zir kohl-lined eyes.

"That's what they are meant to be, isn't it?" zir asks in hindsight, still managing to look embarrassed.

"Yep, got it in one," Sparky reassures zir.

"My mum wanted to make us some proper balaclavas, but can you imagine wearing one in this heat?" she adds, making a face and fanning herself with her hand.

Stabby gives her a brief, tight hug. "You're awesome, the lot of you."

Sparky gives zir a doubtful look. "You really are easily pleased, fam."

Stabby lets out a little laugh and shakes zir head.

"Am not. I am going to glorious battle against fascism with my mates, dressed as an Art Nouveau ninja. Whatever happens next, this is going to be one of the high points of my life!" zie exclaims, raising a fist in the air with a little jump.

"If you put it that way…" Sparky agrees.

They kit up quickly and jump into the van. The streets of the city are nearly deserted. There are no more trams and only night buses cruise through the streets, like the sole survivors of a public transport apocalypse. Clusters of revellers walk home or to the nearest discotheque, and the Area C cameras, which control access to the city centre for congestion charge purposes, are switched off.

Truly off, as in a member of the team has hacked into the system and made sure no data will be recorded until the following morning and the control centre will only see a rerun of the data from the previous night.

Since her wheelchair couldn't fit in its customary place at the back of Sparky's van with all the extra gear they are carrying, Webby is watching over them from her remote location somewhere in the Isola, sending her feelers through streams of information, on the lookout for potential danger and more of those pesky surveillance cameras.

In the previous weeks, Stabby has scouted diligently for the access and egress routes with the least number of them to make Webby's life easier, pacing back and forth along the streets and alleys of the city centre in one of zir many disguises, and has eventually found one that requires minimal intervention.

While Webby works her magic, they are functionally invisible, like ghosts in the techno-surveillance machine.

Sparky drives like all the demons of hell are at their back, she always does, and the rest of the gang hangs on tight, grinning in exhilaration or trying not to puke, depending on who you ask. The van, loaded to the maximum with all their gear and then some, sways like a drunken camel.

Their target is Piazza Della Scala, the small square between the Duomo and the Teatro Alla Scala, where the Town Hall is situated.

On the morrow, one of the main leaders of the far right will stage a rally there, allegedly to protest the law on the *ius soli* right of citizenship and the threat of "ethnic substitution" so dear to white supremacists all over the world, hoping to boost the campaign for his election to Prime Minister with yet another bout of ignorance and hate speech.

The ANPI and other antiracist and antifascist organisations have called for a counter-protest in the nearby, vastly larger, Piazza Duomo.

The members of the Commando will be attending that too, if they don't get arrested, but first they are going to leave a mark on the event, Jugendstil-style.

"We're getting close," Dotty announces, peering at the screen of her tablet, on which Webby is streaming the intel.

"What about the others?" Sprouty sticks his head out of the window to check, and the rest of his words are eaten up by the turbulence.

"They are close behind us, on a different route." Dotty pinches the bridge of her nose. It's not like Sprouty wasn't there when the plan was discussed...

"Time to get the party started, then!" Stabby dials a number on the crappy burner phone zie has bought for the occasion.

"Hannibal is at the gates," is all zie says when the call connects.

***

A few kilometers away, a patrol of Vigili Urbani, the local police, cruising along Viale Forlanini spots a commotion and stops to investigate. They can hear strange noises, like pots being banged against each other hard, repeatedly. There are shouts, yells, and curses.

Drunks, or a fight between gangs, the two officers think. From the sound of it, there are a lot more of them than there are of the police, so they immediately request help and then inch out of the car to check what is happening, pepper spray and batons at the ready. The sounds become even more ominous with every passing moment.

The Vigili cross themselves, heartily wishing that they were allowed to carry guns, and cautiously peer around the corner towards the source of the noises.

Some people are duking it out between the trees of the park as if there was no tomorrow. Swords clang against shields, battle-cries and curses rend the air, as the combatants charge and retreat across the field strewn with the bodies of the fallen.

There are Romans in *loricae* and rectangular shields, Gauls in punk hairdos, chequered trousers and not much else, and a third group of darker-skinned people in white armour, with round shields inscribed with a palm tree.

Carthaginians, officer Bonelli's classical schooling supplies, and, between them and the Gauls, they are doing short work of the Romans, as they should.

He blinks repeatedly, then rubs his eyes as if, by doing so, he could erase those images from his retinas. Part of his brain tells him that he should try to arrest the lot of them for disorderly behaviour and causing a disturbance of the peace; the rest looks at their numbers and those swords and thinks that they definitely don't pay him enough for that.

His colleague has already decided: he has retreated behind the corner and is clutching the St. Michael medal hanging from his neck as if his life depends on it, curled in a ball and very grey in the face. His lips move in a mute prayer.

Bonelli sighs and rolls his eyes. These are not ghosts from the Second Punic War, he tries to convince himself. There is no such thing as ghosts. These must be some assholes intent on playing a prank on honest people, but he will show them.

Yes he will, as soon as the reinforcements arrive, he tells himself. *Any minute now*, he repeats, pressing the call button on his radio handset over and over.

***

Meanwhile, on the far side of Parco Sempione, close to Cimitero Monumentale, a flash mob has ensued, much to the bafflement of the law enforcement.

Citizens have taken to the streets with streamers of cloth, plastic balls, bowling pins, and hula hoops and are now pretending, awfully for the most part, to compete in an Olympic gymnastics event.

A trio of elderly Chinese ladies from nearby Via Paolo Sarpi, allegedly alumnae of the National Gymnastics Academy of Beijing, are sitting on a public bench and act as judges, raising numbered placards and yelling scathing comments about how even in their eighties they would be able to do much better.

In Parco Solari, naked cyclists and skaters have taken over the scene, 1920s swing music blaring from their eighties-style ghetto blasters. Nearby residents are leaning out of windows and balconies, clamouring for the police, the army, the Avengers...*anyone* to make the din stop.

In Largo Marinai d'Italia, the park built on the grounds of a former Austro-Hungarian fortress, a six-foot-five, copper-skinned, very muscular woman dressed in a Victorian gown and armed with a huge parasol is leading a crowd of similarly dressed people against a cluster of scared-looking Austro-Hungarian soldiers.

"Independence or Death!" she yells with a strong Brazilian accent.

There are pagan rites at Parco Nord; mass pillow fights explode in Viale Padova; dancers perform around a machine that blows giant soap bubbles in front of the Lambrate station; a torchlit, 17th century penitential procession marches down Corso di Porta Ticinese so that the plague of racism and intolerance will stop, and, to top it all,

Charles VIII of France has descended through the Alps yet again and a few Milanese knights are engaged in strenuous battle with his bodyguard at Stazione Centrale.

The whole city has exploded into insanity all at once.

Random, mostly innocuous, spontaneous gatherings spread all across the map as late-night partygoers in various states of inebriation join the impromptu festival. Most people don't know what it is all about, but it does not matter.

It's Saturday night, it's summer, the music is on. That's all they need to know. People play, dance, act out of context and have fun.

The law enforcement is at the end of their collective wits. Patrol cars are zooming around the city, heading to the sites of the disturbances to restore public order and make sure everybody goes home and stays there. Officers are debating whether to call in people from the day shifts, and intelligence analysts are tearing their hair out, asking themselves how they could have missed something so big, how it could get organised right under their noses in spite of their strict surveillance of social media.

The transmissions on the police frequencies are increasingly frantic with a jumble of calls and counter-calls, shouted instructions and even a couple of on-air, public nervous breakdowns.

From her perch at the center of the network, Webby grins and contributes to the chaos, generating nuisance calls, while Stabby types frantic streams of instructions to zir accomplices on the group's encrypted chat, directing the performers to draw the law enforcement farther away from the city centre and avoid disbandment or arrest for as long as they can.

***

Piazza della Scala is the eye of this perfect storm of joyous chaos, but the atmosphere is no less frantic. Dawn rushes towards them, inexorable. They will have to be well out of the way by then and there are a lot of actions to coordinate still.

Stabby represses a surge of anxiety. Zie has planned the operation with a reasonable amount of grace time to allow for delays and mishaps, but zie can't help but feel the pressure.

"This is much worse than managing a scientific grant…" zie ruminates, checking the progress of the various units on zir tablet.

Thankfully, the first wave of troops is on time: a false rubbish collection vehicle and assorted civilian trucks have converged on the site, disgorging a small army of co-conspirators and several tons of extra gear.

A squad of gardeners, under the direction of Sprouty and of Loopy's uncle, starts unloading bags upon bags of soil from the back of the skip.

The rich, dark loam spreads on the flagstones, raked by expert hands, then the gardeners unroll bright green tiles of grass upon it, as if laying down a carpet.

Flowering plants appear, placed in slightly raised flowerbeds: dahlias, daisies, marigolds, sunflowers, and flowering lavender and rosemary bushes. Their clean, crisp aromas permeate the air, their colours light up the night.

Little by little, a garden takes shape around the statue of Leonardo da Vinci and his apprentices/boyfriends, scrupulously laid out according to the plan tacked on the side of the gardeners' main truck.

Dotty directs the operations with an iron hand, armed with charts, diagrams, and a laser theodolite.

She has spent long nights calculating the angles of incidence of the sun all over the square and has even taken a leaf out of Stabby's book to check the data for herself.

She's borrowed her mum's best Sunday dress, a delightful halter-top number done in a turquoise, ochre and gold print with a matching headscarf, hidden her very recognisable rainbow locs in the soft folds of a turban, and, disguised as a wealthy Nigerian tourist, has pretended to take endless selfies next to her similarly dressed sister and cousin in order to take solar irradiance measurements with her phone.

They're really pushing the limits of the technology and of their half-improvised equipment, there is no margin for error and she wants it to be perfect.

It is not just a matter of professional pride: this issue matters a lot to her.

Her dad is Italian, so she has gotten double citizenship right from the start, but many young people she knows and cares for, including her baby cousins, born in Milan from extra-EU parents, are on the edge of uncertainty as they approach their eighteenth birthday because the government refuses to recognise that they are as Italian as anyone else, no matter how loudly they ask for it. She is going to do anything in her power to push for change.

"No, move that lavender half a meter to the right!" she instructs, taking another measurement.

I can go on like this all night, she thinks, repressing a face-splitting yawn.

***

"The knights have been dislodged from the Station." Webby's message pings on Stabby's tablet, alongside the current disposition of the police forces in the area. The biologist curses inwardly and calls Tanky, the leader of the knights, directing them to form up for a rear-guard action along Viale Abruzzi.

"Get ready for pickup," zie alerts another accomplice, setting vans running towards the knights.

"Shall we bring the Longobards in?" Webby writes.

Stabby mulls over the thought. It's only about three AM and one of their main disturbance events has already been almost dispersed. They need the extra bodies in the way.

"The Longobards and the Elves, I think," Stabby writes back.

"On it," Webby confirms.

Soon a few more coloured dots appear on the map: the Longobards, in red, are clustered around Viale Monza, where they are acclaiming Theodelinda and Authari as their new legitimate sovereigns, while the Elves, in green, are locked in a ferocious battle against a bunch of Goblins in Corso di Porta Vittoria.

"It does pay off to have friends in different subcultures," Stabby writes.

"Hopefully these units will last a bit longer than the HEMA folks," Webby counters. She doesn't sound very convinced.

They are still a long way from being finished and the last thing they want is for some police to wander their way while they are still doing their thing.

***

The gardeners finish their work slightly ahead of schedule. They pick up their gear and shove it pell-mell in the back of their vans and hop on board for a quick retreat, leaving the floor to the electricians and engineers.

The first van arrives on time with five people, a load of cables and connectors, and part of the payload.

"Where are the others?" Sparky asks.

The squad leader shrugs.

"We came a different way."

"They'll be here soon," Loopy tries to reassure her, but his eyes betray exhaustion and worry.

Sparky nods and pats him on the back, but whips out her phone nonetheless.

"Where are you folks?!" she asks.

"We're getting there, we have a flat tyre." Leccy sounds way too chill about it, given the situation.

"Four EngDs and two PhDs between the six of you and you can't change a bloody tyre?!" Sparky yells, temper rising. She lives up to her nickname in more ways than one.

"We're trying! With all the stuff you asked us to carry, the van's too heavy to lift!" Leccy sounds a lot less calm than before.

Sparky stamps her foot on the ground, mindful of the flowers, and bites her lower lip in frustration. Leccy and her team are carrying three more pieces of payload and quite a bit of the IT stuff. They need to arrive at battle stations as soon as possible.

"What's going on?" Loopy is at her side again, silent as a shadow.

The engineer covers her phone with her hand. "Leccy's van has broken down. We need to mount a rescue and recovery action."

"Damn..." Loopy curses, but he's already looking around for a solution.

"Let's unload our van and start setting up the stuff that's already here. Then someone can drive to them and pick up the rest."

"Or tow them," Sparky butts in, nodding to herself. They surely have enough rope and chains in the back of their vehicle to pull it off, literally.

"That too. Do you want me to go?" Loopy offers.

He knows how to drive quite well, thanks to the lessons of his father, who used to be a semi-professional racing pilot, but he does not feel incredibly comfortable behind the steering wheel. His real talents lie elsewhere.

She shakes her head.

"You hold the fort, mate. I'll go."

Loopy nods and throws the back doors of the van open, yelling at the others to hurry up and help him. Bundles of cables start to appear, hauled by the volunteers, then bulky slabs of material, wrapped in green tarpaulin.

"Hey Leccy, I am on my way. Just send me your coordinates, all right?" Sparky turns back to the phone.

The data pings on the chat almost immediately and she forwards it to Stabby.

"Clear a path for me!"

"On it, fam!" the biologist replies.

Sparky jumps back in the van, turns the transponder back on to allow Stabby to track her, and docks her tablet on the dashboard, tapping away until it displays their custom, real-time map.

Swarms of dots are moving about, some with a clear intent and purpose, some approximating quite well a Brownian motion.

A notification appears, then a path through the maze of narrow, one-way streets of downtown Milan.

Webby has pulled some open-source path minimisation algorithm from Github and tweaked it to respond to the movements of the grey dots representing the police. With it equipped and a bit of luck, it will be no harder than a run of GTA, Sparky thinks.

"All clear! Have a safe trip!" Loopy yells from the back.

The engineer revs the engine and pulls off at speed with a squealing of tyres, disappearing almost immediately around a bend.

***

"Come on, folks! Let's put our backs to it!" Dotty instructs, clapping her hands together. She is the first to follow her own advice, putting to good use her athletic form, honed by years of semi-professional rugby.

They move in groups of four, carrying what at first glance looks like colourful window-panes and placing them in the slots left by the gardeners, solidly secured in weighted floor-mounts, which they have disguised with trays of flowers.

Their work was conceived to be used and enjoyed, not to stay safe behind barriers. They have designed the sturdy mounts to prevent the solar stelae from tipping over when kids eventually try to climb upon them, or if people bump into them, so that the safety of the users will be guaranteed.

They're not exactly lightweight, their creations.

Loopy wipes the sweat from his brow and wishes they had kept some of the gardeners around, or recruited a few more of Dotty's friends from the rugby team.

From the other side of the stela, Sprouty seems to second his sentiment. He's the tallest of the gang, but he's also built like a bundle of spaghetti and his freckled face is all red from the effort he's putting in.

It's worth it, though.

Upright and unveiled, the stelae glimmer and glint with a multitude of colours in the glow of the streetlights. Multicoloured tesserae create patterns and figures at the back of Dotty's solar concentrators.

Loopy's grandmother and her colleagues at the Civic School of Mosaic and Stained Glass, the youngest of whom is sixty-six, have been working hard to assemble them by hand, one sliver of coloured glass, stone, or ceramic at a time, silver heads bent on the task with intense concentration and purpose.

Medieval stained glass, art nouveau revival, trencadìs, theirs is a disappearing art, but tonight it shines in the spotlight, as bright as the stars, and perhaps upon seeing this a few young people will be captivated enough to try their hand at it.

Two of the ten stelae, plus the centrepiece, are still somewhere out there in the back of Leccy's van, the largest of the fleet, and those which are in situ have to be hauled by hand one by one and slotted in place with the help of a pulley rig.

The arrangement slowly takes its form, gaping in places like the smile of a six-year old, but the next wave of troops has already arrived, and they waste no time in getting to work.

AV technicians from the Accademia Della Scala, including Loopy's brother Prof Racket and up-and-coming Italo-Eritrean rapper Ahmed Brown, are placing loudspeakers and other pieces of kit in strategic locations to maximise the acoustics of the square.

Trailing cables sneak out from each piece of kit, running along guides laid through the garden to reach their destination at the bottom of the stelae. Every new connection put in place is double and triple-checked to everyone's satisfaction. Come the morrow every bit of the setup will have its role to play.

Once all the ground equipment is in place, Loopy swaps his sneakers for a pair of climbing shoes, chalks up and climbs fearlessly on the façade of Palazzo Marino, using the bugnato and the protruding frames and decorations as hand- and foot-holds, a heavy-duty cord tied around his waist.

Racket and Brown place a chunky bouldering mat underneath and hover around it anxiously, but Loopy seems totally confident and assured.

It's a V4, maybe a V5, nothing he hasn't conquered before in the gym and on the crags, only a bit taller than his usual highballers, he judges. He doesn't usually get the chance to climb solo, totally unsupported, and he's loving it.

He tops out on the balcony on the first floor and unties the cord from his waist, pulling on it to retrieve the pulley mechanism. He installs it on the rail and threads the cord through, letting it drop back to the ground.

Prof Racket and his crew load up first one speaker, then another, and finally a large banner, hand-lettered with an Art Nouveau font on a quilt of old bedclothes.

Loopy installs each piece, aligning it with loving care, then uninstalls the pulley and lowers it down to the ground.

He climbs down the same way with unhurried, easy grace and is off again, up another building, almost as soon as he touches down.

***

Sparky's rescue run is surprisingly uneventful. From the low pinging noise in the background, she infers that Stabby and Webby must be pulling the strings of the decoy units to give her the maximum possible berth.

She ignores all the still-functioning traffic lights and drives the wrong way up quite a few one-way streets and before she knows it she has reached her destination, a fairly inconspicuous street in the maze of ex-industrial facilities between Viale Ripamonti and the Rogoredo station.

"Wow, that was quick. Even for you..." Leccy comments with a low whistle as Sparky skids the van to a stop.

"Any joy swapping that tyre?" Sparky asks.

"Not a chance. The jack can't cope." Leccy shakes her head. She still looks calm, but her fingernails have been bitten nearly bloody.

"I have another one in the back, but we have to be quick. It's past four AM already. Our window of opportunity is narrowing."

Leccy nods.

"And we have the centrepiece. Let's get cracking."

They have just managed to get it in place underneath the van when Sparky's phone rings.

"You gotta get out of there! Nuddy has been arrested, the naked cyclists have broken ranks. They are running your way!" Stabby's voice betrays a very worrying hint of panic that makes the engineers perk up in spite of fatigue and pay attention.

Sparky runs back to the front of the van and checks the map: a group of pink dots is shooting down Viale Ripamonti, followed by a cluster of grey dots. They are approaching quite fast and, even if they don't come exactly their way, soon they will be closing their main escape route.

"Damn! Damn! Damn!" she exclaims, tapping her fist on the dashboard.

"Are we screwed?" one of Leccy's comrades asks.

"Depends. How much do you care about the van?" Sparky retorts.

"Less than about not getting arrested," Leccy replies, seconded by all her crew.

"Then forget about the tyre. Who of you lot has ever played GTA?" Sparky asks.

A ginger guy with a massive hipster beard raises his freckled hand.

"Let's swap vans, then." She throws him the keys.

He looks so surprised he nearly fumbles the catch.

"Are you going to drive it like that?!" another engineer asks, paling visibly.

"I am."

The front left tyre looks quite deflated and with that much weight on the van it is going to deflate even more as it goes. The whole thing is going to pull left with all it has: it's going to be a wrestling match more than a drive if she wants to keep it on the road.

Sparky is not really relishing the prospect, but the alternative is definitely worse, and beggars cannot be choosers.

"The rest of you are going to ride with him. The lighter the van is, the better."

The ginger hipster nods and cracks his knuckles.

"Lead the way and I'll follow."

"That's the spirit!" Sparky approves.

She hops in Leccy's van, adjusts the seat and mirrors and turns the key. The powerful engine purrs like a tame tiger, but the whole frame is vibrating slightly, as if in pain.

"I know, I know…" she croons, smoothing her hand gently on the dashboard. "We'll get you fixed up as soon as this is over." She revs the engine and pulls away from the kerb.

***

From her pad, Stabby follows the tortuous progress of the rescue mission.

Sparky is driving a lot more slowly than usual, turning into side roads and doubling back to avoid notice and pursuit.

Time is running out and if they get caught, that's it, end of the line: the installation will be incomplete, all their efforts will have been for nothing.

And the worst is that zie can do nothing about it: the naked cyclists are not responding to zir messages and zie has no other nearby units that would be able to run interference and steer the police any other way.

"Come on, fam… Come on…" zie whispers to zirself, eyes glued to the screen.

The bright yellow dot of Sparky's transponder inches closer, slower and slower. Her van finally arrives, with Leccy and her crew on board, but she is not there.

"She's right behind us," a ginger hipster reassures, but the road is empty.

Five tense minutes pass until another van barrels into the square, sparks flying from one of its wheels.

"Gods, she made it!" Sprouty exclaims.

The front left tyre is so flat that the metal rim is dragging on the tarmac and, rather than stopping, the van grinds to a painful halt amid the thunderous applause of the members of the Commando.

Sparky slides out of the driver's seat, stumbling like a drunk, bathed in sweat, but here is a victorious grin on her face as she lets her friends hug her and pat her on the back.

"*Fast and Furious* has nothing on me."

"You were awesome!" Stabby agrees, grinning almost as widely. Zie wishes there was more time to celebrate zir friend's feat of bravery and ability, but it's half past four and the sun will be up in less than an hour. They are too close to miss their target.

"Someone fix that van! Everybody else, let's unload and set up. We're nearly there!" zie orders.

"On it!" one of Prof Racket's mates exclaims. Stabby remembers that in real life he works as a car mechanic.

The central stela is the largest one, twice as large as the others, and it is nearly an "all hands on deck" job just to get it out if the van and into the pulley rig. It's backbreaking, but ultimately worth every drop of sweat, every molecule of lactic acid.

There it finally stands in its allotted place, gleaming with colour and gold, a celebration of the city and a monumental, dazzling "fuck you" to the people who were supposed to talk there on the morrow and all they stand for.

The members of the Commando stand before it with a mixture of pride and awe: they can hardly believe they did it.

"It's beautiful, isn't it?" Loopy comments.

"Of course it is. You designed it," Stabby replies.

Zie is pretty proud of zir scientific accomplishments, but this… this is something larger than zir, than any of them. The moment feels solemn, almost sacred, and fills zir with a joy so fierce and sharp that it is almost painful. Zie cannot help the tears that spill out of zir eyes.

Loopy embraces zir, letting zir hide zir masked face against his shoulder.

The sky is starting to grow lighter in the East, velvety black fading to lighter and lighter shades of grey. Hints of pink start to creep in at the edges. It's nearly half past five in the morning.

"We need to go, folks." Sprouty's voice breaks the magic, dripping with regret.

Stabby wipes zir eyes with the back of zir hand and nods.

"Let's move, before they catch us on the way out."

The Commando retreats in good order, filing out of the square towards their safe places in their now-empty vans.

***

The Sun pays them no heed and continues to rise, painting the sky with a thousand shades of crimson, vermillion, and gold, and as it climbs upwards through the heavens, waking up birds, trees, and all manners of creatures, its rays start to hit the stelae.

Photons bounce through the solar concentrators like steel balls in a pinball machine and finally hit the high-efficiency, multilayer, mini solar panels hidden in the joins between the concentrators.

Photoelectrons cascade between the different layers, amplified at each step, like an avalanche gaining speed as it rolls.

Electricity courses through the cables laid out in the garden, flowing towards the Raspberry Pis, the hard drives, and the speakers.

Music starts to play, a jaunty electro-swing song, filling the air with its lively rhythm and the defiant sound of trumpets.

The first Vigili arrive soon, lured by the sound. After that long night of insanity, they look exhausted and ready to arrest the Pope if he looked at them the wrong way. They expect more people in costumes, or drunks, or nudists, but what they find leaves them completely stunned.

Piazza della Scala has turned into a garden overnight, as if by magic. Grass grows soft and inviting where the flagstones should have been, and flowers fill their senses with a riot of colours and smells.

PLEASE, STEP ON THE GRASS, a small placard says, penned in an ornate, elegant script, but the officers don't dare.

If you step in the land of faeries, you might never come back... one of them thinks.

Among the grass and flowers, a group of freestanding, stained glass windows gleams in the morning sun.

It is as if someone had stripped down a cathedral to its essential elements and planted it in the middle of a garden, thinks another, who had briefly attended the Fine Arts Academy before giving up art for a career in law enforcement.

The ten lateral panels depict events from the history of the city, forming a sort of nave leading up to a huge central piece: the Austrians build the Teatro Alla Scala, Byzantines fight against Ostrogoths, Queen Theodelinda of the Longobards has her son Athaloald crowned in the old Circus, Roman engineers build the Forum, Insubrian merchants trade with long-haired Etruscans from Genova and bearded Greeks from Marseilles, citizens from all countries in the world arrive to work and study, sightsee and live. All the people who have made Milan their own are represented.

On the huge altarpiece, a blond, tattooed Insubrian chieftain and a distinctively African Hannibal Barca stand underneath the sacred hawthorn tree of Belisama on the eve of the Second Punic War. They clasp their hands in alliance, under the benevolent gaze of the goddess, whose golden insignia gleam among the foliage.

MILAN WELCOMES EVERYBODY, declares a large banner that hangs from the Mayor's balcony, penned in the same hand as the placards.

***

While the Vigili are paralysed by their almost-mystical experience, people pass by along via Manzoni, retail workers on their way to the shops, early morning tourists, late-night partygoers dragging themselves home at dawn. They stop, gape in awe, and take a picture. Many end up on Instagram or Facebook. The images go viral in a matter of minutes, pinging across the globe via the internet.

An early spike in Japan is produced by a quartet of friends from Osaka, who are in Milan on a leg of the one-month tour of Europe they organised for their retirement. Minako, who has worked 40 years as a graphic designer in a magazine and has a certain eye for art, realises immediately she has stumbled on something truly unique. She snaps a picture with her phone and sends it straight to her daughter, who is a dealer of contemporary art, and she in turn manages to get it immediately published on an influential Japanese art blog.

Before long, its English-speaking counterparts are taking up the piece of news and dragging their local correspondents out of bed to obtain a fuller coverage of the extraordinary clandestine installation. They get beaten to the best spots in the crowd by the reporters from the city's main newspapers, duly alerted via an anonymous call from Webby.

The crowd increases with every passing minute. Cameras snap endlessly as people wander through the garden, admiring the art and enjoying the lush greenery. A few people sit down with drinks and ice creams, enjoying the music. A garden is a garden, after all, even though this one is temporary and illegal. It's just a better reason to seize the moment.

***

By the time the law enforcement gets its collective act together, it is quite clear that they will have their work cut out for them to clear up the crowds and remove the installation without causing a major public disturbance. It will be impossible to do both in time for the right-wing demonstration to happen as scheduled and it's too late to move it to a different venue.

The trucks carrying the stage and AV equipment start to arrive, but they have to be turned back. There is no space for them to park safely and the last thing they want is a confrontation between the right-wingers and the public, especially since the first representatives from the antifascist counter-protest have begun to appear.

The Mayor arrives on the scene a while later. She takes a good, long look at the newly redecorated Piazza, takes a deep breath of flower-scented air, then crosses the garden to her office.

"I am deeply sorry, but the demonstration has to be cancelled and will have to be re-scheduled to a later date," she informs the organizers, glad that she is not video-calling them, because she wouldn't be able to hide her grin.

If it had been up to her, she would never have given them the authorisation to organise anything, but higher directives had bound her hands. Secretly she is glad that the Commando has done the dirty job for her. They really have gone all the way with their madness this time.

She immediately issues a very ambiguous declaration that does not condemn or approve the whole stunt and gives vague instructions to restore the square to its former state.

No matter how much she likes them, the Commando Jugendstil have graduated to organised crime with last night's events. She can't declare for them, but she doesn't have to.

She knows for sure that, as soon as the news is out, there will be a petition asking for the art installation to be preserved. The pressure will mount, and she will have to bow to it and keep the blasted garden.

"What a hard job..." she thinks, stifling a laugh as she stretches in her chair.

From the window she can still hear the music. Suddenly being in the office on a summer Sunday morning doesn't seem half as bad.

THE HEAVENLY DREAMS OF MECHANICAL TREES

Wendy Nikel

Trees were never intended to be sentient beings, or God would have created them that way, back in the Garden.

Ailanthus ponders this sometimes as the sun's rays prickle her leaves' tiny solar panels and the tubules of her stems absorb the afternoon's deluge. If the Tree of Knowledge had a voice, would it have cried out to warn the Tempted? Or would it, too, have been deceived by the Serpent and the false promises falling from its golden, forked tongue? Had it spoken, might the Tree have saved its offspring? In a way, the trees' first parents had failed them, too.

Though admittedly, Ailanthus is not a natural tree, composed of wood and leaf and bark. No, she was created by another hand, forged of copper and steel and gold, in a factory not far from the Wind Forest. Its fumes are familiar to her. As soon as they're inhaled, they're processed through her leaves and exhaled again in a form fresh and renewed. The humans planted her here, she and her brethren—miles and miles of eight-armed trees-that-aren't-trees in a forest-that-isn't-a-forest. A second Eden, created to save the world.

Whether the other trees spend their days in philosophical ponderings, Ailanthus has no way to know. Though her branches scrape theirs when the wind blows just right and their roots are irreversibly entangled, their creators gave them no means by which to communicate, so their solidarity is one of silence. Thus, Ailanthus spends her days processing the air, dreaming her dreams, and wondering what she'd say if she had the words.

Something—no, *someone* stirs at the edge of the forest and Ailanthus shifts her attention from the skies, from the impossible flight of black-feathered birds and the way they pick the copper from her leaves' veins for their nests high in her cloud-closest branches.

***

"—with enough energy to power a hundred households for a hundred years in each and every tree."

"They're not trees." Bita's voice was hostile, accusatory. She knew how she sounded, but she didn't care. She hadn't wanted to come here anyway. The trees here cast eerie crisscrossed shadows and the wind whistling through their branches seemed a whisper of warning.

"*Bita.*" Aunt Gigi's disapproval manifested itself in gradually deepening lines. Each wrinkle was unique: some longer, some thicker, some that oddly hooked themselves about along the contours of her face.

That, Bita thought, *is how a tree's branches ought to be.*

"Well, they're not trees," Bita said. "Not real ones, anyway. The real ones were each different. Complex and magnificent. Not like these things. These aren't even plants; they're machines—cold and hard and ugly."

"You know how long it took to build this wind forest? Decades. If it weren't for these trees and the others of their kind, Earth would be a wasteland. You understand that, don't you?"

"Of course I do," Bita said, trying to keep the annoyance from her voice. Since she was small, she'd listened to her aunt's lectures about the bark beetles whose population, unchecked in increasingly milder winters, had decimated the world's pine and spruce before moving on to other trees. "That's why I wanted to study botany."

"Botany." Aunt Gigi snorted. "Why waste your time studying the things of the past? We need intelligent young people like you to continue the march of progress, to increase efficiency, to solve the problems of rusting roots and corroding xylem and phloem and… and these birds! Shoo! Go away! Menaces, all of them, but they're endangered species now, so what can you do? There, doesn't that sound like a problem for a scientist to solve? How to keep them from picking apart our trees without driving them into extinction as well? Or better yet, figure out how to make these trees reproduce so we don't have to replace their rusting and broken parts every decade."

Bita had stopped to study one of the trees' eight identical branches. Sure, it carried out the chemical processes of a real tree—photosynthesis, respiration, transpiration—and even produced a "green" source of energy as a byproduct, but calling these mechanical structures "trees" was like calling a light bulb the sun.

"Please, Bita. At least consider it. We're terribly understaffed. We could use your help, and I know you could use the work."

Bita sighed and placed her hand on the nearest tree's trunk. Through the steel bark, she sensed the rushing fluids, the transference of energy pounding through the metal like a cold, mechanical heartbeat. And somehow, deep within the vibrations, somewhere among the hums and clicks and whirring of parts, Bita swore she heard a quiet voice say, "Please."

***

Ailanthus knows she's not long for this world. The harsh corrosion of her inner, movable parts produces friction and uncomfortable burns. The birds have stolen the copper from her uppermost leaves again this spring, yet not one of the trees' keepers have come around to replace them. Without these sun-nearest panels in optimal condition, she functions more slowly, barely eking out two-thirds of the energy she'd once produced each day.

The Creator once commanded the trees to reproduce: *the fruit tree yielding fruit after his kind, whose seed is in itself, upon the earth.* Perhaps His blessing is what the steel forest lacks. There was no booming, powerful "Let there be" as Ailanthus and her brethren rolled across the conveyer belt and down the assembly line, as branches were welded to trunks. There was no anointing of their roots as they were placed in the ground, no sprinkling of holy water on their leaves. Nothing but indifferent mechanical procedures and wearying nine hour shifts and the afterthought, generations later, of fruit and seed and renewal and the bitter realization that what was once deemed the world's greatest solution was really no solution at all.

***

"I told you, Steve, they want me to do the impossible. They think a botanist is some sort of wizard, some sort of Dr. Frankenstein to bring dead objects to life." As she passed by each tree, Bita placed her palm on it, just long enough to hear the rumble of its inner workings. In the months she'd been working at the Wind Forest, she'd done this to each tree she passed but had never experienced that small, pleading voice again. Either she'd imagined it, or she was going crazy. Mama would've said it was a sign, a message from God, but Bita hadn't believed in that sort of thing for years, since her prayers for Mama's recovery had gone unanswered.

"These forests were supposed to solve the earth's problems," she said, frowning, "but we've only created more. The factories that manufacture new trees and replacement parts are using more energy than these worn-down acres can produce. They want me to make magic, to make these trees self-replicate like the trees of the old days used to."

"What if you had a seed?" Steve asked. "An acorn, or a piece of fruit, or pinecone? Could you do it then?"

Bita sighed, recalling all the seeds lost in the electrical fire at Svalbard. "If I had a seed? A real, viable seed? One that somehow, by some miracle, wasn't destroyed by the blight? Well, we wouldn't need these broken-down scraps of metal then, would we? It would take some time, but we could fill these rusted forests with living trees instead. Can you imagine? No more rust, no more clanking of branches when the wind blows, no more harsh glimmer of the afternoon sun reflecting off the metal panels. They say that the old trees used to have their own unique scents, that you could tell by just smelling whether you were in a forest of maple or cedar or pine. And the fruit—"

"We have fruit." Steve looked insulted, as though her words were a personal slight.

Bita laughed. "No, we don't. We have blobs of protein injected with artificial flavorings and synthetic vitamins."

"You're not going to be one of those mothers, are you?" He laughed as he took her hand.

"What do you mean?" It was Bita's turn to look insulted now.

"The kind who's obsessed with keeping her children from the evils of processed foods. Who'll spend a fortune on groceries to get real wheat and corn from halfway across the world."

"Who said I wanted to be a mother at all?"

***

Ailanthus wants nothing more than to be a mother. Nothing more than to give life. If she had the means, she would be her kind's Eve without a breeze-whisper's hesitation. *If* she had the means.

She's been listening to the young woman, watching her as she tries to solve the forest's "sustainability problem," a problem Ailanthus equates with death. Not only her own—that she might bear bravely—but that of the forest itself.

Is there an afterlife for a forest of steel? A bright city of glory where branches won't rust, where their limbs won't snap in strong winds? And there, will they be reunited with those who've gone before? Their ancestors of fragrant wood and soft leaf?

***

"The numbers don't look good, Bita."

"Just six more months," she begged.

Not five years earlier, it was Aunt Gigi pleading for help, and now how the cogs had fully turned. Bita placed her hand on one trunk, then the next, searching for hope amid the rusting forest. Its rattling had grown so loud the women had to shout to be heard, but still Bita strained her ears, leaning in close, for some sign of that small, trusting voice.

"They're pulling our funding," Aunt Gigi said.

"Then I'll work without pay."

"We need to consider other viable options."

They both knew that there were no other *viable options*. Without the trees, the carbon dioxide levels would rise too quickly. Without the trees, everything would die.

"We need to start looking for solutions elsewhere," Aunt Gigi said.

Bita pressed her hand against another tree's trunk. "Please…"

And from somewhere deep within the clanking, clanging tree trunk, a single syllable emerged.

"Yes."

***

Ailanthus has never encountered the thing the woman calls a seed, but each day, she pushes her roots out farther, searching. The seams and joints creak as they unfurl the years' worth of gnarls and reverberate as they clash against those of her brethren.

The woman presses her hand to the metal trunk and speaks of a long-ago time, when in this place stood a true forest, with branches eternally vibrant.

"Evergreens." The whispered word echoes through Ailanthus' branches, burrows deep in her soul.

Weeks pass. The woman wearies, resting her back against the trunk as she scribbles thoughts and ideas onto a plastic tablet, then shakes her head and erases them. The sweat on her brow is slick against the trunk's steel plating, but still, Ailanthus searches, calling upon her silent brethren for help.

Her roots extend, each tube stretched thin, breaking apart rock and ever searching. With the additional effort, she barely creates enough energy to keep her own processes functioning, much less power anything else. Around her, her brethren crumble and fall, carried away in beak-sized bits by the birds alighting on every branch, pecking and dismantling each leaf.

Lightning ignites the abandoned ruins, far on the forest's edge. Only the woman's swift call for help saves Ailanthus from the same fate.

Ashes to ashes, dust to dust.

***

The tree was dying. Its energy output was less than ten percent what it was just weeks ago. Still, Bita wouldn't give up. She shooed the birds from its branches and sheltered it from the rain, all while she sat in the shade of its branches and tried to devise a solution.

She soon ran out of spare parts to dull its rattling and materials to patch the rusted holes in its trunk. When a sparrow alighted upon it, it looked so natural a movement, Bita didn't even think to shoo it away until it had already tucked itself inside.

Perhaps that was what did it in, in the end.

Within moments of the bird's nesting within its trunk, the tree gave a jolt and a shudder, its branches extending one final time. The gears ground to a halt, and it let out a groan.

"Don't give up," Bita pleaded. "Look. Just look what once was."

She held up the image on her tablet of a lush, green tree in the center of a garden. *Quercus wislizeni*: the live oak.

The tree gave no sign of seeing.

***

Her limbs are immobile. Her gears are rusted stuck. Yet in that stillness comes a silence she's never experienced before. All her life has been filled with noise, the noise of mechanical parts clinking and clanking and shifting and moving. A noise she's associated with life.

But now, in the silence, she can hear those around her. Their dying thoughts fill her consciousness. The noise, the bustle, the wheels of progress which they'd so desperately tried to keep moving… that was the thing disconnecting them.

In half-whispered thoughts, Ailanthus calls upon the others. She tells them what to look for, where they might find it. And then, she waits, saving her last reserves of energy.

***

Bita fell to her knees, head bent against the metal panels so corroded that she could almost, just almost, imagine that it was the roughness of true bark. Her hand dropped to the ground beside her, and there she felt…something.

There, protruding from the black soil, entwined in the mechanical tree's roots, was a block of amber. Within it was something she'd only seen in pictures of long ago: the battered, half-broken, yet undeniable form of an acorn.

***

Ailanthus' branches never rust. Her leaves are always bright. She looks down upon the cloud-swirled sphere, at the bright blotches of green.

Evergreen.

NEW SIBERIA

Blake Jessop

1.

I fall backward off the solar collector, and for an instant my splayed fingers brush the dawn. The drop is long enough to try naming constellations I don't recognize in the alien sky. I hit the sand on my back. The impact is surprisingly soft; I survive it. Air rushes out of my lungs like I've stolen it and my new world wants it back. I am unwelcome, and the desert swallows me to drive the point home.

I yell her name. I can't pronounce it as well as she pronounces mine. Amphisbaina. Try it. She slithers down from the array with the speed I once managed in the snow of Arkhangelsk. I go blind, drowning in silica, but I can feel her move. The desert is a muted membrane, like the surface of cloudy water, and when she bellies down and reaches for me with both hands I have already broken the surface tension and disappeared.

Amphisbaina pulls me backward from the quicksand with a long hiss of effort. The sheath she wears scrunches up as she writhes across the face of the dune. I scrabble inelegantly as she pulls. I can feel the subtle power of her tail; her entire torso adheres to the surface of the desert, reading it, and she waves herself the way I might have, once, if I were treading water. My shoulders tumble into her chest and we flop onto firmer ground.

"Nadezhda," she says, her breathing a hiss, and I hear her layer *you clumsy creature* into the three Cyrillic syllables. Nagan speech is panharmonic. They use tone to shade meaning, not adjectives. Amphisbaina chastises me with my own name.

I struggle to my feet, shaking sand from my gear. Individual grains are forming chemical bonds with my sweat, leeching water out of me.

I travelled between the stars to settle here, to save my species. We found a new earth, a chance to start the great voyage over, only to discover our new home already occupied.

Learning to communicate, our hosts selected *Naga* to describe themselves. They call us what we call ourselves, *Human*, because they're far better at learning our languages than we are pronouncing theirs. Amphisbaina does a little shimmy and the sand drops from her easily. She straightens her sheath. Her scales are just a few shades darker than the dunes. I would say she stands my height, but I do not know the right verb. She rears, I suppose, at my eye level; leans back against her long tail and crosses sinuous arms. There is a little sympathy in her posture. Faint pity.

"Watch," Amphisbaina says, and searches for a word, "your step."

2.

There are only so many ways to become sapient. Evolution converges. We killed the Earth, destroyed the Garden of Eden, and have taken up residence with the snakes.

The fleet calls us vanguards, which is flattering, but what we are is laborers. Zeks, if I were cynical, sentenced to build the city. I am not cynical at all. I believe in my work, I'm just afraid that I will never find meaning in it. That's fine. We fled here not to become lovers or artists, but to survive. I can live with it.

The giant solar panel is set flat atop a pillar, one of many that glare upward in an uneven tile across the dunes. There is a spiral groove in the column that makes it easy to slither up. Handholds have been hurriedly welded on to accommodate my less graceful appendages. I started the day's work by falling off the massive hexagon, so Amphisbaina lets me climb first this time, spotting for me. I scramble up, again without setting my safety line. I've wasted enough time, and I've always been prone to doubling bad bets. Adrenaline still floods my limbs, and I'll shake if I don't work. This is the first time I have looked forward to brushing silt from the interlocking panels.

I am unused to this work. On Earth I was a botanist and spiritual counselor. Similar jobs; seeds and scripture both whisper to me about the shape the world, if I listen closely. I never imagined planets as having edges, but they do. We took ours past one. With more time we might have done better, but as it was, our Bolthole Drives could only work once. Humanity spread to the cosmos like dandelion spores blown on a solar wind. It is hard to admit you've killed a planet; like arguing with a lover until you know you will never speak to him again. The shame erodes you, even if it was your ancestors who did the damage, who taxed you without your consent and brought you into their collapsing biosphere to die. We fled into the dark instead.

The strange thing about bending spacetime is that you don't actually spend any time doing it. The jump was subjectively instantaneous. I fed my fellow travelers soy and consolation. I could not have saved anyone if we went astray; just helped them live and die as they drifted into the infinite. We did not miss, however, so I never had to guide them through starving to death in deep space. We found our new world in an endless summer, every bit as beautiful as our Lagrangian telescopes had suggested, but not nearly as bountiful.

Our Garden of Eden turned out to be a desert planet. This irony was not lost on us, but finding radio transmissions rising to greet us defied irony. I helped write the protocol for this infinitely unlikely eventuality; my greatest contribution finished long before we jumped. Humanity considered finding an inhabited world only as a matter of form; the odds against it were astronomical. We jeered at fate, and our skepticism proved too tempting for the gods.

3.

Broad daylight here is broader than any I have ever known. I need to rest.

"You eat," Amphisbaina says, "all the time."

Gross, her lilt explains, *in both senses of your word.* She ate before we set out, and won't again until after we return. I watched her lever her jaws wide and swallow something that faintly resembled a spinghare in its entirety. It will last her a full week. Nagans are mesotherms, only slightly warm-blooded. They are spare, precise creatures who never so much as contemplated pillaging their world. Amphisbaina, who somehow made her meal look graceful, watches me suck down soy protein gel with her arms folded.

Rather than landing in a cloud of scintillating vapor and turning this world into another Plymouth Rock, humanity petitioned. We floated free, lost bone density, and waited to be heard, entombed without warmth or seasons. There were doomsayers and hawks who suggested that we had an avian's right to kill snakes. They were overruled. We learned this much conquering the Earth; we must do right or nothing at all. The Naga listened.

Rather than a moment of victory, which would have been easy enough, we experienced the great relief; the Naga accepted our petition, and we descended to begin civilization anew. What I expected, as a botanist, was to plant seeds, but water is precious in an eternal summer. My life's study is unexpectedly outdated; it doesn't take much water or many botanists to grow soy. Producing energy is easier, but requires many more hands, so I clean the solar collectors that power our New Siberia. In this very apt cosmic joke, Amphisbaina teaches me to survive.

Her world's habitable zone is wide and consistent. Temperatures drop toward the poles, which makes them the third world. Too cold during dust storms to comfortably support unprotected life, even in summer. Local life, anyway. It's undesirable, like living in Russia, so that's where the Nagans allow us to settle. The atmosphere is oxygen rich, but thin, so it gets cold when the sun sets. Our hosts weave blankets for the night just as we do.

In the weeks since I met Amphisbaina I have found comfort speaking to her. First as a recitation then, later, when I understood that she genuinely prefers to listen, as a reassurance. This meeting has long been the dream of both our species, whether we admit it or not. This is not the mythic garden, however, and we are hardly gods, so we keep our hopes quiet. Distance remains between us. At first I thought Amphisbaina was taciturn, alien. I think now it is simple preference; she likes listening to me.

I sometimes find her daring, flashing intelligence difficult to deal with. She hurts my pride with every command about where to put my feet. Solar collectors are no more her profession than mine; yet she became an expert scarcely seeming to try. Being a stellar voyager and lagging behind her makes my spirit ache and scours my confidence. I have been trying to guess why she's really here. Part of confession is knowing what to ask, and when. I finish eating and we take up our tools again.

"It hurts you to be here with me," I say. This is the Russian way of addressing serious sentiment; directly.

To clean each solar cell we drag a microfiber weave across it, one at each end, leaving contrasting trails in the dust. Amphisbaina stops and considers me. I feel like a mouse. We don't yet know how to read one another's faces, so it's easy for her to be mysterious.

"It does," she says. *It does.*

There is no subtext in her voice. No allegory. Just that.

"I understand," I say, "I know the cold. I was born there."

As I speak I close my eyes and struggle to reveal myself the way she does. The way I would in prayer. I try to say*: to join you I sat and shivered in the dark, trying to memorize your language. Trying to decipher your faith. Praying to you instead of God. Begging to be let into the light.*

She stares at me. When Amphisbaina listens, she seems to devote her entire body to the effort, as though she could smell truth, see emotion in the heat of my skin. She listens, even after I stop speaking. I think I've touched her. Now I wonder how. Wonder where.

"I..." she says, and pauses so long that I think she may have decided not to answer, "…declined a mating opportunity."

It's so pedestrian, I laugh. It took my species thousands of years to stop doing that. And we have stopped, almost. I'm here because I'm obsolete, not unwed.

"Thank you for telling me the truth," I tell her.

"You make it easy," she says, and the lush hiss of her voice is beyond my skill to read.

4.

"We must take shelter," Amphisbaina says, tasting the air. *Now.*

I don't question her instincts, even armed with triangulated weather ladar from the colony ships. All the technology in the spiral arm isn't as good as her forked tongue or the tiny, scaly dips beneath her nostrils. Even distant, which she has been since we met, Amphisbaina likes to listen. She senses everything.

Without overture, the Naga reaches out and touches the spot between my brows, trails a smooth finger down the bridge of my nose. I start.

"Feel," she says; "breathe." *A storm is coming.*

I try sniffing the air. All I smell is sand, heat, and the organic aftertaste of the gel. She gives a shake of the head, not unkindly, and I start unpacking the storm shelter. We cover a vast acreage during our seven day shift, far from help and far from home. Dust storms are usually brief, but as violent as Siberian blizzards. As I lay out long polymer tent poles, she surprises me again.

"Finish the garden story," she says. *It will ease the work.*

Amphisbaina recently divined my former profession, and I think she finds it a little ridiculous. She is a modern animal, not given to superstition, but I can tell she loves stories. Nagan society was late-industrial when we arrived, and Amphisbaina is obviously educated. I started at the beginning, and have come as far as the garden.

"The serpent convinces Eve to eat from the tree of knowledge. She convinces Adam, the male, to eat as well, and the fruit grants them an understanding of good and evil. God casts them out of the garden, either because they have lost their innocence or to take it from them, depending on your interpretation."

Amphisbaina shakes her head a little. I know her well enough to recognize this gentle bobbing as a gesture of reflection, not impatience. When she speaks, there is both pride and laughter in her voice.

"I am fortunate to resemble your serpent," she says. *Perhaps all your eating isn't so bad.*

It's my turn to laugh. I have much better eyesight than Amphisbaina, but she has seen straight into the heart of the story. She really ought to be teaching at a university instead of laboring with a refugee. If nothing else, humans have been a boon to the Nagas' schools. We share our technology freely. Manna from heaven.

"I'm not sure," I say. "Neither Eve nor the serpent end up being the hero of the story."

"We shall see," Amphisbaina says. *Shan't we?*

5.

"Prepare," Amphisbaina told me before she went below. *For a shock.*

The storm crashes over the dunes like a tsunami. A boiling wall of dust extends the width of the horizon and crashes toward us like a wave that could drown heaven.

"Amphisbaina!"

She's still underneath the array, in the lattice that holds the panels, cinching our shelter down. I cannot speak with her clarity, but my voice carries the fear every mammal has for storms.

The Naga whips herself up the trunk and through the hatch just as the storm hits us. The wind slams her back into the hatch cover, bending her in two. It would have crippled me. It just pins her.

My family tree is populated with dancers and soldiers. I know how to count both time and cost, how to decide what life is worth. Fear and courage are the same thing. I bolt through the flap and crawl along the panels to her.

The gale is a horizontal hammer. I scale sideways like a spider, my pair of legs for once making life easier. Our hands clasp and I pull Amphisbaina free. We tumble back to the shelter, roll over each other like wrestlers practicing their holds.

The electroactive struts snap rigid as the storm batters the shelter and I drag Amphisbaina in with me. We struggle to close the flap against the scything sand. After days of baking stillness, the sudden howling cold is almost unbelievable. Our careful little emergency space is dusted with sand. I reach for her.

"Your back," I say. Amphisbaina takes my hand to steady herself and flexes her spine.

"Just bruised," she says, but doesn't let go immediately. *Thank you.*

We take stock. Amphisbaina's suit heater has given its life to save her vertebrae. Twisting out of her gear, we check everything she carried. The heater, radio, her unitool: everything is scrap. The wind bellows and makes the layered carbon fiber canvas strain like muscle under tension.

"Trouble," she says, and her tone grades it perfectly. *Serious, verging on life-threatening,* it implies, adding, *though I am not afraid.* I hear her clearly.

What she's driving at is obvious. Her suit heater is dead, and the storm is going to get worse before it gets better. We can leech residual power from the solar array itself, but it won't amount to much. The polymer struts need electricity to stay rigid enough to fend off the storm. With the energy we have we can power them or the shelter's built-in heater, but not both. Without stability we die, and without heat we freeze. All we can do is pray that the storm will not last.

It does. After a while, Amphisbaina speaks.

"What are you doing?" she says. It takes a moment for me to realize what she means.

"Shivering," I say. My breath frosts a little; Amphisbaina's doesn't.

At first I try to make her laugh. I describe riding a bicycle, my two ungraceful flippers flailing around on a cogwheel. I want her to move, burn calories, make heat. She laughs softly, a kind of sweet hiss, but her lids, first one set then the other, droop. She is not made for this. We are going to run out of time.

More accurately, she will. I won't. I make my own heat, even without a summer sun.

A thought. I was hedging, trying to imagine how I would save myself in the tundra. There is a method, particularly if you're two. The idea makes me blush, then blush again for prudishly discounting it. I am a colonist, a traveler, and an apprentice, but first I am a Russian.

Step one, drink emergency vodka. I am not joking. Amphisbaina watches with languor I recognize as dangerous. This is something our species share. The spirit moves me. Step two.

"Make a pile out of all the fabrics." I say, "No, all of them. Take off your clothes. In Siberia we have a way to survive this."

I prepare quickly. It only feels slow; cold stretches time. I have to help Amphisbaina slide out of her sheath. I pile everything we have on top of her; the emergency blanket, the spare shelter canvas, her clothing, mine. Shivering, I wolf down the rest of the gel. I need calories. Tiny hairs rise on my arms and in the small of my back. I wish there were more vodka, and then burrow into the nest.

Amphisbaina is coiled. Fetal, is how I imagine it, with her back to me. There is a shock when I touch her, but it doesn't last. I can feel the drugged vestige of surprise as she hunches her shoulders backward, toward me. Toward warmth.

We lie together. I tense muscles in the order dancers do. Try to focus on generating heat. More and more of her eases into contact with me, until we touch along our entire length. Her tail moves between my calves.

What Amphisbaina does then, if I were lying with a human, you'd call rolling over. What it involves is a kind of gentle, rippling twist that shifts her body through two compass points without any sense of distinct motion. I shiver when her belly comes into contact with mine and she lets out a hiss that can only be satisfaction.

We stay that way. I wrap my arms around her and, as if basking in a glow, she lets hers encircle me. The feeling is one of infinite cool smoothness. Metaphor fails me; if I said ophidian I would only be describing the experience as it is. What's really happening to us is the intimacy of shared heat, of survival; giving and receiving not in the moment of crisis but gently, over time, with no distance between us at all.

"You are so warm," she says, the same way mammals talk about miracles. *Almost unbelievable.*

She is right. That's what I am. Potential energy. Waste heat. Humans radiate it whether we want to or not. It's why we're explorers. The long night passes, and we wait for the light.

6.

"Nadezhda," Amphisbaina says. She pronounces my name perfectly, with the precise sibilance of native Russian.

"The storm is ending," she says. *Dawn has come.*

The tempest breaks the same way a fever does: all at once. The mad fluttering of canvas slows, then stops. Rising unselfconsciously from the nest, Amphisbaina carefully unzips the shelter door.

Sunlight pours in. She basks. Flicks out her tongue to taste the warmth. I don't know how I smell, but she doesn't seem to mind. Light courses around her and sets our world spinning again. Close heat, a summer breeze, and sand. We're going to have to dust the array again.

Amphisbaina glances back at me over one smooth shoulder, arms loose by her sides. I blink, and dig around for something to eat.

GROVER: CASE #C09 920, "THE MOST DANGEROUS BLEND"

Edward Edmonds

Detective Ishani Grover walked into the room at 3:15 AM, wiping rain off of her forehead, and stopped short when she saw the carnage. The remains of Ash Snort were splattered across the weather manipulator's gravity generator, across its consoles, across the walls. She hadn't seen this kind of carnage since the Terra War. Blood, entrails, cartilage, and other pieces of Snort clung to everything like dust. Her eyes went from slightly blurry to wide awake when the smell hit her; she felt sick but pushed it away, breathing carefully until she steadied herself. She was a professional. She had over a hundred cases under her belt and she had solved all but one. This was a test for her. It was important, political in more than one sense. There was no room for sickness in moments like these.

She took out a metal thermos that was attached to her side, and opened it. Inside was a strong tea, brewed using some plants from local greenhouses. She wished it were coffee, even as she felt guilty for the thought. She couldn't remember a time when coffee wasn't a rare commodity—global warming had made it nearly impossible—but the solar greenhouses were just starting to get enough room to produce it with the other foodstuffs that sustained the population. It was still rationed; the tickets gave enough coffee grounds for two cups a week. She had both yesterday.

Yesterday was glorious.

Today she could have used it more.

There was movement across the room; a man finished a conversation with another officer, and then walked towards her. He was average height, but otherwise, he was attractive. He had brown hair and a broad build, indicating some power beneath his suit and tie, but its pressed edges suggested he wasn't security. No, he was definitely a ministry man; only government types wore suit and ties to murder scenes. Impracticality was virtually a symbol of government, right next to the flag. Perhaps he was a well-dressed meathead—wasn't anything possible?—but the way his eyes searched hers out as he got closer made Ishani doubt that. He was a thinker, this one. Probably just here to deliver some documents; maybe he knew one of the deceased?

Either way, he didn't belong. She didn't mind for the moment; a bit of eye candy never hurt anyone, especially when less-appealing things were slithering down the wall.

"Detective Ishani Grover?" He offered his hand and she took it. She gripped it and he gripped it back. Good man. Nothing pissed her off more when one of them gave her a limp handshake.

"Yes?"

"My name is Ali Gayth. I'll be your ministry contact for this investigation."

"My what?"

"Because of the impending storm," he explained. "The ministry wants me to help you with the investigation."

"Ah." Government oversight. Great.

The engineer's death came at a poor moment. This weather generator was built on an island near the Florida coastline, and it was hurricane season. In fact, a hurricane was projected to hit the coastline within a matter of hours. Since the generators were perfected some forty years ago there hadn't been major destructive damage caused by the weather—the engineers who ran them used them to manipulate gravity to divert the storms into largely uninhabited regions, of which there were plenty now after the Terra War—but if the engineers couldn't operate the system, the hurricane could move into one of the new settlements along the river. It could risk the lives of hundreds of people, and there weren't a lot of those left nowadays. Ash wasn't the only one who could operate the device—three more engineers were on duty, and could pick up the slack—but the death of an engineer now made the settlers nervous.

And, as she was reminded by her CO, settlers still had votes.

"Look," she started to say, but he held up his hand.

"I'm not here to get in your way. I'm just here to help."

"Then, piss off." The words tumbled out of her mouth before she could restrain them. The man looked shocked for a moment, but then smiled, probably taking it as a joke. She smiled back at him. Better that way, probably. *Smooth, Ishani. Smooth.*

Ishani broke off from the conversation to look across the room. The locals had already cordoned off the scene, and the solar fence lit up the whole area outside the windows and the entrance she had already come through. Aside from the carnage, the control room looked like it was well maintained; there wasn't any sign of a fight, nothing obviously broken, no chairs kicked over. She knew the gravity generator could rip biological matter apart. Her superiors wanted answers, and it would be an easy one to give. Mistake. Engineer blown apart. No danger, huzzah. Another notch on her belt.

"Ma'am?" Ali asked.

"Detective, you mean." She looked over. "All right, if you're here to help, I'd love some coffee. I'm going to interview the other engineers, ask what they think happened, and when."

"Way ahead of you," Ali said. He pulled a notebook out of the inside pocket of his jacket. "The second engineer, fellow named Gregg Melqart, said that the gravity manipulator was turned on while Ash was inside. Tore him to shreds. Said he felt it go on around midnight but since Ash was on duty nobody checked it until Engineer Sheila Porter came on duty at one. Then, she started screaming, and everyone came running. Also, I'm out of coffee rations, so you're out of luck there."

"Aren't there failsafes?" Ishani tried to ignore the twinge of annoyance she felt. The information was good. It was still *her* goddamn crime scene. She licked her lips, dry and unsatisfied; she had really hoped he had coffee.

"Apparently, not working. They've been waiting on parts from the maintenance crew, but since the maintenance crew is on strike..."

"So he died because of a government workers strike. Which is why the ministry sent someone to come here. PR and damage control."

"I'm here to help," he interjected. "PR is incidental to the investigation."

"You ministry types don't get involved for that." She shook her head slowly. She was starting to get angry, and had to contain herself. "You're here for politics, Mr. Gayth."

"I just gave you information. Doesn't that mean something?"

"It means you started an investigation without the lead detective because you wanted political leverage." Her lips were pursed; she took a step back. "Excuse me."

She walked away, intent on leaving, but heard footsteps behind her. She looked over her shoulder. He was following her a couple of steps behind.

"Didn't I make my contempt for you obvious, Mr. Gayth?"

"I still have to come with you."

"According to whom?"

"Your boss."

He was probably right, and she felt annoyed.

"Fine. Follow, if you need." She turned around.

"I also interviewed the other two engineers. I have notes, if you'd like."

She ignored him. She'd talk to all three engineers herself.

She found engineer Sheila Porter in the staff room. The sight of the staff room shocked her; empty cans were strewn across a broken table in the middle of the room. One can oozed a brown liquid that pattered onto the floor. The walls were yellowed from tobacco smoke—which Ishani was pretty sure was not supposed to be smoked inside—and a small hole had been kicked into the northmost section. Ishani eyed the hole, but it was impossible to know when it happened, and judging from the state of the rest of the room, it was hard to say if it was relevant. She filed it away in her mind for later and looked over to the engineer. Sheila was slumped into a recliner off to one side, snoring softly, her legs level with the rest of her body. Ishani walked over to Sheila and looked down at her, wrinkling her nose at the smell of whiskey.

Ishani looked over to Ali. "Glad to know our best and brightest ministry engineers are so thoroughly vetted," Ishani told him. Ali looked downward, and Ishani grinned with savage glee at his discomfort. "Didn't you talk to her earlier?"

"I did. I didn't get much out of her." Ali looked down at Sheila. "She started drinking almost immediately after Ash Snort died."

"Did she say anything interesting?"

"She said it was all her fault."

Ishani cocked an eyebrow at him.

"All her fault?"

Ali shrugged. "She's pretty drunk. Could just be grief."

"Or it's a confession."

"Or, it's a confession."

Ishani looked down at Sheila's prone form, letting her mind block out the offensive odors that hung in the air around them. Ishani reached down and shook her.

Sheila suddenly groaned, and then startled awake when she saw them. Her arms flailed, tripping the lever at the side so she sat straight upright. Her head lolled sideways, and her mouth opened slightly several times before closing. She looked up at Ishani, her eyes unfocused and glassy.

"Who fuck are you?" Sheila asked. Her words slurred, and she spat as she cursed.

Ishani took out her badge. "Detective Ishani Grover. I'd like to ask you some questions."

Something stirred in Sheila's eyes. She held out her hands.

Ishani gave her a questioning look.

"Arrest me," Sheila said. "I did it. I fucked up." Sheila's words slurred even more to a point where Ishani almost couldn't make the words out. She leaned her head downwards and started to cry, sobs escaping her throat. An awkward silence followed. Ishani considered reaching for her handcuffs but thought better of it.

"What did you do, Sheila?" she asked.

"Fucked up."

"How?"

Sheila howled, sobbing uncontrollably. Ishani started to get annoyed.

"Sheila, you need to talk to us."

Sheila continued to sob. Ishani sucked in some air, and her arm twitched. Arresting her would be so easy. Ishani could let her rot in a jail for a while until she got some answers. And in the meantime she could catch up on the sleep she'd lost. Her eyelids dragged down.

There was a special place in hell for early morning crime scenes.

Ali walked over to her, offering Sheila a handkerchief. Who the fuck carries a handkerchief nowadays? Sheila accepted it, blew her nose, and continued to sob. Ali put his hand on her shoulder and rubbed it, and for some reason, Ishani felt even more annoyed than she had before.

"Sheila Porter," Ishani began, but Ali put up his hand. Maybe it was just the audacity of the gesture that stopped her. She went to speak again, but Sheila's voice broke in.

"I fucked up."

"How?" Ali asked. His voice was soft, gentle.

"I didn't install it properly."

"Install what?" Ali asked.

"Failsafes," she said. Ali looked up at Ishani and caught her eye. Ishani swallowed her pride and nodded back to him. He continued to press.

"You mean the broken ones?"

Sheila shook her head furiously. "The new ones," she said, her voice still shaky but strengthening. "Parts came in yesterday."

"Did the other engineers know?" Ishani cut in. Sheila looked up at her, her eyes clearing slightly, and shook her head. "I just put them in, but they were all, well, doing other…other things." Sheila's voice wavered again and pitched higher, but she took a couple of steadying breaths, and kept going. "But when Gregg told me that the failsafes didn't work, I knew, I knew." She paused, and then broke down into sobs again.

For the next ten minutes, both Ishani and Ali tried to coax more information out of Sheila, but only succeeded in driving Sheila into a greater frenzy. After a few minutes, Ishani motioned to Ali to leave, and they closed the door of the staff room behind them. Ishani knew when a witness needed space, and she was glad to be in the fresh air again. She signalled to one of the police officers to keep an eye on her as they walked away, and a young man with a pimply face took up watch by the door. He couldn't have been much older than a teenager. Human power had always been short since the Terra War—almost three quarters of the human population had died—but still, she wished that the team here was a little more experienced.

"She seems pretty beat up about it," Ali started to say, but Ishani cut him off.

"This is my investigation, Mini Man."

"Pardon?" His eyebrows went up.

"You cut me off in there."

"I did it because I knew arresting her wouldn't have done her any good, or you."

"That isn't your decision to make." Ishani's frustration, formerly aimed at Sheila, now rebounded back to Ali. Her face flushed and she pushed his chest with her forefinger. It was solid muscle. She pushed the thought aside. "You are here as an observer, a politician. I am a detective with ten years on the force, and I have seen more murders and death than you probably ever will. So, you need to fuck off, capiche?"

The murder and death may have been an exaggeration, but it had the intended effect. Ali opened his mouth to argue, as if to say something back, but then closed it again. She could see him shaking. Good. She'd touched a nerve.

After a few moments, he took a deep breath, and then let it out. "Okay. Sorry. It just seemed like a good idea at the time."

"Apology accepted." She nodded at him, noted that he still seemed angry, and looked purposely away into her notebook. His feelings were not what was at stake here, and she wanted to make sure that he understood that.

She took out her cell and opened a chat box.

GROVER: CHECK THE FAILSAFES. NEED TO KNOW IF NEW ONES WERE INSTALLED.

ORTON: AYE CAP'N.

Edgar Orton was the resident techie assigned to work the investigation, and she had known him for a long time. He would be able to tell her if Sheila was telling the truth.

She looked at her briefing information. There were two more engineers on site, plus a dozen other support staff. She wanted to talk to the administrator, but he had not arrived yet. All of them would have already given statements to the authorities. She felt like sleeping standing up. But something was bothering her. She couldn't quite place it, but it nagged at the back of her mind. She shook her head. Time to go see the other engineers.

***

Most engineers tended to be small people; the small ducts systems and narrow catwalks favored smaller people. At nearly seven feet tall, and broad-shouldered, Melqart was a veritable giant; Ishani wondered if they had to modify the duct system just so he could crawl through it. He had black hair that fell past his shoulders, and muscles rippled underneath his shirt. He had a plain face, but a handsome one, with gray eyes and a scar underneath his chin. When she found him, his head was leaning back on his cot. His eyes were closed, and he had on headphones that plugged into a jack in the wall. When she came in his eyes opened and he pulled them off, sitting up.

"Hello." His voice was deep, velvety. She could smell his cologne: smooth, expensive, probably pre-war. Ishani smiled despite herself. What was it with crime scenes and attractive men?

She pulled out her badge. "Detective Ishani Grover. I just need to ask you a few questions."

He nodded and leaned back into his cot. "About Ash, I presume."

She nodded.

"Anything I can add to what I told him?" He nodded in Ali's direction. Ishani ignored him.

"I'd like you to take it from the beginning, if you don't mind."

"That's fine." He sat up, strands of bloodstained hair falling forward.

"There's blood in your hair," she pointed out. He reached up, found the blood, and sighed.

"Went to the control room after it happened. It's hard to wash out."

"You certainly have quite the hairstyle, Mr. Melqart."

"Gregg." He smiled. Ali coughed next to her, and she sighed internally.

"Mr. Melqart," she said, waiting for the implication to sink in for both men around her, and then continued. "Where were you when all this happened?"

"In here," he replied, motioning around him. "Lying down. Listening to some music."

"What were you listening to?"

"Electronic Rap. New CD by The New Earthians. Want to listen?" He motioned the headphones towards Ishani, but she waved her hand. She knew the band. They were terrible, and she was grouchy enough as it was.

"No, thank you. Carry on."

"Well, I was in here. I must have dozed through Sheila's screams, or the headphones blocked them out, but I was in here when John burst in and told me to come with. I ran into the room with him, and saw, well…" He left the sentence hanging in the air.

"So that's all you know from the night? You didn't see anything?"

Gregg looked up to the ceiling. He looked tired, and there were bags under his eyes. "Just slept in here, as I said. Been sleeping a lot lately."

"Why?"

"Trying to quit coffee. Health reasons."

In the back of her mind, she debated asking him for his rations, but decided it wouldn't be professional. "Okay, so what do you think happened?" she asked instead.

"Failsafes broke. Maybe an equipment malfunction?" Gregg shrugged. "Really hard to say."

"And if the failsafes weren't broken? Would anyone wish Ash Snort any harm?"

"Pretty much everyone." Gregg shrugged again. "He was a bit of a dick, as much as it pains me to say. Too much bad energy. He would yell at everyone for anything breaking. You should have heard him yelling about the broken failsafes, told everyone how dangerous it was, how anyone who broke it should be fired. Kinda ironic now, thinking about it."

"What do you mean?"

"Well, he was the most concerned. None of us really thought about it since we usually take other precautions. It shouldn't have been activated. And now the machine fires up and kills him when he's on duty. Dude was right all along, and couldn't stop it." Gregg looked far away for a moment, then drew his attention back to Ishani. "I hope whatever happens to him after this life, he's a bit more at peace now. Bad way to go."

"You would have thought he'd be more careful then."

"I suppose."

"What if the failsafes were put back in beforehand?" Ishani asked him, eyeing him carefully. Gregg's eyes widened a little, and he raised one eyebrow.

"Well, we wouldn't be having this conversation then, I guess."

"Are you aware that the new failsafes were put in beforehand?"

"No, I wasn't." Gregg's eyes stayed wide. "I checked them after and noticed they didn't work, but I figured they were the old ones. What does that mean then?"

"That's what I'm asking you."

"Well." Gregg brought up his hand, scratching the back of his head. "If the failsafes weren't installed properly, it would do the same thing as a broken one."

"And if they were?"

"Well." Gregg thought for a moment more, then shrugged. "I don't know. Someone would have had to flick them off, override them, or get around them."

"Can that be done accidentally?"

Gregg nodded. "Yeah, but you would need to enter in a password to override, and then have your accident. It'd be pretty hard to accidentally enter in a password. Power surge could do that too if the software had a bug."

"Is there any reason why someone would disable it?"

"Not really. It wouldn't help anything. Ash wasn't a cowboy either; he was very by-the-book."

Ishani thought about that for a moment.

"Did him being by the book create any conflict between him and everyone else?"

Gregg gave a short laugh. "It annoyed the hell out of us. Not much beyond that though. Ash was always the kind to dot his i's and cross his t's if you know what I mean. Did every one of our records, no matter how insignificant. If his shift started at eight, he would be there at eight, not seven fifty-eight, not eight-o-one. He knew the letter of his job and he'd stick to it no matter what."

"Did it annoy the hell out of anyone in particular?"

Gregg thought for a moment, and then gave a noncommittal shrug. "Nobody really got upset about that. We all got along. Only person who never got along with Ash is Sheila."

"Oh?" Ishani pounced. "What happened there?"

"Ash and Sheila used to bang, I think." He grinned a little. "Knew each other since school. Had some pretty vicious talks sometimes, especially when Sheila got into the booze. I don't know what to make of that, though. She seems very broken up."

"Did they argue a lot?"

He nodded. "About anything and everything. It didn't take very much. Sometimes if John was bored he'd just get them going."

"What about?"

"Well, Ash was a neat freak and hated drugs of any kind. Took every chance he could to talk about the evils of booze or coffee or aspirin or lord knows what else he heard was going around. Sheila was a party girl so they'd fight about that. Sheila's parents for another. Her folks are Wind Changers. Ash hated them with a passion. Didn't think Sheila was too fond of her folks either, but I don't think she liked to hear people insulting them."

"Wind Changers?" Ali interjected. Ishani jumped; she had almost forgotten he was there.

"A cult. Believes that our solar tech is the devil or something," Gregg answered. "Thinks modifying weather goes against God's plan. I don't know much about them beyond that though."

Ali nodded.

"Thank you for your time, Mr. Melqart," Ishani told him. Gregg Melqart nodded, putting his headphones back into his ears. Within a few moments, he looked asleep.

As they walked away, Ali spoke. "So what do you think?"

"First, tell me what *you* think." She was curious, despite herself.

"I think Sheila now has motive, method, and opportunity."

"Pretty convenient, don't you think?"

"What do you mean?" His face scrunched up into a cute expression. "You saw her. She's a wreck. She screams guilt."

She shook her head. "When one person gives you all three in one interview, you should corroborate your sources." God, it would be easy to just leave it right at that; oh look, Sheila confessed, time to go to bed. Ishani refused to let herself. She identified with Ash a little that way; she would dot her i's, cross her t's. "She seemed too beat up about it for it to be an act."

"Lots of murderers regret what they did."

"Yeah, maybe. But I don't buy it, not yet at any rate. Let us talk to the last engineer first, Nelson, go from there."

Just then her phone went off.

ORTON: CALL ME WHEN AVAILABLE.

She loved Orton; others would just call, but he always sent her a message first for fear of interrupting her. She still called immediately.

"Hey." He was a thick, bug-eyed man, and his face filled the viewscreen. He answered on the first ring and dispensed with all pleasantries. "Failsafes were installed and working, but power was cut to the dorms and redirected to the generator. Some code here looks like someone tried to program it to it to take from the reserves but there wasn't enough and the backup systems took from the lowest priority area. The failsafes were in the software, but this basically forced a backdoor through the hardware."

"No chance it was an accident, or a bug?" she asked. He shrugged.

"It would be pretty specific for a bug. Could be a virus, I guess, but definitely man-made, and had to be installed with someone who knew the place."

"Thanks Orton, you're the best."

The man's heavyset features beamed for a moment, and then blinked out.

This changed matters. They knew for almost certain now that they were dealing with a murder, or maybe even sabotage-gone-wrong.

Either way, it would change the tone of her investigation. She was glad she didn't take the easy answer. She couldn't afford another mistake at the agency.

"When Sheila is awake, we need to talk to her again." She told Ali what she'd found out from Orton. "For now, we still have one more engineer to talk to."

***

When they found Nelson, he was in one of the electrical rooms, fumbling with wires underneath a console. She checked her watch; it was nearly four in the morning now. It had taken them nearly twenty minutes to travel to the generators from the dorms. She wondered if any of these people slept.

"Whore-lady piece of shit second-rate tech," Nelson said, accompanied by a growl after a series of sparks shot out of one side. "Shoulda bloody thrown you out with the last hurricane, watch the wind blow you around like the tech garbage you fucking are, fucking fuck fuck."

With a hum, the console, previously off, came alive, and buttons started to flash on the main screen in the middle.

"Fucking right." John Nelson pulled himself out from underneath the console. He was a small, wiry man, with a thin scrunched-up face and a hooked nose that made Ishani think of the front of an airplane. Whereas some people would be bashful about expletives, Nelson only grinned when he realized he had an audience. He sneezed, half-catching it with his hand. A shower of dust shot out in front of him. He wiped his hands on a pair of filthy-looking jeans, then offered a handshake.

To Ali.

Ali took his hand reluctantly. John then looked at Ishani. "Sorry ma'am. I know I ain't supposed to swear in the presence of a lady, but these machines, well, sometimes they need a touch of love to get moving."

"Charmed," she replied coolly. Then she offered her hand. "I am

Detective Ishani Grover. This is Ali Gayth, he's from the ministry."

He looked at her hand for a moment, then shook it. His handshake was limp, and Ishani narrowed her eyes at him. "I just need to ask you a few questions," she said.

"Figured someone would want to come talk once Ash got blown up. Didn't figure it would be so quick." Nelson reached down to pick up an assortment of tools that had been spread on the floor around him, and he started putting them into a toolbox off to the side. "Figured they'd wait 'til morning, on account of people sleeping."

"Nobody here seems asleep," Ishani commented.

"Hard to sleep when you just saw the insides of someone you know spread across your living space." He said this without much emotion in his voice, as though it were a commonly-held fact. "Besides, we just got a shipment of parts in. Lots of work to do if we want to beat the storm."

"You would probably have to get moving soon, huh?"

"Tomorrow is when we need to turn it on." He nodded to Ali, and then hefted his toolbox. "Well, tonight now, actually. If there's a good time to die, it probably wasn't now. Put our schedule back at least another hour. If you want to chat, I have a diagnostic to do in the other room, I can talk while I work."

He pushed past them through the doorway; he smelled intensely of body odor, and it took all of Ishani's self-control not to gag.

"Besides," Nelson said over his shoulder, "already told all this to that fellow there what I saw and know. Don't see why I gotta repeat anything. I have stuff to do."

"I'd just like to hear it directly from you."

Nelson put the toolbox down to enter a code into the door. "Waste of time," he muttered. The door slid open. He picked up the toolbox and walked through it, and Ash and Ishani followed. This new room was bright, so bright they had to shield their eyes. Light streamed in from glass windows to either side. When they cleared the glass windows, and Ishani's eyes adjusted to the new light, she noticed they were in a room that looked like the one Ash Snort had died in.

"Another generator?" She looked around, eyeing the different features.

"Yes ma'am." Nelson set his toolbox down near one of the consoles. Without the blood, gore, police tape or other activity, Ishani could see the details of the room a lot better. A long cylindrical generator sat in the middle of the room, submerged into a network of wires that clung to it like suckerfish to a whale. A ladder ran along the edge, and as she got closer she saw that the generator stretched several floors beneath them. Information streamed across screens all around her, each console bearing labels that she assumed pertained to the generator's function. The outsides of the generator and the consoles were all plated with a variety of different metals, giving the place a hodgepodge look. With metal being so expensive, and few of the old plants operational, she assumed they took what they could get to keep the place running. Nelson pulled out a panel, a copper-piece in between the stainless steel around it, and pulled out one of the parts. Immediately, all the doors hissed shut.

"What was that?" she asked. Nelson looked up and grinned at her.

"Safeties are still on, miss, you don't worry your pretty face. The doors just shut whenever you muddle with the equipment. Containment measure."

Ishani nodded, still looking at the equipment around her. It all seemed so vast. She had never been inside one of the weather manipulators. She wasn't even sure how they worked, just that they found a way to manipulate gravity to affect the weather. Weather generators across the world worked in tandem to push storms to the right areas. The work the engineers did was extraordinary.

"So what else you need?" Nelson started pulling out tools from his toolbox, spreading them around him. Ishani looked back at him.

"Did Ash have any enemies here?" she asked, but Ali was already starting to speak.

"What's this?" he asked. As Nelson worked, Ali had circled around to stand next to Nelson's toolbox. Now, he pulled out a piece of paper. It was shiny, folded, and bright green.

"Hmm?" Nelson looked over to Ali, ignoring Ishani.

Ishani took a step towards Ali and took the paper. It was a brochure, and the words "Give unto God what is God's" were written in big, blocky letters across the front. She immediately knew what it was. Ali had a smug look on his face; he probably thought he was hot shit, and she felt like slapping the look off his face.

Nelson shrugged. "I don't know. Looks like some Wind Changer crock. Maybe ask Sheila. I don't know where it's from."

"Why Sheila?" Ali asked.

"Her folks are Wind Changers. Lord knows her and Ash would get into it over it."

"Isn't this your toolkit?"

Nelson shook his head. "We share 'em."

"Do you know who would bring this?"

Nelson shook his head again. "Nobody on staff I know of is one of them." He turned back to his work, pulling a box of wires out.

Ishani thought about what she'd just heard. Would one of the engineers be lying about being a Wind Changer? It seemed antithetical, but, she supposed, one of them could be converted. It could have been one of the other staff members she hadn't met yet, but that also didn't seem likely. The machinery looked complex, specialized; she would run background checks on the others, but it seemed unlikely anyone but the engineers could have programmed the machinery. She yawned slightly; she wished she'd had more than a small amount of tea to keep her going.

"So, Nelson, back to my earlier question. Did Ash Snort have enemies?"

Nelson shook his head. "Nah, he spent most of his time enforcing regs or gambling with Gregg, and he was really only ever good at the latter. You know, funny enough," he said, then stopped. His head jerked up, and he seemed to be listening for something.

Her phone went off. A voice came on from the other end, but then her phone blinked and powered down. Out of battery power. She swore, putting it away.

"Shh!" Nelson snapped. He didn't look at her; instead, after a moment, he jumped up to one of the consoles. His fingers flew across the board. A moment later Ishani heard a slow whine, then a deeper pitch underneath it, and felt a sinking in her stomach, as though an invisible force were pulling her to the floor.

"What the hell is going on?" Ali asked.

Nelson didn't answer. He pressed his right hand down onto the console and with his left rapidly typed in a multitude of codes. Ishani felt the pressure continue to grow, and she took a step towards the exit; to her horror she discovered she couldn't move, and she dropped to her knees as the force around her continued to build. Next to her she saw Ali try to move but he seemed to be pulled upwards, and his feet left the ground. The pressure was also inside her chest, and it felt like she was being pulled apart on the inside. She thought of the remains of Ash Snort, and tried to scream. She couldn't breathe, and nothing came out.

With a gasp, Ishani felt the pressure release. She collapsed. Ali hit the floor hard. Nelson was breathing heavily, his head resting against the console.

"What the hell?" Ishani got out between breaths.

"Power," Nelson started to say. Then, the console exploded. The spot where Nelson was standing was replaced by a fireball, and he screamed as the flames engulfed him. He ran a few steps and tried to drop but tripped over his tools, and he careened into the space near the generator. Ishani tried to get up to stop him but he stumbled over and fell, his screams reverberating in the space around the generator. After a few moments she climbed to the edge and looked down; his body was splayed out on the floor, still burning, and unmoving.

"Jesus Christ," Ali muttered, walking over next to her. He was unsteady, gripping a railing.

They stood there for a minute, side-by-side, trying to catch their breath, too unsteady to move. Nelson's neck was bent at an odd angle, obviously broken. Ishani tried to move but found her legs were weak, and she too put her hands on the railing to keep her strength. She trembled, and looked over to see him trembling too. She tried to open her mouth to speak, but didn't know what to say. This had gone wrong, so wrong. Nelson had spent more time repeating what he said to Ali to her. What if he knew more? What if he had the key to the whole investigation, and she didn't get it because she wanted to prove a point about this being *her* investigation? She looked at Ali, his features all drenched with sweat. This man almost died. She almost died too. And they were no closer to figuring out what happened than before.

Pride goeth before the fall, as the Wind Changers might say. Were they here? What the hell was going on?

The door behind them slid open, and the young police officer she had seen earlier stood in the doorway. His face was purpled and enlarged, but he held his back straight. He walked over to her and saluted.

"Ma'am," he said, seemingly unaware that anything was amiss. "We have a situation, we—" He stopped. His eyes caught the blackened console, and then they found the body of Nelson below. His eyes went wide.

"Mr. Nelson fell to his death," she said. "I'll need Orton to look at the system, see what happened. The generator turned on and almost killed us, and the console exploded after. What were you going to say?"

He swallowed, touching his bruised skin. "Ma'am, engineer Sheila Porter… She's gone."

***

Ishani knew she should get some sleep. The two police officers on duty had switched off and were now hunting down Sheila Porter; her name had appeared on a ferry manifest bound for the mainland, and had almost arrived there, but the storm delayed it long enough so that they managed to catch the ferry before it disembarked.

Sheila was not on board. It was disappointing, but nobody was in a mood to give up. All that meant was that she still had to be on the island. It was now six in the morning. A spare bed was offered to Ishani as a courtesy. Instead, she stood in a watchtower to watch the storm.

In the distance storm clouds raged, twisting left and right in a macabre dance that was as potentially deadly as it was beautiful. A bolt of lightning snaked across the sky, and set fire to something in a distant, uninhabited ruin. She knew the ministry would have people watching, making sure the fire didn't spread. That the danger was contained. She had seen those storms when the generators failed.

Was Sheila a Wind Changer? Had she witnessed the destruction that nature could inflict on them? Had she seen the damage they could inflict on nature, for that matter? So many years of climate change, so many failed warnings, and then, eventually, war. Who would want that to happen again?

A figure came up to the railing next to her. Ali.

"Pretty," he commented. Ishani nodded, listening to the generators below her bellow.

"They're powered by solar, and use the heat they produce to feed back into the system. Only a fraction of the energy is wasted, even with the limited metal supply. It's really cool to watch." Ali produced a flask from inside his coat, and Ishani looked at him with raised eyebrows.

"Thank God things still ferment," he continued as he took a swig. He winced a little from the taste, and Ishani smiled.

"You don't seem like you like it."

"Not the best," he admitted, and laughed. "Hey, I'm off my shift, and I nearly died. I deserve a shot."

"Fair enough." She smiled. "It would almost be worth taking a picture. Headline: Ministry Man, drinking on job." She mimed taking a picture using her phone.

He grinned nervously. "You wouldn't."

"That depends."

"On?"

"If you're sharing."

His smile eased, and he passed the flask. She took it and had a swig. It was awful, but it was alcohol. She took another gulp and passed it back, wiping her mouth on the back of her hand. He took it back and looked inside.

"Jesus, you must like it."

"Not the best," she replied, grinning. "But hey, I'm off my shift, and I nearly died, so, you know."

He laughed again. "You're my kind of girl," he said, pulling from the flask.

"Oh?" She flushed slightly, but her mouth formed into a smile she hoped was wry. "Are you flirting with me, Ministry Man?" She looked at him. He must not have realized what he'd said, because he looked like a deer in headlights.

"Relax," she said, holding up her hand. "You can take me out for dinner, but you better hope you have some coffee rations stored up. I am craving that stuff hard."

He gave a short, dark laugh. "Maybe I'll ask Ash."

"Huh?"

"He had a small fortune in coffee rations." Ali leaned over the railing, looking at the ground below. "Found them in his room. More than he should have."

"Really?"

"Yeah. Heard the other officers mention it."

"Weird." Something was bothering her, and her head started to cloud. She quickly shook her head as if to clear it. "So, he just had them lying there?"

"It was hidden somewhere, I guess. Place looked like a mess. He must not have cleaned for awhile."

"Weird. He seemed like a real stickler for organization."

Ali shrugged, draining the flask and making a face. "Hard to say. Some people change between home and work I guess."

"I guess," Ishani said to herself, turning back to the storm. The storm was still there, rolling through. The fire that had started was now out, contained, manageable. More lightning shot through the sky but none of it seemed to make landfall. The storm would continue into the Midwest. A few farms would get some needed rainfall, but the storm would abate without killing anyone.

"Ali," she said. "How do you think he got those coffee rations? You can't buy them in bulk, right?"

"Nope." Ali sighed as he spoke. "And you can't really hoard them either. You're given a certain number and they have an expiration date. Otherwise we'd have people save them up and cash them in, ruin the supply for everyone else."

"So, if Ash has them, he would need to have gotten them from someone else, right?" The picture was becoming clearer in Ishani's brain. So beautiful. So simple. Like so many crimes, so petty and stupid.

"I suppose so, yeah."

Ishani calculated some things in her head, retracing her steps from the day.

"And Nelson said there was a power outage in the dorms?"

Ali thought for a moment, then slowly nodded. His eyes started to widen as he understood the implication. Ishani stood up, pulling out her gun and radio.

"What are you doing?" Ali asked.

"Going to catch a murderer."

***

"Over fucking coffee rations?" Ishani burst into Gregg Melqart's room, startling him. He started awake, his hands struggling to get the earphones off his head.

"Wha?" he muttered, looking back and forth between her and Ali.

"You weren't going to quit coffee, you lost your fucking rations." She waved her gun at him when he tried to move. He put his hands up. His blanket fell across his chest, dragging the earphones down. "Ash had all your rations."

"Did not." He wiped his eyes quickly.

"So where were yours?"

"I, uh, tossed them into the incinerator. Told you I'm trying to quit," he said, a note of anger in his voice. "That isn't a crime, is it?"

"Bullshit, they're worth enough to trade, and when Ash turns up dead and those rations are in his room, and the whole place is roughed up, it looks awfully suspicious."

"So?"

"So, Ash was OCD about everything. He hated messes."

"Listen, I was in here, listening to music the whole time." He gave a deep yawn, and scratched his belly. "Told you that."

"Oh, were you?"

"Yeah, I was."

"You're lying, because there was no electricity in the dorms that night." She motioned to the wall plug in. "You didn't have power. Your earphones wouldn't work. You thought the reserves would be enough but they weren't. But then again, you'd know that if you were here."

Gregg's mouth opened, closed, then opened, then closed. His eyes were clouded, tired. He said nothing.

"No," she said, "You were too busy rushing back, and you're too tired to think about those things I'm willing to bet. It takes twenty minutes to get from the dorms to the generators, maybe fifteen if you're quick. The rooms may not have locks but you made quite the mess looking for those rations."

"I don't know what you're talking about," Gregg said, but his voice was shaky.

"I'm sure," Ishani said. "You overplayed your hand, Mr. Melqart.

Trying to frame Sheila was a nice touch, and I love how you tuned us into the whole Wind Changer stuff—all very nice bullshit—but Sheila isn't her parents, and as far as killing Nelson, she was genuinely upset and probably still way too drunk to pull that off. We caught the ferry before it hit mainland too, thanks to the storm. Sheila wasn't on it. I'm sure we'll find her body, and when we do, I'll have enough grounds to charge you with murder. Get it? Grounds?" Gregg's eyes were wide, and he shook slightly as she laid it all out in front of him. "As in coffee grounds?" She spat. "I'm glad they won't serve you coffee in jail, you dumb fuck."

She tossed a pair of handcuffs on the bed, and waved her gun at it expectantly. He picked up the cuffs, looking at them as if in a dream.

"Cuff yourself. You're under arrest."

***

A couple hours later, they found Sheila's body. It had been hastily dumped out of one of the windows, and had landed in a pile of brush. Gregg Melqart was in custody and asking for a lawyer, and Ishani was looking forward to going to bed. She waited at one of the island's docks with Ali.

"Strange it wasn't better hidden," Ali remarked. "Everything else looked well planned."

"He was probably banking on us chasing Sheila off of the island, rather than look closer to home."

"Bit of a gamble."

"Mmmhm," Ishani mused. "But then again, he obviously wasn't very good at gambling."

Ali chuckled, and a silence grew for a few moments. In the distance, the ferry lumbered towards the island; it was a small craft, and its solar panels were all they could see from this distance. It was rapidly approaching the island; Ishani checked her watch. ETA ten minutes.

"It was nice working with you," she said, slowly. "I may have been a bit harsh, so I apologize."

"It's fine." He waved his hand. "You ended up figuring it all out. Didn't mean to get in your way."

"Well, you did, a bit," she said, then, seeing the look on his face, quickly continued. "But you also helped a lot. And it was your observation about the coffee rations that helped me catch him."

"So, that was a thank you?"

"Don't push your luck," she chided, but smiled.

He smiled, and nodded to her. The ferry was closer now, and she could see its bridge, the metal siding, the spray of the motor as it pushed water behind it. They watched it approach, and slowly it drew up to them. It docked, its captain tossing over ropes to tie the craft to the shore.

"So are you out of coffee rations?"

"Huh?"

She looked at him. His brown hair was disheveled, his suit was crumpled, and he smelled slightly of alcohol. But, all things considered, he did save her life. It was worth a date.

"I said, are you out of coffee rations? Or have you forgotten about dinner?"

He smiled, looking once again like a deer in the headlights. She grinned, grabbed his hand, and pulled him towards the ferry.

AMBER WAVES

Sam S. Kepfield

Ryan Baumann pressed the firing stud on the electromagnetic gun. The drone tumbled from the sky and was lost in a shimmering gold field of ripe wheat.

"Score one for the good guys," he said in satisfaction, walking along the dirt and gravel road to retrieve the drone. He had a fire extinguisher from his Jeep, in case the drone sparked or caught fire. The last thing he needed was a fire right at harvest time.

The drone lay in a twisted mess half a mile east. He turned it over in his hands. There were no markings, of course, but he could have Sadie run a serial number check with the FAA in ten minutes. Ryan would bet that it was owned by Phytek. In a control room somewhere in California, there was a blank screen and an alert to local reps to retrieve it.

Ryan stowed the EM gun in the back of the Jeep and resumed his original task, fixing a malfunctioning wind turbine. He climbed the fifty feet to the motor, and began undoing bolts on an access panel. He was on the last bolt when the wrench slipped off the bolt and out of his hands and fell fifty feet to the ground, landing in the tall grass at the base of the windmill.

He swore, and wiped at his forehead with the bright red bandana. It was easily over a hundred today, the fourth day in a row, with the relative humidity not much lower. No rain for three weeks running. Kansas summers had always been bad, and he had thought as a kid they couldn't get worse. A few billion tons of CO2 and methane had proved him wrong.

It wouldn't have been a big worry, except that it was the

beginning of June, and the wheat that stretched in every direction was ready to harvest. And as if that wasn't stressful enough, the satellite images from this morning showed a big front moving down from the north, meaning that at best there would be rain, which would turn the hardpan ground to mud and slow the harvest. At worst, it could bring a hailstorm that would flatten his crops. Some things about a farmer's life never changed.

His boots hit the baked soil at the foot of the turbine. He retrieved the wrench from the ground, and took a swig of Gatorade from the cooler in the back of the Jeep. A drone—one of his—whizzed through the air a hundred yards away, and a beep sounded from the smartpad on the driver's seat.

"Get your butt back up on the windmill, plowboy," said the tinny voice from the pad.

"Slave driver," Ryan told Sadie, his wife.

"I heard that. A nice tongue-lashing when you get back."

"Yes ma'am." He grinned. "May be a while. This turbine is giving me fits."

"You keep saying you're the brains of the family, dear. Prove it."

"With pleasure. While I've got you, can you run an FAA check on a drone?" He read off the model and serial number. Sadie made a kissing noise and promised to get on it.

It took an hour for him to find the problem on the turbine. The yaw drive was out, meaning that the turbine was not receiving data from the wind vane, and would not rotate into the wind. The turbine would still run, but it would generate less power than usual. A quick check for parts on the pad told him that a replacement drive would cost a thousand dollars, which he could afford, but would take four days to arrive, which he couldn't.

Nothing to be done about it today, so he replaced the access panel and tossed the faulty drive into the back of his jeep.

Halfway down the path to the dirt and gravel road, another vehicle turned in and blocked his path. He approached and stopped the jeep. Sadie jumped out and planted a big kiss on Ryan's lips. She was a tall woman, with her hair in a ponytail and sparkling blue eyes, dressed in denim shorts and a white t-shirt.

He kissed her back. No makeup today, but she didn't need it. She had that pale blonde, freckled look that still made his heart skip—and the few small lines around her eyes made her all that much sexier.

"Hey, babe," she said. "Brought you some lunch." She broke away and retrieved a blue cooler from her truck. "Got your favorite. Lupe's tamales."

"I hope you brought about a dozen, 'cause that's how hungry I am," Ryan said. Lupe Mendoza, who ran the No Walls café in town, turned out authentic Mexican and Tex-Mex, famous all across southwest Kansas. He used real meat, not lab meat, and grew the spices used to flavor them.

"Two dozen," Sadie said, setting the cooler on the tailgate of Ryan's Jeep. "I had a hankering for them, too." She opened the cooler and they dug in.

"Get a hit on that drone?" he asked between bites.

"Yep. Registered to Vesta AgTek. No flight plan on file."

"Vesta? Why would they be snooping on us? They don't have any holdings around here."

"Wrong-o, my love. They are a wholly-owned subsidiary of GCF Industries, which produces fertilizers, pesticides, and transgenic seed crops, including wheat. They've patented the new drought-resistant transgenic hard red winter wheat hybrid DX-107."

"You did your homework, honey," Ryan said. Sadie gave him her *of course I did* look, one of cheerful accomplishment. They had met when he was majoring in Agronomy at K-State, and Sadie was majoring in Ag Tech, with minors in political science and computer science. It had proved a winning combination of talents. In their eight years of marriage, they had devised a division of labor. Ryan took care of the field operations and maintenance, which was why he was in a sweat-soaked shirt guzzling electrolyte replacements to prevent heat stroke. Sadie did the tech work—using a fleet of a half-dozen drones to check the condition of their three thousand acres, growing wheat and soybeans and milo. She also did the finances, figuring out what they could afford in the way of equipment, supplies and online services. It had made Ryan swallow some pride, but he had to admit she was far better at it than he was. On top of that, she was a hell of a cook. "So what's that have to do with us?"

"They're pretty vigilant about patent infringement."

"And?" Ryan had a sick feeling where this was going.

"They may think that we planted some of their wheat without permission."

"We didn't. We bought this from the elevator." The H112 hybrid was supposed to produce higher yields, up to 120 bushels per acre, and was drought-tolerant.

"Which might have been playing fast and loose with the contracts," Sadie said.

"What it really is about is our land. We're one of the few operators around here who haven't sold out, and we're trying to make a run at a sustainable green operation and succeed and it's driving them nuts."

"You're right. We're not out of the woods yet," she pointed out. "We need a couple more good harvests to get the machinery paid off, and then we can *really* expand."

"Still want the greenhouses for strawberries, huh?" It was her dream, a large greenhouse to grow fruits. Properly done, in a controlled climate, strawberries and blueberries and grapes could realize huge yields. What she didn't eat outright or can, she could sell at the local farmer's market or co-operative.

"Mmm-hmmm. I *looooove* strawberries and chocolate," Sadie said around a bite of the tamale. She winked at him. "And we can expand in other ways, too." Unlike their grandparents and great-grandparents who needed big families as cheap labor, Ryan and Sadie hadn't started popping out children at a young age. That hadn't stopped Sadie from bringing up the subject with increasing frequency over the last year. He knew she was thirty-three, knew she was feeling a deadline looming, knew she felt awkward at the barbecues and fairs without children running around her and shouting and laughing. He knew she felt an emptiness in her life. And he knew she would be one hell of a great mother.

But Ryan had a built-in conservatism about such things, a genetic trait that had ensured survival through the lean times and the fat. And part of it, he had to admit, came from his relationship with his own father. Troy Baumann had been a stern taskmaster who suffered fools lightly, including his own son. Having his wife die of cancer when Ryan was ten made his father permanently bitter. When he reached his teen years, they'd had shouting matches over matters that were trivial. And when his father died seven years ago, Ryan had a hard time summoning sorrow. He worried that he'd imbibed too much of the old man's anger at the world to ever be parent material.

There were times, though, when Ryan looked at the friends who had stayed here without a break for college, and he envied them. Don Barnes, his friend from high school, worked on computers at the local Navstar dealer, had two boys, ten and eight. On the visits to Don's spread five miles on the other side of town, Ryan would get to thinking that it was time.

"I reckon we could." His reply was a little too quick. *Not now. Not again*, it said.

"Paul thinks it's about the land, too," Sadie said, changing back to the business at hand. "Vesta has been buying up some small acreages here in Hodgeman County, and in Finney and Ford as well. He'll be ready for them." Paul Harmon was their attorney, who ran a practice in Wichita that specialized in agricultural law. He had also gone to high school with Ryan, and after passing the bar came back home to fight for the natives against distant agricultural combines.

"I started one of the harvesters on our north half-section, since the moisture in the wheat was down. We'll get a truckload and run it in to the co-op and see if they'll take it."

"How's the rest of it look?" He unwrapped another tamale, his fourth.

"The spectral readouts from the drones say that our half-section to the east will be ready by the end of the week. The moisture sensors on the beans show soil temp and moisture are low-normal, so you may need to run the center pivot." The huge arm of the irrigation system, anchored to and run from a well planted in the center of the field, used microdrip irrigation, with long hoses falling from the pipe to the ground, to conserve water.

"Good," Ryan said, sobered. "God, I always hate this time of year."

"I know," his wife agreed. "I need to sleep for a week after it's done."

They'd both grown up on farms in this area, two counties apart, and were used to the frenzied hard pace of harvest. Even with robot harvesters and semi-independent grain trucks, it was still a time full of 20-hour days and backbreaking labor. But that wasn't what was bothering him. "No. A dozen things could go wrong and wipe out a crop." He looked to the north horizon, where a hazy strip of clouds had formed.

"We'll be fine," Sadie assured him, putting her chin on his shoulder. "We've made it this far." She kissed him, slow and passionate.

"If we didn't have all this work..." Sadie treasured rural life, especially making love under the stars or a full moon. Babies hadn't been part of the deal then, though.

"I know." She smiled seductively. "When we've got it all in the elevators. Promise." She glanced at his pad. "I better run before you ravish me. Gotta check the weeders running on the soybeans." She kissed him and got back in her truck, and he watched her drive off.

He made a circuit that afternoon of the three half-sections of wheat they had planted. The moisture content was low enough they could begin harvesting; anything above 13 percent would be rejected, since moist wheat could spontaneously combust and a blow a grain elevator to the moon. The lone robot harvester had halted, its bin full, on the last field. Ryan headed back to their homestead to get the truck, keeping a worried eye on the sky. The hazy dark line had become a line of cottony thunderheads, with a dead-gray bottom that spelled trouble. The best they could hope for was some needed rain that might slow down the harvest a few days. The worst could be a tornado, or even worse, hail.

A thick shelterbelt of cottonwood and cedar concealed the Baumann homestead. The original, a large two-story house, stood empty on an adjacent section of land. Built by Ryan's great-grandfather in 1920, it had housed four generations that worked the land.

The current Baumann farmhouse was visible only as a small hill covered in prairie grass, with a limestone-lined entrance. Ryan and Sadie had taken a page from early Great Plains history, and built two stories down. Nearby stood an old barn, built in the 1890s by a previous tenant driven out by drought and crop failures. George Baumann purchased the land around 1910, and kept the barn for extra storage. Ryan and Sadie had painted it red five years ago, and placed solar panels on the roof. Smaller equipment and tool sheds flanked the barn.

He parked the Jeep in the large Quonset hut that housed the trucks and other equipment, tossed the faulty yaw drive on a workbench, and walked toward their house. Ryan descended the steps into the dugout, and felt a chill as he entered the large underground foyer.

Sadie was frowning, hunched over the computer in the kitchen alcove, a cup of tea by her side. She looked up when he entered.

"I'm going to take a truck out," he said. "Harvester's full, and we need to get the grain in."

"Better hurry," she said, turning one of the three computer screens to him. It displayed a satellite image map of the area. A green line was advancing from the north, with red and orange and yellow splashed behind it. "Front's moving in quick."

"I don't need a computer to tell me that," Ryan said, taking a pitcher of ice water from the refrigerator and swigging from it. "We got maybe two hours. Get everything tied down."

"NOAA says one and a half."

"I'll trust my senses over a satellite," Ryan said, heading out the door. The heat hit him like a sauna when he closed the door behind him.

At least, he reflected, he didn't have to worry about the house being damaged. The first homesteaders, confronted by a lack of timber and stone, had simply dug into hillsides, put a roof over the hole, and covered it with grass. It was cool in summer, warm in winter, and the only real drawback was keeping the cattle from grazing on the roof and falling inside and smashing the furniture. The Baumann dugout was bigger—about four thousand square feet, on two levels, with four bedrooms and two baths. Everything ran on the solar panels built on top, which he could see retracting as he drove the truck out of the shed. And he didn't have to worry about the house blowing away in a tornado and winding up surrounded by Munchkins.

He was almost to the field when he was stopped by a black pickup truck. Two men got out, giving him a quick view of white lettering on the doors that read GCF. It was a diesel model, not an electric. GCF was paying a pretty heavy carbon tax to impress the locals.

The men were both dressed in khakis with black polo shirts, wearing sunglasses. One was taller with dark hair, the other shorter and stockier, with blonde hair, both done in a military-style crewcut. They looked like security guards. They definitely weren't farmers. Everyone Ryan knew wore dirty jeans and pearl-buttoned shirts or t-shirts with ball caps this time of year. And the locals damned sure didn't wear loafers.

"You're Ryan Baumann," one said, walking up to the truck. A

statement, not a question.

"I am," he said. "I'm pretty busy. Got a load of wheat to haul in before that hits." He gestured to the storm clouds in the north.

"This is about a drone registered to our company," the taller man said. "About three hours ago one of our drones was shot down with what we think was an electron gun. We'd like it back." The words were polite. The tone was not.

"Come by tomorrow and talk to me."

"Mr. Baumann, under the Federal Drone Aviation Act of 2022, 49 U.S.C. section 407, it is a federal offense to destroy a properly registered drone while conducting—"

"State law prevents you from conducting unauthorized surveillance." He noticed the small packs clipped to their belts, with the body cameras on their collars. "And that's all I'm saying. I've got a lot to do, and I don't have time for this." He put the truck in gear, and drove around the pickup, leaving the two behind in a cloud of dust.

The anger was still there when he pulled up beside the harvester. Corporate agriculture wasn't new—big mechanized farms had been around since the 1970s. Corporate goons were new. He called Sadie, who reported that the solar panels were retracted, and the wind turbines were also off. The turbines would descend into the ground partway, putting twenty-five feet of the tower out of harm's way. If they were damaged, the blades and turbine could be replaced, and the tower would still be functional. He warned her about the GCF enforcers. She laughed it off. "I'll take the Fifth. Besides, we're better armed than they are."

The harvester was a large boxy machine, with huge tires in front, and a twenty-foot header that cut the grain. It had taken two passes up and down the length of the field to fill the bin.

The control pad for the harvester was on the truck seat. Ryan swung out the auger, and wheat poured into the truck bed. He put on a bandanna to keep out the dust, took a shovel off the side of the truck, and climbed into the bed. He used the shovel to spread the grain evenly, pulling his feet up to keep them from being buried. After pulling a tarp over the grain and fastening it, he was done.

A quick message to the elevator on his pad told him that there were at least ten other trucks in line waiting to unload. Adding in the trip, it was going to take two hours to dump the load and get back to the house. The storm clouds were moving in, and he admitted that maybe the satellite had been correct after all.

He decided that the grain could stay in the truck overnight, and he would unload it tomorrow. There likely wouldn't be much else he could do if the fields were muddy. Programming the harvester to head back to the house, he guided the truck over the bumpy field onto the dirt and gravel road.

The storm clouds blocked out the sun as he pulled the door to the shed shut. The wind from the north picked up, blowing powdery dust from the fallow field north of the house.

Sadie came running from the house. "Harvester died," she said.

"Where?"

"Two miles over and two north." She was heading to her pickup truck, Ryan in tow. Right by the old house.

"Batteries were fully charged this morning when I towed it out," Ryan said.

"Yeah. There was a power surge, and then it went offline."

"Damn. We have to go get it." It was a $100,000 piece of machinery, and they weren't about to leave it to the mercies of a summer storm, even unloaded. And he had a pretty good idea what had happened to the harvester.

Sadie climbed behind the wheel of her pickup. Ryan retrieved the EM gun from his Jeep, as well as a pump-action 12-gauge shotgun. Sadie looked at him, questioning, but didn't press it. She had figured out the cause, too. The pickup sped out of the compound, fishtailing as it hit the road.

Halfway there, Ryan spotted a black pickup speeding north a mile distant. He could make out small lettering on the doors. *Knew it*, he thought. Ryan retrieved the EM gun from behind the bench seat. Standing beside the truck, resting his elbows on the bed of the pickup, he took aim.

"I don't think you have enough range," she said.

"We'll see. If not, no harm." He pressed the firing stud. An invisible electron beam leaped out, and hit the pickup. Even though it was diesel-powered, it had electronic systems which promptly died. The pickup slowed to a halt, and Ryan smiled. "Got him." Sadie took the EM gun and stowed it in the cab, and made the gravel fly as she put the truck in gear and hit the accelerator.

The harvester was stalled in the middle of the road just short of the crossroads. Halfway down stood his boyhood home. Sometimes he'd stop out here and imagine the arguments from the barn or the porch.

The hell are you going?

Into town. I'm gonna meet Kevin and Duane.

We got work to do yet. Get those repairs on the tractor done.

Been working all day, they ain't got the parts in town, and the shop ain't open.

Think you can take off like this?

I have a life.

When we're done, goddamnit.

Get off my ass! I didn't kill her. The goddamned cancer did. Quit acting like it's my fault.

Sadie whipped the pickup in a U-turn, going into the ditches, and then backed it up. Ryan got out and unfolded the tow hitch on the harvester, signaling Sadie to back up farther with his hands. She stopped, the tow ball directly under the hitch—naturally, since she'd done it countless times. Ryan clamped the hitch to the truck, and they took off for home with the leaden clouds above whirling about. Rain began pelting the truck halfway there.

Ryan sprang from the truck and opened the door to the Quonset shed, and he was soaked by the time Sadie joined him to sprint to the front door.

As they reached the door, Ryan looked up. "Goddamn," he said, barely audible over the clatter of the rain on ground, trees, metal and wood.

"What—oh, no," Sadie said as she beheld the rotating wall clouds to the southwest which meant only one thing—a tornado was coming. "Get inside," she said, opening the door and pushing Ryan through.

They both shivered in their soaked clothes as they entered the foyer. Sadie began stripping first, and Ryan followed suit. She threw the garments into a laundry basket in the kitchen, and then sat at the computer station. Ryan returned bearing dry robes and towels.

"Nothing we can do now but wait," he said.

"NOAA radar says it's going to go through here in thirty-five minutes."

Ryan looked at the multicolored blotches on the screen. One bright red spot was marked POSSIBLE FUNNEL CLOUD SIGHTED. He couldn't tell how close it was to their fields. "It only takes thirty minutes to wipe out a year's work," he muttered.

"Stop being so damned gloomy," Sadie told him. "At least we're safe down here. And when you get right to it, that's all that matters." She looked up at him with her pale blue eyes, and he realized she was right.

"Give me an outside view."

"Ryan, for God's sake, there's nothing—"

"Do it." Sadie tapped commands into the keyboard, and a view from a small videocamera mounted on the barn flashed on the screen. The lens was flecked with raindrops, but they could see trees bent in the wind and debris flying past. The horizon blended with the slate sky. The camera panned, then stopped.

"Damn," Sadie whispered. To the southwest a dark finger dipped from the clouds.

"It's over by Mike Hoffman's place," Ryan said.

"Moving this way, though."

"Can we get a drone up?"

"Forget it." She began typing and mousing, and another screen came up. "KTTV has high-altitude drones with infrared cameras and radar tracking it."

Ryan went to the front door, opened it halfway, and peered out. "Rain's quit."

"Yeah. Looks like this is an F2. We've been through worse. Remember three years ago?" An F5 had torn through the western part of the county, wiping out Colston, a small town of maybe fifty people and a grain elevator, finishing what drought and warming had begun.

KTTV also had storm chasers out, and Sadie had their transmissions on the second screen. Ryan had always thought these people should be committed to a mental hospital. Anyone living in Tornado Alley tried to avoid tornadoes, not drive toward them.

The funnel cloud touched down, throwing up dirt and grass and wheat—someone else's for now. Sadie had the sound down, so they weren't treated to the various expletives and excited babbling from the storm chasers.

They watched as the funnel raced across the fields, tracking it moving northeast. It reached the edge of an area outlined in green—the border of their holdings. Ryan moaned as it began tracking across the northern part of their fields.

"Easy, babe," she said. "It's not going to hit much. It's only a hundred or so yards wide. And we're insured." The storm moved along a line, grazing the northern end of their fields, finally exiting and moving on to wreak havoc on others.

"Guess we better survey the damage," she said. They dressed, and Ryan drove them west and north to the storm's footprint. The Jeep kicked up mud and gravel, and the fields had turned to gumbo under the downpour. No harvest for a couple of days, then.

A football field-wide swath had been blown through the amber waves. Ryan stood there quietly, somberly looking at the damage.

"Not much damage," Sadie said. "Those transgenic stalks were supposed to take more punishment. I guess they lived up to the hype." She squinted, and then pointed to the field. "It's not all bad." She smiled. Ryan looked to where she was pointing. A crumpled heap of metal lay in the middle of the field. It was black, and they could see wheels poking out of the wheat, still spinning.

"Were they inside?" she asked.

Ryan craned his neck, narrowed his eyes. "Nope. Over there, by the Miller's shelterbelt." Two tiny figures dressed in black and khaki were trudging along the road, no doubt griping about being marooned in the middle of nowhere, shaken about their close encounter with nature in its rawest form. "I don't mind losing a few bushels if it's for a good cause."

The storm was passing, the clouds were breaking up. The anvil-shaped cumulonimbus clouds and the base clouds were scudding to the northeast. He looked toward the west, toward the stand of cedar and cottonwood that he knew so well.

It was flattened.

Ryan drove the Jeep slowly toward the wreckage, and stopped alongside it. The trees had been snapped like toothpicks. And the house—the house was a tumble of wooden debris collapsed into the basement. He climbed out of the Jeep, and silently gazed at the ruins.

No voices.

"You know," Sadie said, "we're not going to have much to do the next day or so. Harvester'll sink in the mud. So will the center pivots." She moved closer to him, put her arms around his neck.

"Might be able to work on the barn, get that wiring replaced."

"You could," she said, smiling. "I was thinking more about tonight."

"Anything in particular?"

"I thought maybe," she said, unbuttoning his shirt, "we could see about—expanding."

Ryan caressed her back. "I think it's about time."

GROW, GIVE, REPEAT

Gregory Scheckler

Alex fidgeted on the porch next to her robotic doll, Miss Lasagna, who was her oldest friend.

"How much longer?" said Alex.

Dusty and fray-haired, her robot checked online shipping records. "They should arrive within the hour. Is the coop ready?"

"It's not too wet." Alex took a deep breath of farm-fresh Wisconsin air. "I smell geosmin and 2-methylisoborneol. They indicate eukaryotes and prokaryotes whose biosynthesis created volatile organic compounds. Did you get that?"

"Correct," said the doll. "The smell of rain is caused by many microorganisms."

"But do you know what this means?"

"At only eleven years old you have mastered biochemistry?"

Alex reached down off the porch, and rolled mud in her fingers. "The dirt is ready. Maybe this season our chicks won't all die."

Last season had been terrible. Mildew infected the beans and blight ate the tomatoes. And one night she forgot to put the chicks into their coop just before lightning shattered the dark and a thunderstorm flooded the low ground. The next morning, she found the chicks drowned, huddled together into a small mass of feathers. Ever since witnessing their limp wings, Alex had grown a permanent scowl. Her family couldn't afford more chicks. They scrounged all winter, and like most homes, their pantry harbored too little food. The bitterness and hunger resolved her heart, pushing her to avoid more mistakes.

"Is the coop warm enough?" said Miss Lasagna.

Alex ran to the chicken house, which she'd helped remodel. She scuffed her overalls on its solar siding, the cheap kind from Barnard's Hardware downtown. The coop's pipes and barrels absorbed the sun's warmth. One side housed a handful of old chickens, and the other side was empty, waiting. Beneath a small awning, a weatherproofed computing console revealed a suitable temperature. Behind the coop they had wildflowers for butterflies and bees, and a small garden of beans, spinach, tomatoes, potatoes, and more beans, and a fat pile of compost that fed into the coop. She checked beneath the coop for the nutrient cycles from crushed insects that had been trapped into secondary composting bins and then into slow, rotating drums that smashed them into a useful protein shake. Shoved by solar-powered micropumps, the shake piped onto a drying rack where it evaporated into tiny pellets to feed the chicks. Their small home-farm's compost cycles and flowers became the insects' food which became new waste cycles and then the chickens' feed, and clean water, and ultimately the chickens themselves, and their eggs. The land's terroir infused her family's home-farm chickens through their fragrant shared history: long ago mile-thick glaciers scrubbed limestone into tiny flecks of dirt, creating the smell and texture of their world. Alex said, "It's ready. We're really just made of water and fancy dirt patterns."

"No," said Miss Lasagna, "I'm made of plastic, metal and little lightning bolts."

"Let's be friends anyway."

"Yes, please." Miss Lasagna's left eye loosened. She rotated her head toward the road. Crunching gravel beneath bicycle tires. Chuckles Lancy, Alex's only friend besides Miss Lasagna, rode his beat-up bike down Howler's Lane and up the driveway. He skidded to a halt, and nearly tipped over his bike's rusty trailer-cage full of toy animals that his father had given him. People around town whispered that his father had ditched and run. And he had. But every holiday he sent Chuckles animal dolls, which Chuckles loved and took everywhere and called the 'best overcompensation ever.'

Alex scowled, but unlike other kids, Chuckles never seemed to think Alex was stern and unhappy. Maybe Chuckles believed her frown meant she was thinking through problems. He said, “Are they here yet?”

Before Alex could respond, a postal drone buzzed across the field. It clunked to a stop. Its lift-arm set a wide box on the porch. Chirps sang from the package’s air holes. A strange, unnatural noise also grew: three wee whistles whose tone went on a bit too long.

***

Alex freed two dozen chicks from the box: Amber Whites, Barred Rocks, and Golden Bantams. Their feathers fuzzed against her fingers, and made Chuckles giggle. Mom set out seed, and bug pellets, and wilted spinach.

Chuckles pointed to a side of the box secured by foam cushioning, where he found three gelatinous cubes that pinched their tiny mouths and wobbled their nipple-like wing buds. He said, “You do have Blockies!”

The Blockies squeaked another long shrill note, warning that they required attention. Alex called up the Blockie’s guidebook, skimming over their directions. She placed the planimals onto shelving along the top of the coop. She clamped wires onto their wing buds, linking them to the console and solar panels. She pushed thin feeding tubes into their mouths, connecting to the wet feed of processed insects. Chuckles squirmed when she slipped waste hoses into their cloaca. The Blockies’ hybridized plant cells, infused with heme and modified proteins, built viable and fatty muscle-like tissues. Funny cubes of unthinking plant meats, the planimals twitched inside their cubby holes, flexed by well-timed jittering of electricity and warmed by orange lamps. At the end of their guidebook, a brightly colored webpage from Blockie Technologies said the ‘Grand Prize for Most Efficient Home Farming’ included five free Blockies per year for life, plus enough funding to build a new sustainable home-farm ecosystem. Alex registered their Blockies. Winning could solve their food problems forever.

Mom's bracelet buzzed, and she glanced at it. "Chuckles, your Mom's messaged. Time to head home."

He said, "But what are all of their names? Toy animals and real animals always have to have names."

Alex's Mom said, "Time to go. You know how your Mom is…"

"All right." Chuckles jumped up onto his beat-up bicycle. "Come by for *Space Survivor: Mars* later?"

"Once I finish my schoolwork," said Alex. Chuckles took care to ride on the side of Howler's Lane. Alex crept over to the chicks and held a grayish-brown one. "Well, I think you're Beebee, and that's your sister Skeezy."

Mom placed a hand on Alex's head and said, "These are farm animals not pets. We might not get to keep them anyway. You know the local politics. Do try not to name them."

"Oh, you say that every year. But why? Chuckles' toys all have names. And Miss Lasagna has a name and she's not even alive."

"And what's my response to this issue every year?"

Alex scowled, and ran her fingers over the turf beneath the chicks' feet. "You always say, 'Miss Lasagna isn't going to end up on our dinner table this winter.'"

"Please don't eat me," said Miss Lasagna.

Alex hugged the doll. "Silly-head, we don't eat robots."

Mom crossed her arms. "The chicks and the Blockies aren't pets. Let's not have a repeat of last year." Mom marched back to the porch. As soon as she was inside the house, the chicks all turned to Alex as if of one mind. The Blockies quivered.

Alex whispered, "I'm still going to call you Skeezy. And maybe you're Picasso and you're Betsy-Boopsie. And soon you'll meet Maisie and Mrs. Chocochip and her baby and Frumpy Bob and the others."

She leaned up to the strange fleshy planimals. "And you three, what should I call you?"

The lights registered enough warmth, priming the Blockie's cells. Alex said, "Okay Lumpy, Grumpy, and Doc, you three Blockies got no brains. So I'm in charge here and I will do my best."

***

The next day, hurtling down Howler's Lane, Mr. Hank's box truck squealed to a stop and shoved a cloud of road dust over the yard. He wobbled over to their house and stapled papers to the door. He and his truck bobbled to the next house.

Alex took the papers and began crafting a paper airplane. She folded a fuselage along the words "By order of the Township of Benville, Wisconsin…" She creased a nose cone. The edge of the outer wing displayed "all home-farm chickens must be relocated due to immediate public health concerns." She focused on strategic folds for airfoils. She tossed her paper airplane. It spun and plummeted into Miss Lasagna's grip.

Alex fumbled with Miss Lasagna's eyeball and shoved it back into the doll's head, linked to the home networks. She sat her next to Mrs. Chocochip, who cooed. Her elegant feathers and dark eyes featured in Miss Lasagna's pictures. The doll took portraits of Maisie and Frumpy Bob too.

"This is all wrong," said Alex, "They shouldn't take my friends."

***

Alex strapped Miss Lasagna to the handlebars of her recycled bicycle, and pedaled along pastures to Chuckles' house.

They crowded down in front of the Lancy's wallscreen. In *Space Survivor: Mars,* Commander Maxwell wanted to save the Martian farms from an ugly fungus that destroyed spinach crops and threatened the blue-green algae that produced the planet's oxygen. But evil forces declared Spinach Was Bad. Maxwell had a fit. Spinach Is Good. For reasons of public health and preventing the fungus from spreading, the bad guys (all robots, of course) took his spinach away and Maxwell stomped into their production facilities and stole all his spinach right back and blew up their bad robot leaders. Maxwell thundered his war-cry, "Nobody takes my spinach!"

"Chores dear," said Mrs. Lancy from the kitchen.

Alex helped Chuckles measure his Eco-Pod's efficiency ratings. Smaller than Alex's coop, the pod was a Barnard's kit donated to Chuckles and his mom. He said, "My Mom's been working so much. But I can do some of this. Sixty-one. That's great! What's your efficiency rating?"

"Oh, just a little more," said Alex, still distracted by the loss of her chickens.

Later that night, Alex couldn't sleep. She printed dozens of Miss Lasagna's photos of her birds. She snuck out and rode her bicycle down the road. She stapled the pictures on outdated utility poles, all the way to the city farming facility at the blind corner where Center Street wound back onto Dead Man's Hill, a slippery gravel incline. On every photo she wrote, "Nobody Steals My Chickens!"

***

Mr. Hank and his city truck rumbled into their driveway.

Alex yelped and jumped into her closet to hide, embracing a picnic basket. Her chickens were disease-free, she was sure of it. She did the testing herself. And they were her friends. She pressed the basket's lid down as hard as she could, until she had to pinch her forearm so that she wouldn't cry.

Dad cursed at Mr. Hank, who said, "We've been through this. Law's the law, like it or not."

Alex snuck out of the closet to the stairwell, better to hear the adults.

Mr. Hank's voice sounded flat. "The city facility's safe and healthy. You have my word."

From inside the truck, Frumpy Bob squawked as loud as the ten foot tall SuperChix, the robot rooster attraction who frightened and delighted children every year to the county fair. Mrs. Chocochip pushed her head out of the basket and pressed against Alex. She pressed the chicken back down, for her baby. Frumpy Bob let out a hellacious rooster howl. Mrs. Chocochip smashed out of the basket and flew down the stairs. Dad caught the hen mid-air and passed the chicken to Mr. Hank.

Dad glared at Alex. “Young lady, we are not law-breaking misfits.”

Tears ran down Alex’s cheeks. She clutched the basket, which still contained Baby Chocochip, who chirped.

Mom said, “Oh Alex, you didn’t?”

“I’ll take care of her baby, I will, they’re my friends, I had to, Momsy, I had to.”

“No, we have to do the right thing, and send her with the others. It’s best if Baby’s with her mother.”

“That’s what Miss Lasagna said.”

Alex trudged downstairs, and set a cup of meal worms in the truck. Baby Chocochip was so hungry that she dunked her whole head into the worms. But then all of the chicks and chickens disappeared with Mr. Hank, who drove them away. Mom cradled Alex. Although she sobbed on the outside, on the inside Alex birthed a heart-sized thumping welt of anger.

***

At midnight, Alex shoved her anger through her feet, and pedaled as fast as she could with Miss Lasagna strapped to her handlebars. She turned to Chuckles’ house. She tapped a window pane. Chuckles, surrounded by his dolls and half-asleep, said, “Huh?”

“Can I borrow your bike and wagon?”

“Okay, but wait for me.”

Alex rode the bike and wagon to the city farming facilities. Chuckles wobbled on Alex’s rusty bike. Alex prowled along the main barn, a wide metal building with big exhaust fans and waste processing units, community vegetable gardens, a greenhouse, water tanks, and a butchery. They crept through a gap between a door and its chain. Inside, except for a handful of warming lights at chicken pens, the main barn was dark and still. Chickens clucked. Alex found her flock. She counted the chickens and charted them from memory:

Skeezy, Frumpy Bob, Mrs. Chocochip, and Maisie. She stuffed them all into the bike wagon's cage, even Baby Chocochip.

She pedaled into the center of the road. Chuckles rode after her while Miss Lasagna's eyes recorded the ride. Something big and clunky hurtled down the hill.

"Pull over!" yelled Chuckles.

But Alex pedaled harder. A truck's headlights cut through the darkness, slicing down Dead Man's Hill.

Chuckles squealed. Alex lost balance. The bike's wagon torqued and twisted, slamming into the road. The cage burst open and Frumpy Bob and Maisie bolted into the air. Their wings shone in the light like stained-glass angels. The truck veered and clipped the wagon's back corner. Mr. Hank yelled and counter-steered. Blood splattered across Alex's face and arms. The truck slammed onto its side, smashing into the city farm's storage tanks. Water pounded the road and pooled into a wide pond of mud, spinning feathers, two smashed bicycles, a ruined wagon, and Chuckles, limp and red-headed. Alex clawed at the cold, germ-ridden mud.

***

In the morning, Alex sat upright in her hospital bed, while a doctor checked her pupils and forehead. She wiped a spot of chicken blood off of Alex's ear. "Just a minor concussion. You're a lucky young lady."

"Chuckles?"

Dad said, "Broken arm. He's in surgery right now."

Alex stared away from her parents, to an empty patch of wall scrubbed raw by antiseptic soaps. She said, "Miss Lasagna?"

Mom said, "Her hair's more frayed than ever. Perhaps you can repair her."

"Maisie?" asked Alex, "Mrs. Chocochip?"

Mom hugged her. "Frumpy Bob and Maisie didn't make it. You could say they saved your life, by startling Mr. Hank into steering away from you."

Circled by the darkness of exhaustion, Dad's eyes sank into his skull. He said, "We're glad you're okay. But there are consequences for your actions."

"I just wanted to get my friends back."

"You snuck out. You could've been killed, or Chuckles…he's only nine and Mr. Hank's banged up bad. And the city farm…"

Mom and Dad took Alex into Mr. Hank's room. Covered with wires and plastic tubing, he swelled like a Blockie. He murmured.

"I believe," said Dad, "that you owe Mr. Hank an apology."

"I'm sorry," said Alex.

"Not enough," said her Dad.

Monitors next to Mr. Hank beeped and tiny screens brightened against a background aroma of triclosan, triclocarban, and chloroxylenol—old-fashioned antibacterial soaps. Alex said, "I never meant for anyone to get hurt. I thought it would just all work out. I'm sorry."

"Look kid, maybe I should've had the truck on autopilot," said Mr. Hank. A flash of anger crossed Dad's face.

Mom flexed the muscles of her forearms. "The city's got to repair the community farm facility and Mr. Hank can't do that right now. Since you caused some of this problem, what do you think you can do to help resolve this situation?"

"I should help at the city farm?"

"Yes," said Mom.

Alex stiffened her posture. "I'll reassign my schoolwork as service to the city farm."

Mr. Hank's face spasmed. "Fix the water or the whole system fails."

He wheezed. The skin along the back of his hands bunched up underneath adhesive tape that held intravenous tubing in place. Alex felt the same, full of blips, bruises, and taped-together wrinkles. Her willpower deflated into a memory-picture of dark mud cut open by the bright wings of Frumpy Bob.

***

A handful of protesters lined Center Street near the city farm when Dad delivered Alex and left her under the guard of Elaine Hollis, a long-time city employee who had bio-active tattoos on her forearm that synced with the farm's computers. A backhoe surrounded the barn's north corner where contractors puzzled over how to rebuild the water filtration and containment units. Elaine showed Alex the basic systems.

"Where are your Blockies?" asked Alex.

"We don't do planimals. They'd need newer systems, which we can't afford unless we get a much bigger budget or greater efficiencies."

She assigned Alex to feed, clean, monitor, and account for all of the chickens held in various pens and coops, about thirty household's worth of birds, including the last of Alex's friends. Skeezy and Betsy-Boopsie and Picasso shied away from her touch, and too many others were gone. Their loss was her fault. She inspected the remaining chicks, and marked each one's health by feathering, size, and beak color. She set Miss Lasagna into their cage and two chicks sat on the doll's battery-warmed lap, paying no mind to her loose eyeball.

That night Alex couldn't sleep. Her heart thumped and her anger thickened. How could she be so stupid? The chickens deserved better. She drew maps of all of the farm's systems, cycle after cycle chained together across the chickens, water inputs and drainage, solar power panels, and vegetable gardens. She worked until exhausted, sleeping on the floor surrounded by her drawings.

***

The flock of protesters expanded overnight.

Inside the farm, Alex found two of her chickens dead. She took them to Elaine, who tested their blood.

Elaine slumped into a chair and reviewed her tattoo's readouts across her forearm. "It's the illness. We can't save them all. We have to cull them."

"What caused the infection?"

"Water-borne variant of avian flu H5N12, damned epidemic. We haven't had enough clean water. And some of yours…they were in puddles of mud… maybe they got contaminated… If the tanks and filters hadn't been ruined. We have to test them all."

They coaxed chickens into walking on bioreactive paper. Their footprints turned the paper bright orange, a warning sign. Elaine said, "I'm sorry, Alex, but testing shows the cull has to include all of your family's chickens."

Alex bit her tongue.

"And Alex, I want you to be in charge of informing the other families. This is your fault, after all."

"It is not my fault that viruses exist."

"No, but it's your fault that Mr. Hank crashed and ran into the water. The broken filters catalyzed this infection."

Alex flexed her fists until her fingernails ground into the flesh of her palms in the same painful way that bad memories cut into her brain.

"Yes, ma'am," said Alex, "Farming always means tough decisions." She passed a series of drawings to Elaine, and a memory chip. "I wasn't fast enough with this. But it's better now than never, right?"

Elaine swiped the memory chip over her tattoos, which revealed preliminary diagrams and equations along her forearm. She threw the diagrams up to a large wallscreen, then tracked the systems and pored over the designs. Her eyes widened, and she tapped furiously along her arm. "Kid, you did this?"

Alex nodded and felt the pain in her hands. "New efficiencies. You said it was that or a bigger budget. And I have no money. So I trimmed out the unnecessary parts. If we reset the solar panels, and turn compost bins into a bug farms, then we could maybe even put in a bunch of Blockies for people who can't have their own home farms."

"We're in for a rough few days, but this is wild," said Elaine, scanning the screen. "Just really wild…"

***

The next day, inside the barn in a quiet corner and away from crowds of protestors, Elaine and Alex gathered sick chickens. Skeezy's unsteady heartbeat pulsed her soft feathers. Alex sucked back her sniffles. "I'm sorry, but you have an illness. I know you don't get the logic that we must sacrifice some to save the flock. I apologize for my part in this. I wish I'd known you for much more time."

Alex wiped back her tears and forced herself to concentrate. She injected Skeezy with an anesthetic, and then a poison. The hen wheezed and dropped into lifelessness in her arms. Alex did the same with the others, and apologized to each. She and Elaine threw all of the dead into the furnace to disinfect them and recycle their bodies into electrical power for other parts the facility. At the shock of killing her old friends, Alex grew sullen. In the butchery sink, she washed her hands and wiped her eyes, a stiff-lipped, bitter farm-girl with a permanent scowl. Her sadness frightened her, and she buried it deeper into the recycling furnace of her lungs.

***

Alex supervised when Mom killed the first planimal. She disconnected the wires pinned to Doc's wing buds. His mouth puckered, and then opened wide. Mom squirted an intensive saline solution into him and after about a minute Doc let out a little wheeze. But he had no brain and no pain.

They wrapped Doc in a big towel and Alex struggled to help lift his thirty pounds of dead weight onto the kitchen table. Mom made the first slice, bisecting Doc from mouth to cloaca across a series of tiny organs, dark red plant-meat filled with fluids that oozed onto the table top. Alex severed the organs and pulled out their fibers. The meat squeaked. She dropped the organs into a bowl, where they slimed and slithered, wet and ruddy. The faint scent of geosmin rose up from the meat, the dirt's perfume-proof that Doc came from their farmlands.

Alex sliced each half into thirds. She shaved these into one-inch slabs of meat. Seventy-two slabs in all, enough planimal protein for at least that many servings of dinners. It wasn't hard to imagine the wealth if she won the contest: five Blockies per year would feed them well if they ate planimal meat almost every day. They dunked the slabs in cold water and vacuum-sealed them into biodegradable freezer bags.

"It's a lot easier than the chickens," said Alex. "No feathers."

"And less work to raise them. And cheaper. And fewer germs," said Mom, whose hands were covered in the grease of planimal meat.

A wave of relief passed through Alex's abdomen. She said, "It's nicer to chickens not to kill a chicken when you can grow a Blockie. Chickens think. Chickens know things. Blockies are part plant, have no significant brain, and feel little to no pain. We should farm more Blockies."

"A fine moral calculus," said Mom.

Alex held the packages of planimal meat. "If everybody knew..."

***

Mr. Hank leaned on a pair of crutches and adjusted the cybernetic exoskeleton that braced his injured legs. His voice fluttered, gravelly and weak. "Elaine's been showing me your plans."

Alex stared down to the dirt along the floor. "I killed my friends and Chuckles hates me and no one gets it."

Mr. Hank wiped his brow and said, "I know the feeling."

Beyond the farm's main doors, a large group of protesters camped in an empty pasture. Someone threw red paint and chicken feathers on one of the city trucks. Alex shivered. Mr. Hank got a call from Miss Lancy. He turned to Alex and said, "They got to the Lancy's Eco-Pod, infected it with a fast-acting fungus. It's sabotage. Lost the chickens and then the pod...their Blockies too...the Lancy's are ruined. Going to be a rough winter, I'm afraid."

Alex asked, "Who would do such a thing?"

"She suspects counter-protesters, or protesters trying to make things even worse for all of us."

"I can't tell who's good or bad anymore," said Alex.

"You can figure it out," said Mr. Hank.

Alex slouched. "No, I can't."

Some people were pro-Blockies. There were anti-Blockies, a pro-Natural clique. Some ate meat, some ate only egg and dairy, some were vegan, some gorged on nuts, some gorged on anything. And there were almost-anythings, people who ate everything except the Blockies, not because of ethics but because they said they tasted bad. And there were open-source farming plans versus seed licensing, patented plant hybrids versus the free plant movement. And decentralized individual farms versus localized city farms, versus centralized factory farms, and every degree of difference among them. And huge vertical hydroponic farms in the cities, powered by solar cells and windmills. And still not quite enough food or distribution to feed the entire planet.

Alex said, "Everyone's busted into factions."

Mr. Hank said, "See? You care. You're a good one. The good ones do what they can to help us all."

"Why won't they help each other?"

Protesters blocked the road to the city farm. Dueling sides yelled across the road at each other.

Alex marched out to the middle of them. She hollered at them. "But this is my fault. You have to let me help fix the problems. All the creatures need water and feed. They'll die if we don't help them."

Someone yelled, "They're dead already."

The blockade refused to let anyone pass. Their sweat filled the air with a tense mixture of salted anxiety, and sulfurous hints of rage. They chanted "No designer meats!" and "Planimals must die!" versus "Planimals protect us" versus "City Farms are our right" versus "My taxes, my choice!" versus "Home-farm Independence" versus "Nobody Takes My Chickens!" decorated with pictures of Alex and Maisie. "Planimals are Vegan" versus "Unnatural Fake Meats =

Disease."

The crowds closed in on each other. Someone shoved Alex. She fell and bashed into someone else. Fistfights broke out. Mr. Hank winged a crutch at the protesters. Cops arrived.

***

Alex sat in the living room. She crammed her hands along the sofa's cushions.

Dad said, "I don't know what's gotten into you. First the theft. Now a street fight. And cops? This isn't like you."

Alex turned on the wallscreens and focused them on daily newsfeeds. They spat about droughts in the West, stranded food crates at seaports, acres of bioengineered soy that contracted a lethal bacteria, more reports of the new bird flu, and agribusiness protests nationwide.

Dad scowled. "There's no easy way out of these tensions for any of us."

"Yes there is," said Alex. "Grow safe food. Give it to people. And then do it again. Grow. Give. Repeat."

"Is that what's fueling you? Idealism?"

"Dad, no."

"A dream of Utopia? Everyone happy on the old home-farm?"

"Dad, no. It's no fantasy. I killed them all. I killed our chickens. It was my fault."

"It was your responsibility, not your fault. You didn't invent viruses. You weren't manually driving the truck instead of letting it drive itself. But responding to the accident, and recognizing the infection, that's the responsibility."

"You treat me like I'm some adult."

"In a way, you are. You do think in advance of your years."

"I'm just eleven."

"That's true."

The wallscreen's debates surged over home farming operations versus Eco-Pod ownership versus leasing, to jobs to factory farms to shipping costs to individuals' rights versus environmental realities to grandiose assertions that home-based farms provided distributed sets of systems which could be called a necessary national defense. Every report was good, and bad, mixing confounding confusions. But Alex's muddied thoughts melted away during footage from a huge rally in Chicago when the outspoken head of the Blockie Technologies, Dr. Nancy Corvalier, shook her fists. "We're a non-profit. And that's why Blockie Technologies is committed to keeping all of our ideas freely available worldwide." People cheered. "We know we can't all afford everything. We're not the rich ones who can buy their way out of trouble. We have to use our wits."

Alex knew how that felt. Her family never was among the well-to-do.

Corvalier said, "We urge everyone to set aside our differences."

That's what I said, thought Alex, *grow, give, repeat.*

"We strive for the higher purpose of finding the best ways to feed the world. If together enough of us can achieve seventy-five percent feedback cycle efficiency ratings for our Blockies, then we could feed the entire planet with healthy planimal meals every day. Imagine a world without hunger and you imagine a better humanity."

Corvalier's idealism fueled Alex's focus. She wrote at a fevered pace in her notes and sketches, scattering them throughout the room.

***

The Torvalds had a nice house but an ugly, unkempt garden. Mr. Torvald sniffed at Alex.

"Due to a city-wide epidemic some of us lost our chickens at the city facility. Your chickens got infected and had to be killed before the other chickens got infected. Reparations and food credits can be acquired by application through the City Bursar. I'm sorry."

Torvald said, "Oh good grief." He turned away. "Marge, they sent that angry kid to tell us she killed our chickens!"

From the distance Marge said, "Well tell that punk we don't want her stinking science smarts!"

Alex said, "But if instead of chickens you used… Planimals can help us all. If you grow them right, everyone eats."

"No one wants that crap," said Torvald. He slammed the door.

The next house had a flat porch and a scruffy dog in the window. The Kuang home. Alex knocked. A teen answered.

Alex said, "Due to a city-wide epidemic…"

"Oh baloney. Government tool."

"No, the planimal process. We can improve it, I'm certain."

"My parents can't afford those."

"Neither can mine. But the city will give you food credits and compensations. It's all arranged. I could show you how to build much more efficient Eco-Pods…"

"They voted against that scam. I would too, if I were voting age. Bye now."

The Mousaka's home had shutters and peeling paint. Alex knocked. A hunched, elderly woman answered. Alex said, "Due to a city-wide epidemic…"

"You're from the city?"

"Yes, for school service."

"My son used to work for the highway service until the autopilot road builders took his job."

"I'm here about the chickens."

"Are you from the city?"

"Yes, due to a city-wide epidemic…"

"The highway service was such a good job…"

"Is your son here? Can I talk with him?"

"Oh no, dear. He's long gone. Left me all alone. Children grow and forget their parents."

"I'm sorry, ma'am."

"Are you from the city, the food service? I'm so looking forward to today's meals."

"They bring you food?"

"Yes, every day. Very reliable. I can't cook anymore. Can't follow the directions."

Alex said, "I'm not the food service."

"Well, goodbye then."

"Bye," said Alex.

She imagined marching straight through the protestors back to the city farm, but she still had to report to Chuckles and Miss Lancy. The Torvalds, the Kuangs, the Mousakas—none could accept the planimals, or like Mrs. Mousaka, who couldn't even cook for herself, maybe they couldn't manage to farm a planimal.

Alex knocked on the Lancy's door. Chuckles answered, and he glared at her.

"I have to share news from the city," said Alex. She passed him a report, and recited her speech in a practiced, flattened tone. "Due to a city-wide epidemic some of us lost our chickens at the city facility. Your chickens got infected and..."

"My body hurts," he gestured with his arm in a 3d-printed geometric cast. He flushed and choked back tears. "I'm not allowed to talk with you."

"You just did talk with me."

Miss Lancy pulled Chuckles aside and said, "It's nothing personal. I'm afraid you proved to be a bad influence. So you and he can't play."

"I'm sorry," said Alex.

"Your dumb ideas hurt us!" said Chuckles.

"I'm sorry," said Alex. She scowled and Chuckles backed away. "I had to kill all my chickens too."

"Goodbye," said Miss Lancy, closing the door.

Alex yelled through the door. "I'll find a way to help you. I promise."

Her legs hurt. Her mind reeled. The families she spoke to may as well have been her own flock of undead chickens, eyes burned out, clucking and yelling at her for killing them.

***

That evening Alex dozed, shuddering as if she felt her arms slap the road. She heard the crunch of twisting metal. Frumpy Bob squawked. Skeezy and Maisie burst into the air, their faces lit up by the truck's headlights, their open beaks shocked and widened. Alex tried to breathe to calm herself, but her guts convulsed. She wailed.

Mom held her until Alex had no more air in her lungs. Alex gulped and began to sob again.

The pounding welt of her anger had been spinning for days. It felt awful and good to let it out, to let herself wail and cry. The welt of her heart slowed its spin, crystallized, and became a deeper concept. Alex calmed and choked back her sniffles. "I may have a different idea."

Alex took Mom to the wallscreen and tapped on pictures of their coop's feedback cycles and computer programs.

"How much? Prove it," said her Mom. Alex called up the Blockie's anatomical maps, circuit diagrams, and looped feedback cycles.

Mom said, "How do we test your idea?"

Alex shifted into full attention on the screen. "First we get the programming right. And fine-tune their sensors. Is that even possible?"

"Maybe?"

"And Mom, this isn't about the contest. I don't care about that anymore. This is much bigger."

After another hour shuttling back and forth between programs, Mom fell asleep. But Alex's calculations felt too easy, which on principle bothered Alex awake.

She drew more diagrams, layering feedback cycles and lists of every person she'd ever met: Mom, Dad, Miss Lancy, Chuckles, Mr. Hank, Elaine Hollis, her schoolmates, the Torvalds, the Kuangs, and all the families and numbered charts for all the people in town.

She tracked population dynamics and farm tactics. She drew new diagrams on the wallscreen, across series of hundreds of feedback cycles looped together with energy input and output equations, caloric restrictions, vitamin and mineral needs, micro-pumps and plans for printable, bendable circuitry to be implanted in the Blockies, and flocks of chickens tending the fields, enriching the compost for all. She re-organized all of her plans into a website and a free book. She put Miss Lasagna's photo of Baby Chocochip on the cover. She titled it *Inseparable: The Easiest Path to Get Over 80% Efficiencies with Planimals, Chickens, and People, Including You and Your Neighbors.*

She placed the book on discussion forums for home farming. She set an automated program to repeat links to the book's information wherever people discussed chickens. She collapsed into slumber, on the floor and among piles of her diagrams and drawings. Miss Lasagna pulled a blanket over her.

***

Dr. Nancy Corvalier arrived in an electric pick-up truck with dark windows. Alex held Miss Lasagna's tiny plastic hand. The doll's eyes recorded the scene. Mom and Dad watched from the doorway.

Corvalier said, "I love your book. And I've read so much about you, but do you know what it is about heroines?"

"No."

"Compared to stories, heroines are always smarter and more complex in real life."

Alex smirked, but kept her eyes down. Miss Lasagna kept her own eyes up. Dr. Corvalier knelt down to Alex's level, and said, "And who is this fine robot here?"

The doll's servomotors rotated her neck until she looked into Corvalier's eyes, and said, "I'm Miss Lasagna, pleased to meet you. Alex is feeling a bit quiet these days."

"Could you two show me your Blockie ecosystem? I'd very much like to see your innovations."

Alex walked to the coop, with Miss Lasagna in tow. Corvalier ooh'd and aah'd over Alex's newest designs. Corvalier sniffed the breeze, and said, "Now smell that air, a perfect farm-fresh soil, excellent musky dirt."

"Calcium carbonate crushed by glaciers," said Alex. Her eyes still faced the ground where most of what she saw was Corvalier's black lace-up hiking boots, a practical, unobtrusive style. "I know about the contest's efficiency percentages. They aren't realistic measures. They're just marketing. A rough tool. And I'm okay with using it for rough ideas and for marketing since you're trying to help people. But the real thinking is subtler, and in the design compromises and balances for feedback into linked waste and re-use streams, even evaporation, you have to include people. People are a part of the equation. Everyone in the community. I mean people's inputs and outputs, also, our innovations."

"Good." Corvalier tapped her boot against a stone. "Then we can discuss tough balancing acts and put this contest aside, after a little publicity, of course."

When the photo crew arrived, Alex held Miss Lasagna, who waved her plastic hand, but Alex scowled. She accepted the grand prize with annual free Blockies and money to build or remodel an extensive home farming operation. She pulled on Corvalier's sleeve and said, "Can you take me to Chuckles' house? I need your help to tell him something."

***

Behind the Lancy's house, a ruined Eco-Pod stank of fungal rot, and in front, a crushed bicycle made a deranged lawn sculpture. Alex insisted that her parents stay in the car. Corvalier, Miss Lasagna, and Alex approached the Lancy's front door. Miss Lancy answered and Chuckles watched, big-eyed and wary, from the dining room.

Alex said, "I won the grand prize but I'm giving it to you. Dr. Corvalier can arrange the paperwork."

Corvalier shook out a big double-take, and said, "Are you sure Alex? That's a lot of food and resources."

Miss Lancy's face flushed. "This is too much…"

Alex said, "I'm certain. Maybe you can share some dinners

sometimes? Maybe we can grill Blockies? Maybe we can watch *Space Survivor: Mars* again?"

"I don't know," said Chuckles. But he showed his Commander Maxwell doll to Miss Lasagna. The dolls walked up to each other and hugged. Miss Lancy smiled so widely that she almost cried.

Alex produced a memory chip full of new drawings and plans for a new farming operation at the Lancy's home. She showed them to Corvalier and Miss Lancy, and said, "See? This automates so that a single parent could gain well-balanced feedback cycles, as much as eighty percent ratings on average. Hook up pipes from the home, and air venting from the bedroom, with a little heat exchange from the basement and the more industrious folks could get up to two or three percent more with a bit of daily maintenance. This is how we solve world-wide problems. Little by little."

They chatted over the plans. Chuckles listened and hugged his mom.

***

In their dining room, Dad popped open a bottle of champagne. Alex's neighbors chattered and cheered. Dad pranced and curtsied when he gave Miss Lasagna a tiny glass. Alex kept a new chick, Baby Montague, in the fine and comfortable hollow of her overall's front pocket.

Corvalier offered a toast, "To the end of world hunger."

"Hear, hear!" said Mom and the others.

Corvalier added, "It won't be done in a day, but one step at a time and we're getting there. To the future."

Everybody toasted again. Alex stepped around the old wooden table, frowned with concentration, and 'helped' Miss Lasagna drink her glass of syrupy-sweet bubbly. The doll said, "Hear, hear! Sometimes we just have to out-think the present-day."

Mom said, "The future? We'll have to give it up to Alex."

"To me?" said Alex.

"Yes, up to you. You'll have choices we never had. Good choices.

Maybe you can start a farm on Mars?"

Alex cuddled into Miss Lasagna, careful to protect Baby Montague. She missed her chickens. "Well I'm the kind of woman who gets things done. Miss Lasagna and I think this is going to be difficult. But she says she's up to the challenge."

They arranged their dinner of Blockie steaks, kale and sweet potatoes in a roasted garlic sauce, with a sprig of rosemary and small slices of strawberry and sugared Wisconsin ginseng. Alex got to sit at the head of the table, with Miss Lasagna who wore her sequined party dress and a crooked pink bow in her frayed hair. Baby Montague poked out from her pocket, her feathers more full than ever, her scent nuttier and closer to the Earth. She rustled and cooed when Alex stroked her back where her feathers felt soft and smooth.

At the end of the evening, Alex tiptoed back to her room and fell fast asleep, smiling to herself. She dreamed of building a planimal farm on Europa, in a floating dome above the moon's ice-cold surface. And they had enough oxygen, nitrogen, hydrogen, carbon and complex molecules for people and plants and planimals and real live bugs and chickens, even Mrs. Chocochip and her baby who shared a basket-like spaceship and who wore fat silvery spacesuits and rounded helmets.

CABLE TOWN DELIVERY

M. Lopes da Silva

Pella cursed beneath her breath as she yanked on the rusty levers of the hopper. The left rear leg kept sticking. With a growl and a fierce pull she freed the frozen gear just in time, preventing the four-legged vehicle from tipping onto its side. She hit the emergency brake and slumped back in her seat, listening to the groan of the hopper's legs. Pella blinked as sweat prickled her eyes. She'd been driving the hopper for over twenty hours, and halfway through the desert the air circulator had cut out. Hot, stale air reeking of metal and old paper sat in the back of Pella's throat like an unwanted lozenge. She rubbed the back of her neck, grimacing at the knotted muscles.

Pella brought up the schedule on her flatpad—no time to dawdle. She was due in Cable Town in eight hours. And if she was late in Cable Town, then all the rest of the stops on the line would suffer. People had been waiting for years. Pella thought longingly about sponging the grime off the back of her neck, but instead unset the brake and got the hopper in motion again. She checked the battery levels; the solar panels plastered all over the hopper's body like an insect carapace had finally sucked up enough juice from the persistent summer sun.

She activated the prop; a power-chomping propellor extended from the top of the hopper's body, then began to spin. Slowly, the hopper lifted into the air. As soon as the hopper's feet were scraping oxygen, Pella set the four limbs of the vehicle to the limp flight stasis mode that made her think of jellyfish arms.

She punched the radio on, expecting static and getting plenty of it, but soon fragments of a song began to fight the snarl of white noise. Pella raised the volume slightly. As the signal strengthened, and the song clarified, Pella realized that it was one that she knew. She raised the volume higher as drums and bass and flutes joyfully peppered the air, and hummed along. It had been a long drive, and would be longer yet, but Pella loved her job. She grinned as she drove the hopper through the beige-blue sky, forgetting the ache in her neck for a while.

***

Arc sat at the edge of the cable car's open door, gently swinging her legs. Her dad would give her hell if he saw her sitting like that, but he was helping Lyka open a stall at the Complex. Arc loved the way her legs felt suspended over the steep concrete canyons, the forbidden hot winds from the desert toasting the tips of her toes. She could feel the gentle sway of the car as it rocked at the joint of the cable suspension above. The winds weren't too strong, today. Arc frowned. She put down the glittering paper she'd been cutting with a pair of rusty shears, adding the heavy tool on top of the sheet as a paperweight. If the winds weren't very strong, the Kite Festival wouldn't get much business, and if there wasn't much business, maybe dad and Lyka would have to go back to rat hunting.

Arc closed her eyes, listening to the metallic creaks and groans of all the cable cars suspended from thick black lines along the city's skyward corridors. Dad called it "the free music". She liked to listen to the free music, which would build with every ripple and swell of the wind, and dwindle with its passing.

Cable Town was a city built on the cavernous carcasses of several other cities. Odd structures were improvised along the planes and sides of collapsed skyscrapers, tenaciously clinging to the concrete skin like brilliant particolored mold. These buildings were built from salvaged scrap, and often dripped with edible succulents, which residents would plant on any surface that could manage to hold a bit of dirt in the face of the persistent heavy winds.

Above the buildings the endless rows of cable cars spanned, creating what Lyka called a "town of treehouses" (Lyka had seen trees before—this was a sore point with Arc, who had never seen any). Wind turbines loomed above like languidly-spun spurs. Bridges criss-crossed the sky at lower, less windy junctures. The view down any Cable Town alley was a dark scribble of angular lines and boxes above a seemingly bottomless pit.

Arc had lived in Cable Town for all eleven years of her life. Lyka, her big sister, had lived in another place called Sum City, but she didn't remember much about it, and their dad had to be in a rare mood to talk about the past. If prodded, he would just shake his head and say, "We're better off." Arc believed him.

It wasn't that rat hunting was bad, exactly, it just didn't pay very well anymore. That's why they'd saved up and leased an extra car just for Lyka to grow her rare tea shrubs—a greenhouse in the sky—and painstakingly followed her every instruction for months and months on end.

If they didn't at least break even at the Kite Festival, they'd have to surrender the car—rare plants and all. They'd already worn out the patience of the Cable Town bankers, who flashed their brass knuckles alongside every bright smile these days. Her dad had forbidden Arc to help out at the Complex, cautioning her not to let the rope ladder down for anyone she didn't know.

Arc picked up the skeleton of her box kite, testing the strength of her amateur weaving at the joints. One of the corners fell apart after her prodding, and Arc shoved the collapsed mess away in disgust. Lyka had promised to show her how to make a kite this year, but she'd forgotten in all the flurry of preparation for the festival. Arc drew her knees up to her chin for a proper sulk. The bottoms of her feet felt shockingly cold on the metal floor of the car after the warm summer sirocco.

That was when she started to hear it—a stuttering mechanical drone reminiscent of a cicada. But this sound was louder, deeper than the voice of an insect; Arc grabbed one of the tethers secured to the car walls and stood, squinting at the dusty sky. She thought she saw something that looked like a flying tower. With a deep frown, Arc leaned out over the void, her knuckles white on the tether.

Suddenly the drone was oppressive, booming; a shadow fell over Arc's torso and she twisted up to see a massize metal shape block the sun. The cable car tilted, and Arc glimpsed the remains of her kite—paper, shears, and mangled frame—begin to slide out the open doorway. Arc leaned over, reaching for the supplies, and just managed to grab them.

But her hand slipped off the tether.

With a scream, Arc plummeted into the abyss.

***

Pella caught a glimpse of Arc's fall; a smudge across the flat screen depicting the live feed under the hopper's belly. Immediately she yanked a lever, and the vehicle began to rapidly descend.

"Damnit, damnit, damnit," Pella growled, squinting at the falling, shrieking child below her and trying to calculate properly. They only had a few seconds. Pella made a decision and yanked a lever in conjunction with another one.

In response, the right front leg of the hopper swung out in space and then halted with a shuddering creak inches alongside the child. Arc seized the metal limb. Pella hoped that the child was hanging on tightly. Locking the limb in place, she abruptly shifted the hopper's trajectory. The prop whirred fiercely. Arc shivered, struggling with a sudden bout of nausea as the hopper bounded *up*. She buried her forehead against the shiny metal limb she clung to.

"Are you okay down there? Just nod once if you are. Twice if not. I can see you." This voice crackled from a speaker hidden on the hopper's body.

Arc nodded once.

"Great! I'm going to go as slow as I can, but I've got to make it to the Complex in the next eight minutes, so I'll drop you there." There was a pause, then the speaker crackled to life again. "Well, not 'drop you.' Drop you off, I mean. You'll be fine, is what I'm saying. Oh, never mind. Just hold on!"

Arc peered through her eyelashes nervously, watching the hopper navigate wildly through the windy corridor of bridges and cables, then squeezed her eyes shut again.

***

The Complex was a cleared, flat spread of concrete surrounded by shops set up in the remains of old apartment buildings. The space was used as a market on most days, but also frequently served for festivals and dances and performances.

Pella had parked the hopper on the far northeast corner of the concrete field. She patted the side of the hopper affectionately. "Here you are, folks! Just give her a few minutes to charge up and you can walk right in. All download devices need to go through the digiwash first. Traditional books and other media are stored on the first and second floors."

Arc hovered behind Pella's leg. She'd seen Lyka's stall at the western edge of the Complex while the hopper had landed, and wondered if Lyka had seen her. A crowd had quickly gathered around the hopper, and while some of the people there seemed interested in the spectacle of the child being gingerly lowered to the ground by a robotic limb, the majority of the crowd were definitely interested in something else.

"What is this?" Arc asked when Pella had a moment.

"What do you mean?" Pella replied, smiling good-naturedly at the child. She was relieved that Arc appeared unhurt.

Arc pointed at the vehicle. "This machine, for starters."

"Oh, that's a hopper. The long legs are good for crossing the desert."

Arc frowned, puzzled in spite of herself. "Why is that?"

"You ever been to the desert?"

"No," Arc sighed, "I'm not allowed outside of Cable Town."

"That's probably because it's all rocks and torn-up earth—it's completely unstable. The legs help pick your way along the route."

Pella was greeted by a friendly individual in long mottled violet robes, and detoured into a short conversation. Arc rubbed the sides of her arms nervously. She wasn't supposed to be at the Complex today, but maybe her dad would understand that there'd been special circumstances. Arc imagined her dad yelling at her about leaning too far out of the cable car and grimaced. She ducked further behind Pella.

Finally the conversation ended, and Arc tugged at Pella's elbow. "But I mean what is this? Why is everyone grouped up?"

Pella grinned, her eyes merry. "You don't know, huh?" She looked down at a bulky gray flatpad that she plucked from a bag at her hip. "That's right—there hasn't been one of our hoppers by in twelve years, now." Pella leaned forward a little, lowering her voice in mock conspiratory. "So think—is there anything you want to see or hear or learn about? Anything at all? It could be an animal, or a place, or a person, or how to make something."

"Trees," Arc blurted out. "And how to make a kite," she added after a moment.

Pella nodded, tapping the skin of the hopper. "All that is inside. And more! Stories, too. And songs, and art."

"How much?" Arc frowned skeptically.

Pella laughed. "For nothing!"

Pella's laughter was picked up by some bystanders who had overheard the conversation.

"It's a library, kid!" someone called out from the crowd.

Arc shifted on her feet awkwardly. She still didn't know what that meant, and she hated being the subject of laughter.

Pella shook her head. "Don't pay any attention to them. Yes, it's a library, and I'm a librarian, but you'll figure out what that is in time." She scrabbled in one of the pouches on her belt, and pulled out a few coins. "I can pay for a drink with this here, right?"

Arc blinked, looking at the coins. "Yeah. At least three drinks, if you want tea."

"They have tea here now? I hope it's cold. Why don't you buy us two, and come back with change?"

Arc smiled, slipping the coins into the deep front pocket on her trousers. "Okay!"

***

Arc crouched beside the stall, peeking over the top of the low fabric wall. She could see Lyka and her dad working, brewing and chilling and serving tea for the people lining up. It was good to see them so busy, and Arc felt a pang of pride at her sister's hard work being so well received. Arc hung back, waiting until her dad's back was turned, and Lyka was alone.

Arc whistled—one note, low—and Lyka looked up. When she saw her little sister crouching by the booth, she groaned beneath her breath. Darting a glance over her shoulder to confirm that their dad was still busy, Lyka approached Arc.

"You're not supposed to be here. Dad's going to be upset."

Arc handed over Pella's coins. "Two iced teas, please."

Lyka rolled her eyes. "Where did you get this money from? You need to go straight back home."

"It's an order from the librarian. She saved my life when I almost died today."

Lyka sighed. "Fine, don't pay any attention to me. But you're going to need to go home after you drink these."

"I'll miss the Kite Festival if I go home."

Lyka marched away from Arc, poured two iced teas from the noisy refrigerated taps running off the solar cell roof of the festival stall, and returned with two pressed palm leaf cups and change.

"Stay out of dad's sight, and don't get into any more trouble, Arcling."

Arc smiled up at her big sister. "You're awesome, Lyka. The stall looks great."

The corners of Lyka's mouth twitched up. "Glad you think so. Now scram!"

Obediently, Arc darted off into the crowd.

***

By the time Arc returned with the drinks, the doors to the hopper had opened, letting in streams of people, some holding books that they'd been hoping to return for over a decade. Arc saw Pella leaning against the front of the hopper's entrance, smiling and chatting with the patrons. When Pella caught a glimpse of Arc in the crowd, she smiled and gave a slight nod. The child darted forward, offering one of the iced teas to Pella, who took a long swig.

"Ah, that's good! I haven't had tea in forever. I mean, hot mint brewed in a cup, sure, but not real tea like this."

Arc listened to the babble, smiling proudly. "My sister made that. With my dad. We all helped, but it was mostly her. I thought there wouldn't be anyone here today because the wind was so weak, but there's a good crowd!"

Pella arched an eyebrow. "'Because the wind is so weak?'"

Arc nodded. "It's the Kite Festival today. They're going to launch the kites tonight."

Pella grinned. "Oh, there'll be enough wind for that. I had a few bad gusts nipping my heels across the desert earlier. You'll see."

Arc shrugged. "I guess people showed up anyway. For the library."

The woman removed a grimy rag from a pouch on her belt and swabbed at the grease along the back of her neck, guzzling more tea. The cold liquid eased the raw patch in her throat. When she finished, she gestured at the hopper.

"Why don't you go in and take a look? Just grab one of the flatpads by the door—it'll walk you through the place."

Arc finished her tea, depositing her empty cup on a designated compost heap nearby, and headed toward the hopper. It had been a strange day, and yet she hoped it would go on and on; Arc hadn't been this happy in years.

***

The inside was packed with people slowly milling about, most of them gazing down at their flatpads. After Arc answered her own device's prompts for language and other settings, she picked the option to borrow the flatpad for the week, then return it at the end. If she didn't return it, apparently the librarian would just track down all the equipment anyway. Patrons with their own recording devices could download as much media as they could carry. And of course, there were always the physical books to check out.

Arc had read exactly five books, total; her favorite one had been a book of fairy tales. Interesting things were always happening in stories like that—heroes sprang up in the unlikeliest of places.

"How may we help you?" a recorded voice from the flatpad asked gently.

"I…need a book on trees. And to know how to build a box kite."

"Digital or physical media preferred?"

Arc frowned. "I guess digital is all right." She thought for a moment. "And maybe a physical book, too—one with fairy tales in it."

The device presented a list of book titles, with descriptions Arc could interact with. After fussing for a bit, she selected a few books, then hit the download button. She glanced up—in her casual meandering, she had ended up bottlenecked by an entrance. Turning sideways, Arc squeezed past two adults covered in holographic tattoos, muttering apologies along the way.

A faint chime rang out from Arc's flatpad. "Main library," the device announced.

Arc looked up and saw a room filled with books; the metal walls were fully converted to shelves that spanned from the ceiling to the floor, and every shelf was neatly packed with the spines of books. Patrons carefully removed these books from behind taut elastic cords, flipping pages and pausing as they read.

"What's it like to be a librarian?" Arc asked suddenly.

Recorded clips of Pella's adventures began to play on Arc's flatpad. Amazed, Arc watched as Pella piloted the hopper through fantastic storms, and narrowly avoided wild animals that charged at the vehicle with unchecked fury. She watched Pella singing songs to herself as she navigated along empty stretches of snowbound tundra. She watched Pella hang suspended from a curious sling as she repaired the underside of a frozen hopper limb. She watched Pella sort the shelves, and run maintenance checks, and fix the damaged books and flatpads. She watched Pella meet new and exciting people in dozens of places that Arc did not know.

It was dizzying. Arc grinned, imagining a life of endless adventure, delivering the pure magic of ideas to strangers who would soon become friends.

***

Arc exited the hopper in a daze, the dazzle of the setting sun speckling her vision with fiery dots. Her imagination swirled with idylls of towns and cities and trees and libraries. She'd never suspected the sheer multitudes of thoughts there were to think!

As the dots dispersed, Arc could make out a silver-haired woman in expensive silk handing Pella a few rolls of coins, as well as some boxes of mushroom bread and water.

Pella said, "Thanks for paying the maintenance fee, it's always a pleasure setting up in Cable Town—is this mushroom bread? You didn't have to do that!"

"It's a pleasure having you here. We'd love to have you stay longer if you could."

Pella laughed awkwardly, scrubbing her scalp with her fingernails. "Ah, well—you know how the schedule is! But I'm on time and here for the week, Mayor Trenton."

The mayor smiled. "Feel free to come over for dinner while you're in town. I'm in the red and blue car at the top of Zephyr Way."

Pella tipped her chin down. "Thank you! I just may at that."

A hand landed on Arc's shoulder, eliciting a yelp. She looked up, and saw a man she didn't know at the other end of it. He grinned at her in a way that she didn't like.

"Hey, kid—where's your sister? She owes me some money."

"Hey! Take your hands off that kid!" Pella began to stomp over to the strange man, who kept Arc's shoulder pinched like a vise.

"Stay out of this—it's not your business," replied the man.

"You're right, it's mine." This new voice belonged to a deep, gravelly voice struggling to be patient. Arc shrank slightly from the voice, even though she knew it was likely her salvation. "Let my kid go." Arc smiled at the bearded man, but her smile quickly wilted beneath his stern stare. Regardless, the fingers gripping her shoulder loosened, and she fled to stand by her dad's side.

"Your daughter still has an outstanding debt with us, and the collection deadline is due tonight."

"Then why are you harassing this one? She doesn't have any debt with you."

The strange man grinned again. "Not yet." He gave a short bow to the group standing there.

As he straightened up he addressed himself to Arc's dad. "I'll be coming by later, Bedlam Green."

***

Her dad frowned deeply, crossing his arms in front of him. "Why are you here? I thought I told you to stay put!"

"I'm going to run away and become a librarian!" Arc cried, grabbing Pella's elbow.

Pella's face dropped in shock. "Ah, what's going on now?"

"Arc…" Bedlam sighed. "Enough fooling around."

"I mean it!" Arc shouted, glowering up at her dad. "You never listen when something's important to me, and this is important!"

The awkward silence was only partially alleviated by the noise of the crowd.

Pella cleared her throat. "Now, being a librarian is a tricky thing. It requires years of studying. And you have to be good at fixing things, and solving problems, and being alone sometimes."

Arc's eyes started to smart. She rubbed at them with the back of her hand. "I can learn! I can be your apprentice! I can go with you when you leave at the end of the week, and you can train me how to do everything."

"Arc," Bedlam began, his eyes darkening.

"Actually, would you mind talking with me for a moment, er, is it Belgan Greeg?"

Pella had interposed herself between father and child.

"Bedlam Green," he corrected her.

"It'll just take a moment," the librarian assured him.

He peered into the face of the woman for a long moment, then nodded. Arc watched as her dad stood listening to Pella for a while, then spoke his piece. Arc couldn't quite make out what anyone was saying. The silver-haired mayor had joined the conversation now, and Arc wondered if the adults would ever let her take part.

***

They all sat on the roof of the hopper, holding cups of cold tea as the hot summer winds began to pick up. Even Lyka had joined them after closing up the tea stall. She paid off the bankers with a sackful of coins and followed that up with a list of stern threats if she ever caught any of them near her family members again. Bedlam sat next to Pella, embroiling her with endless questions. Lyka turned to Arc and ruffled her hair with a goofy smile.

"So I'm a big success, and my little sister is going to be a librarian! We're an impressive bunch."

"Not a *real* librarian, a 'library volunteer'," Arc reminded her, "it's not like I'm going to leave Cable Town."

"*For now,*" Lyka added. "But you'll get to run Cable Town's first library in the meantime! That's a big, important job!"

Arc bit her bottom lip. "It's only going to have a few books to start with."

Lyka laughed. "I'm sure that problem won't bother you for long."

Arc thought about that.

Suddenly, the music of the festival performers died away. Kites covered in every hue of palm paper were carefully removed from parcels and baskets. Tiny candles were placed at the hearts of these kites and lit, and in first a trickle of action, then a steady current, the kites were released.

No one in Cable Town remembered where the Kite Festival came from, or who had started it. Arc wondered if the librarians might know. She thought about libraries, and collecting knowledge, and how to fill a bookshelf with only a handful of books. She had ideas she wanted to run by Pella.

Arc listened to the free music as the wind rippled through the cable cars, and sent the glittering kites scattering through the night like stars.

WOMEN OF WHITE WATER

Helen Kenwright

Berta poured tea into her cup, stirred in a little honey, and took a sip. The knot in the small of her back relaxed a little. She leaned back and gazed up at the lattice of bamboo that arched over the patio of the café. She idly followed the movement of the thermo-conductive petals the bamboo bore, as they tilted this way and that to catch the sun, twinkling iridescent blue. Stems of green cable carried the energy they captured down the arch and into the earth. From there they burrowed underground to the generators that powered the fountain, the booths, and the residential treatment village that made up the Wellness Centre. The flowers basked, the sun warmed the courtyard, and Berta enjoyed a precious moment of peace, trying to mind her own business.

It didn't work.

A group of youngsters from the art therapy booth arrived at the café. Fluttering like butterflies as they found places to sit, things to say. Searching for clues as to who they were in the faces of other people.

Berta knew who she was. She had made peace with it a long time ago. In fact, she knew a great many things. It was her job, after all.

Inevitably, the butterflies flitted her way, no doubt to "keep her company".

Emily was the first to arrive at Berta's table, followed quickly by Sable and Noah.

For reasons she would never understand, a woman in her fifties taking a work break alone, to drink in a little fresh air and a cup of tea, was an immediate cause for concern. As if, left unattended, she might spontaneously break a hip or fall into a deep depression, mired by the weight of her years. In fact, Berta was in excellent health, and believed herself to have the energy and constitution of a woman half her age. She didn't dislike other people. She had Goldie and Reg. Her brother, Freddie. And Andrea, although Andrea was her apprentice and she didn't like to blur lines. That was, as far as she was concerned, quite enough.

"So," said Emily (because young people didn't seem to say 'hello' these days). "How was your morning?"

"Hot," said Berta, and sipped her tea, refusing to make eye contact.

"It's a real scorcher, isn't it?" said Emily. "Proper Yorkshire summer. I was just saying to Sabs..."

Berta popped her listening face on, and tuned out. Their voices washed over her like background music, while she attended to the deeper, more important things. It suited everyone: they didn't want to listen, they wanted to speak, so excited by the full and enormous knowledge they thought they held that they had an overriding impulse to share. Constantly.

They knew nothing.

The courtyard was paved with repurposed concrete slabs, cracked at the joins to allow moss and tiny plants to grow. Through it Berta could feel the hum of the earth, the pull of gravity. The pressure of a coming storm filled her ears, and through it all she smelled jasmine, green tea, and fear. A river in full flow, smashing through tree roots and churning silt.

Berta snapped her attention back to the butterflies.

"Which one of you is it?" she said, cutting Emily off in mid-flow.

"I'm sorry?" Emily looked offended. Never mind. She'd get over it.

"One of you knows something wrong. Bad. Hidden and forbidden. You may as well own up, secrets like that never end well."

The three of them looked at each other in confusion, their sweet, smooth brows temporarily wrinkled.

Emily was the first to come up with a response. "Oh, would you like to give us a reading? I've always wanted to—"

Berta stood up. They flitted back, as if she'd startled them. She drained her cup, and turned it upside down in the saucer. Because that's what they always used to do at Grana's house, and it's the oddest traditions that stick.

"Child, I do not do 'readings'. People are not books. They are a chaotic mixture of hormones, emotions and information fighting for domination of one small, fragile soul. I look into that soul and find the truth, however dark or terrifying it may be. Do you really want me to do that to you?"

She scanned their faces, tempting any to break their mask, to let the truth come to the surface and be named. But none of them did. All she saw was the usual mix of fear and confusion that her gifts tended to put in people.

"Have a lovely afternoon," she said. She picked up her bag and walked away with a loud, messy sneeze. Knowing played havoc with her membranes.

***

Berta stretched out her legs, and crossed them at the ankles. She looked out across the valley of White Water: to the forest in the distance, the jumble of cottages and workshops of the village below, and the gleaming silver line of the river that separated the two. Berta had never fancied living more than two floors up herself, but Andrea's apartment certainly had a stunning view. They sat side by side on the balcony, surrounded by the smell of earth and growing things from the plants that swarmed over the exterior of the building. The evening was very warm, but thankfully too dry for the midges. A bullfinch hopped about to Berta's right, his eye on the juicy buds of the forsythia bush in the corner of the balcony. Finally he took the plunge, dived in close, and tucked in to his supper, just a few inches from Berta's elbow.

"Such tiny hearts," Berta murmured. "Such courage."

Andrea looked up from her laptop. "Are we talking about people, or something else?"

"Birds," said Berta. "People are spineless."

"It's still bothering you. The thing from yesterday with the art therapists."

Berta fixed her eyes on the rail and the thermo-conductive ivy that wound its way through real twists of clematis, almost, but not quite, blending in. "What thing?"

"You should look into it, if it's bothering you."

Berta folded her arms across her chest, and shrugged. "None of my business. I only mentioned it as a point of instruction. 'Don't go where you're not invited,' that's what I say."

"Yes, I know, but don't you think that sometimes people invite you at a subconscious level? They might have thrown that truth your way because they needed to, without even realising it."

"In which case, it's still none of my business. I only deal with conscious requests, from conscious people, in full control of their faculties. It's called consent."

"I'm not saying you should rush in without permission. But you could ask. Isn't it a bit like a cry for help?"

"The only cries for help I listen to are the ones where people look me in the eye and say 'help me'."

Andrea opened her mouth, hesitated, closed it again.

Andrea was a clever girl. As well as being Berta's apprentice in the Knowing, Andrea was the main accountant for the whole of the West Riding. She kept tabs on the exchange of credits, transaction records, trading between communities. Berta had little interest in such things, but she was proud of Andrea for being able to focus on numbers when her talent was still on the raw, untrained side. Berta was well aware that she'd been a nightmare in the early stages of her own apprenticeship, all wild emotion and barely a logical thought in her brain. Andrea was approachable, too. Kind. Respectful of the human fragilities that Berta found frustrating.

"Excellent," said Berta. "I'll get the kettle on."

***

The Village Hall was near the south bank of the river. The building nestled under a meadow-roof that currently sprouted a swathe of cornflowers, harebells and teasel dotted with bright scarlet poppies. Its concertina windows opened out onto a terrace that was bordered by a vibrant country garden. These borders were tended by any who had time to spare, including Berta. She pottered among the perennials, plucking a blown bloom here, pinching out an over-eager stem there. It put a song in her heart, one that often burst out in the form of a purring, contented hum. Occasionally, she would whistle, and Goldie would tease her for it. She took no notice. The garden was bursting into the full glory of summer right in front of her, an orgy of flowers and fruit, insects and birds. If that wasn't worth singing about, Berta didn't know what was.

She picked a couple of handfuls of ripe strawberries from beneath the bee-covered borage, and sat down to share them with Goldie.

"African daisies are looking good, Bert," said Goldie. He sprawled in his deckchair, dressed in fuchsia-pink shorts and crop top that revealed a lot of saggy cleavage and wrinkled belly, the silvery line of an old Caesarean scar, and a fresher, shorter one just below his rib. Marks of honour, he called them.

"Daisies look after themselves, mostly," Berta said.

"Trick of good gardening. Ecosystem balancing, they call it."

"If you say so. I just don't put things in if they take much effort."

"Hey, is that your girl? Ann, is it?" Goldie pointed at a figure on the path.

"Andrea. So it is." Berta popped another strawberry in her mouth.

Andrea waved as she approached. She was carrying a basket full of fabric and ribbon.

"What's that for?" said Goldie. "Doing some dressmaking?"

"Bunting. For Midsummer Festival." Andrea put the basket down and took the seat next to Berta's. "That breeze is delicious."

It was. It carried the scent of the river, fresh-cut grass and the meadows.

"I'll go see if Reg has got the tea urn on." Goldie stood up with the customary grunt of the achy-jointed. "He gets distracted."

Berta watched Goldie go into the Hall.

"I saw Emily today," said Andrea.

"That's nice," said Berta.

"She's in love with Noah."

"Ah. Told you it was a whole load of nothing. Teenagers. Pfft."

"She's really upset."

"Best she spoke to you, then."

"They were raised next door to each other. Best friends all through school. Dated for a few months, over the winter just gone. Then he dumped her."

The corner of Berta's eye twitched.

"Didn't even give the poor kid a reason," said Andrea.

"She'll get over it," Berta said. "Fancy a strawberry?"

***

A silver-grey cat frequented the Wellness Centre most afternoons, strolling casually through the entrance and stopping first at Berta's booth. She called him the Gentleman, because he was a stately, well mannered creature, with a white throat that reminded her of an Edwardian cravat. He radiated confidence and had a big, rumbling reassurance of a purr. She scratched him behind his ears, and ducked through the bead curtain into her booth. He followed her in.

The air inside was heavy with the accumulated impact of years of incense-burning, persistent sandalwood and rose. Her booth was festooned with rich silks and baubles: red drapes, gold fringes, tiny glass beads suspended from the ceiling on spider-threads. In front of her was a crystal, spiky and polished, sparkled with fragments of gold. Well, it was probably gold. She'd never really looked into it.

Her power was nothing to do with the crystal. But some people felt better thinking it did.

The Gentleman hopped up onto a cushion on the bench beside her. Evidently even he was finding the sun too hot this morning. He set about washing, getting stuck into the nooks and crevices of his fluffy feet.

The bead curtain rustled, and Sable's head poked through. Emily's friend. There was a smear of clay on her cheek. "So," she said. "You busy, Dr. Berta?"

"Good morning."

"Andrea said you had a prob with your air-con?"

"Did she?"

Sable stepped into Berta's booth. She had a screwdriver in one hand and what looked like a set of cogs in the other. "Yep. She said you might be okay for a trade."

"I might not."

"'S okay. I'll do it anyway. No clients for sculpture this morning and I had these parts printed up last night just in case."

"What do you want?"

"It's kind of complicated. I hope you don't take offence."

Berta looked at the Gentleman, who opened one eye, sighed, and closed it again.

"Try me." The girl had the good sense to blink at Berta's tone.

"Uh…she said she'd give me a session, if I did this for you. Because she owed you for a job you were going to do for the Midsummer Festival."

"I am unaware of any such transaction. So the whole arrangement unravels. Don't you think?"

"I…guess? Do you still want the air-con fixed or not?"

"Do you know what you're doing?"

"Sure." Sable waved the screwdriver dismissively. "I went to engineering workshop last winter. My folks run the mill upstream at Flyling Moor."

Berta took a moment to consider. It was very hot, and showed no sign of easing off. Furthermore, she had an appointment with Cid that afternoon. They didn't call him Sweaty Cid for nothing. All the incense in the world would count for nothing in the face of his armpits on a hot day.

"I suppose you could take a look."

"Sure!"

Berta watched Sable as she worked. The girl tickled her fingers over the rounded sides of the unit like she was petting a dog. She found a release catch Berta hadn't even noticed and the control panel came loose. Sable peered inside. "Aha!"

"Yes?" said Berta.

"I was right. The gears on the solar converter's melted. Have you ever had this serviced?"

"I'm sure I did. Once."

"A lot of folks are having the same issue right now. I'll have it up and running in two shakes."

"Appreciate it," said Berta, with a kind pat to Sable's arm. "Don't you worry. I'll settle with the accountant."

***

Berta was enjoying her deliciously cool booth at the end of the day when Andrea came through the bead curtain and sat in the client chair.

"Afternoon," said Berta. She pulled a flask out from under the table and poured tea into two china cups. "Rosehip. Tell me what you think."

Andrea breathed in the steam, gave it a good look, and took a cautious sip. Then another. Then a third. "Mmmm. That's actually pretty good. One of your Grana's recipes?"

"Maybe. What did you find out from that sculptor-therapy-mechanic girl?"

"Sable. You are perfectly aware of her name."

"Ah. Getting over-involved, are we?"

"It's called compassion, Berta."

She would have thrown just about anyone else out of the booth for that. But Andrea Knew. She was just making a point.

"Very well. In your compassionate opinion, Andrea, what's going on with Sable?"

"Thankfully little. She's a happy little soul. Everything goes into her pottery, I think. She's done a beautiful set of herb jars for the Hall."

"So it's the boy then."

"Interesting thing there. She slept with him."

Berta's eyebrow shot up.

"Around the time he split up with Emily, by the sounds of it. Didn't hurt her. But perhaps it hurt him. Perhaps he left Emily because he liked Sable, and now he's heartbroken because Sable isn't bothered?"

"May the magic of the wild places save me from a teenage love triangle," said Berta.

"And again, Berta, they're not teenagers. They're only a few years younger than me."

"Oh, hark at you, all of thirty years under your belt."

"Relationships are complicated, however old or young you are."

"That's as may be. What I Knew wasn't as simple as a bad choice of bedfellow. It wasn't that simple. It was deep. Dark. Tragic. The whiff of the forbidden about it."

"D'you think Noah intends to hurt one of them?"

"Maybe. I'll keep an eye on him. You should, too."

Andrea nodded, and took another sip of tea. "Nice and cool in here."

"Oh, all right," sighed Berta. "What d'you want?"

***

White Water buzzed with all the excitement and promise of Midsummer. The Festival went back as far as human history, but since the cataclysm it had found fresh importance. A celebration of survival. Of community. Of respect for nature in all her moods. Grana had told Berta tales of the old times, when the world was one big village and no one had a sense of home. Berta could scarcely imagine living somewhere she didn't know everyone. It had its problems, for sure, especially if people had secrets to keep. But on days like this, when everyone came together to celebrate the longest day of the year, the sun, the river, the earth and all their gifts, she loved White Water with all her heart.

Berta arranged homemade cakes on a bench that already groaned with food. The cakes were the centrepiece, a tower of sponge and gingerbread, buttercream and ganache.

Andrea came up and kissed her cheek. "Thank you."

Berta grunted. "Grana's recipes."

Andrea squeezed her around the waist. "Of course."

Berta rubbed at whatever must have just got in her eye. Grana had loved Midsummer, too. The night of magic and wisdom, she'd called it.

Goldie appeared at Berta's other side, and put his arm round her as well, crossed over Andrea's. His breasts squished tight into Berta's arm as he squeezed her. "You did good, Bert. The old girl would be proud."

She might just be, at that.

"Look at the pair of you, getting all soppy," Berta said. "Has Reg got that urn on yet?"

The Hall was a picture, swathed in bunting and strings of fairy lights that twinkled out of the doors, through the garden and down the grassy bank to the river. Most of the village turned out for a picnic tea. They flocked to the stalls to play skittles and guess the number of beans in a jar. The Gentleman wandered around the trestle tables of the hot food stall, ready for any bits of fresh, flaky fish that might enter his domain. A cricket match pottered on for most of the afternoon, and a band sent banjo and guitar riffs rippling down the valley, melodies tripping around each other in an intricate swirl of joy.

Reg and Goldie danced against the backdrop of the slowly setting sun, their skinny shadows stretching across the grass. The heat had yet to leave the air, but Berta noticed clouds to the west, heavy with rain. Never mind. They'd have a few fair hours yet. As the light faded, candles were lit around the Hall. Berta sat with Andrea in the garden. Andrea's friend Matt brought them huge slices of cake and glasses of last year's elderflower champagne. A slender young man passed by juggling with fire, and Matt stared at him, clearly besotted. Andrea and Berta exchanged knowing looks.

Then Berta noticed Emily and Sable. They were sitting on a large blanket, surrounded by a crowd of other fluttering youngsters. Including Noah. He looked miserable.

"Oh dear," said Andrea.

"Teenagers," muttered Berta.

Andrea didn't correct her.

Freddie rushed up to them, flushed and excited because his team had finally won the cricket. Berta let his enthusiasm wash over her, pleasantly infectious. But her gaze kept slipping back to the young people on the blanket: Emily and Sable sitting too close, touching too much, while Noah glowered beside them.

***

Andrea picked up a dripping plate from the rack. "I think Noah's gone home," she said. "Matt saw him headed up Westgate with his mum."

"She never was one for parties," said Berta. "Freddie, pay attention. That's not clean." She slipped a bowl back into the sink.

"Oops," said Freddie. "Sorry, Sis."

"It'll be dark soon," Andrea said. "I'll finish this if you like."

"I'm not so old that I can't walk home in the dark," said Berta.

"You've done it now, Andrea," said Freddie. "She'll be here 'til three in the morning, just to prove a point."

Berta snorted a laugh.

Andrea pulled her hair back off her neck and wafted it with her dish towel. "It's so hot. Is it ever going to rain?"

No sooner were the words out of her mouth than there was a roll of thunder. The storm was a good way away yet, but it was loud enough to rattle the doors of the Hall.

"Be careful what you wish for," said Freddie.

***

Berta wove her way through the revellers on the lawn, collecting the last few plates to wash up. The air was thick and still, the heat suffocating even at midnight. But the youngsters didn't care. They danced on to the driving beat of the band, faces lifted to the darkening sky. Under the sound of the music the river rushed, swollen from the storm which had broken farther up the valley. She saw Emily, and Sable. Emily was in tears. Sable comforting her. Noah stood with them. He must have come back after walking his mother home. He looked too-tall and awkward, his head down.

Berta put down her pile of plates, and marched towards them. But before she got there, Noah broke away, first at an awkward trot and then a loping run.

Berta followed. She kept her eyes fixed on him because, as fit as she was, she had no illusions about who would win in a running race between herself and a young man with long legs and something he urgently needed to get away from. Besides, running was a sweaty, undignified sort of thing to do.

Noah was headed for the river.

Berta walked faster.

He reached the bank of the river where the boulders were. The spot where the fishers fished from, where children would sit and dangle their feet in the water. But the river was in flood now. As Noah climbed up onto the tallest boulder, water surged. The river swept the boulder into its flow and knocked Noah clean off his feet.

Berta ran.

***

She caught up with him downstream, where the willows clustered around a twist in the river's course. A duck sheltered her ducklings in the lee of a few stray rocks, watching her with beady little eyes. Berta had no fear of the River of White Water. But Noah clearly did. He thrashed and cried out and was drowning in the face of overwhelming panic. Berta cursed, hitched up her skirts and waded into the water.

The river roared in her mind, silver and gold twisting around an image of Noah, pulling him away from her. "Now, now," she murmured. "You know that's not how this works, Sulis. Give him back to me."

She lunged forwards and caught him before he went down again. Her arms wrapped tight around him, holding his slender, drenched body close to hers.

And then she Knew.

***

When he'd finished puking up the river, Noah sat on the riverbank and cried. Berta waited, wringing out her socks. Wet skirts and shirts and whatnot could be coped with, but she detested having damp feet.

"When you're done, young man," she said, "we need to talk."

He looked up at her through long, wet eyelashes. "Why? You already know, don't you?"

"I find it's best to be clear. Especially when the person in question didn't give permission. Besides, there's more to the craft than knowledge. Knowledge isn't the same as wisdom. I think you probably need the full package, don't you?"

"Emily hates me. You saw her with Sable tonight." His head drooped. "I saw you watching us."

"She loves you. She was trying to make you jealous. Why didn't you talk to her about it?"

"What, and tell her that the dad she thought was her dad, the nice, decent one she thinks the world of, isn't actually hers at all. That she has the same loser father as me? How the fuck is that supposed to help?"

His shoulders convulsed, and he started to cry again.

"May magic and the wild places save me," she muttered.

"She's my sister," Noah said. "I fell in love with my sister."

"I see. And where did you get that idea, exactly?"

"My father told me. They had an affair, him and Emily's mother. Just after I was born. He promised her mother he wouldn't tell anyone, but when I Emily and I started to get… close… well, he had to."

"Naturally."

"You don't look shocked."

Berta laughed. "In the name of the wild river, boy, it would take more than a bit of adultery to shock me."

"It's incest." Noah said the word as if he was afraid it would hide under his bed and strangle him in the middle of the night.

"Listen carefully, Noah. She's not your sister."

He looked up again. "What?"

"You silly boy. If you thought about it for ten minutes you'd realise. Your dad lied to you! He's done a lot of that, you know, over the years. Your mother's quite a regular of mine. So was Emily's mother, once he'd broken her heart too. But Emily was nothing to do with it. You know this, in your gut."

"But why would he say it if it wasn't true?"

"People lie for more reasons than you can count. Knowing your father, I'd say he was jealous. He never forgave Emily's mother for refusing to leave her partner for him. Always bore a grudge, that man. Last thing he'd want is for his son to be with her lovely daughter. To his mind it'd be like you were getting a bit of what he couldn't have."

Noah blinked at her. She watched the lies shatter; truth connecting with truth to blossom in his heart.

"She doesn't even look like him," Berta said. "She's got her father's eyes. Haven't you noticed?"

"I thought it was a coincidence."

Berta sighed. "Don't they teach genetics in that school anymore?"

"Oh."

Berta waited. The rain started, the tail of the storm, pitter-pat on the river in front of them.

She gave up on her socks.

"Then," Noah said.

"Go on. Go find her. Have fun. There's still two hours before sunrise."

Noah's grin broadened. He laughed. He sprang to his feet, the darkness lifted from him, and then, to Berta's absolute horror, he plucked her from the ground and twirled her around, the stars spinning through the sky, like a fairground ride. She shrieked and smacked his back until he let her go, pretending to scold him.

"Sorry. Thank you." His eyes shone. He ran off, back to the music and the young people. Berta hid her smile behind her hand, even though there was nobody to see her. Then she went to the edge of the swollen river and stood, letting the water rush over her feet.

"Well done," said Andrea. Berta realised she'd closed her eyes for a moment. Andrea stood beside her, her feet bare too.

"I have no idea what you're talking about," said Berta.

They each put an arm around the other.

"Midsummer," murmured Berta. "The night of magic and wisdom."

"And the river," said Andrea.

"Always the river," said Berta.

UNDER THE NORTHERN LIGHTS

Charlotte M. Ray

Until the mini-blimp crashed in the pond, my life had been average and boring. But the splashes—first from the repurposed camper, then a few seconds later, from the solweave patchwork bubble, and a minute after that, frantic, human-made ones—those splashes changed everything.

And that is how I met Krista. Sputtering and flailing her arms, teal and purple hair a mess, climbing out of the old camper while cursing a blue streak.

"Need a hand?" I shouted from my boat. Well, it was more of a raft, which worked better most of the time since I only used it in the shallow lake for checking the hydrofarm. And, apparently, fishing up Kristas.

"I'd be delighted," she replied in a foreign accent. She had made it up on top of the camper, and occupied herself by hauling in the bubble and, to my surprise, folding it in on itself.

"It's not rigid?"

"Nope, I didn't see any benefit in that. I figured it should be easy to stow, in case of storms, for example. You wouldn't want the wind to blow it away, right?"

"You built it?" I don't know why I asked. I already knew she had, which thoroughly impressed me. I got the feeling she would continue to impress me, too.

She looked a few years older than me, or just laughed so much that she had started developing lines at the corners of her eyes early on. Her big, clear eyes were blue as the summer sky reflected in the water.

"Hey, how much weight does your raft carry?" Her words served as a splash of cold water in the face, helping me focus on the conundrum at hand instead of on the curves beneath her kinweave flight coveralls.

"Enough to carry both of us, but not nearly enough to salvage the camper. Sorry."

"Okay, we'll figure it out later. I'm Krista, by the way. I'm going to Svalbard to see if there's anything left of the seed bank there."

I took the wet hand she held out. "I'm Hien."

***

Since she was already drenched, she decided to dive back inside the camper to get her essentials out: a pocket-AI, batteries and chargers of various kinds, and a soaked bag of clothes.

By the time she surfaced for the third time, a bunch of other people on rafts and in boats had shown up, tossing questions at me that I couldn't answer. Apparently, since I had found her first, I should already know everything about her. And apparently I was now responsible for her well-being. Never mind that she hadn't listened to me when I asked her not to risk drowning by diving for her stuff.

But I didn't mind offering her a place to stay for a while.

"Let's go. We need to get you something dry to wear, and food, too."

"I don't want to impose," she said, her sky blue eyes telling me she meant it. She would understand if I couldn't or didn't want to help any further, and she would get by some other way.

It took a few moments for me to refocus on anything else than her pretty eyes and the inner strength shining in them. "I…it's not a problem." I sounded like a frog with the cold of the century until I cleared my throat. "I have plenty of space and food. I really don't mind."

As it turned out, my "plenty of space" only felt big and open when devoid of Krista. Her presence in my home made it feel warmer, cozier, even though she spread things out to dry just about everywhere. She set her chargers in a row on the porch railing to catch the sun. Her kinweave jumpsuit hung from one of the roof beams to the side, giving off a faint blue glow as the draft from the open window made it sway, the kinetic energy instantly turning into heat to help dry it.

Krista herself looked gorgeous in the flannel pyjamas Mrs. Solheim, my neighbor, had brought her, along with some toiletries and what she claimed were leftovers from a stew she happened to have made the day before. But I knew Frieda, and I knew what this stew tasted like both when it was days old and when it had been made a couple of hours earlier, and this was as fresh as they came. Not that it mattered if Frieda wanted to tell a little white lie so Krista wouldn't feel like a burden.

***

Krista absolutely blew my mind in every way possible. The girls I had grown up with were like boring, gray moths where Krista was like a colorful butterfly, except that she had a purpose. She had a plan, and she wasn't going to let something as silly and insignificant as a crash and a little water get in her way. No, she told me, it was just a minor setback. Yes, she said, she would rebuild the solweave bubble and the rotor, and make sure whatever had caused the mishap wouldn't happen again.

I offered to help, of course, while a small voice in my head hoped we either wouldn't succeed and she'd have to stay, or that at least the repairs would take a long time. That maybe she'd start to like it here and not leave even if we did manage to fix it. But I would never sabotage her.

Krista smiled and sighed happily when she woke up on the inflatable bed in my living room and told me how much she loved the smell of fresh coffee. She smiled again when we stepped outside and she took in the buildings with the solar mosaic walls that mimicked the living flowers and trees all around us. She did the same when we stood on the shore of the lake, along with all the people who had come to help raise the camper.

The only problem with all this was I didn't have time to talk to her. I mean, of course we talked, but only about the problem at hand. And other people talked to her, too, people who knew more about winches and ropes and pullies and things. I did all the things I was asked to, of course, which mostly consisted of speeding off to get this-or-that from Elias' garage or helping keep a rope taut. Others were the brain, I was just the muscle. But at least I made myself useful.

We did the heavy lifting by hand, instead of using bots, because the ones we had that were powerful enough were also too heavy for our boats and rafts, and not necessarily completely waterproof. Krista's camper needed to be towed to dry land as soon as possible, even if none of us thought anything inside could be salvaged.

We did have our pocket-AIs, naturally, but they only confirmed what Krista and Vladi planned, Vladi with his long beard firmly curled around his fingers as he pondered, Krista tossing out ideas and suggestions seemingly at random until he nodded and grunted agreement. And still, in the midst of all this, she had time to look around and smile, as if the dark green pines and spruces in the distance had been put there by a long-forgotten artist, just waiting for her to show up and appreciate it.

"You're so lucky to live in a place this beautiful, Hien," she said that evening, when the camper stood outside in my yard. Water dripped from it into a shallow trench Frieda's grandkids, Stefan and Mariam, had dug quite happily for half a liter of strawberries. I allowed them to pick their reward themselves from my manual outdoor farmland. Judging by the red juice stains on their faces, quite a few extra berries made their way into their stomachs, but that was to be expected. Encouraged, even, because the more they picked, the less I would have to do.

"I suppose it is, but I've lived here all my life. I hardly notice it unless something special is going on," I replied.

"Special like what?"

I wanted to say "like you", but managed to stop myself. "Uhm, like the midnight sun, maybe. That's pretty awesome. Or, well, it's not actually midnight sun, we're still too far south for that, but it doesn't get properly dark here in the middle of summer. And sometimes you'll have pink and purple and red streaks of clouds set against the not quite dark sky, and maybe the full moon will look gigantic when it rises, and yeah…" I felt my cheeks heat up. "That's nice to look at," I finished, sounding completely lame.

"I hope I get to see that before we get the mini-blimp fixed. Although, I suppose I'll be following the midnight sun when I can continue on my way," she mused. She didn't know her words made my heart ache. Already. After only a day, only a few conversations, I knew I didn't want her to leave. At least not yet, not for a long time.

***

We spent the next day following her AI's directions in breaking apart the camper to dry it all out. It guided us in a childlike, cartoonish voice, which cracked me up every time I heard it. Krista looked a little embarrassed when I asked about it, but to me, it felt like we were breaking new ground. I knew something private about her now, something I got the feeling no one else knew.

"I can change it into something more serious if you want," she said, then continued before I had a chance to reply. "I figured being alone in a self-built blimp that I hadn't tested for long flights yet was a little risky, so I wanted the AI to sound the opposite of serious. You know?"

"I would have done the same if I had thought of it," I smiled. "But I'd probably have set any alarm to be in a stern voice. Like an officer in an old war movie."

"You like old movies too?" Gleefully, she said, "AI, run the test for total systems breakdown warning."

An alarm sounded, a tinny klaxon that merged into an "Atten-shun!" barked by a harsh male voice, then turned into a forlorn foghorn, and the "Atten-shun!" again. The racket continued for a minute or so, all kinds of warning noises running into each other. I could see Krista laughing, but couldn't hear the sound until she hit the AI's reset button.

"So you couldn't just have one. You needed all of them." My own voice sounded strange to my ears in the ringing silence.

"Yeah, I had to make sure there was at least one warning sound that would wake me. Maybe fewer would have been enough." Her eyes sparkled. "But at least it worked." Her face became serious and a shudder went through her. "I think a bigger bird of some kind hit the rotor. A goose, maybe? I'm just glad I crashed here, and in the water, instead of in the middle of a forest or the sea or something."

She sat down on the porch steps with a thump, her face pale. "How about a little break?" Her voice was strained, and before she had time to hide her hands, I saw how they shook.

"Sounds good. I'll get us something to drink."

I went inside and rummaged around for a lot longer than I needed to. I wanted to give her time to calm down. She didn't seem to be the kind of person to show her fears and insecurities to just anyone. I mean, who does? But it felt as if it was even more important to Krista than to most other people to keep up a brave and competent face. And if she ever opened up to someone, it would be all the more precious. Forcing the issue would probably only serve to push her away, which was the last thing I wanted.

Eventually I ran out of plausible little things to do. I had switched a few batteries into the charging hub, not because I needed to, as I didn't use much electricity in the summer, but to have something to do. And hey, who knew if next week would be unusually cold and cloudy and dry, with no winds to speak of. Then the power-mosaics on the outside walls wouldn't have anything to generate power from. No sun for the solar panels, no wind or water to move the microkinetics. Plus, as long as Krista stayed here, there'd be two of us who needed warm water. I set the house-AI to recalculate power usage for two inhabitants until canceled.

When I went back outside with two tall glasses of fresh strawberry juice, Krista looked more relaxed. She stared out across the pond, to the village where all the gleaming power-mosaics and solar-glass clad greenhouse balconies glinted in the light. Her eyes widened in surprise when she took a sip of the juice, and before I knew it, she'd drained the whole glass. I gave her mine, smiling and feeling proud.

"Do you know where I can get more solweave?" she asked. "I think the bubble was damaged in the crash, but until I can spread it out properly, the AI can't make a proper analysis."

"The nearest town is only twenty kilometers from here. There's a manufacturing plant there. We could go tomorrow, maybe? Their AI will be able to suggest the most efficient fixes."

"Sounds good," she said and flashed me a smile that disappeared as quickly as it had appeared. "You know, it's nice to have someone to talk to again. It got a bit lonely with only the AI. And it's also nice to not be judged…" Her words tapered out. "But then, you people here—" Her arm made a wide sweep to encompass the whole village. "—you seem to be more open-minded."

I waited for her to continue. It didn't take long, and when she did, her words came slowly, in a guarded voice.

"I live in a community where people are content with what they have. And rightly so, in a way. We have everything we need. But to me, it feels isolated. When I started to work on the mini-blimp, the others didn't want to know about it. They think it's completely unnecessary to travel, to go anywhere else."

I hmmed. In truth, the people in my village weren't much different. If I were to build a mini-blimp, or any kind of flying machine, or consider moving into town, they'd be concerned. They'd ask why I wasn't happy with what I had, and what they could do to help me be happier. They wouldn't understand that some people had a need to experience more of the world, for real, not only through virtual reality travel programs.

"The only person who helped me build it is a little girl, Qiuyue. I doubt she'll ever forgive me for not taking her with me, but I think her parents would have had a few problems with that." Krista gave me a sidelong glance. The look challenged me to laugh or ridicule her next words. "My best friend is a ten-year old girl, and I miss her like crazy."

I nodded. It wasn't a laughing matter to me, who didn't have any close friends at all. "Is there anyone else you miss?" I asked, fearing her answer.

"Well, I wouldn't have thought so, but there's old Mr. Mwabi. I used to hate having to help him with the hydrofarm, because his knees are so bad. I never understood why he didn't have the AI-bot get his produce, not until it hit me that he wanted someone to talk to."

"Old Mr. Mwabi, huh?" I was fishing for more information. I needed to know if she had another man on her mind. I mean, it's not like I thought she might fall for *me,* but still, if I had competition for her heart, I wanted to know. Just in case I ever mustered up enough courage to do something about my attraction. And just in case she ever gave me a sign it might be welcome.

"Old, as in probably over 80 years old. Cranky and irritating, but I still miss talking to him."

She noticed my relief, of course, and giggled, which made my cheeks heat up again. "Hey, a guy's gotta know who he needs to fight over the princess, right?"

I joked it away, but there was a little too much truth to it. If she realized that or not, I couldn't tell. Fortunately, she didn't ask, and she didn't dwell on it.

"Anyway, I'm planning on going back. Eventually. If I actually manage to get to Svalbard and then back...provided I can get the solweave bubble fixed."

Relieved at the change of subject, I stretched my legs. I should spend more time on the exercise bike, I decided. Before, I hadn't cared how I looked, or how other people saw me. But now I worried that she would look at my legs and think they were scrawny, or that my average, slim body type that spoke of my Vietnamese father's heritage wasn't to her liking. And still, I could change *those* things. But what if she preferred blond hair and eyes as blue as her own? Round eyes and a big beard? Someone who had more to offer than fresh strawberries and a pretty view? Or if she didn't like men, or anyone at all. Not that any of that mattered since there was no reason for her to stay here any longer than it took to get her blimp airborne again.

"What exactly is it you need from Svalbard, anyway?" I asked, finally able to silence my thoughts for a while.

"Seeds for all kinds of plants my community could use, but especially strawberry seeds."

I chuckled. Then I realized she wasn't joking.

"My great-grandparents came from northern Swenomark. They fled to southern Polmany when the waters started rising. It's been sort of a legend in my family that there's something magical with strawberry cakes, and well, I want..." She paused, again letting her eyes convey a warning before she told me something important. "I want Qiuyue to have a cake like that for her birthday, at least once."

"Don't you have any strawberries closer than this? Or in Svalbard?" It didn't make sense. But Krista's expression softened, so I must have asked the correct question. Or maybe it was just because I hadn't laughed.

"They're watery and tasteless. I can't imagine that a cake with that kind of strawberries would be legend-worthy, so I decided to go directly to the source and get seeds for every kind of strawberry in the world." Her jaw clenched a little. "So okay, you can laugh now."

"Strawberries are no laughing matter. Come, let me show you something."

I stood up and held out my hand to help her up. When she actually took it, my heart skipped a beat.

I lead her down the path to the greenhouse. She stopped dead in her tracks as she took in the vertical troughs and the bots checking humidity, temperatures and light. Her eyes widened and her nostrils flared when the scent of ripening strawberries reached her. Her mouth popped open when realization hit.

"I...you...oh. But...the juice? It must have had more in it?"

"No, only strawberries." I grinned. "From my manual field outside. I sell the ones I grow in here. They're almost as good, but not quite."

"May I?" Her eyes shone.

"Of course." I ordered the nearest bot to bring us some samples.

I've never seen anyone enjoy my produce with such clear delight before. In between mouthfuls, she smiled and made wonderful small sounds of pleasure.

"Don't eat too many of these, it gets better," I said. I lead her through the greenhouse and out the back door.

"This," I presented with a flourish, "is where my private stash comes from. I tend to these myself, by hand, and they get to ripen under the real sun. Have a taste." My heart thumped with both pride and anticipation.

She picked one, a challenging look in her eyes. She made a show of it, slowly bringing it to her lips and nibbling on it, but when the first taste hit her, she popped the whole thing into her mouth with a moan. I hurried to pick some more, offering them to her one at a time.

"These are what legends are made of. This is what I need." She gobbled another one. "Would these grow about 1500 kilometers south of here?"

"They might, but they wouldn't taste like this. The soil is different there, and the water, and the natural light, and the temperature. All kinds of factors come into play."

"How do you know so much about this?"

As we went back to the house, I told Krista about how I became a strawberry farmer.

As so many others, the floods had forced my great-grandparents to flee. Mine had lived in Finlonia since the 1990s, and didn't want to leave their new homeland, their children's only home. They returned as soon as they could and started the strawberry farm, and I was the fourth generation to care for it.

"But where are your parents?" Krista looked concerned. She had probably figured out I lived here alone—it wasn't as if I had introduced her to a lot of people.

"When I was old enough to take care of myself, they started joining a caravan bound for southern Russia every autumn. After a few years they decided to stay there permanently, helping Mediterranean dolphins that were trapped in the Black Sea."

Krista stared at me, her eyes blazing with anger for me. "How old were you?"

"Sixteen. But I didn't mind. Frieda—Mrs. Solheim, that is—took care of me. I got used to being alone during the winters, and I liked it. My parents were, and still are, doing something very important to them. And it's not like my farm bots aren't programmed for any and every possible challenge, and even if that all was to fail, I have savings to add to the globucks."

Her left eyebrow arched, then straightened as she figured it out. "Oh, we call the universal income grant basebucks. But 'universal' could mean every galaxy in the universe…and you call it global 'cause it's only for this world. Clever, if a little facetious."

That's another reason I liked Krista. She was smart, and never afraid to let her opinion be known.

***

Krista's reaction to the strawberries I cultivated, both in the greenhouse all year round and out in the open during summertime, made my head spin. I had to check my physmon to see that the clenching in my chest and elevated pulse weren't signs of a heart attack, but it only suggested a few deep breaths to ease my lightheadedness.

She noticed, of course, and looked at me for a long time with a sort of calculating expression that sent electricity down along my spine. I couldn't tear my eyes off her, and wanted more than anything to be brave enough to reach out and touch her.

A loud beep from her pocket-AI interrupted the moment. Krista glanced at it, swallowed, cleared her throat and said, "The inside parts of the camper are ready for active drying. I need to manually adjust the windcatchers to fan, though."

It sounded almost like an apology. I didn't understand why. I mean, it's not like she had the space for a proper AI-bot in the camper, and probably not enough spare energy for one either way. But I did.

"We can use one of mine if you want."

"They're busy, though." Her gaze swept over the greenhouse.

"It's fine. This time of year their batteries charge faster than they use them, so they can work longer. And it's not like a few hours make a difference for the berries." I didn't wait for her to object, but instead linked one of my bots to her pocket-AI for instructions.

In the morning, we hailed a sturdy transport-bot to get Krista's bubble to the solweave manufacturer. According to her pocket-AI, the camper should be dry enough to reassemble in a couple of days, and by the time we'd be finished with all the work on that, the bubble should be fixed.

The cavernous solweave plant was cool. I dawdled in the clothing-section where multiple AI-bots printed out part after part of perfectly designed and colored solweave pattern parts. I recognized trouser legs only because of their length, and the backs of jackets—I think, at least. What I didn't understand was the volumes. Did people need and use all this? Or was the plant delivering for a bigger area than I had realized?

Not that it mattered. Krista had already moved on, into the industrial side, and had her AI communicating with the order receptor.

"I want to avoid unplanned, urgent landings in the future," she said. "Looks like caging the rotors is the first step, then making the bubble bigger to carry the extra weight. But then the actual bubble starts to weigh more, which means adding an extra rotor and cage, which makes me need a bigger bubble… Damn." Her shoulders slumped and an annoyed crease appeared between her eyebrows. "And what's worse, once I get to the last part of the journey, I can't exactly land for the night and check or fix things, so I'd need to take a proper AI-bot with me."

I must have looked confused. Krista sighed and made her AI project her route on the wall.

"It's about 450 kilometers over open water from Hammerfest to Bjørnøya, and then another 250 to the southernmost part of Svalbard. That's at least three nights total over the sea."

I shuddered at the thought of Krista, alone in the camper, helplessly tossed between angry clouds and harsh, cold waves, struggling to manually adjust ropes and fans and sails and what-nots, while the pocket-AI frantically shouted out warnings and failure reports.

"Sails."

"Huh?"

"Sails," I said. I don't know where the thought came from, but it felt right. "Make it a boat. Don't fly. Float." I saw when Krista's brain caught up with my idea. She stopped seeing me, and instead saw possibilities, and started babbling so quickly that I couldn't keep up. Her pocket-AI did, though, and soon projected a completely different construction than the oblong bubble of the mini-blimp onto the wall.

"You're a genius, Hien." She grinned at me. "I still have to get to Hammerfest first, so I need the bubble fixed. I don't know why I never thought about just making the whole thing into a boat for the last leg, though."

"Because it still means you need a proper AI-bot," I said, sad to see the excitement on her face fade. "You'd have to stop in Hammerfest to rebuild, which could take days."

"And we're back to square one, because I still don't have one, and even if I did, the extra weight and charging it would mean a bigger bubble and so on."

"At least you wouldn't need it powered all the time if you only brought it to construct the boat." Another idea started to form in my mind, but I didn't know what she'd think about it. In all honesty, I didn't know what *I* thought about it either, but I did know it was one of those ideas that would haunt me if I didn't just say it. "What if… what if I came with you?"

The words seemed to echo in my head. Time slowed to a crawl as I watched her turn to face me, her eyes a deeper blue than I'd ever seen them before.

"But—" She shook her head so strands of teal mixed in with the purple. "Hien, you have a…you live here. I can't ask you—"

"But you didn't ask. I offered," I cut in. "Never mind. We'd have to change your design too much, and we hardly even know each other. If you don't—"

"No, no, it's not that. Of course I trust you, and I enjoy your company. We seem to understand each other, but this would take weeks. You can't just take off like that, can you?"

I considered it for a while, then dove in head-first. "I don't see why not. The greenhouse farm is automated, and it's summer. If I take one bot off, the others will have enough energy to work a few extra hours per day." The words tumbled from my mouth without much input from my brain. "We could rebuild your hydroponic into an aeroponic farm, which would decrease weight a little. We could bring a bunch of my windcatchers, too—in fact, if I'm not going to be home, we could utilize most of my energy producers."

"You're crazy. Why would you even think about this?" Her smile took the edge off her words.

"As you said, we get each other. I enjoy your company too, and, well, it would be an adventure." I hesitated, but I might as well be completely honest. "It feels as if I was only existing until you crashed into the pond, and you woke me up and now I feel alive. I can't explain it better than that, but I do know I don't want to go back to sleep."

Her arms around me, her body pressed to mine, made my physmon beep, which made both of us giggle.

***

It took almost two weeks before we could leave. First our AIs needed time to consider and calculate all kinds of different things, from carrying capacity to food intake to weather prognosis, and then they needed time to come up with the actual blueprints and building plans.

We worked day and night and ended up pulling two of the AI-bots from the farm. I hired Mrs. Solheim's grandkids to help out with the strawberries to make up for it, which they didn't mind in the least. They probably ate more than they picked, but there were still plenty to ship out every day.

We ended up with a strange construction that looked almost like a snowman with wide, iridescent wings. We encased the camper in a solweave halfbubble, then came the repaired original bubble, and on top of that a smaller bubble that housed and powered only the AI-bot. The wings were a mix of solweave and kinweave, with windcatchers attached, and when in motion would generate enough power for the four rotors.

Every day as we worked, people came to gawk and talk and help and question the sanity of the whole thing. They probably thought we were crazy, and that's how I felt, too. But at the same time, the more I got to know Krista, the more I wanted to go with her. Except for the farm, I didn't have anything keeping me here. The only reason I hadn't gone to see more of the world before was a lack of purpose. I'd simply never felt the need to do so. I had been content, but I knew I wouldn't be anymore. And every day, the thought of not working with and talking to Krista became more and more impossible.

Finally, one sunny day, we had completed all the changes on the AIs' lists. We had packed and stowed everything, made sure we had plenty of food, and then we simply up and left.

It really felt that easy, which surprised me. When I looked down at the pond, at my cabin and my greenhouse, at the people I had known all my life, tiny as ants as they waved up at us, I expected trepidation or even fear. But none of those feelings made it through the haze of exhilaration and happiness as the pond shrank into only a sunlit dot far behind us.

The craft itself—I couldn't call it a mini-blimp anymore, since it looked nothing like one—made a lot less noise than I had anticipated. A soft purr and a slight swaying were the only signs that we were actually airborne, and of course, the fact that we couldn't go outside. I didn't mind that part, not at all. The cramped space inside the camper put Krista and me in close proximity all the time, and she seemed to enjoy it as much as I did.

There was one single cot to sleep on, but I had brought the self-inflating air mattress that could be hooked up to a windcatcher. Every time I set it up, it would generate just a little more energy than it used to fill up. I had a kinweave blanket and pillow too, whose soft glow may not be necessary in summer, but helped a great deal with the waking up-process during dark winter mornings.

I hadn't thought much about what we'd be doing while flying north, other than looking at whatever lay beneath us and keeping an ear open for AI reports. Luckily, Krista had. Her pocket-AI had years worth of movies and books and games and music of all kinds to enjoy if and when she didn't feel like planning one of her many dream houses. Just for fun, she claimed, but I noticed the longing in her voice, and found a new longing inside my own heart: to help her achieve that, in reality.

The first few days flew by, both literally and figuratively. Our systems held up perfectly, and the farther north we traveled, the more hours of sunlight we had, giving us more power. It almost felt as if we were chasing the sun, daring it to stay above the horizon throughout the night.

The landscape changed, too. The shallow ponds and lakes became scarcer. Forests and hills were surrounded by grasslands, not water, and soon those hills became mountains, the trees lower and more gnarly. We didn't see any settlements, but we were trying to avoid them anyway, since we didn't want to explain ourselves to anyone who might be able to contact us.

***

On the fifth evening, we set down earlier than usual, after the AI informed us there was a high chance of Aurora Borealis that night. Even the AI wasn't sure if or how that might affect our crazy craft, but neither one of us wanted to find out.

We landed right on the bank of a stream with the idea that refilling our reservoirs with fresh water would mean less energy to clean what we already had. Also, I just thought it looked nice. We were surrounded by open flat land, that faded into hazy, blue hills in the distance.

The air this far north had probably always smelled this crisp. We had watched a documentary from Before, showing us reindeer and a glass-igloo hotel, local entrepreneurs making and selling natural remedies such as lichen wraps, calling it Saami shamanistic power. The AI made adjustments to our kinweave suits before it deemed it a good idea to go outside.

The stream ran quickly enough for us to consider it worthwhile to detach a few windcatchers and toss them in, as tiny makeshift waterwheels that we connected to kinetic receptors. I picked them at random, but Krista arranged them in a colorful pattern so they looked almost like a tropical flowerbed underwater.

It didn't take long before the mosquitoes showed up, attracted by the residual heat from the solweave and our bodies. They came in clouds, their high-pitched buzzing almost louder than the zapping sounds the adjusted microcurrents on our kinweave suits made.

Krista laughed and ran straight into the cloud of insects, twirling and waving her arms to catch as many little bloodsuckers as possible with the electric sparks. I made her AI start playing music for her to dance to as I sat down on a rock and simply enjoyed watching her. My own suit zapped away, bringing down mosquito after mosquito as soon as they came close enough. I didn't think I'd ever felt this happy in my whole life, and doubted I could get any happier.

"Come on, you need to move or your suit will run out of energy and you'll get eaten alive," she said as she danced towards me. She pulled me up before I had time to protest and held on to my hands as she made me stumble along with her twirls, the red light of the setting sun painting highlights in her hair.

"Maybe we should slow down," I said after I'd barely avoided stepping on her toes for the third time. I couldn't focus with her so close to me, my hands still in hers, my heart pounding in my chest. I couldn't look away from her eyes and the intense gaze in them. They looked green in this light, like the dwarf birches and heather plants covering the ground.

The music changed into something slower—the AI had probably heard me—and Krista melted against me. We had bumped into each other in the close confines of the camper many times over the past few days, but never lingered even when I, at least, had wished for more. This felt nothing like that, nothing like gently holding her shoulders to move around her. This was Krista, confusing me, making my head spin with fragments of thoughts and wishes and fears and what-ifs. The one clear thought I had was to wonder how the AI had programmed the suits to only zap mosquitoes, not human hands, and hers were traveling together over my back, and mine were split, one at her slim waist and the other at her neck, under her hair.

Until I untangled it and plucked a buzzing mosquito from her cheek, careful to only use my fingertips so the suit didn't get close enough to accidentally zap her. She swallowed audibly as I couldn't help myself, but drew my fingers down her face.

"You know what happens when a person picks a mosquito off someone's face?" she asked, her voice husky, enticing, her eyes staring into my soul.

I shook my head, unable to form words.

"They have to kiss her. It's tradition."

"Is that so?" I croaked the words out and shuffled my feet until it didn't feel as if I'd fall over from a stiff breeze.

She nodded. "It is now."

Soft lips met mine, and it felt as if my suit's bugzappers had turned inside out and trickled down my spine. She tasted like strawberries, and I couldn't stop sipping and tasting and feeling, my mind blank, euphoric, as if I was floating on—

"Oh wow." She pushed herself away and stared behind me. "Hien, look!"

Well. Obviously our first kiss wasn't as earth-shattering for her as it was for me. But I turned to look, and to hide my embarrassment too, and my mouth fell open.

The sky, still the deep orange of a midsummer sunset, was alight with gigantic green-yellow streamers, dancing like we had done moments before, twirling, flaring up, changing colors and waning, only to appear again in new and different flowing arches.

"AI, visual recording," I said, and added, "Up. The sky." I wasn't capable of saying anything else, but I did manage to move myself in behind Krista so I could both hold her and look at the same cosmic display she saw.

I barely had time to get those few words out before the tops of the green bands turned into a deep crimson, flared impossibly high and settled back to green and yellow.

I felt Krista draw in a deep, shuddering breath. "I'm going to take this as a sign, Hien," she said. "If you're okay with that."

"Eh?" I had a stupid moment. Given the circumstances, I don't think anyone can blame me.

"About you and me. How we met and now this." She hesitated for a second, and I've never heard her sound as vulnerable as she did when she spoke again. "Please tell me I'm not wrong. Tell me I haven't misinterpreted you."

I would have told her if I had been able to speak. Instead, I turned her around to kiss her again, hoping she would understand my answer. Words would come later, soon even, because she needed to know how she had changed my whole life in the short time I had known her, and how I hoped she would continue to do so. But for a while longer, I needed to simply enjoy the magic of this moment.

***

We spent a couple of days by that stream, coming to terms with our changed relationship. It felt like the most natural thing in the world. Dreamlike to me, because I had to constantly check with myself to see that I was awake, that this was real, that I could touch and kiss Krista whenever I wanted. And even more unbelievable, she touched and kissed me, too, whenever she wanted.

The mosquitoes never stopped coming, but the Aurora Borealis did. Eventually we had enough of zapping bloodsuckers, gathered up our improvised waterwheel flowerbed, and continued on our way.

The remains of Hammerfest made both of us sad. We had thought we would want to stay there for a few days, explore the ruins, but decided to continue to Bjørnøya and Svalbard as soon as possible. We got to work on converting the craft's bubbles on a tiny, rocky beach by the outlet of a fjord on the day before midsummer's eve.

There's not much to tell about the rest of our journey. At least, not much that isn't too private to share. The largest of our solweave bubbles turned into an air cushion, the middle one combined with the wings into a big solsail, all the rotors except one submerged, and the original bubble served to keep us on track.

Krista had a bout of sea sickness, but I was able to care for her until she got used to being rocked by the waves. The never-ending sunlight kept us going at a steady pace both day and night, and we made good time.

Bjørnøya was nothing more than a bunch of rocks, inhabited by birds, and it looked too harsh and desolate for us to want to make landfall there. We didn't need to, anyway, as we weren't flying in a blimp anymore.

During those days, I learned just how incredibly rare it was to see Northern Lights in the summer. Krista just smiled and said it had to be about as rare as crashing a mini-blimp into a lake and being rescued by a strawberry farmer who just happened to be one's soul mate.

We found the seed vault cared for by a community of maybe fifty people and a bunch of bots. They welcomed us and helped us find what we needed, and that was that. As I said, reaching Krista's original goal didn't make much of an impact on either one of us, not compared to how we had found each other. And how we had started making plans, how every moment we weren't otherwise occupied, we used the AI to help draw blueprints and calculate material needs, talking and dreaming about our future.

Mrs. Solheim arranged a party for the whole village during our stop-over to collect my things. Until that day, I hadn't realized how much people cared about me. They looked sad that I was leaving even after I told them I would be overseeing the farmbots remotely, and that they would still get all the fresh strawberries they could eat, and that both Krista and I would spend our future summers with them.

"Are you sure you want to leave your home?" Krista would ask me in the week leading up to our departure.

And I would reply, with a smile, "Are you sure you want to be my home?"

We both said yes. Every time.

ABOUT THE AUTHORS

Julia K. Patt is a writer, teacher, and editor living in Maryland. Her science fiction has appeared in *Clarkesworld, Escape Pod*, and *Luna Station Quarterly*, among other places. Follow her on twitter (@chidorme) or check out her website juliakpatt.com for more.

DK Mok is a fantasy and science fiction author whose novels include *Squid's Grief* and *Hunt for Valamon*. DK has been shortlisted for four Aurealis Awards, two Ditmars and a WSFA Small Press Award. DK graduated from UNSW with a degree in Psychology, pursuing her interests in both social justice and scientist humour. DK lives in Sydney, Australia, and her favourite fossil deposit is the Burgess Shale. Connect on Twitter @dk_mok or www.dkmok.com.

Jennifer Lee Rossman is a science fiction geek from Oneonta, New York, who enjoys cross stitching, watching *Doctor Who*, and threatening to run over people with her wheelchair. Her work has been featured in several anthologies and her debut novel, *Jack Jetstark's Intergalactic Freakshow*, will be published by World Weaver Press in 2019. You can find her blog at jenniferleerossman.blogspot .com and Twitter at twitter.com/JenLRossman.

Stefani Cox is a Los Angeles-based speculative fiction writer and lapsed urban planner. She's an alumna of the VONA/Voices of Our Nations Arts writing workshops and an associate editor for *PodCastle* fantasy fiction podcast. Stefani also works as a communications consultant, and spends her free time practicing yoga, hiking, and being an insatiable bookworm. She holds a master's in City and Regional Planning from UC Berkeley. Find her on Twitter @stefanicox or her website stefanicox.com.

Shel Graves is a reader, writer, and utopian thinker who lives by the Salish Sea. She works as a caregiver at Pasado's Safe Haven, a non-profit on a mission to end animal cruelty. She earned her MFA in Creative Writing at Goddard College. She keeps her writer's journal at shelgraves.blogspot.com. Talk to her @Utopianista on Twitter and see pictures of her furry companions @Sheltopia on Instagram.

Holly Schofield travels through time at the rate of one second per second, oscillating between the alternate realities of city and country life. Her short stories have appeared in *Analog, Lightspeed, Escape Pod*, and many other publications throughout the world. She hopes to save the world through science fiction and homegrown heritage tomatoes. Find her at hollyschofield.wordpress.com.

Jerri Jerreat's fiction has appeared in *The New Quarterly, The Antigonish Review, The Dalhousie Review*, and *Room*, among others. Another science fiction story appeared in an anthology *Nevertheless: Tesseracts Twenty-One* by Edge Publishing. Jerri is an Ontario paddler who has lived in Vancouver, Ottawa, St. Catharines, and in Tübingen, Germany. She now lives under a roof of solar panels on an ancient limestone seabed near Kingston, Ontario. Visit her website at JerriJerreat.com.

Jaymee Goh is a writer, poet, reviewer, and scholar of science fiction and fantasy. Her work can be found in *Lightspeed Magazine, Strange Horizons*, and *Science Fiction Studies*. She is the editor of *The SEA Is Ours: Tales of Steampunk Southeast Asia* and *The WisCon Chronicles Vol. 11: Trials by Whiteness*.

Commando Jugendstil is a real-life small collective of Italian solarpunk creators who aim to conjugate green technology and art to make cities a better place to live in and build creative communities.

Tales From the EV Studio is a posse of emigrant Italian writers who specialise in historical fantasy, archanepunk and scriptwriting for comics. This is their first foray in the realms of solarpunk.

Wendy Nikel is a speculative fiction author with a degree in elementary education, a fondness for road trips, and a terrible habit of forgetting where she's left her cup of tea. Her short fiction has been published by *Fantastic Stories of the Imagination, Daily Science Fiction, Nature: Futures*, and elsewhere. Her time travel novella, *The Continuum*, was published by World Weaver Press in January 2018, with a sequel forthcoming. For more info, visit wendynikel.com.

Blake Jessop is a Canadian writer, lecturer, and poet. You can read more of his science fiction in the *2018 Young Explorer's Adventure Guide* from Dreaming Robot Press, or follow him on Twitter @everydayjisei.

A native of Niagara Falls, Ontario, **Edward Edmonds** is a teacher currently living in Saskatchewan, Canada. His works have previously been published in the literary magazines *Inscribed*, *Steel Bananas*, and *dead (g)end(er)*. You can find Edward on twitter @ededification if he's not haunting your local coffee shop.

Like much of **Sam S. Kepfield**'s fiction, "Amber Waves" draws upon the author's decades-long residence in his home state of Kansas. Sam was raised in Western Kansas, attended Kansas State University and the University of Nebraska, and currently resides in Hutchinson. He is the author of two books and numerous short stories.

Massachusetts author-artist **Gregory Scheckler** crafts science fiction stories and cartoony artworks. His writings can be found at World Weaver Press, Crow's Mirror Books, the *Berkshire Eagle*, the *Berkshire Review for the Arts, The Mind's Eye*, and *Thought & Action*. When he's not writing or artmaking, he and his wife can be found skiing and biking the Berkshires, watching their neighbor's chickens, or tending their solar-powered home.

M. Lopes da Silva is an author and fine artist living in Los Angeles. Her work has appeared or is forthcoming in *Electric Literature, Blumhouse, The California Literary Review*, and *Queen Mob's Teahouse*, and anthologies by *Mad Scientist Journal*, Gehenna & Hinnom Press, and Fantasia Divinity Publishing. She recently illustrated the Centipede Press collector's edition of Jonathan Carroll's *The Land of Laughs*. Find more at mlopesdasilva.wordpress .com.

Helen Kenwright writes hopeful speculative fiction, and is currently working on a steampunk/solarpunk novel about history, humanity and unexpected consequences. She has an MA with distinction in Creative Writing from York St John University, and runs the Writing Tree, an organisation offering online creative writing tuition and support. She teaches creative writing for Converge, a project at York St John University which offers educational opportunities for people recovering from mental ill-health, and for the University of York's lifelong learning programme. Find more at www.helenkenwright.com or on Twitter at @hnkenwright.

Charlotte M. Ray lives (physically) in Finland with her husband and their computers, and (mentally) in whichever imaginary world she is currently occupied with. She is fascinated with new and upcoming tech, and secretly wishes someone would invent a brain image-to-text converter and teleportation. Her story "Addie-cted" appeared in the WWP anthology *Covalent Bonds*.

ABOUT THE ANTHOLOGIST

Sarena Ulibarri is Editor-in-Chief of World Weaver Press, and she is also a fiction writer who has been published in *Lightspeed, Fantastic Stories of the Imagination, Weirdbook*, and elsewhere. Her solarpunk story "Riding in Place" appeared in the anthology *Biketopia: Feminist Bicycle Science Fiction Stories in Extreme Futures*. She lives in a solar-powered adobe house in New Mexico, and can be found online at SarenaUlibarri.com and @SarenaUlibarri.

Thank you for reading!

We hope you'll leave an honest review at Amazon, Goodreads, or wherever you discuss books online.

Leaving a review helps readers like you discover great new books, and shows support for these authors who worked so hard to create these stories.

Please sign up for our newsletter for news about upcoming titles, submission opportunities, special discounts, & more.

WorldWeaverPress.com/newsletter-signup

SOLARPUNK: ECOLOGICAL AND FANTASTICAL STORIES IN A SUSTAINABLE WORLD

Edited by Gerson Lodi-Ribeiro
Translated by Fábio Fernandes

Imagine a sustainable world, run on clean and renewable energies that are less aggressive to the environment. Now imagine humanity under the impact of these changes. This is the premise Brazilian editor Gerson Lodi-Ribeiro proposed, and these authors took the challenge to envision hopeful futures and alternate histories. The stories in this anthology explore terrorism against green corporations, large space ships propelled by the pressure of solar radiation, the advent of photosynthetic humans, and how different society might be if we had switched to renewable energies much earlier in history. Originally published in Brazil and translated for the first time from the Portuguese by Fábio Fernandes, this anthology of optimistic science fiction features nine authors from Brazil and Portugal including Carlos Orsi, Telmo Marçal, Romeu Martins, Antonio Luiz M. Costa, Gabriel Cantareira, Daniel I. Dutra, André S. Silva, Roberta Spindler, and Gerson Lodi-Ribeiro.

MORE SCIENCE FICTION
FROM WORLD WEAVER PRESS

Campaign 2100: Game of Scorpions

Larry Hodges

The year is 2100, and the world has adopted the American two-party electoral system. When it comes to the election for president of Earth, the father-daughter team of Toby and Lara Platt are the cutthroat campaign directors who get candidates elected by any means necessary—including the current president, Corbin Dubois of France. But when an alien lands outside the United Nations, claiming to be an ambassador from Tau Ceti, Dubois orders her attacked. Toby resigns.

The alien survives—and so, it seems, might Dubois's corrupt reelection campaign, now run by Lara. But Toby vows to put his daughter out of a job. He challenges the two major parties—one conservative, one liberal—and runs for president himself with a third-party moderate challenge. He's a long-shot, but he's determined to fix the problems he created in getting Dubois elected.

Amid rising tensions and chants of "Alien go home!" the campaign crisscrosses every continent as father and daughter battle for electoral votes and clash over the ideas and issues facing the world of 2100 in this bare-knuckle, fight-to-the-finish political campaign. The world is watching. And so is the alien.

"Larry Hodges is an insightful political commentator and a kick-ass science-fiction writer. A dynamite novel full of twists and turns; this futuristic *House of Cards* is both entertaining and thought-provoking."
—Robert J. Sawyer, Hugo and Nebula Award-winning author of *Quantum Night*

"A tense, taut political thriller that rings much truer than you would suspect, given that it won't be happening for another 8 decades."
—Mike Resnick, Hugo winner and editor of *Galaxy's Edge* magazine

MORE SCIENCE FICTION
FROM WORLD WEAVER PRESS

THE CONTINUUM

A Place in Time, #1
Wendy Nikel

Elise Morley is an expert on the past who's about to get a crash course in the future.

For years, Elise has been donning corsets, sneaking into castles, and lying through her teeth to enforce the Place in Time Travel Agency's ten essential rules of time travel. Someone has to ensure that travel to the past isn't abused, and most days she welcomes the challenge of tracking down and retrieving clients who have run into trouble on their historical vacations.

But when a dangerous secret organization kidnaps her and coerces her into jumping to the future on a high-stakes assignment, she's got more to worry about than just the time-space continuum. For the first time ever, she's the one out-of-date, out of place, and quickly running out of time.

"Nikel's inventive spin on time travel and eye for sumptuous detail make her writing a treat to read."
—Publishers Weekly

"*The Continuum* packs a staggering amount of well drawn world-building into a short space, making for enough time travel adventure to launch a series...full of heart, humor, and thrilling action and adventure scenes that make for a fun, fast read."
—*Foreword Reviews*

THE GRANDMOTHER PARADOX

A Place in Time, #2
Wendy Nikel
The Rules must be broken again.

Far Orbit

SPECULATIVE SPACE ADVENTURES
Edited by Bascomb James

Featuring stories by award winners **Gregory Benford, Tracy Canfield, Eric Choi, David Wesley Hill**, and more, with an open letter to speculative fiction by **Elizabeth Bear**.

"Put aside all of your preconceived notions of what 'sci-fi' is—whether you think you love it or hate, it doesn't matter—pick up this book and get to reading!"

— Good Choice Reading

Far Orbit Apogee

More modern space adventures
Edited by Bascomb James

Far Orbit Apogee takes all of the fun-to-read adventure, ingenuity, and heroism of mid-century pulp fiction and reshapes it into modern space adventures crafted by a new generation of writers. Follow the adventures of heroic scientists, lunar detectives, space dragons, robots, interstellar pirates, gun slingers, and other memorable and diverse characters as they wrestle with adversity beyond the borders of our small blue marble.

Featuring stories from Jennnifer Campbell-Hicks, Dave Creek, Eric Del Carlo, Dominic Dulley, Nestor Delfino, Milo James Fowler, Julie Frost, Sam S. Kepfield, Keven R. Pittsinger, Wendy Sparrow, Anna Salonen, James Van Pelt, and Jay Werkheiser.

MURDER IN THE GENERATIVE KITCHEN

Meg Pontecorvo

With the Vacation Jury Duty system, jurors can lounge on a comfortable beach while watching the trial via virtual reality. Julio is loving the beach, as well as the views of a curvy fellow juror with a rainbow-lacquered skin modification who seems to be the exact opposite of his recent ex-girlfriend back in Chicago. Because of jury sequestration rules, they can't talk to each other at all, or else they'll have to pay full price for this Acapulco vacation. Still, Julio is desperate to catch her attention. But while he struts and tries to catch her eye, he also becomes fascinated by the trial at hand.

At first it seemed a foregone conclusion that the woman on trial used a high-tech generative kitchen to feed her husband a poisonous meal, but the more evidence mounts, the more Julio starts to suspect the kitchen may have made the decision on its own.

"Mysteriously delicious. Tastefully romantic. With a GMO garnish."
—Terry Bisson, author of *Bears Discover Fire and Other Stories*

"*Murder in the Generative Kitchen* by Meg Pontecorvo is a compact little story with a lot to say. Readers will find a fresh take on Asimov's three laws, see a twisted future where vacations are paid for by the courts, and learn that the same old arguments will still be contested long after we're gone."
—Ricky L. Brown, *Amazing Stories*

"With Murder in the Generative Kitchen, new author Meg Pontecorvo cooks up and dishes out for you not one, not two, but three original sci fi premises. Enjoy and digest them well!"
—David Brin, author of *Existence* and *The Postman*

World Weaver Press, LLC
Publishing fantasy, paranormal, and science fiction.
We believe in great storytelling.

WorldWeaverPress.com

Printed in the USA
CPSIA information can be obtained
at www.ICGtesting.com
LVHW010054140824
788135LV00003B/375

9 780998 702278